Tara Pammi can't rememb[er] wasn't lost in a book—espe[cially] was much more exciting th[an] at school. Years later, Tara's wild imagination and love for the written word revealed what she really wanted to do. Now she pairs alpha males who think they know everything with strong women who knock that theory *and* them off their feet!

Lorraine Hall is a part-time hermit and full-time writer. She was born with an old soul and her head in the clouds—which, it turns out, is the perfect combination for spending her days creating thunderous alpha heroes and the fierce, determined heroines who win their hearts. She lives in a potentially haunted house with her soulmate and a rumbustious band of hermits in training. When she's not writing romance, she's reading it.

Also by Tara Pammi

Billion-Dollar Fairy Tales miniseries

Marriage Bargain with Her Brazilian Boss
The Reason for His Wife's Return

Born into Bollywood miniseries

Claiming His Bollywood Cinderella
The Surprise Bollywood Baby
The Secret She Kept in Bollywood

Also by Lorraine Hall

A Son Hidden from the Sicilian
The Forbidden Princess He Craves

Secrets of the Kalyva Crown miniseries

Hired for His Royal Revenge
Pregnant at the Palace Altar

Discover more at millsandboon.co.uk.

AN INNOCENT'S DEAL WITH THE DEVIL

TARA PAMMI

PLAYING THE SICILIAN'S GAME OF REVENGE

LORRAINE HALL

MILLS & BOON

AN
INNOCENT'S DEAL
WITH THE DEVIL

TARA PAMMI

MILLS & BOON

CHAPTER ONE

SHE WAS NOT just broke. She was in a mountain of debt. And now that she was finally ready to admit her blunders and bawl her eyes out and beg him for help, the one man who'd loved her was gone.

Yana Reddy walked through the quiet, dark halls of her grandparents' house like a night wraith wandering through the dark woods from one of her favorite fantasy stories.

While her younger half sister, Nush, had always proclaimed her love of fairy tales, it was the much darker fantasy tales populated with demons and ghouls and djinns that drew Yana's interest. Especially one particular author she'd fallen in love with at a young age. Even then, her tastes had been drawn to the forbidden.

Now her grandfather leaving notes for his three granddaughters from beyond the grave appealed to her. She pulled the crisp folded letter out of its envelope and pushed it back in again without reading it, like she'd done a hundred times that day—the day they'd officially said goodbye to him.

Unlike both her half sisters, Mira and Nush, who'd burst into happy tears at one last note from their beloved Thaata, she knew the moment she'd seen her name written in that beautiful cursive script, that she wasn't going to read it.

Not yet.

Maybe not ever.

That would be her punishment. Plus, the possibility of a forever unclaimed present appealed to the contrarian in her. One last ploy to annoy Thaata.

A few hours ago the house had been full of extended family, friends and people who'd loved and respected her grandfather, who'd started a software company called OneTech, which his protege Caio Oliveira had turned into a billion-dollar venture.

Thaata had believed in second chances. Only Yana had never been able to use one to prove herself worthy like her sisters had done. To make him look at her with respect and love. Not frustrated resignation and the pain that he couldn't reach her.

Their alcoholic father had clearly preferred variety in his sexual partners for none of the sisters shared a mother, so Yana's grandparents had been the only responsible adults in their lives, and had essentially raised the three girls.

But all through her childhood and adolescence, Yana had resented them for it. Had chosen, in her early teens, to go and live with her flighty, unreliable, beautiful mother, Diana, instead of what she'd considered to be the much stricter regime of her grandparents.

By the time she'd realized the irreparable damage Diana had done to her, it had been too late. She'd trusted a woman who had, in return, emptied out all of Yana's bank accounts to pay for a cleverly disguised gambling habit.

Worse, in the last few months, Diana had ruined Yana's credit by borrowing off her credit cards when she'd refused to carry on funding her extravagant spending.

Closing the door to her grandparents' bedroom behind her, Yana fought the grief that had kept bubbling up like lava. If she let it out, it would burn her through, leaving nothing but ashes. She walked around, trailing her fingers over Thaata's things—

a worn-out leather diary on his nightstand, a biography title on his desk and a picture of her, Mira and Nush with him.

It had been taken during one glorious summer where Yana hadn't fought with him or her grandmother, when Diana had gone to live with her brand-new second husband.

How could you have made such a wrong choice? she wanted to scream at her teenage self. How could she have chosen to live with her mother, who'd shown her nothing but neglect and abuse, over the grandparents who'd only wanted the best for her?

A woman who'd eagerly asked Yana about the *assets* that Thaata might have left her only a day after his death. Yana didn't have to wait for the reading of the will to tell Diana that whatever assets Thaata might have left her would be all tied up so that she couldn't touch them for a very long time. A witness to Yana and her grandfather's arguments more than once, Diana had believed it.

She'd left instantly, leaving Yana with a crippling debt. Just…breezed out of her life with barely a goodbye.

Almost nearing thirty now, Yana's modeling contracts were coming few and far between. As she didn't want to be a model for the rest of her life, she'd already given up on most of the networking necessary to stay current. She thought again about the new career—a work in progress for some years—she'd hoped would take shape before her life had fractured into tiny fragments.

For a second she considered asking Mira or Nush to help her sort out the mess her life had become. But she couldn't. And not just because they were finally moving forward in their own lives with men they loved.

Hitting rock bottom had cleared up one thing for Yana— she'd fix her life by herself. It was the only way to restore her own faith in herself.

Grabbing the keys of Thaata's vintage car and one of his cigars from a secret compartment in his dresser, she tiptoed back to her room.

Rummaging through her closet, she grabbed a black leather corset top and skinny jeans and got dressed. Pushing her feet into stilettos, she tied her hair into a high ponytail, slapped on mascara and lip gloss without looking at the mirror and rushed to the garage.

The crisp night made goose bumps rise up on her skin as she drove with the windows rolled down. With the engine humming sweetly and the scent of the cigar smoke filling her nostrils, she felt a measure of peace, for the first time in weeks.

Running away again, a voice very much like Thaata's taunted, but Yana refused to listen to it now just as she'd done when he'd been alive.

Yana knew who the man was the moment the double doors of the secluded VIP lounge of the night club opened. He stood framed by the archway bathed in beams of purple lighting.

She knew even though it was dark and quiet.

She knew before that distinctive gait brought him to the chaise longue over which she'd draped herself, having fought off three different men who'd wanted to take her home.

She knew because she'd always possessed a weird extra sense when it came to *him*.

A Yana's stupid-for-this-man sense.

A basic, lizard-brain *wanting* that screamed she was prey even though he'd never played predator. A let's-ditch-any-self-respect-and-make-a-play-for-him urge.

Nasir Hadeed.

World-famous fantasy author, current political strategist and retired investigative journalist, reclusive billionaire and most important of all—her stepbrother for just four years.

They'd only ever spent a few months under the same roof out of the four years his father had been married to Diana. During the time when she'd transformed from a gangly, awkward fifteen to a leggy, brazen, stupidly confident nineteen, who'd imagined herself to be a tempting seductress.

Already, Nasir had been successful, renowned and respected in literary circles and the political world as a just-retired war-zone correspondent.

Twelve years older than she was, he'd not only been incisively brilliant in ways Yana couldn't comprehend, but also effortlessly suave and stunning with a roguish glint in his eyes that the world didn't see. His brilliant, award-winning tracts on war zones and world issues hadn't captured her heart, though.

It had been the fantasy novels he'd written, garnering worldwide acclaim that had thoroughly captivated her. Those brief months she'd spent with him had been in a different universe in which he hadn't loathed her. An alternate, upside-down timeline.

He'd indulged her overlong, extravagant breakfasts at the palatial mansion that had been his father's house in Monaco—when she'd demanded to know why a loathed character had to be redeemed or a favorite one had met her demise—with a dispassionate fondness and that dark smile. As if she were a stray dog he'd pat on the head and throw a few morsels of affection at.

But thanks to her behavior on her nineteenth birthday, when he'd returned from the incident overseas that had given him all those scars, he'd written her off forever.

How Yana wished she possessed one of those time stones he'd written about in one of his novels. So many wrong and questionable and self-defeating decisions she could erase with one turn of the stone. Especially when it came to Thaata and him.

Two men—two of the most important men in her life who'd influenced her, made her want to be more than who she was. One of them, her grandfather, was forever gone now thinking the worst of her, and one was determined to think the worst of her forever. She wiped at a stray tear that flew into her hair, donning the superficial persona that had become like a second skin now.

Because if Nasir pitied her, she'd just fall apart.

One signal from Nasir to the nearly invisible bartender and bright lights illuminated the dark corner. Immediately, he moved to block the glare that made Yana blink gritty eyes.

Shards of light traced the blade-sharp cheekbones, the hollows beneath and the wide, thin-lipped mouth. And the scar that bisected his upper lip and zigzagged through his left cheek—the remnant of a near-fatal knife wound that had changed the trajectory of his life. And hers, in a way.

Awareness pressed down on her as he took her in with that quiet intensity. She'd never understood how there could be such intense energy between them when they detested each other.

"Hello, Yana."

A full body shiver overtook her and still, she lay there, stupidly gaping at him, gathering her armor, which had already been battered by grief and loss. "Am I in hell, then?"

In response, he shrugged off his jacket and draped it over her mostly exposed chest and bare shoulders. She'd always marveled at how cruel and dispassionate Nasir's kindness could be. Still, she couldn't sit up. Couldn't get her heart to stop thundering away in her ears. "Go away, Nasir. I'm in full party-girl mode and as we both know, you're lethally allergic to that."

It was like craving the warmth of the sun but spending years trying to figure out how to ignore its existence in the sky.

Of course, the hateful man sat down on the coffee table, cornering her. Despite the dark, even with her stomach hurting because she'd barely eaten anything the whole day, even with her head in a weird limbo of grief and self-directed rage, warmth unspooled low in her belly at the familiar scent of him.

Bergamot and sandalwood—it was as if a chemist had experimented and figured out the perfect combination of scents that provoked all of her sexual fantasies and then doused Nasir Hadeed in it.

Two minutes in his company and Yana wanted to kiss the man senseless and curse him to whatever hell would torment him the most. The only constants in her life were her abiding love for her sisters and this mad obsession…for Nasir.

She took a puff on her cigar, blew out a ring like a photographer friend of hers had taught her. Not her fault that Nasir chose to sit right in that space.

Shadows created by the interplay of darkness and light gave his face a saturnine cast. As if those stark features needed to be tarred with any more harshness. Light, amber-colored eyes, deep-set and invasively perceptive, met hers. The large beak of his nose—which should have rendered him ugly but instead made him look intellectual—made it effortlessly easy for him to look down on her.

"How are you, Yana?"

She took another puff of the cigar. "How did you know where to find me?"

"One of your staff followed you here and called me."

Raising a brow, she went for insouciance that she didn't feel in the least. "Keeping tabs on your favorite supermodel, you naughty man?"

Something flitted in and out of those thickly fringed eyes, too fast for her to catch it. "I was nearby when you tore out of the garage as if a demon was chasing you."

"I didn't realize I was so important to you that you'd come all this way to pay your respects to my grandfather," she said, going on the offensive.

There was no other way to act around him. Shields up one hundred percent and donning titanium armor, like the prickly heroine in her favorite sci-fi show. Also based on a novel this very man had written.

Seriously, her obsession with him had no chance of petering out when she gorged herself on every word he'd ever written—novels and articles and newsletters and political treatises—like a wanton glutton.

"Clearly, it was a self-indulgent fantasy to imagine I'd find you behaving like a responsible, normal adult in the throes of grief." The cigar that she'd barely taken two puffs of was roughly yanked away from her lips and put out with a pinch of fingers that should have burned him but drew not even a quiet hiss. "That's a disgusting habit and a lethal one, too."

"Did you miss me so much that you came all this way to harass me, Nasir? No one else to look down on and feel better about yourself?"

"I came here because I need you."

Yana sat up with the force of a coiled spring that had been stretched too far back, for far too long. Her head swam, the reason anything from starvation to the special kind of dizziness only he could cause. "Huh! The world is upside down today, I guess. Or I'm traveling through parallel universes like Uzma does," she said, mentioning the intrepid heroine of his latest novel. Plucking her phone from her jeweled designer clutch, she opened the camera app and thrust it in his face. "Care to repeat that so that I can record it?"

Silence lingered, full of his infinite patience and her childish taunts.

"Fine." She straightened her posture on the chaise, tucking her knees away from his. They were both tall people and in the tight space of his legs, her awareness was on steroids.

She tried to not linger on the way his black trousers bunched at his thighs, or the way the white shirt open to his chest drew her gaze to the swirls of hair on dark olive skin. Or the large platinum-faced dial of his watch on a corded wrist. Or the long, bare fingers that had once—only once—lingered on her jaw with something almost bordering on tenderness.

"I have a serious proposition for you."

God, even after all these years of mutual dislike and loathing, even after he'd married another model, a woman a few years older than she was, whom she'd nevertheless considered her mentor and close friend, whom he'd had a child with, even after he'd blamed her for helping his marriage to Jacqueline combust, how could she still feel this giddy anticipation? When was she going to get over this…ridiculous fascination with him?

"How interesting," she said, pouring her excitement on thick even as her belly twisted into a knot. Leaning toward him, she mock-whispered, "But my kind of propositions are not usually your…*forte*."

A muscle jumped in his jaw, the scar twisting with the action. He thrust a hand through that thick, wavy hair he usually kept military short. "Oh, believe me. Having found you in a nightclub two days after your grandfather's death, smoking a cigar, looking like you do… I'm questioning my common sense in even being here."

"Ahh…now, that's the guy I know and love to loathe." A tinkling laugh escaped her. "Come, Nasir. You might be a diplomat in the biggest political circles and the hottest bachelor on the planet but it's the lowest denominator of you I get, no? Let's not try something new today, of all days. I've had enough shocks, thank you very much."

Remorse flashed through those usually inscrutable eyes. "I'm sorry for your loss, Yana. I know that grief takes different forms—"

"You don't know anything about my relationship with Thaata."

"Fair enough."

Irritation and hunger and something more danced across Yana's skin as she studied him.

"It's about Zara."

His daughter. Her facade fell away like snakeskin. She reached for his hands but pulled away at the last minute. "Why the hell couldn't you have opened with that instead of insulting me?"

"Your worry about her is real." He sounded stunned.

"And you're an ass."

Feeling caged, her breaths coming shallow, she stood up. Her foot had fallen asleep on her, forcing her to grab him to keep her balance.

His white linen shirt proved no barrier to the firm muscles underneath and the heat coming off him. Under her fingers, his abdomen clenched.

The sensation of his hot, hard body under her touch stung her palm. His grip on her tightened as she tried to yank herself away. "Damn it, Yana! Stay still." The tips of his fingers pressed into her bare arm; one corded arm wrapped around her waist. It was too much contact and hyperventilation wasn't far away. "Or you'll ruin that pretty face and any hope of—"

"What's wrong with Zara?"

Now that she'd managed her overreaction to his proximity, she could see the exhaustion beneath his calm. It made the light, slightly raised tissue of his scar stand out in stark contrast to the rest of his skin. Worry and fatigue carved deep grooves around his wide mouth.

An answering pang vibrated within her chest.

"She's fine, physically. But losing her mother at that young age, even one as mostly absent as Jacqueline was...the doctors are saying she's not adjusting well to the loss." His Adam's apple moved up and down as he swallowed. "We've tried everything. It has been...painful to see a bubbly, extroverted child like her withdraw to that extent. I'm at a loss as to how to help her."

"Children are much more resilient than we give them credit for. With support, Zara will get over losing Jacqueline."

"Have you gotten over your mom's neglectful, bordering on abusive behavior toward you?"

Something hot and oily bellowed under her skin. "That's none of your business."

"I'm just saying Zara shouldn't have to go through this alone."

"How is she alone when she has you?"

"I've tried my damnedest to get close to her. Don't pretend as if you don't know how things are between us. How Jacqueline messed everything up. How she tried to cut me off from my own daughter."

"I don't want to talk about Jacqueline."

"I don't, either." He rubbed a hand over his face. "This is about Zara. Not you, not me and definitely not her mother. She lights up when you text her or video call her. She talks for hours about your chats, your emails, the cards you send her from all over the world. That collection of keychains you've given her over the years… Every single one is worn down for how much she plays with them." A shuddering sigh made his chest rise and fall. "She keeps asking for you, Yana."

Yana jerked away from him, wobbled again and braced herself against the back of a dark leather sofa. Shame coiled tight in her chest. "I'm sorry I haven't been to visit her recently."

Damn it, how could she have forgotten all the promises she'd made to Zara when Jacqueline had fallen ill? Why had she gotten involved when she had such an abysmal record at handling expectations? What about being the child of two absent, neglectful, narcissistic parents equipped her to handle a fragile child? "Between losing my grandparents only months apart and work—" and keeping her head afloat while her mother robbed her blind "—I… I've been scattered."

"Nothing new in how you live your life, then, huh?"

His criticism stung hard and deep.

She loved Zara. Loved her despite the fact that Jacqueline had used Yana's tumultuous feelings for Nasir to feel better about her crumbling marriage. Despite the fact that he loathed the very sight of Yana.

Under the guise of fixing her hair, she dabbed at the tears prickling behind her eyes. Her failure rubbed her hollow.

She had failed Zara. After vowing to herself that she wouldn't let the little girl feel alone in the world like she'd once felt.

The vague headache that had been hunting her all day returned with a vengeance, making her light-headed. Or was it the fact that she'd skipped lunch and dinner and her sugar levels were falling fast? "No, nothing new."

A soft curse escaped his mouth.

Nasir never cursed and if she was feeling normal, she'd have recognized it for the win it was. Suddenly, she became aware of the heat of his body at her back and her dizziness intensified. His fingers landed on her shoulders, the rough pads deliciously abrasive against her bare skin.

"I'm sorry. I came to ask you for help. For a favor. To…beg you if I need to. And yet, I can't seem to stop insulting you."

"Nothing new in how you talk to me either, then, huh?" Yana glared at him and sighed. "I want to see her. I do. Zara's important to me, one of the few important people in my life. But…" She rubbed at her pounding temples. "Right now things are impossible to get away from."

"That's where the proposition part comes in."

"Not necessary. I love Zara as if she were…" She bit her lip, heat flooding her cheeks.

My own, she'd been about to say. Which was laughable even in thought because she was the last person who should be responsible for a young girl. She couldn't even manage her own life without sinking into debt and self-rage.

Nasir's amber-colored eyes gleamed. "And yet, you don't act like she is. She's seen you once since Jacqueline died."

"I just told you I've been busy with shoots and—"

"I've heard whispers that you're completely broke. If that's true, I really don't care how it happened. I'll pay all your debts and pay you whatever sum you demand on top if you come spend the next three months with Zara."

"No."

Her answer reverberated in the quiet around them, the darkness amplifying it.

No, I don't want to be anywhere near you.

No, I don't want to spend three months under the same roof as you.

No, I finally have enough self-preservation to not cut myself down just because you hate me. No, no, no.

Even if that meant breaking her promise to Zara.

"I know you have no way out of the financial hole you've dug yourself—"

"No."

"Because your modeling contracts are drying up—"

"No."

"So my bet is that any assets you have will be seized soon and—"

"No."

"Damn it, Yana! You need this as much as Zara needs you."

"No," Yana repeated, even as the word continued to ring in her ears and her vision was blurring and fading and she felt nauseated and dizzy and...

"Yana...look at me. Yana! What the hell have you done to yourself now, you..."

He's really beautiful. The errant thought dropped into Yana's fading consciousness.

Nasir grabbed her and pulled her to him, and she could finally see the amber flecks in his eyes and the long, curved lashes casting shadows onto razor-sharp cheekbones. He was looking at her as if he didn't loathe her. As if he was actually worried about her. As if he...

No, she couldn't spend three months with the man she'd loved for half her life.

Not that she loved him anymore. *Not at all.* The tightness in her chest was only an echo of what she'd once felt for him.

Yana fainted and in the flash of a second before she lost consciousness, she had the disturbingly pitiful thought that Nasir had caught her. That he hadn't let her fall to the ground.

CHAPTER TWO

NASIR HADEED WALKED the perimeter of the VIP lounge like a caged predator as the young doctor that had been dragged from the exotic restaurant downstairs examined Yana. He glanced at his watch for the hundredth time in the last half hour, a powerless ire simmering under his skin.

She'd remained unconscious for three and a half minutes. It had, however, felt like a hundred eternities. His heart hadn't yet calmed down from its rapid pounding rhythm.

Despite his long career in war-torn zones and some of the most dangerous places in the world, despite having tasted the loss of a woman he'd loved once that had forever calcified his heart, he'd never been so terrified as when Yana had folded into his arms like a cardboard doll. Amidst her litany of *nos*.

The saving grace had been that he'd shouted for his body-guard/assistant. Ahmed had had the presence of mind to immediately commandeer a doctor.

Nasir had rubbed her arms up and down as soon as he'd carried her to the chaise longue. Even with her light brown hair hanging in a limp, messy ponytail, her lips chapped and even bleeding in a couple of places for she had the habit of worrying her lips with her teeth, her face a sickly sheen of white, she was still the most stunningly beautiful woman he'd ever seen.

Worse, not an hour in her company and he was cursing

her recklessness, his own decisions that had led him to need her, and the universe all in one go.

And his weakness when it came to her, too, for he hadn't been able to stop running his fingers over the jut of those legendary cheekbones and the sharp, elongated tip of her signature nose that had skyrocketed her to fame at the tender age of sixteen.

Once she'd recovered consciousness, he'd moved to the far end of the cavernous lounge. To give her privacy and to get himself under control. *Ya, Allah*, what was wrong with him?

He'd chased her halfway around the world to this damned nightclub because he needed her for his daughter. And yet, all he'd done was insult her, over and over again.

Where was the diplomat the world lauded? Where was the responsible father of a five-year-old?

I always get the lowest denominator of you...

If only she knew how close to the vulgar truth she was. How she inspired and invoked and ignited his basest instincts. When she taunted him. When those gorgeous brown eyes landed near his mouth and skidded away. When she simply fluttered about in the locus of his own existence.

Her soft whispers as she spoke to the young doctor, the quiet but husky chuckle, the trembling shoulders...everything about her called to him.

If only he could see the beautiful, vapid, vain teen she'd suddenly turned into one summer, he'd have no problem dealing with her.

His disastrous marriage to Jacqueline Yusuf—a sophisticated model and businesswoman he'd once considered his equal in every way—had completely cured him of the stupidity of trusting his judgment when it came to women.

But Yana...had always been indefinably stubborn and refused to be slotted into any one box.

He couldn't look at her and not remember the fifteen-year-old who'd shyly hero-worshipped him the first time he'd visited his father and his new wife. Or the one who'd begged for his autograph on a first edition. Or the passionate, sweet teenager who'd yelled and cried when he'd killed off her favorite character, or the hug she'd given him with an endearing smile on her suddenly stunning face when he'd brought that favorite character of hers back to life in the next novel.

He couldn't not see the nineteen-year-old who'd shocked him by walking through his room ditching pieces of clothing on the way to his bed, boldly declaring that she loved him with all of her heart, body and soul.

Or the girl who'd lied to her mother that Nasir had kissed her. Or the woman who'd looked as if she'd been dealt a staggering blow when Jacqueline, her friend and mentor, had introduced him as her fiancé. Or the woman who'd barely met his eyes when she'd stood by Jacqueline's side when they'd gotten married.

Or the woman who'd lied more than once to help hide Jacqueline's many affairs from him. Or the woman who'd stayed by Jacqueline's bedside for the last few weeks during her battle with cancer.

Or the woman who had miraculously managed to carve a place for herself in his young daughter's heart. Or the woman he'd touched in tenderness after Jacqueline had died, not a few minutes before his lawyers had discovered that Jacqueline had been preparing to sue him for solo custody of Zara, and Yana would have been the character witness to prove his negligence toward his daughter.

And yet, he'd learned, only after Jacqueline had died, how Yana had spent hours entertaining Zara, watching her, cooking for her, reading to her while Jacqueline was supposed to have been looking after her, how much attention she'd bestowed on his daughter when it should have been her mother doing that, how many times Jacqueline had dropped her off with Yana.

Yana Auntie this, Yana Auntie that... It was all his five-year-old girl would speak of. Just when Nasir had written Yana off entirely, the blasted woman revealed a new, complex dimension to herself that had dragged him back under her spell.

She loathed him and yet, she was capable of genuinely loving his child. What was he supposed to make of her? If only this ridiculous attraction he'd fought for so long would fade.

But he needed her and damn it, he needed Yana well again and ready to spar with him.

He needed her to not look like a lost waif, one hard breath away from falling apart. He needed her to fight him tooth and nail so that he didn't have to feel guilty about how he'd talked to her tonight.

She *had* just lost her grandparents—the only responsible adults she'd known in her life. And he'd done nothing but insult her and minimize her very real grief.

He'd never met another woman who provoked such extreme reactions in him. Not even Fatima—the woman he'd loved a lifetime ago—had tied him up in knots like Yana did.

From the tendrils of tenderness that had swamped him as he'd held her, to the rage that she didn't care enough about her own health. Even back then, he'd only learned of her diabetes when she'd gone into shock due to low sugar levels. It had been reckless and naive and foolish at sixteen. Now, almost thirteen years later... Had she still no sense of self-preservation?

What if he hadn't been there to catch her when she'd fainted and force feed her the bar of chocolate when she'd recovered consciousness? What if no one knew her whereabouts and she'd lain there for hours, going into shock? What if he'd had to inform his child that her Yana Auntie had taken seriously ill, too?

And he was inviting this…train wreck, this selfish, infuriatingly stubborn woman into his precious little girl's life.

Into his own life.

Into his space—his haven, which he allowed no one into.

It was like issuing an invitation to chaos and mayhem and sheer madness to reside in his house, in his head, in his heart.

"Here, sir," said Ahmed, stalling his walk, a bottle of water in his hand.

Nasir shook his head, too tired to reprimand the older man for addressing him using the honorific.

"Is Ms. Reddy okay, do you think?"

On cue, Yana laughed, leaning toward the young doctor.

He *wasn't* jealous of her attention toward the damned doctor, or her laughter or whatever it was she was saying to him. *He wasn't.*

"It was a miracle you caught her, Inshallah," Ahmed continued, unaware of his employer's roiling emotions. "Or she might have really hurt herself."

Nasir grunted and restarted his perambulations of the lounge, cutting closer and closer to where the doctor was now entering her phone number into his own cell phone. If he gritted his teeth any tighter, he was going to need dental work.

"Did the doctor say what caused the faint?" Ahmed asked.

"She probably forgot to eat." Nasir cleared his throat. "She's diabetic."

"I remember. Anything else you need from me?"

"No, get some sleep. We'll leave for London first thing tomorrow morning."

"Ms. Reddy has agreed to spend time with Zara baby, then?" Ahmed inquired, all polite affability.

Yana's multiple *nos* echoed inside Nasir's head like a chant. She hadn't simply refused him. No, she'd looked horrified—as if he'd invited her to sacrifice herself at some demon's altar.

He usually encouraged that impression of himself in most people, including his extended family and friends. That she saw him as some kind of autocratic, unfeeling beast grated, though.

"Sir?"

"No, she hasn't agreed." He bit out the words. "But she will. Even if it means I have to—"

"I know that you and Ms. Reddy don't see eye to eye, but I will not support kidnapping the young woman, sir. Even for Zara baby's sake."

Nasir laughed, the tension in his muscles relaxing for the first time in days. His bodyguard's strait-laced morality and hero complex never ceased to amaze him. "Things are going to be hard enough dealing with her, Ahmed. She doesn't need you as her champion."

"Beg your pardon, sir, but your father taught me that everyone deserves a champion. Ms. Reddy does, too. Especially since I've never seen you treat anyone with the kind of…" Ahmed broke off, then cast him an arch look that communicated everything he didn't say. "Have you forgotten how much your mother loathes Ms. Reddy?"

"She'll understand that Zara needs her," Nasir said, but even he didn't believe it. His mother's reaction to his bringing Yana home was a bridge he'd cross when he came to it.

"I just think bringing Zara baby to her could've been easier," Ahmed added with infinite patience.

"And let her drag Zara around like unwanted luggage just like Jacqueline did? Let my five-year-old daughter be exposed to alcohol and drugs and parties and toxic behaviors like her mother did? Should I also expose her to all the lurid gossip about her mother and her lovers that's still flying around even after all these months?"

"You're holding your wife's past mistakes against Ms. Reddy. I've never known you to be so...cruel." Ahmed sighed. "It *is* a hard situation. But if Ms. Reddy says she cannot make it, then she must have a good reason. I have seen her with Zara baby and she adores her, just as much as the little girl adores Ms. Reddy."

The conviction in Ahmed's voice only fortified his own. "Don't worry, Ahmed. I won't make you a party to this. You can catch a different flight." His jaw tight, Nasir stared at the woman who was sure to cause him untold problems once he was in his house. "But by kidnapping or some other way, she's coming home with me."

"Who's kidnapping whom?" Yana asked behind him.

Nasir turned around to find the young doctor glancing up adoringly at her, his arm propping her up. "Everything okay, Doc?" he asked, wishing he could laser the man's arm off with his vision.

"I'm fine," muttered the irritated voice next to him.

Whatever the doctor saw in Nasir's face, he replied hurriedly, "Ms. Reddy's vitals are all good. Just exhaustion brought on by weakness."

"Glucose levels?"

"Normal. The chocolate bar you fed her helped stabilize her. She just needs lots of rest, hydration and proper meals."

"Ahmed," Nasir said, somehow holding on to the last thread of his patience.

His bodyguard escorted the reluctant, dazed doctor out the door while he was still shaking his cell phone in Yana's direction in the universal sign of "call me."

Finally, Nasir turned his attention to her.

Yana stood leaning against another high-backed lounger, her fingers fiddling with the jacket he'd draped over her. *His* jacket.

It hung on her shoulders, the thick collar drawing his gaze to the smooth skin between her small breasts and the one button holding it closed farther down. The tie holding her hair together had fallen off and now the golden-brown waves fell past her shoulders, the edges curling up.

"Don't treat me like an idiot," she bit out, all huskiness gone.

She still looked pale to him, but at least the fight was back in her. "Don't act like one, then."

"Just because you've caught me out at a bad time doesn't mean you get to look down that arrogant beak of a nose at me."

"You fainted, Yana," he said, gritting his teeth again. "And didn't respond for three and a half minutes."

Even the obvious fright in his tone had no effect on her.

"It's been a horrible few weeks. No, months. Seeing you just made it worse. I told you but you didn't listen."

When she wobbled, Nasir caught her at the waist. She fell into him with a soft thud, a quiet, enraged growl escaping her mouth. He felt her anger, her grief, her resignation, as if they were his own. Felt the force of her aversion to him.

"I hate you," she whispered, almost to herself. "I hate that you're the one who found me when I'm at my lowest."

Nasir let them wash over him, hoping the venom and rage in her words would dilute his own awareness. Her face close to his, her warm breath feathered over his jaw. Then there was the prick of her fingernails into his forearm. The wildcat was doing that on purpose and yet, the sensation only made his arousal sharper.

This was how it would be every minute between them—

she cursing at him and he…would be in a constant state of arousal. It was funny, really, how they'd come full circle. She loathed him now and he couldn't be near her without his body betraying him like a damned teenager.

For a man who'd seen that heaven and hell could exist side by side on this very earth, maybe this was just punishment for his cruelty toward her. When she'd been nineteen and had needed firm handling and kind words and not his blistering wrath. When she'd been his bride's maid of honor at their wedding, Jacki's nurse at her bedside, a grief-stricken best friend with his child sobbing in her arms.

For a second he indulged the idea of telling her what her nearness did to him. Of shocking her as she constantly did him.

Would she be disgusted by his near-constant desire for her? Would she call him a roaring hypocrite as he deserved? Or would she simply count him as one among the scores of lecherous men that hit on her?

Slowly, feeling as if he'd run a marathon with no victory at the end, he tugged the neckline of her jacket higher.

"Can you please stop manhandling me? I'm all sweaty and gross. And why the hell did you cut open my top?"

"You were hyperventilating even before you fainted." He'd thanked the dim lighting of the lounge as the leather of her corset top had splayed open under the sharpness of his penknife. He didn't need more pictures of her naked perfection in his head. "That damned thing was so tight it's a miracle you could breathe."

Earlier she'd been too cold. Now her skin was warm as he held her up. The indent of her tiny waist, the slight flare of her hips, the jut of her hip bone, the smooth warmth of her skin…everything about her was fragile in his fingers.

"Let me go," she demanded.

"You'll kiss the floor the second I do," he said, holding himself rigid and stiff. Even with the aroma of cigar and the leather of the nightclub clinging to her, she smelled good.

It had been too long since he'd held a woman like this. Since he'd had sex. Since he'd worked out the pent-up frustrations of his body instead of engaging his mind.

Learning of Jacqueline's affairs had put him off relationships. Swiping left or right or whatever the hell side he was supposed to, casual dating or sex with strangers...he hadn't been fond of it in his twenties. At forty-two, the very idea of taking some strange woman to his bed made him want to hurl. And yet, every inch of his body was buzzing with an electric hum now.

Ironic that the one woman who made him react this way at the most innocent of contacts was someone he could never have. Even for a casual fling.

"Escort me to a cab, then."

"No."

"Have Ahmed drive me home, then."

"No. And for God's sake, stop arguing with me just for the heck of it."

"Or what?" she said, thrusting her face into his with a belligerence that got his blood pumping.

"Don't push me, Yana. We'll go to my hotel suite, where you'll eat, sleep for however many hours your body needs and then, in the morning, we'll finish our discussion."

"I don't want to spend another minute around you." She stepped back from him, palms raised. "If I have a heart attack next, it will all be your fault, Nasir."

He'd had enough. "You can screech and scream like a banshee for all I care. I'm not letting you out of my sight anytime soon."

Without batting an eyelid, he picked her up and threw her

over his shoulder, fireman style. God, she weighed so little that he didn't even breathe hard, though it had been a while since his job demanded something so physical.

To his eternal surprise, she fell quiet. And he knew it was because she was on the last reserves of her energy. The chocolate bar would only prop her up for a while. Her quiet resignation rid him of any guilt that he was railroading her when she was feeling this weak.

She needed looking after as much as his five-year-old did, at least for a little while. Resolve renewed, he forged through the screaming throes of the nightclub.

Barely a few minutes later he crossed the foyer, then pushed the button for the elevator with Ahmed at his back. Thank God he'd booked a full suite at the same hotel. Still, they'd caught more than one curious hotel guest's attention. More than one eager paparazzo's prurient gaze.

But at least he had her now.

CHAPTER THREE

THE UNIVERSE WAS really cruel, Yana thought, as the man she'd taught herself to hate—and, oh, how easy he made it for her—placed her on his bed with a tenderness that stemmed from all the wrong reasons.

She rolled away from him using energy she didn't have and instantly regretted the impulse. It was *his* bed she was rolling in; his suite he'd brought her to. That heady cocktail of clean sweat and his signature scent clung to the sheets.

If she closed her eyes, she could still feel the hard dig of his shoulder over her belly, his muscled back smushing her breasts, his corded forearm at the tops of her thighs, holding her in place. Even more shocking was his sudden devolution from the veneer of the starchy, uptight, no-public-display gentleman he'd always shown the world.

Who was this Nasir who had no control over his words or his actions?

Slowly, she sat up, cataloging the exhaustion sweeping through her. She was hungry. Tired. Her mouth felt dry and gritty. But she hadn't had a fainting spell in years. Not that Nasir would believe her.

The stress of the past few weeks, her new medication and the fact that she hadn't eaten all day…they were excuses, however valid. She'd let herself drift into chaos again.

But better Nasir who found her than Mira or Nush or God

forbid Caio—who took protective instincts to a whole other level. Her sisters would've been very upset at how close to burnout she'd edged. They'd have blamed themselves and that was a vicious cycle she'd never enter again with loved ones.

At least with Nasir, she'd had a lifetime of dealing with his contempt.

But if there was one thing they had in common, it was the stubborn tenacity once they decided on a course.

She saw it in his face now, in the tight set of his jaw. In the edgy energy that imbued his usually elegant movements. He'd decided that Zara needed her and he was determined to drag her with him. But as much as she adored Zara, how could she be a stabilizing influence on her when her own life was only two streets away from utter mayhem?

Brow furrowed, Nasir approached the bed as if she were a wild animal he hoped to not provoke. Yana splayed her arms over the thick headboard behind her and straightened. "I won't bite, Nasir." When his jaw tightened, she grinned. "I mean, I know you're much too conventional to enjoy something so…outside the box."

"Good to see your usual…spark back. As for what I enjoy…" His gaze skidded toward her mouth and away so fast that she wasn't sure if she'd imagined it. "Just because I don't advertise my desires for all the world to see doesn't mean they're all vanilla."

A shiver of pleasure ran down her spine—keenly felt after the miserable past few months. Damn, but the man could play.

With each step he took toward her, fantasies she'd buried years ago roared back to life. Done in pale pinks and warm yellows, the luxury suite amplified the stark, forbidding sensuality of the man. There had always been something almost ascetic about him. And like in the stories of celestial women who seduced sages, Yana had always imagined herself to be the one who broke through his reserve.

Coming to a stop at the foot of the bed, he rolled a bottle of water toward her on the silk sheets. She emptied it in a matter of seconds, wiping the water that dripped down her chin with the back of her hand. All the while, his gaze seared like a physical touch.

"One would think you'd take better care of your body seeing how it's your only livelihood."

She held her automatic response by the last frayed thread of self-control. Her dreams for the future, her hopes for a different career... He hadn't won the privilege of hearing about them. On the contrary, she wouldn't be surprised if he mocked her for having them in the first place. Curling her lip, she said, "One would think you'd have more capacity for empathy and understanding given you've seen the worst of the world."

His mouth flinched.

Had she wounded him? Was that even possible for a mere mortal like her?

"You're right. I have been overly judgmental when it comes to you. But that shouldn't preclude you from—"

"Please, Nasir. Try to understand. I cannot come with you." She let him hear her frustration, let him see her powerlessness in granting him this wish.

Amber-brown eyes searched hers. "Of course, you can. It's a choice you make to put someone else's needs, a child's needs, before your own." Hands tucked into his trouser pockets, he studied her with dispassionate intensity. "Tell me what I can do to sweeten the pot."

She raised a brow, calling on all the haughtiness cameras had taught her to fake most of her life. "How pedestrian and predictable of you, Nasir. Like every other man, you think you can buy me. Even my grandfather couldn't rise above bribes to make me behave."

"We both know you're in a financial hole. I'm giving you an easy way out." He rubbed a finger over his brow. "I admit I'm surprised you're not running toward me to snatch my hand off."

"Or you underestimate my loathing for sharing a roof with you."

Their gazes met and held. Memories swirled across the distance between them.

Long, dark nights spent in Jacqueline's Paris apartment watching over her as her death drew nearer. In those few weeks she'd spent at her friend's side, an intimacy of sorts had developed between Nasir and her. A byproduct of being so close to mortality, no doubt.

It had been more insidious than physical attraction, more dangerous. An intense curiosity in his eyes—as if he meant to peel away her armor and see beneath. As if, for the first time in their history, he found her interesting.

She'd even seen a flash of admiration in his eyes, and if she wasn't careful, she'd begin chasing it all over again. Like her mother was forever chasing the impossible win at the gambling tables. Like her dad with his alcoholic binges.

Addiction was in her genes. Only her drug of choice was this man's approval. And desire. And respect. And want. And her own need to bring him to his distinguished knees.

Not a week after Jacqueline's death, he'd turned on her. Accused her of conspiring with his late wife to separate Zara from him permanently. Accused her of cozying up to him even as she'd planned to betray him again. He'd consigned the worst motives to her actions and written her off as a backstabbing bitch, without giving her a single chance to defend herself.

His consequent cruelty was a shield Yana couldn't let go of.

"If I was wrong about you—"

"If?" she bit out. "Is it any wonder that I find rotting in penury more appealing than being saved by you?" She let out a huff, breaking eye contact and adjusting the oversize jacket around her shoulders. As if all of this was nothing but a nuisance she could shrug off. "Why couldn't you have just brought Zara to me?"

"Because she's already gone through too much upheaval in the last few months."

"Fine. You can oversee our visit together, looking down your beaky nose and holding me up to your impossible standards. I'd love to spend time with her here."

"Or you could be smart and just accept my help. It's not like you have a thousand other offers."

"Arrogant of you to assume that I don't have people who'd dig me out of my financial hole as you call it. All I have to do is ask."

"Like who?"

"Like my sisters, who are both independently wealthy," she blurted out, hating his arrogant assumption that she'd been abandoned by one and all. That no one found her worthy just because he didn't. "Like Caio, who's my grandfather's right-hand man and my brother-in-law, and the new CEO of OneTech. Like Aristos, my other billionaire brother-in-law."

"And yet, you haven't confided in any of them, have you? Why is that, I wonder?"

Every minute with him was a danger to her persona of shallow supermodel. "How do you know you haven't caught me right before I did that? As tacky as I can be, even I know not to ask for handouts just two days after my grandfather passed away."

"I don't believe you. I think you hate the thought of asking them for help. Of letting them see how spectacularly you've failed in managing your life. Especially when one of your sisters is a doctor and the other's a…coding genius. After all, you have that stubborn pride to contend with."

Dismay filled her at how clearly he could see through to her deepest wound. But then, no one else knew her flaws as well as he did.

She was saved from responding when his phone gave a series of loud pings. His frown went into scowl territory with each swipe of his fingers.

She pushed onto her knees. "Is it Zara? What's wrong?"

"Some imbecile snapped a pic of us going into the elevator." A pithy curse flew from his mouth. "It's clear it's you and me." His scowl changed direction. "You don't care?"

She shrugged, examining his reaction. His privacy was sacrosanct to him. No one even knew where his permanent residence was. "That cute doctor, can we make sure he doesn't leak that I fainted?"

A shrewd glint dawned in his eyes. "You don't care about being linked with me but you don't want anyone to know you fainted?"

She blurted out before she thought better, "I don't want my sisters to know."

"A hint of a rumor about you and me just months after Jacqueline's death…"

"Everything that mattered to me is…already gone. So please, keep your threats of destruction to yourself."

It was not some dramatic threat or a bait for pity.

The resignation in her eyes burned Nasir with its honest edge. And for a second, he felt the most overwhelming urge to save her. From herself, if required.

God, he was as arrogant and egotistical as she called him.

"Not even if Zara were to hear of that kind of gossip about her Yana Auntie and her father?"

"She's only five." She jerked her head up, her golden hair spreading around her face as if she were a lioness shaking out her mane. "She wouldn't hear such…lurid gossip."

"And yet, she knows the name of every one of her *uncles* who visited her mama on photoshoots at work. She's aware that her mama was fobbing her off on you even before she was gone. She's confused and heartbroken, Yana."

Her curse rattled in the silence between them. She looked stricken and yet she rallied. "I'm not an easy fix you can use when you're overwhelmed and then throw away like some dirty Band-Aid when you're done. You threw me out of her life, Nasir. You told me to never return."

"So you'll punish Zara for my mistakes?"

"I'm not." She pressed a hand to her chest as if it physically hurt. "There's bad blood between us. It won't be long before she catches on to it. That's more confusion you're dumping on her."

"Then we'll start afresh with a clean slate."

She laughed then and it wasn't just mockery. The glint of tears in her eyes, the bitter twist to her mouth, spoke eloquently. "Hell has more chance of freezing over before you'll see me as anything more than—"

"So this is about your ego, then?" Frustration and a powerless feeling burst out of Nasir. That he was being a beast to Yana was unforgivable. But that his past actions should now so adversely affect Zara, too, made him sick to his stomach. That he had forever calcified his heart as an unhealthy coping mechanism for an early loss in life, resulting in his worry that he wouldn't be able to connect with his own daughter, was a constant niggle at the back of his head.

"That I rejected your seduction attempt all those years

ago? That I lost my temper over your continued lies about Jacqueline's affairs? That I'm telling you to your face that you're reckless and irresponsible and that you should get your life under control after you fainted in my arms?" he said, unraveling under the onslaught of a perfect storm of worries. "You're so insecure about one rejection ten years ago that you would abandon a child you claim to love when she needs you the most? Are you still just as desperate as you were back then for my approval?"

He couldn't bear to look at Yana's stricken face at his harsh words. He couldn't swallow the bitter lump in his throat that said he was no better a parent for Zara than Jacqueline had ever been.

"I don't want anything from you." Her whisper could have been a shout.

"Whether you accept my incentives or not is moot now. I know how to get you on the plane."

Large brown eyes searched his.

"I'll leak news of your debt to your sisters."

"You wouldn't."

"I will do anything to make Zara smile again," he said, grabbing the jacket he'd discarded earlier. "To not repeat the mistakes I've already made. So yes, I would tell the world that the incomparable Yana Reddy is so deep in debt that she can't even afford her own medication. That her team has jumped ship. Your sisters will pity you and—"

"You're a bastard."

"You know I am. So why sound so surprised?"

"And how do you know I won't fill Zara's mind with lies against you?" He didn't miss the cornered look on her face. A bitter smile pinched her mouth. "You've given me enough material over the years."

Some uncivilized part of him only she brought out wanted

to growl like some wild animal at the threat. He was still fixing all the damage Jacqueline had caused by filling his daughter's tender heart with horrible lies about his apathy as a father. Still fixing his own blunders. For Yana to threaten him...

Nasir made himself take a deep breath. Forced himself to go with his instinct, to listen to his heart and his gut, instead of the more rational facts and fears. "I don't know that for certain," he said, the words coming more easily than he'd have imagined. Coming from some place he'd shut down a long time ago. "But I do know that however much you loathe me, you care deeply about Zara."

It was the dig about her wanting approval from Nasir that stuck like a craw in Yana's throat.

His words had cut her open as if he'd taken a scalpel to her skin. But examined again, out of his infuriating and overwhelming presence, as the blistering-hot water pounded out the soreness in her muscles that always accompanied her fainting spells, Yana acknowledged that it was the very truth that she'd spent years running from.

She'd always chased approval and validation—from her mother, from her grandparents, from her career, from Jacqueline. And she'd sought it in the most harmful, chaotic, childish ways possible.

For years, she'd wished she'd been smart and self-sufficient and self-composed like her older sister Mira. Then Nush had come into their lives and she'd wished she were full of hope and love and magic like her little sister was. Not forgetting that genius brain of hers.

Yana had always wished she were someone else. Someone more grounded, someone cleverer, someone more easygoing, someone less chaotic, someone healthier... The list of things she wasn't yet wanted to be was as long as the number of thugs Diana owed money to.

Even as Yana desperately wanted to be seen and appreciated and loved for herself at the same time.

Talk about confusing her little brain.

What Nasir was wrong about, though—and how she'd have liked to tell him that to his face—was that she'd sought his approval all those years ago with her pathetic seduction attempt. Or that she'd offered herself as some kind of cheap bargain. Or that she'd wreaked some sort of petty revenge afterward because he'd dented her ego.

As the hot water restored her sense and composure, she saw the root of her obsession with the blasted man.

Nasir was one of three people—her sisters Mira and Nush being the other two—who'd given her approval without her having to earn it with good behavior or better grades or by making restitutions because she'd ruined her mother's career simply by being born.

He hadn't judged her for being her mother's daughter or criticized her for being her chaotic, messy self, or mocked her for following him around with puppy-dog eyes anytime he'd visited. The four years she'd spent under the same roof as his father, the few months Nasir had joined them in between assignments and visits to his mother, he'd been unflinchingly kind to her.

Already making her name in modeling, Yana had been exposed to men and women wanting things from her. Her mother wanted the fame and fortune she'd lost by giving birth to Yana at a young age. Her alcoholic, mostly absent father wanted forgiveness in his rare moments of sobriety. How could she forgive someone who held no significance in her life except as a sperm donor?

The simple acceptance she'd received from an experienced, worldly man like Nasir had been like standing in sunbeams. Giving her the thing she'd craved most, he'd made her feel worthy of it.

There was magic in such unconditional acceptance.

She'd fallen for him with all the passion and intensity of first love, ready to sacrifice everything at his feet, follow him around the world with her heart in her eyes. Hence her pathetic seduction attempt. Just thinking of it now made her cringe in the shower.

And when he'd inevitably rejected her, with such brutal, cutting words that she'd forever lost not only her self-esteem but also his trust, she'd shattered. When her mother had found her running back to her room, tears running down her cheeks, Yana had lied to her that he'd kissed her.

Letting out a feral groan, Yana pressed her forehead to the pristine tile of the wall. It had been the stupidest trick she'd ever played in her life. In one stroke, with one foolish lie told out of the fear of making Diana angry, she'd made Nasir loathe her.

It was the same way she'd behaved with Thaata, too. The more she'd wanted her grandfather's approval, the more she'd acted against her own self-interests, against her own well-being.

Never again. Never again would she let her self-worth be decided by anyone else. Not her mother. Not her grandfather. And definitely not Nasir.

Stepping out of the shower, Yana wiped the moisture from the large mirror and stared at her reflection. A smile broke through the worried twist of her mouth. She'd been in that chaotic, self-damaging place before and she'd clawed her way out of it. This time there was the added motivation of ensuring a five-year-old's well-being and happiness.

A girl just like her, wanting nothing but love from the

adults around her. A chance for Yana to make sure Zara's life was different from what her own had been. She'd give the little girl all the attention and affection she'd always craved from Jacqueline, like Yana had craved from Diana.

And just maybe this three-month stint with Nasir and Zara was the universe throwing her a bone. She needed a place to recoup the loss she'd sustained, recover from her mother's betrayal and plan how to get her life back on the right path. On a different path. A path chosen by her and her alone.

She'd do it all without letting herself be swallowed up by the man who'd made her believe in herself a long time ago.

CHAPTER FOUR

IT WAS A month later that Yana found herself aboard Nasir's private jet on the way to one of the tiny islands that made up Bali, after her last modeling shoot for a while. She hadn't wanted to keep him waiting once she'd agreed to his proposition, but it was impossible for her to just check out of her world for three months at a moment's notice, just because he demanded it. When she'd presented him with the various demands on her schedule, he'd agreed that she couldn't leave with him readily enough. But of course, she should've known that he wouldn't simply take her at her word.

As if things weren't confusing enough, he'd stayed with her, followed her wherever work took her, staying at the same penthouse suite at the same luxury hotel when she'd returned for Nush and Caio's wedding. The picture of them together in that elevator had run in an online gossip rag, which had eventually come to Mira's notice.

Yana had given her sister a sanitized version of their fight and their subsequent agreement. Ever the practical and strategic Reddy sister, Mira had given Yana the best advice.

Treat it as a job. Be professional.

While Yana could see the simple yet profound wisdom in it, barely an hour since they'd taken off, she'd found it hard to implement.

Tapping her fingers on the armrest of her seat now, she

studied the understated elegance of the aircraft's interior. Thanks to her modeling career, she'd traveled all over the world, to exotic destinations, no less. But her mode of transport hadn't always been this luxurious. Still, she could catalog the minor differences from when she'd traveled in such a cocoon of luxury.

The aircraft was state-of-the-art, but like Nasir, there was a quiet, industrial-type elegance to it rather than the flashy extravagance that most rich men she knew exemplified. Neither did she doubt that it was an efficient mode of transport for a man who traveled all over the Middle East and South Asia, instead of being a status symbol.

She'd had a month of him trailing her like a shadow, showing up at her shoots and events and even at her meetings with all manner of people, but Yana was still nowhere near used to his presence.

For the first time since she'd known him, she was going to get an exclusive glimpse into his very private life. When he and Jacqueline had been married, all the parties and gatherings that Jacqueline had hosted, even as a couple, had been at her apartment in Paris, or in New York.

Yana had even overheard a fight between them when he'd refused to open up his estate—wherever it was—for one of Jacqueline's "outrageous, drunken soirees" as he'd called them.

"You're jumpy and fidgety. Is there something you require?"

Straightening her pink satin jacket with exaggerated care, Yana counted to twenty before she turned to face him. For the past hour, she'd tried to treat him as part of the very elegant, luxurious background. It shouldn't have been hard with his long nose buried in the documents in front of him.

"Is the fidgeting and jumpiness bothering you?" she asked, with a saccharine sweetness that made even her teeth ache.

If only she could continue to ignore his magnetic presence. But it was like ignoring the sun while orbiting him in the sky.

"No." His answer came so reluctantly that Yana laughed. "Lies."

"Okay, fine, yes. It bothers me. Do you need something?"

"No."

He returned his attention to putting away the documents in front of him.

Yana studied his profile, drawn as ever to it. His hair had grown long enough to curl thickly over his brow and reach past the nape of his neck. Dark circles hugged his eyes and there was a gauntness to his features that made his cheekbones stand out.

As she watched, he shrugged off his jacket, undid the platinum links at his cuffs and rolled back the sleeves of the white shirt, revealing strong forearms covered in dark hair. Her gaze leaped to his fingers undoing the buttons at his throat, eager anticipation fizzing through her.

The plain, platinum face of his watch—Jacqueline's gift on their second anniversary—was a much-required reminder to stop mooning over him.

Pulling off the glasses that gave him a serious, sexy professor vibe, he let that perceptive gaze rest on her. He didn't do an inventory of her. But she knew that he had noted every little detail about her, from her dyed strawberry blond hair to the deep V of her top.

A shiver ran down her spine. Suddenly, she wished she'd tried to nap, or at least pretended to have fallen asleep for the duration of the flight. "You didn't have to wait for me to join you."

"I promised Zara I'd bring you back with me, no matter when I returned this time. I couldn't take any more chances of disappointing her."

His tone was, for once, affable. And yet, whether it was habit or some other defensive instinct, she felt the prick of his distrust. Took long, deep breaths through her nose, reminding herself that one of her own ground rules for this trip was that she'd be polite. No losing her temper, no riling him up and definitely no staring at him like a lost puppy, salivating with her tongue out and begging for a cuddle.

"I promised you I'd be there. I don't break my commitments."

"As that is something I'm not aware of, it made sense to stay and make sure."

"Do you have to turn everything into a character assassination?" she said, instantly regretting the combative words.

Why couldn't she just let it be? He was trying to be polite, trying to put that whole clean-slate nonsense into play. Acting as if they were nothing more than two strangers who'd shared and lost a common friend.

His long, rattling sigh told her she'd completely missed the mark. "The stakes are very high for me. Can we agree on that?"

She nodded, heat streaking her cheeks at his gentle tone.

"Good. Let's say it has nothing to do with you and your character and everything to do with my own shortcomings."

Picking at a loose thread on her cuff, she gave him another nod.

He was worried about how to reconnect with Zara after all the damage his marriage, and Jacqueline's lies and his own aversion to engage in a fight, had caused the little girl. It was etched into his features.

"I have some conditions," she said, deciding to steer the conversation to a necessary topic. Maybe that was even the best way to act, moving forward. Ignore the little blips of her temper, the squeaks her heart made whenever he was near.

He raised a brow at the sudden shift away from their argument. "Conditions? Isn't that something you should've discussed with me before you got on the plane?"

"You might have no faith in me, but I decided to show some in you. Even though…" She shook her head, cutting off that line of thought. "I just believed that you would be amenable to whatever I asked for so that these three months with Zara, *for Zara*, can pass with the least amount of aggression between us."

A long finger rubbed over his temple, even as one side of his mouth curled up. "You have given this a lot of thought."

"I've decided to treat this like any other contract. Professionally. I mean, I *have* had a lot of experience dealing with arrogant, egotistical, petulant men, who think they are a gift to the world. So why not draw from my almost fourteen years of experience?"

His reluctant smile turned into a full-fledged one. The sudden flash of his even white teeth and the deep groove it dug on one side of his face… She barely buried the sigh that wanted to leave her lips. God, the man's gorgeousness was lethal when he smiled like that.

"So what are they?"

"What are what?" she said, stuck in that sticky place.

His smile deepened. "The conditions you have for me?"

"Oh, yeah," she said, making a big show of pulling out her notepad from her giant clutch and opening to the right page. She had no doubt that a full-blown blush was painting her cheeks and lowered her head to hide the evidence. "You already took care of my debts. That was my first condition."

"Ahmed dealt with all that mess. He decided it wouldn't do for me to know all the gory details."

She looked up, surprise and relief rushing through her. Though she had a feeling it hadn't been Ahmed's decision so much as Nasir's. Which meant his belief that *she* had accrued that immense debt was being propagated further. And she needed that barrier between them, needed him to think she was reckless with every area of her life. "Remind me to thank Ahmed."

She looked down at her list and hesitated. A month ago she'd wanted to never set eyes on her mother again. To completely wash her hands of her. After this last betrayal, she'd thought herself incapable of caring the smallest amount about Diana.

And yet, over the past few weeks of having a clear goal and vision for her own life, of talking to Zara over video calls, of watching her sisters move on in their lives, she'd realized it wasn't in her to just walk away. To close her heart off. To abandon her mother when gambling was a mental illness.

What if Diana needed a fresh chance like Yana was getting from Nasir, albeit at a high price? Would she ever be happy if Diana wasn't also in a good place?

Her decision was driven not just by common sense but compassion and a sense of duty, too. Breaking away from toxic patterns, suddenly felt like it was within her reach. She could move forward with her own life then. But of course, she needed help. First, to gain a spot in that clinic she'd researched; second, to be able to pay for it; and third, to convince Diana to give it a try.

She'd decided to add the first two to Nasir's list.

"I need a recommendation for a rehab clinic. I've done my research and found one that's nestled in the Swiss Alps, but it's expensive and very exclusive. They usually only take people based on recommendations. From big shots like you."

His gaze immediately latched on to hers. "Rehab?"

"Yep. I've decided to tackle the bull by the horns, so to

speak. For my gambling," she added, her throat dry over the lie.

Instead of seeing relief or even the self-righteous "I knew it" that she'd expected, a thoughtful look entered his eyes. "I'm glad you decided to seek professional help. Is it that bad, though?"

There was a tenderness to his voice that her brain wanted to cling to. Or was it her stupid heart? "How about we leave it to me to be the judge of that," she said tersely, because she didn't want him to probe.

"Of course, you're the judge," he added in a kind tone.

She sighed. Every dialog between them felt charged. Or perhaps she was making it so. "Some of us develop unhealthy, damaging coping mechanisms to deal with life." She wasn't addicted to gambling but she was addicted to something else, all right. "Not all of us are perfect with iron-clad control like you."

His mouth twisted with bitterness. "Not only am I far from perfect, but I'm only realizing now how *my* unhealthy coping mechanisms have hurt others. At least you're self-aware. I have been deliriously, arrogantly oblivious of my own failings."

Now it was she who wanted to probe. That wanted to dig and dig until he was fully revealed and unraveled in front of her. That he'd hurt Jacqueline with his inability to love her was common knowledge between them. And yet, he'd never seemed to mind much before. She'd never seen a single hole in his convictions and beliefs about how he'd conducted his life.

Instead of giving full rein to that fascinated part of her, she forced herself to look down at her notepad.

"I will personally speak to someone on the board of administration," he said into the building silence. "Just let me know the timeline."

She nodded, running her finger down her scribbled list. "The next few things are not that big of a deal. I'm charging you twenty million euros for the three months. I'd prefer a bunch of chaperones as a buffer while I spend time with Zara and…"

His laughter was loud, booming around in the intimate space, pinging all over her skin. She looked up and lost her breath.

Head thrown back, muscles of his neck clenched tight, he was a study in masculine beauty. Attraction and desire tugged at her, a hook under her belly button pulling her closer, urging her to touch that smile, to taste that smile. Damn, she had it bad.

"What's so funny?" She went for irritation to hide her helpless attraction.

It was several minutes before he sobered up. "You are one expensive nanny, aren't you?"

A smile twitched at the corner of her lips. "Well, I guess I am. And please, before you come out with insults that I should be doing this out of the goodness of my heart, out of my love for Zara, don't. That's the price of me spending time under the same roof with you. Knowing that you will be overseeing everything I say, judging me, and…" It was hard to stay detached or antagonistic toward him when he looked at her with that smile stretching his sensuous lips.

"Fine. Agreed. You will have enough money at the end of three months. And believe me, we will have chaperones galore."

She turned a page on her notepad, gathering the courage to ask the most important question.

"Is that it?"

"I want Zara to spend one month out of every year with me going forward. It could be two periods of two weeks or four different weeks. I want that written into a contract."

"No."

Neither of them was surprised by his instant, biting answer.

The surge of rage and something else—a sharp helplessness, in her expression—told Nasir he'd given her the answer based on the rules and rationale that drove him. Had he been too quick to reply without thinking it over?

She tapped a pink nail incessantly over the table. "That one condition is non-negotiable. If you don't agree, I'll turn around and leave the second this plane lands." Every word was enunciated with a staggering conviction behind it.

"You're springing this on me at the last minute," he said, pushing for time.

Her brown gaze was pure challenge. "My relationship with Zara needs to exist outside of my relationship or lack thereof with you, Nasir. That's what adults should do. Put their differences, their egos, aside, for the sake of a child. I don't know what the future or the aftermath of these three months—" she said, laughing, with no actual humor in the sound "—is going to look like. This way, I'm ensuring that regardless of what happens between you and me, Zara always has me in her life. And not just as some patch-up you bring in when things get bad."

For the first time in his life, Nasir was speechless. Golden hair flying around her face as she bit out each word, Yana looked like a lioness defending her cub. "You're a natural at this, despite the fact both your parents neglected you."

She tilted her chin. Whatever fragility he had seen that first evening at the nightclub was all gone now. "It makes me even more empathetic to Zara's plight. She's just a child. No child should have to starve for attention or affection. Or get lost in adults' mind games." She played with the ends of her hair, her thrust delivered with an efficient, but impersonal bluntness he was coming to appreciate about her. He couldn't even get mad because she was right; Zara had gotten lost among his and Jacqueline's conflicts. "As for Diana messing up…" Her throat moved hard. "I've realized there have been good things in my life, too. It's on me whether I move forward with gratitude or bitterness."

"You sound very wise," he said.

"You sound shocked," she retorted with a cutting smile.

Clearly, in the past month she had returned to some sort of routine. He hadn't missed the fact, seeing he'd shadowed her wherever she went. Meals, regular exercise and medication on time, he could see the changes in her face. That gaunt, lost waif look was gone, leaving her effervescently beautiful.

He liked her like this—full of passion and conviction. Suddenly, he realized he had seen her like this before. Before she'd entered the modeling world as a far too naive and impressionable girl with only her mother's greedy, grasping behavior as a guide. Forced to grow up too fast. Acting out in the form of reckless, paparazzi-attracting, almost orchestrated publicity stunts.

There was a contentment to her now that he found extremely satisfying and that in turn was disconcerting, to say the least. He didn't want to be invested in Yana's happiness or well-being. Or only so far as it affected her relationship with Zara. God, that made him sound like an utter bastard.

"You look different," he said, unable to help himself.

She scrunched her nose, and even that twitch was sexy. "Good different?"

"Good different, yes." He didn't miss the hungry expectation in her eyes for more, but refused to cater to it. It was better if they behaved like polite strangers.

"Maybe the fact that—" she giggled, moving her hands in an arc toward him, encompassing the aircraft and the notepad, and everything else, her gestures getting wilder and more expansive with each passing second "—I'm making you pay through the nose is the cause of the change?"

"A small price to pay, then. Your happiness is quite the halo around you."

She gave him a regal nod in response. Then she studied her fingernails, going for that casual vibe that she never could quite pull off. "I think sometimes we have to hit our lowest point to see that things aren't as bad as we thought, that they can still be fixed."

He returned her somber nod, marveling at how deeply her words reached inside him. He'd been at that lowest point once. But unlike dreaming on a different vision as Yana was doing or moving forward, he'd simply shut the world out. Had stopped caring about anyone. Had withdrawn into his mind, into his books, into his career. Even when he'd met and married Jacqueline, he'd designed his marriage to fit around his life. And of course, it had fallen apart in a spectacular fashion.

Because somewhere in the past fifteen years, he'd stored away his heart outside himself. And then, suddenly, he didn't know how to forge a connection with his own child.

"I know a little about being in dark places, feeling like you'll never crawl out of them." The words flew out of his mouth. "Or feeling as if you deserve to be there."

"Don't tell me the great Nasir Hadeed hit points of low confidence in his esteemed life."

"I will save you from the gory details, then," he said, trying to inject humor back into his voice. "It is not a good feeling when our idols turn out to be hollow, no?"

"I didn't idolize you," she said with a fake outrage he didn't buy.

He worried that she'd probe. It was unfounded.

It was becoming more and more apparent that Yana wasn't anything like the flimsy illusion she weaved for the entire world.

"So, are you in agreement about me having Zara for a month?"

"If I insist on being present while you do?"

"Because you don't trust me to look after her?" she asked with big eyes. In that moment she looked as beguilingly naive and full of insecurities as his five-year-old. "I'd never put Zara at risk."

That it was a promise and not some outraged declaration made his chest ache. "No. I want Zara to see that we're not at each other's throats."

She nodded, taking his lies for the truth.

He had no intention of spending time with her on a regular basis, no intention of seeing her again after these three months were up.

And still, he wasn't able to help himself from prodding her. From poking at her sudden composure.

Suddenly, it felt as if he was standing behind a wall she'd erected. He shouldn't miss the messy, volatile Yana he'd once known, but he had a sudden feeling that this defensive barrier was a fundamental part of her.

"If that's a problem for you—"

"You keep thinking I'm still hung up on you. I'm not. Haven't been for a very long time. It might even be the right thing for all of us, because who knows how much time you actually give Zara. This way, you'll be forced to take time off from your work."

And there was the truth, putting him in his place in the perfect way. As only she could. "Yes, fine, you can spend time with Zara every year. But we don't have to put it in a contract."

"We do. I don't trust your good opinion of me will last forever."

And that was, apparently, that.

Pushing out her long legs, she reclined her seat and closed her eyes. Her arms were folded around her midriff, thrusting her small breasts up.

It took him seventeen long seconds to look away from the enticing picture she made even in repose, from her shiny hair to the deep cleavage at the V of her blouse to the long legs bared in pink shorts.

She was right.

He had no idea how the aftermath of these three months was going to look. Because the truth he'd refused to accept until now was that this woman had always threatened his control. Had always pushed and prodded at all the rules he'd lived his life by. She made him want to risk everything again all over. She made him forget the excruciating pain of loving and losing.

CHAPTER FIVE

"YANA? WAKE UP."

Yana tightened her arms around the solid warmth that enveloped her, needing to sleep for another thousand hours. "Get off. Leave me alone."

A soft tap on her cheek, followed by a chuckle, tickled the blurry edges of her consciousness. "We're here. Let's go, sleepyhead."

She was warm, and cozy and so tired, and the voice sounded so good against her temple. Like a deep bass reverberating through her, weaving a web of comfort she'd rarely known. "That's not how you wake up someone," she mumbled, snuggling closer and pouting.

A sigh and a hiss disrupted her pleasant state.

"Ahh... Would you like me to try the Sleeping Beauty method? I don't know my fairy tales properly but I think it involved a kiss."

A kiss? That deep, husky voice was offering a kiss to wake me up? Would it be as delicious as he sounded?

It wasn't a bad way to wake up, even though she'd always found the idea of someone kissing her to save her a bit problematic.

"Come on, Yana. Unless you want me to act on that threat."

Slowly, she blinked her eyes open and found amber-colored eyes gleaming back at her in the dark interior of the car. They were like warm, deep pools, inviting her to sink into them. She frowned. Something was wrong with the cozy picture, in and out of her head. In the past ten years, she'd only ever seen those eyes staring at her with contempt or anger.

It was Nasir. But why was Nasir offering to wake her up with a kiss? Was she dreaming again?

The car came to a sudden stop, forcing her to take stock of the surroundings. Through the tinted windows of the chauffeured car, she spotted a dark gray twilight sky, punctured by thick, tall trees that seemed to stand to attention, watching their arrival.

Her eyes widened as she realized she was in the car with Nasir and that they'd finally arrived at their destination. When he handed her a tissue, she stared at it blankly. A sigh left him before he gently wiped at the corners of her mouth.

Yana sprung back from him as if he were a viper flicking his forked tongue at her. Slowly, she pulled her limbs away from around him, even as her body bemoaned the loss of his solid warmth.

"It's okay. You're okay, Yana," he said so softly that the incongruence of it froze her. He'd never spoken to her with that tenderness. Not in ages. "You fell into an exhausted sleep," he added.

She wiped the corners of her mouth with the back of her hand and repeated the same to gritty-feeling eyes.

"Why am I not surprised that you are such an aggressive cuddler when you're asleep?" he said, a hint of humor peeking through his tone.

"It's information you shouldn't have at all," she quipped, feeling irrationally resentful. Though she knew he'd said it to put her at ease.

"No?"

"No. It's intimate information that's reserved for a lover or a boyfriend or a…"

With a groan, she closed her mouth. Why had he let her wrap herself around him like a clinging vine? Why not be cruel in action as with words and push her away? Then she wouldn't feel this discombobulated around him.

She straightened her shorts and her satin top, which was so badly wrinkled that it looked like she'd writhed on the ground.

No, just in his lap, a wicked voice she'd thought she'd left behind piped up.

With the guise of fixing her hair, Yana tugged at the roots roughly, to restore a measure of sanity to herself. "Where's my jacket?"

One long finger carefully held her unwrinkled pink jacket aloft. "You kept saying you were too hot."

"You should've woken me up or pushed me aside."

"You really think me an unfeeling beast."

"Yes. And I'd like to keep thinking that."

"And why is that?" The soft query came with a silky, but nonetheless dangerous, undertone.

Yana took the jacket from him and pushed her arms through the sleeves, ignoring him. Gathering the messy mass of her hair, she quickly braided it away from her face. Only when she felt a semblance of composure return to her did she turn to face him. "I'm sorry for—" she moved her hand between them, her cheeks heating up "—climbing all over you."

He exhaled in a sibilant hiss, pressing his fingers to his temple. "It's no big deal."

"It *is* a big deal. You're my employer, and I'd like to keep those boundaries clear."

A flicker of irritation danced in his eyes. "Pity you didn't have that rule all those years ago, huh?"

And just like that, the truce that had lasted the whole flight fell apart. Grabbing his wrist, she pulled it up to thrust the platinum dial in his face. "Wow, you lasted a whole nine hours without insulting me. That's got to be a record."

His long fingers grabbed hers. "Wait, that's not how I meant to say it."

"Let me go, Nasir."

"Not until you hear me out."

Of course she knew who he was talking about—Gregor Ilyavich, a sixty-six-year-old infamous painter of celebrated nudes. When he'd approached Diana, who'd also been her manager and coach back then, about painting Yana nude, her mother had been ecstatic. Just as she'd guessed, his nude portraits of Yana had instantly shot her into a new stratosphere of fame. All the big designers had wanted her face on their brand, were willing to pay whatever she wanted.

But the true price for her starry fame had come later—when Gregor had made his move on her. Something Yana chose to believe to this day that Diana hadn't known about. She herself had been a naive idiot who hadn't seen the power play until it was too late.

Thank God the portraits were now out of circulation as a private collector had bought them for millions. Not that Yana hadn't loved them. They had been gorgeous, otherworldly, elevating her to something more than the symmetry and perfection of her face and body. Gregor had pinpointed and then extrapolated things she'd chosen to hide from the world in those portraits—her insecurity and her vulnerability.

But the lurid gossip about her affair with Gregor, the over-the-top speculation that *she* had trapped him for his money, and her tattered reputation as some kind of backstabbing gold digger had left a bitter taste in her mouth.

Her justly deserved humiliation at Nasir's hands two years prior and then the flaming mess that had been her association with Gregor had been enough to confirm her belief that she was never going to get it right with men. Just like Diana.

"Are you forever going to dig up skeletons from my past and dangle them in my face? Is that the plan for the next three months?" A scornful laugh escaped her. "Because we both know there's enough material."

"No. Of course not. I brought it up the wrong way. I just…"

"Just what, Nasir?"

"I introduced you to Gregor at that release party for my novel. I felt responsible." A muscle jumped in his cheek. "I *feel* responsible, to this day."

Her righteous fury leeched out of her, leaving a void in its place. A void that would fill with dangerous things like hope if she wasn't careful. And even with that warning, she couldn't help but say, "What does that mean?"

"You were a very gullible twenty-one-year-old. He was notorious for charming and seducing women who were decades younger than him with the promise of fame and fortune. I was responsible for bringing you to his notice. For letting him enter your life. I hate that he…took advantage of you. That I didn't protect you."

"I was twenty-one. And Gregor coerced me in no way to pose for him. So there, I absolve you of all blame." She raised her palms, forestalling the distressing topic.

"Yes. But I should have looked out for you, should have made sure you knew his background. Abba took me to task for it enough times."

The mention of his dad was enough to make a lump rise in Yana's throat.

Izaz Hadeed had been one of the kindest men she'd ever known. Enough that she'd loved living in his home when Diana had been married to him. Enough that she'd known whatever had brought them together wouldn't last long because Diana didn't know what to do when good things came into her life and so she destroyed them.

Something Yana thought she'd inherited from her mother, in her lowest points, along with good skin and thick hair.

Enough to know that his son—while grumpy and caustic on the outside—had inherited that very same kindness. God, the stupid dreams she'd weaved, imagining them all together as one big, forever family.

Even after he and Diana had separated, even after Yana's own horrible shenanigans and false claims about Nasir kissing her, Izaz had always kept in touch with her. Calling her on her birthday, sending her gifts wherever she was in the world, asking her if she was okay after Nasir and Jacqueline's wedding…he'd made her feel like a cherished daughter.

He'd loved her like one.

She bit her lower lip with her teeth hard enough that the pain held back the tears that threatened to spill. "Ahh, so that's what this is about. Izaz Uncle finding fault with you. That's why it still rankles after all this time."

"It wasn't just Abba's criticism that got to me…" His chest rose with the deep breath he took. She knew it was raw grief at mentioning his father, who had passed not a year ago. Only Izaz's affair and subsequent marriage to Diana had been the biggest divide between father and son—conquered and forgiven years later when he'd reconciled with Nasir's mom. And yet, she remembered Izaz being heartbroken that Nasir hadn't forgiven him completely, that his son had become a hardened man in the subsequent years.

"It rankles, still, because it's true."

In a sudden move she didn't expect, he clasped her cheek with a gentleness that shocked her. When she'd have pulled away, he held firm. Something about the expression in his eyes threatened to break her into so many pieces. His second hand joined the first one, in this assault of kindness.

She felt locked, pinned, splayed wide open.

"The world only saw your confidence, your success, your brazenness. But I know now, as I should've known then, that you were young, naive, so unused to the vipers and Gregors of the world. I should have warned you that he was a predator."

The genuine regret in his eyes forced out an answer. "He didn't…do anything I didn't want him to, Nasir. And if mistakes were made, I was twenty-one and so I'm allowed them."

She didn't know why she was propagating yet another lie between them when she could instead choose to clear the air and admit that she'd refused all Gregor's advances. Especially since it seemed Nasir's main regret, that he hadn't interfered, persisted after all these years.

"That mistake shouldn't have happened in the first place. You should've been—"

She slapped his hands away, his gentleness nothing but a hidden strike. "I think I prefer the version of you that blamed me for my impulsive, lazy, ruinous tendencies rather than this…patronizing one that invalidates my very existence. How dare you feel sorry for me? Or is it disgust over my actions and how you should have saved me from myself that keeps that massive ego of yours boosted?"

"Yana, you misunderstand me."

Without waiting for his clarification, she pushed the car door open and stepped out into the dark night.

She was so very exhausted—all the way down to the marrow of her soul. Just when she hoped that he saw her, *actually saw her*, and was beginning to respect her, he set her back to square one. And however many times she promised herself never again, it didn't seem to stick.

* * *

Her legs felt like they were made of that JELL-O that Zara adored as Yana stepped out of the car without falling face-first into the rough gravel. Not that she'd have managed even that without Nasir's steadying arm around her shoulders.

Once she could trust her legs, she quickly moved out of his reach. His scowl told her he hadn't missed her instinctual rejection.

She rubbed her eyes again, all the different time zones playing havoc with her body's rhythms. There was a chill in the air that nipped at her bare legs and chest. She inhaled deeply anyway, loving the scent of pine and something old in the air. Tugging the lapels of her jacket closer, she raised her head.

It was a big castle—no, strike that—a humongous castle that greeted her. Rather, it was the shadows and outlines of one, since twilight had now given way to thick, dark night. The castle looked like it had sprung right out of one of Nasir's stories. The stories that were situated perfectly at the periphery of dark woods, the ones that housed all kinds of scary and outcast creatures. The ones she'd always liked the best because she'd felt like she'd belonged in them.

Once he straightened, she reached to take her heavy shoulder bag from him. He held it away from her.

She ran a circle around his body, trying to reach for it, bumping into him. "It's fine. I can carry it inside."

"You're being ridiculous, you know that?" When she jumped for it, he circled a hand around her neck with a gentleness that made her pulse leap. The gesture was so unlike him, so much bordering on possessiveness, that she stilled. Every atom in her body stilled. "It's just a damned bag, Yana. Let it go."

Yana raised her hands in surrender, an unholy humor coursing through her at his cursing. There was nothing better than seeing him devolve to her level—whether in vocabulary or gestures or actions. Suddenly, power and something else between them felt more fluid than she'd ever assumed.

"Where are we?" she asked, following him as he began an upward trek from a gigantic courtyard where the chauffeur had dropped them off.

Small, hidden lights dotted across the land illuminated a gravel pathway toward the looming castle. All the tension she'd felt while imagining them together melted away as she took in the fresh air and the beautifully dark setting.

God, she and Zara would have so much fun here. And yet, she didn't miss the fact that it was also quite the deserted location for a five-year-old. Zara would need other kids and activities to engage with. But she couldn't bring that up now. She'd love to never bring it up and not give him a chance to put her in her place but that wasn't an option.

Zara was, and would always be, a priority, even if that meant courting Nasir's special kind of disapproval. She made a mental note for later.

Apparently, they weren't going to walk in through the main entrance, which boasted two solid iron doors with knockers the size of her head. She felt like she was entering a fantasy world.

"It's a small village near Bavaria," he finally answered. "Close to the Alps. You'll see the view tomorrow."

The remoteness of the location was exactly how she'd imagined he lived. Had Jacqueline played queen of the castle?

Jacqueline had been quite the party animal, and their relationship had never made sense to Yana. But she'd put it down to her own conflicted past with him.

Now she knew that she'd been right in her intuition.

The closer they got, the larger the castle loomed with dark gray stone, and tall turrets and, oh, my God, a tower at the back that seemed to look down on the rest of the castle. "There's a tower in your castle?"

"Yes." His laughter at her enthusiasm reverberated in that single word.

"Please tell me you're renting it or I don't know...housesitting it?"

It was all a little too close to one of her fantasies. Fantasies involving castles and Nasir and dark, fairy-tale-esque romance had been the staple of her teenage years. Fantasies she needed to keep convincing herself she'd grown out of.

It was as if all her darkest dreams were taking shape in reality—she and Nasir in a castle, she and Nasir with a lovely little girl, she and Nasir finally meeting under one roof as equals. But there was no danger of that, she reminded herself bitterly.

When Nasir didn't loathe her, apparently he was busy feeling sorry for her.

She sensed his reluctance before he answered her. "No. I bought it. Recently."

"How recently?"

"Right after Jacqueline died," he said, meeting her gaze. Letting her know that he knew what she was doing. "We moved here from her Paris apartment once I took care of the legalities."

She took a shot in the dark. "You bought it to impress Zara?"

The moonlight didn't hide his grimace. "She wouldn't stop talking about castles and fairy tales and dark creatures. You'd left us—" he raised his hand, forestalling her protest and shook his head. "You're right. I shouldn't rewrite history. *I* made you leave. Jacqueline was gone. All Zara would talk about was living in a huge castle with three monstrous dogs and with a forest in the back and..." A long sigh seemed to emerge from the very depths of him. "It was the only bridge I had to build toward her."

"Oh."

He nudged her shoulder with his. The playful gesture stunned her. As did his teasing tone when he said, "I know where she gets that fixation from."

"I just shared everything that fascinated me at her age," she whispered, her mind scattering in a thousand directions.

What had changed in how he saw her? Had he finally understood that she'd always had Zara's best interests at heart? Was that enough to redeem her multitude of sins? And what happened when they didn't agree on something regarding Zara? Would his approval vanish?

"Stories saved me when I was a little girl. *Your stories* helped me escape my own life."

"I'm glad, then, that I got something right with you. Even if it was done unknowingly." His gruff tone hit her low in her belly, the soft underside she sometimes forgot existed.

Something built in the silence between them as he opened the relatively small but actually giant side door, and ushered her toward a dark staircase. And it seemed to stretch and stretch and stretch upward. Endlessly.

Without rancor or contempt or anger or intense mutual dislike coloring and cluttering the space between them, they were unmoored suddenly. As if anything was possible in that space now. As if they were any other couple who were trying to do their best for a little girl they both adored.

"I… I wanted Zara to have the same anchor during a hard time in her own life," she said, clearing her suddenly thick throat. "I didn't mean to create an obsession you'd have to deal with."

"No. I'm grateful for the spark of the obsession you planted. It became a lifesaver for us both."

He rubbed a hand over his face, and suddenly, in the dark corridor, Yana saw his own exhaustion, the emotional toll the past few years must have taken on him. Jacqueline's infidelities, her long battle with cancer, then her death and the full responsibility of Zara's well-being. Then suddenly, he'd lost his beloved father.

It was a lot for one man to take.

Even someone like Nasir, who was fully in control of himself and his emotions and the people around him and even his own circumstances. He was judgmental, ruthless, exacting in his standards for himself and others. And yet, now, beneath all of that, she saw something else, too. Something like regret.

Even just within the past month, he'd followed her wherever she went around the globe, all the while giving time to his own work and returning to see Zara every weekend so that she didn't feel abandoned yet again. It annoyed her how her heart ached for a man she needed to hate.

"Nasir, I'm—"

"You were a better parent to Zara than Jacqueline or I have ever been. For that, you have my eternal gratitude."

Stunned beyond words, she stared at him. That arch of electricity, that taut tug of connection, came again. This time it built faster and louder and stronger.

She nodded and walked on up the stairs, his words sitting like rigid boulders on her chest. Of course, he'd recognized that she loved Zara. And being the man he was, he'd immediately thank her for it, would give her the place she wanted in Zara's life. It was more than she'd expected when she'd said yes to this...contract, the best outcome she could've hoped for.

Relief should have come. Or at least some kind of vindication. All she felt, however, was a confusion, an ache.

"I feel like Maria from *The Sound of Music*," she said, forcing a giggle into her tone. The last thing she wanted was to have an emotional breakdown in front of him, for him to see the wretched confusion in her soul. "Please tell me you don't have several children waiting for me to look after."

"That's a nice fantasy," he said, a thread of some deep, dark, cavernous thing dancing in his words.

Yana stumbled so hard that she almost fell on her face.

His fast reflexes meant his hand on her jacket held her upright just as they reached the landing on the second floor.

"What? Lording over me and Zara like Captain Von Trapp with his whistle? Finding fault with everything I do? Because let me tell you that particular fantasy's already come true."

He opened the door, a grin on his face. There was something really different about him, here in this place. Or was it simply relief that he finally had her where he needed her? "Why do you always assume that I want to think the worst of you?"

"My dear stepbrother," she said, using the term she knew he loathed, placing her palm on his chest in an exaggerated pout, pouring on her fake charm thick, to dissipate the fizzy bubbles in her own chest more than anything else, "it's our history that says that."

His long fingers wrapped around her wrist but he didn't drag her touch away. Her pulse raced under his fingertips, playing a symphony for his favor. "I don't remember it always being quite like that."

"Weren't you the one who taught me that history always has another version? Probably from the one who didn't originally have a voice?"

"What is your version, then, Yana?"

"Does it matter anymore?"

"It clearly does. To both of us."

She shook her head, telling herself it was a lie. "I made a ghastly, horrible mistake, no doubt about it. I knew I'd done something wrong the minute I told Diana you kissed me. I want you to know that I did eventually tell Izaz the truth. I was… I own my part in that, even though I'd like to say I was also a product of insecurity and codependency and…" She sighed and blew out a long breath. "You meted out a rather cruel punishment that would've lasted a lifetime if not for the fact that I came into Zara's life, quite by accident, which ended up, *luckily* for me, perhaps redeeming me a little bit in your eyes."

If she thought he'd dig into the very painful past and pick at the scabs of her *ghastly, horrible mistake*, Yana was proved wrong. If she thought he'd jump at the truth she'd just revealed that his punishment to cut her out of his life had hurt her, she was safe from that, too.

He simply stared at her for a long time, as if weighing her words. "You are right. And you're a better person than I am, clearly, for not holding it over my head."

A humorless snort escaped her. "That's what you expected when you came to see me, wasn't it? Me to hold your own behavior over your head? That's why you were so fast to use all the leverage you had on me."

"And you refused me, again and again, even though I know you want to be here for Zara. Don't think it escaped me that the possibility of being here with me was so distasteful to you that it sent you into a faint."

"Nasir—"

"Don't think I forget for one minute that my beastly behavior toward you might have cost Zara the stability she needs, the love of the one person she desperately craves. I might have failed my daughter all over again."

There was such a note of anguish in those words that Yana found herself reaching for him automatically. In that moment Yana remembered why she'd once admired him so much. There was a quiet dignity to him, even in defeat. "I didn't mean—"

"My relationship with my daughter is a mess I created. I let my unhappiness with Jacqueline, my distaste for her drama, create a divide between Zara and me. I assumed she was better off with her mother than being used as a pawn in a power play between us."

"A little girl would only see it as apathy," she said, unable to help herself.

His throat moved on a hard swallow and his mouth curved in a bitter smile. "I realized that too late. I got so good at keeping people out of my life that I succeeded with my daughter, too."

It was as natural as breathing to want to comfort him. "You and she will get through this, Nasir. I promise you. Things will be better soon."

With his hand at the small of her back guiding her through the darkness, and the tight corridor they were navigating, their gazes held. "You don't know that."

"You're doing everything you can to fix it. Including kidnapping me, blackmailing me, letting me drool all over your Armani jacket in my sleep. Just to make her happy. Just to give her a sense of security. She'll realize all the effort you're putting in soon enough. Zara's a very clever girl."

It was what she'd have done for anyone in such a situation. She'd always been a very touchy-feely person. But when her upper body pressed against Nasir in a tight, warm squeeze, she realized too late that she'd gone too far.

Too far with him, that was.

Because even a little was always too far with this man.

Suddenly, it was impossible to ignore her nipples pebbling against the muscled wall of his side. Her breasts aching and heavy. His hard, denim-clad leg nestled between her thighs, against the place where she'd dreamed of him being so many times. Her spine and her curves melting and molding around him to get a better fit, a tighter squeeze, a harder push.

She closed her eyes, and it was a mistake because the sensations multiplied by a million. Her breath came in soft, shallow pants as she searched in the darkness with her fingers. A liquid ache pulsed through her when she found purchase on his face. His soft, warm mouth that could be so hard with anger at her fingertips. The rough, pebbled texture of his scar. His breath on the back of her hand, heating her up even more.

And without her permission, without her knowing, without her will involved, her body bowed toward him. Offering itself up as some kind of ritual sacrifice at the very altar of the beast she should run from.

Forehead pressed against his shoulder, she breathed in long gasps, willing herself to let go. To step back.

His fingers around the nape of her neck were like bands of heat, brands of possession. Lingering at that sensitive place. Playing through the little wisps of hair there.

"Yana," he said, his own voice a husky whisper, echoing around the walls. "We can't… I can't do this. There's too much at stake."

She jerked back from him so fast and with such force that the hard stone banged into her head, evoking a pained gasp. Hot tears pooled in her eyes at the impact but he was already there. His fingers gently probing and prodding at the back of her head.

She took a tentative step away, putting herself out of his reach. "I'm okay. Let's just—"

"Yana, we can't—"

"No idea what you're talking about," she said, focusing her gaze over his shoulder. "All I did was offer comfort. Maybe even that's not palatable to you when it comes from me."

He searched her gaze in the dim light and nodded. But the truth of their almost-encounter shimmered in the amber depths, and her own senses, whipped into a frenzy of need, taunted her for her lies.

CHAPTER SIX

"WAKE UP, YANA AUNTIE! Auntie, wake up!"

Yana found herself tickled by small hands, but this time she knew who was wrapped around her like a baby koala. Her eyes opened to shafts of pure golden sunlight sliding in through the high windows, bathing her face in a warm light. For a second she lay with her open gaze focused on the high, vaulted ceilings, and yet another gleaming chandelier that reminded her of the castle and her and Nasir's almost-encounter.

Nope, not thinking of the thing that he claimed he couldn't give in to and that had never even happened. Although, the fact that he'd said that he couldn't take the chance...meant he wanted to do it, whatever it was that hadn't happened, right?

"Yana Auntie!"

Smiling, Yana trailed her fingers to her stomach where itty-bitty fingers were digging into her ribs, and caught them with her own. "Gotcha, Zuzu!" As she expected, Zara gave a loud squeal and burst into giggles when Yana shouted, "Tickle monster!" and went for the little belly. Like earthworms in mud—another favorite of Zara's—they rolled together on the bed, giggling for God knew how long.

Her chest burned as if a fire had cleansed away all the loss and grief, leaving fertile ground again. There was nothing like laughing and goofing around with Zara, who gave as good as she got. Eventually, they both ran out of breath.

Sitting up, she pulled Zara into her lap. Tiny arms immediately wound around her neck, with her face buried in Yana's chest. An almost clawlike hold of those little fingers raised a lump in her throat. Yana buried her face in Zara's thick curls. The little girl smelled of sunshine and dirt and strawberries, and it tugged at instincts Yana hadn't known she had.

She'd never given much thought to marriage or children, to stability and putting down roots. Planning her life was Mira's forte, and believing that it would turn out wonderfully was Nush's, whereas hers had been drifting from one mess to the other. And yet, ever since she'd been a chubby, charming baby, Zara had sunk her hooks into Yana's heart and they only seemed to dig in deeper with time.

"You pwomised you'd visit soon." The complaint came in a small, muffled voice as if Zara wasn't sure she had a right to even complain.

In response, Yana grabbed Zara's huge stuffed toy, and spoke to Lila the llama. She told the stuffed toy about how both her grandparents had passed away in the past year, and how much Yana had needed to be around her sisters and why she'd not been able to visit Zara sooner.

Pulling back, Zara stared with a seriousness that belied her tender age. "Your thaata died?"

Yana nodded.

"Like Mama?"

Hand shaking, Yana tucked a springy curl behind the girl's ear and planted a soft kiss on her chubby cheek. "Yes. But—" she trailed her fingers over the little girl's face and neck, straightening her pajamas, slowly tickling her again, forcing an easy cheer into her voice "—I'm not sad anymore. Now that I can hold my Zuzu girl again."

Explanation accepted, Zara sneak-attacked her, and they burst into another bout of giggles, made plans for picnics and walks and movie nights and ice-cream parties. The number of promises the girl elicited from Yana restored her faith in her decision to come.

Suddenly, three huge, excited dogs burst into the bedroom and began to sniff and bark and generally make mayhem around the bed. "And who is this?" Yana asked, eyeing the two shepherds and the pug.

One castle and three dogs... He really had gone all the way in making Zara's fantasy come true. Yana shouldn't really be surprised after his ruthless determination to get her here. How much further would he go to make Zara happy?

"That's Leo and Scorpio. And that one," Zara said, pointing to the cutest among the three, "is Diablo."

As if he knew how extra adorable he was, Diablo the pug lifted his front paws up onto the edge of the bed. Yana patted the sheets and immediately, the three dogs jumped up and went for their faces, licking them.

Zara suddenly fell quiet.

"What's wrong?" Yana asked.

"We're in twrouble." Resolve tightened the little girl's features. "Don't worry. I'll tell Papa I let them on his bed."

Belly dipping, Yana noted the austere navy-blue furnishings, the starkly functional furniture and an entire wall full of bookshelves that shrank the vast bedroom significantly. The bed was a vast king bed with two night stands—one full of Zara's pictures in frames and the other held a pile of books and a pair of reading glasses.

This was Nasir's bed. This was his bedroom. Yana sighed. *Why did all roads seem to lead her to Nasir's bed?*

"I let the dogs on the bed, Papa. Not Yana Auntie."

Nasir stood still at the entrance to the room, wondering if his heart could rip out of its shallow shell at the entreaty in his daughter's words. The doubts in her eyes tore him apart, re-minding him yet again how badly he'd messed up with Zara.

"Don't send her away."

Hands on Zara's shoulders, Yana pulled his daughter into her body, as if she meant to protect her from everything, in-cluding him.

As if she were my own... He hadn't missed Yana's almost slip of the tongue that evening at the nightclub. The picture of them together like that on his bed—one achingly ador-able with jet-black curls and the other, glowingly beautiful with dark golden waves spilling over her shoulders, packed an invisible punch to his sternum. With the sunlight limning their similar golden-brown coloring, they looked like they belonged together.

They looked right, real in a way he hadn't known in so long.

Shaking his head at the fantastical thought, Nasir moved toward the bed. With each step he took, Yana's mouth flat-tened.

Did she truly think him such a beast as to upset his own daughter over something so small? That although he'd un-knowingly made Zara doubt his affection, it made him feel any less awful? Or like Zara, had he only shown Yana the grumpy, grouchy outer shell he'd adopted long ago?

Going to his knees, he gazed into his daughter's eyes. His hand shook as he straightened the collar of her pajamas. "It's true Papa doesn't like dogs in his bed. Because Papa's a grouchy old man who's used to things a certain way. But sweetheart, you'll never be in trouble with me over such a small thing. And definitely not your wonderful Yana Aun-tie, either." His five-year-old's lower lip jutted out in disbe-lief. "I pinkie promise that I'll never send her away again, yeah?" He extended his pinkie toward her and he wondered if his heart had moved into that digit now.

That trembling lower lip calmed and Zara tangled their pinkies. Her smile was a wide beam of sunshine. "Next time I'll close the door so they don't follow me."

He laughed and buried his face in her belly. "You're not promising that *you* won't sneak into your auntie's bed every morning, are you?"

She threw her arms around him again and with the sweet scent of her in his lungs, his pulse calmed. He bopped the tip of her nose before getting to his feet.

His gaze shifted to Yana, and in an instant, a full body flush claimed him as he took in her disheveled state. Her face free of makeup, her wild hair tangled around her shoulders, she looked incredibly young and vulnerable. As if she'd put away the mask she wore for the world. Something almost like approval glinted in her eyes.

"I'm sorry she woke you. I held her off for two hours."

"It's fine. Clearly," she said, waving her hand around the bright sunlight in one of those expansive gestures he was coming to recognize she made when she wanted to hide, "I overslept."

She asked him something in fragmented Arabic while trying to protect Lila the llama from the dogs so that Nasir had to move closer to hear her. When she repeated it, he laughed. Apparently, it was a morning of shocks. Or the month of Nasir pulling his head out of his backside. "You just asked me why you're standing in my bed."

Pink dusted her cheeks and she grabbed the duvet as if she needed a lifeline.

Seating himself next to her, he ignored how stiff she went. There was a wicked joy in making her brazen act falter. "When did you learn Arabic?"

Her sharp profile softened as a gentle smile wreathed her mouth. "When I lived with your dad. He practiced..." Her eyes shimmered with an aching fondness as she swallowed and corrected herself. "He used to practice with me all the time. He taught me a lot of bad words and said I needed to use them against you."

"He always liked you."

"He *loved* me." Her conviction shone so bright and clear that Nasir was taken aback. "He loved me as if I were his own daughter. He'd call me and text me and send me little gifts. Even though you forbade him to have any contact with me."

The profound ache in her tone made Nasir swallow hard. "You kept in touch?"

Her smile grew bittersweet. "Usually me venting about how the world was unfair and he'd remind me that the world didn't understand how wonderful I was." The love in her eyes made him feel like he was lost in a sea of emotions he'd willingly turned off inside him.

It *had* been his condition when his father had reconciled with his mother that he never have any more contact with Diana or her daughter. On an intellectual level, he knew why he'd insisted on that. Diana was destruction itself. And yet, he hadn't given a moment's thought to the fact that Yana had gotten caught in the crossfire. He hadn't wanted to punish her, even though she'd lied about him kissing her. He simply hadn't considered the effect on her of taking away his father's love.

"I did a lot of things wrong by you. I won't shame myself further by offering excuses."

"You thought I was beneath your notice. But he..."

"He what?"

She cast a quick look at Zara and the dogs, who were now playing on the terrace attached to the bedroom. "Izaz Uncle wondered if you never forgave him fully for leaving your mother. He thought the bond between you two never…recovered fully." She held his gaze. "I believe he missed you. *The real you*, he'd say."

Standing up and moving away from the bed, Nasir rubbed shaking hands over his face. Regrets coated his throat like thorny prickles. "Of course I forgave him. My mother wasn't easy to love," he said on a wave of grief. "I… I wish he had just asked me. I'd have told him that it was all to do with me. Not him. He was a wonderful father whatever went on between him and Ammee." He turned to her, feeling caught between the sterile world he'd locked himself into and this new one where pain and loss ruled. "What else, Yana? What else did he say?"

"I'd console him by calling you all kinds of names." Her mouth twitched. "And he'd defend you, say you'd just lost your way. That his warm, loving son was buried somewhere beneath the cold, hard one you'd become."

And here was the proof—that the man who'd loved him with such depth, who'd believed in second chances, had thought Nasir had just lost his way. His father hadn't approved of his lifestyle, or his marriage to Jacqueline, but he'd never interfered because he'd believed that everyone had a right to make their own mistakes. Unlike his mother, though, Abba's concern had been about Nasir's happiness.

Nasir had not just lost his way, he'd actively distanced himself from all the good things in his life. Because losing Fatima had been so painful that he hadn't wanted to feel anything again.

A sympathetic murmur had him unclenching his jaw. He turned to find Yana looking at him with regrets in her eyes. That she could feel his pain when he'd been anything but kind to her…humbled him. "I didn't say it to hurt you."

"I know that."

They stared at each other, she from her cozy position on the bed, he standing under the archway leading to the terrace, as if at a crossroads.

She'd always been an incredible temptation. Easy to resist because she'd always embodied the very drama and loss of control he'd abhorred. And yet now, in revealing his own flaws to him, she was revealing herself to him. Bit by tantalizing bit. Anything between them could only be temporary, yet she was here for his kid and he shouldn't even indulge the mad idea in his head. But it was there, growing every second. He wasn't even sure if he could walk away from her again, like he'd done last night.

"I'm glad you and he kept in touch," he said, forcing his thoughts back. "That he could talk to you about...me."

She nodded. And he could see questions fluttering on her lips, her curiosity in the arch of her brows. He waited. And waited. And waited. The Yana he'd known once wouldn't have half the control she seemed to possess now. Even that felt like a loss to him.

Turning away to look at Zara, she said to him, "Why did you bring me to your bedroom?"

"I was as exhausted as you were." He thrust a hand through his hair as she slowly untangled herself from the mess Zara and the dogs had made of the sheets. A toned thigh, the flash of her pink thong and the shadow of her nipples—the artless show she gave him was sinfully arousing. He cleared his throat. "I think I automatically brought you here because it's the bedroom that's attached to Zara's."

Distaste filled her eyes as she jumped from the bed as if it might take a bite of that delectable bottom. "Wait, this is the room you shared with Jacqueline?"

"No, I told you last night, remember, that I bought this

castle for Zara after Jacqueline died. You know as well as I do that she'd never have moved out of Paris for anyone or anything."

She kept moving until she was standing directly in front of shafts of sunlight. As if they couldn't resist her, either, light beams drenched her, delineating every rise and dip for his pleasure. Golden dust motes created a crown around her stunning face. Her legs…went on for miles, and it was only the background noise that Zara and the dogs created that stopped his thoughts from crossing over to forbidden territory.

"If you can have the staff show me to a new room—" Yana stepped back as he approached, a frown tying her feathery brows. "What?"

He grabbed a colorful throw from the foot of the bed and wrapped it around her, tugging her closer until the edges met in front of her chest. But he didn't let go. He didn't want to. There was something incredibly arousing about arresting her in his embrace, in having her face him like this. Gathering her messy hair, he pulled it back so that the throw could sit snugly around her shoulders. The brush of his knuckles over her nape, her rough exhale coasting his lips, every moment was pungent with an arching awareness.

Tying the edges of the soft throw to hold it together, he backed away.

Licking her lips, she stared at him.

"Your T-shirt is practically transparent."

Yana's belly did a slow, tantalizing roll. Her mouth dried up as if she'd spent hours in a desert. Which she had once for an underwear ad. But this was a delicious burn that seemed to taper off and arrow straight down to her pelvis. She tugged at the T-shirt she'd put on last night, far too exhausted to unpack properly. No bra and a thong with most of her legs bared.

In contrast to her disheveled state, Nasir was dressed in dark jeans and a white T-shirt that made his olive skin gleam. His wet hair was piled high on top, with gray streaking his temples.

But neither the casual clothes nor the gray in his hair or the fact that he looked like he hadn't gotten any sleep last night diminished the sexual appeal of the man one bit. It was too much. Her own skin felt too tight to contain the pleasure and anticipation sparking through her.

It wasn't just the magnetism of his good looks, though. This morning the strain around his mouth had lessened. He looked dreamy, carefree, even, approachable. And that it was because of her presence, even if only indirectly, made delight dance inside.

God, she was such a pushover, and the realization prodded her to brazen it out.

With one wriggle of her shoulders, she dislodged the throw he'd so gently wrapped around her, wishing she could shrug off the warmth of his body just as easily. Nakedness was nothing new to her. Her body, for so long, had been just a tool, another costume, that she put on to please the world. She wasn't going to feel shy or modest about it now.

She cocked a hip and straightened her shoulders in a move she could do in her sleep. "My transparent sleepwear is not my problem." The throw settled like a warm wrap around her cold feet. "Since you're the one who barged in here."

He grinned, and she had a sense of a passionate, almost violent, energy being contained in his body. "Right! The closed door means the dogs and I are forbidden to enter."

"You've got it wrong. Unlike you, the dogs *are* welcome. Even in my bed, Nasir," she retorted, incapable of keeping her mouth shut.

Palm pressed to his chest, he let out an exaggerated sigh that said it was his loss.

It was such a dramatic, outrageous gesture for him to make that she laughed out loud. A pang of nostalgia ran through her. He'd been like this once—playful, witty, as ready to mock himself as he'd mocked her.

And even this felt like madness, to laugh with him like this, to see him try so hard for Zara's sake, to see his eyes travel over *her* with that devouring intensity. The near chant in her head that he was just one of millions of men who derived pleasure at the symmetry of her face, at a body she'd achieved through hours and hours in the gym and nearly starving herself at the beginning of her career, didn't help one bit. It was impossible to see Nasir as just any man, even in her head.

"Anyway, I can't just take your room, Nasir—"

A new voice piped up, interrupting her. "No, she can't. It's bad enough that we have to see her making pretty eyes at you all over again. Didn't you learn a lesson with your wife, Nasir? Yana will only teach Zara more awful things about you."

Yana froze, recognizing that voice. Around her, a deafening silence fell. She felt Zara's little body tucking up against her bare leg and picked her up. Even the dogs seemed to know instinctively that they needed to be wary of Nasir's mother.

It took all she had to bite back a hysterical laugh because she didn't want to scare Zara. Already, she was stiff in Yana's arms. When she saw Ahmed fluttering behind Amina, Yana walked Zara over to him. "How about a picnic as soon as we get ready, Zuzu?"

Her head tucked into the crook of Yana's shoulder and neck, Zara gave her a doubting look. "Pwomise?"

"Yes, baby. It's a lovely day and we'll spend the entirety of it outside. Once you finish breakfast, grab your boots and your scrapbook, yeah? You live right in the middle of a forest. So we have to look for fairies, okay?"

"Fairies!" Zara beamed. "Don't be late, Yana Auntie," Zara said, leaning across into Ahmed's arms. No one could miss the worried frown wreathing her forehead when she cast a glance at her grandmother.

Another thought struck Yana and she rounded on Nasir as soon as Zara was out of earshot. "You've got Zara stuck here, miles away from civilization, with only *your mother* for company? She hated Jacqueline even more than she hates me, Nasir. Is it wise to expose Zara to her brand of cutting honesty?"

"I'd never hurt Zara by showing my dislike for her mother," Amina spoke up.

"And yet, here you are, pouring vitriol in my face the first morning I'm here." Yana's voice shook. "Are you so wrapped up in yourself that you can't see that Zara can sense your feelings?"

Refusing to give Amina another chance to attack her, Yana closed the massive doors to the bedroom right in her face and pressed her back to it. Now she knew what Nasir had meant when he'd said they'd have chaperones galore.

If it was possible that there was a person who hated her more than Nasir did, it was his mother. The woman who blamed Yana's mother, probably justly so, for destroying her marriage. The woman who loathed Yana for being *that woman's* daughter and the one who'd made up a fake kiss from her son.

To trap him just like her mother had trapped his father.

Yana grabbed her bag from the closet and turned to Nasir. "Please book a hotel suite for Zara and me."

"No."

"I'm not staying here with *her*."

"Yana, listen to me."

"And you call me manipulative."

"I never called you that. Not even when you lied about kissing me all those years ago. You're far too reckless and destructively honest to be manipulative."

"You're just saying those things to try and calm me down."

She walked through the vast closet, feeling betrayed. No one could spew vicious truths like Nasir's mom. And she was already defenseless, having barely recovered from her own mom's betrayal, and from the void her thaata had left with his death.

"You should've told me she'd be here."

"Then you wouldn't have come."

"Can you blame me?"

"Only Zara matters, Yana. Ammi knows that." He raised his palms in surrender when she glared at him, his jaw so tight that she could see a vein bulging there. "I promise, I won't let her near you."

"You *can't* ensure that, Nasir, unless you stick to me like last night's gum." A strange tsunami of emotions built inside her, and Yana couldn't grasp it back under control. That Amina might be right, that she'd lose herself all over again over Nasir... "You can't control Amina...her grief, her loss, her...hatred. Not when they're all so raw after losing your dad just last year." She pushed her fingers through her hair roughly. "I get enough of this drama from my mom, and I've already had enough lashes about the past from you. I can't take it from her, too. Not even for Zara. Not when I'm trying to start a new chapter in my own life. Not when you both tried to make sure I lost your dad a long time ago."

Something about how still he stood arrested her frenzy. Yana knew she was losing it, betraying all the anger and resentment she'd tried hard to bury when Nasir had attempted to cut her out of his Dad's life, but she couldn't seem to stop.

Not when he looked at her as if he was seeing her for the first time.

The real, messy, vulnerable, hurt-as-hell her. The girl no one had looked out for. The woman who'd thought she didn't deserve that kind of looking after. That kind of love.

"When I was growing up, I didn't know how deep words like that could wound. How toxic they could make me behave in turn. But not anymore. I can't keep getting battered by you and her, and my mom and all the shadows of my past mistakes. I'll fall apart and where will that leave Zara then?"

His fingers came around her nape in a firm, yet tender grip, stilling her. "Shh...breathe, *habibi*. Breathe for me, baby. You're okay."

"I—"

And then his arms were tugging her to him, and Yana sank into the embrace. It was a gift. As necessary as breathing. She'd been starved for touch for so long. Starved for understanding as she'd tried to hold her life from imploding. Starved for a lifetime of being held like this by him.

"You're safe here, *habibi*," he kept crooning at her temple, holding her as if she was the most fragile, most precious, thing in the world. Her breath came in shallow pants and she was trembling, and he kept whispering endearments as if he meant them. That bergamot and sandalwood scent dug deep into her roots, making a home there. Centering her. His large hands stroked all over her back, soothing her.

He'd been like this once before. A long time ago. He'd been kind and patient and... And he was only being so now because she was very near a breakdown and he needed her to not fall apart. He was a good father and would do whatever was required to keep her here for Zara.

She was in his life just because Nasir loved his daughter—she couldn't forget that.

"No lies," she said quietly, pulling away from him. "You decided it was okay for me to be exposed to your mother's vitriol. You're fine with treating me however you please because I'm an eternal car crash anyway, right? But no more. At least for Zara's sake, ask Amina to keep her mouth shut about Jacqueline." She wrapped her arms around herself, reminding herself that she was steel and ice. "I'll stay but you don't deserve it because you've broken my trust again."

After walking into the en-suite bathroom and closing the door behind her, she leaned against it. Yes, seeing Amina had thrown her. But she was stronger than an angry, bitter old woman, stronger this time than her childish attraction to Nasir. She'd be stronger for herself and for Zara.

CHAPTER SEVEN

NASIR STOPPED PRETENDING that he was getting any work done—even though it was a chapter he'd already plotted multiple times, minutes after he saw Yana walk to the pool with Zara's little hand tucked in hers. As he walked through the myriad corridors of the castle, their laughter floated upward from the multiple open terraces.

For over two weeks now, he'd told himself that work was more important, especially after the forced break while he followed Yana all over the world. But it was a fruitless exercise when all he wanted was to join them both and play happy family in a way Zara had never experienced with him and Jacqueline. Even that startling thought didn't stop his progress.

Every day, after walking the dogs, Yana and Zara promptly arrived at the pool. When Zara went down for a nap under the supervision of her actual nanny, Yana disappeared back inside the castle. Then the two of them would show up in the cozy library in the evenings, either reading or drawing or listening to rhymes. Yana even ate dinner with Zara. He didn't doubt one bit that Yana's day was precisely planned to have minimum intersection with his. Even during that early dinner, she retreated halfway through it to give him time with Zara.

It was exactly the kind of experience he'd wanted for Zara,

with a few structured activities and free playtime, but had been unable to achieve with any of the myriad staff he'd hired. In only a couple of weeks of Yana's being here, Zara laughed, played naughty tricks and was more open and demanding with them—everything that a healthy, thriving five-year-old should be. Even his mother had to agree that Yana had an innate ability to love Zara like a mother.

With him, though, she was an ice queen extraordinaire. A thorn under his skin. The flicker of anguish when she'd said her pain was an acceptable price to him haunted him, day and night. The flash of grief when she'd said that she'd lost his dad, too, showed he'd become a villain in her life.

He knew he'd compounded his mistreatment of her by throwing her out after he'd learned that Yana was supposedly Jacqueline's character witness to enable her to gain solo custody of Zara. Having seen her open love for his daughter, he more than doubted his accusations now. Yana wouldn't have done that to Zara. Jacqueline must have instructed her lawyers to name Yana without telling her.

All of his distrust of her just because she'd claimed he'd kissed her when he'd never even touched her. It had been a stupid, juvenile impulse she'd given in to when she was only nineteen. Had he really behaved any better—a man twelve years older than she was? Had he shown any more maturity than she had?

Now she'd shut him out so thoroughly that Nasir felt as if he had been robbed of something he'd never even realized he had. He'd made peace with his attraction to her. But where did this need to be acknowledged by her come from? To be forgiven for all his multitude of sins?

Wherever it came from, it was so not a good idea. Especially when she'd always be a part of his little girl's life *and his life*. And still, he kept moving, instead of turning back.

* * *

Yana sat at the edge of the pool, praising Zara for everything she did right and for things she tried under the swimming instructor's tutelage. When Yana stood up, Nasir's breath left his body.

Her skin gleamed with a golden-brown sheen that came out of no bottle. The bright orange bikini she wore was basically three triangles that should come with a libido overload warning. Every movement sensuality in motion, she looked like a Bond girl from the eighties, all wild and free and innately sensual.

The swimming instructor and Yana struck up a relaxed conversation. Then she bent and lifted Zara out of the pool and wrapped her in one big towel, tying a turban-esque smaller one around her hair before the nanny came over to fetch the little girl for her nap.

"Do you see how she flirts with that boy? Is this the kind of behavior you want around Zara?"

Nasir's irritation leaped into dangerous territory at his mother's open insults. Of course, he saw the casual flirting, the laughter, the swat on the arm and how her body inevitably bowed toward the younger guy as she chatted to him, how she naturally made him open up and smile back at her.

What he hadn't understood until now was how that effervescence, that wildness, was an intrinsic part of her. Like lightning, she either illuminated or burned everything she touched. And just the idea of burning with her made arousal flood his body.

He cast his mother a quelling look. "Don't, Ammi."

"You will regret—"

"Stop, please."

In just a few minutes Yana had pinned down his mother's inconsolable grief and the outlet of bitter rage she used to channel it. The past year he had given in to his mother's demands to stay with Zara because he understood the sheer magnitude of her loss. He'd lost a woman he'd loved once. While Fatima's face was nothing but a distorted memory now, the hollow loss of it remained.

But now his mother's words were directly harming his own motherless child. That he hadn't seen Zara's reticence with her until Yana had pointed it out...made his very foundation flounder. "If you cannot be civil to Yana, I'll send you away."

"I'm Zara's grandmother. I've helped you look after her all these months."

"And for that," he said, "I'm forever grateful. I want Zara to know you, to love you. Jacqueline's parents are long gone anyway. But everything you say, everything you don't say, about her mother, and now about her precious Auntie Yana... Zara processes all this."

"She is only—"

"You can't have missed that any time Zara spends with you has to be overseen by me at her request, that it's out of obligation."

He could see her heart breaking at his harsh words but the truth had to be said. If she didn't fix her behavior, the damage would soon be irrevocable.

"You're choosing that woman who's a liar and cheater and...whose mother ruined my marriage over me?"

And there was the crux of the matter. "The only one I'm choosing here is Zara. I'm doing what I should've done from the moment Jacqueline told me she was expecting. If you can set your grief aside for one moment—" he raised his palms to hold her protest off "—you'll acknowledge that Zara flourishes when Yana is around. Yana's going to be a permanent part of our life, and I want you there, too. That means you have to let the past go. Yana was only a child herself when Abba and Diana met."

"What about the lies she told about you?"

"She was young and naive, and the only one she had to teach her right from wrong was Diana, who we both know has no moral compass. And I had just dealt her a brutal rejection." He'd never been able to get her stricken face out of his head. He'd turned on her, when he could have dealt the same rejection with a little grace and a lot more kindness.

Instead, mindless with grief and guilt over losing Fatima, he'd shredded Yana to bits. He saw the truth finally, clearly now. Yana had loved him with all the urgency and naiveté and fierceness of a nineteen-year-old.

"If I can let it go, then you can. And Yana's not responsible for Abba leaving you."

"You are attracted to her," his mother whispered in a shaken voice. "How just like a man!"

He didn't dignify that with a response.

"She is not right for you."

Nasir laughed. "I chose Jacqueline but she cheated on me again and again. And believe me, I was no great husband, so I very possibly drove her to it. Yana's suitability is moot because she loathes the very sight of me."

"That's impossible."

"No wonder my ego has always flourished, Ammi."

"If she's that important to Zara," she said, having to have the last word before she walked off, "then you'd better keep your distance."

Having been celibate for more than three years, Nasir wondered if part of what was driving him might just simply be sexual frustration. But he knew it wasn't just a need for release.

Yana's ice-queen act was rattling things he didn't want to delve into. It was time to take not quite a sledgehammer to it, because Yana was far more fragile than he had ever thought her, and not just in body. The most shocking thing, however, was this…strange energy between them. He understood now how much of her natural passionate nature went into hating him. And hating, he knew from his own experience from his marriage to Jacqueline, was not apathy.

He relaxed into the lounger while Yana took her own swim. Let the bright afternoon sun soak into his skin.

When was the last time he had taken a moment for himself like this? The last time he had found this pleasurable fizz run through all of him at the mere idea of a conversation with a woman?

In a smooth, single movement, Yana pulled herself out of the pool. Water glistened over golden-brown skin in shimmering drips, licking at toned muscles and lush valleys and hollowed dips that he wanted to chase with his own tongue.

Yana walked past him, as if he was no more than one of the statues littered around the estate.

Nasir wondered what his life might have been like if he hadn't dictated her life from afar, deciding rights and wrongs for her, and he'd never quite loathed himself more than he did then.

And like a statue brought to life by a sorceress's hand, he suddenly felt all these things he had shut off long ago, when Fatima, the woman he should've protected with his life, had died in his arms.

If she was disconcerted by the fact that he was waiting for her by the pool in the middle of the day when they hadn't even made eye contact for more than two weeks, Yana didn't show it by the flicker of an eyelid. Having toweled herself down briskly, she grabbed a tube of sunscreen and began to apply it to her belly and legs liberally.

Nasir saw all of this out of his periphery, and it was as if she had stripped naked in front of him. Just for him.

The shimmery white gel soaked into her skin like magic

dust, not that she needed it. Slightly angling her torso, she lifted her bikini top and took her breasts in her bare hands with a brisk efficiency that came from parading in front of strangers with a power only a few could own. Once the bikini top was back in place, she reached around her back, twisting herself like a gymnast.

He stood up and grabbed the tube of sunscreen. "Let me help."

She didn't even look up. *Ice queen indeed.* "I can manage, thank you."

He was damned if he walked away now. "Right, it makes you uncomfortable if I touch you. Forgive me."

The slender line of her shoulders stiffened. He'd have missed it if he wasn't entirely too fascinated by her body language. Tension drew a line down her back and spine, giving him a map to her emotions.

"And why would I be uncomfortable if you touched me casually?"

"I wondered that, too." He managed a shrug, somehow keeping his lips from twitching. "But it's a fair assumption based on how you keep jerking away from me."

She snorted and somehow even that was elegant, too. "My body is a tool. I've sold clothes, shoes, hairstyles, cosmetics, jeans and most of all, sex. I've had hundreds of photographers and designers and camera boys and tailors maul me about like I was a mannequin."

Nasir wished he could see her face, the bloom of pink on her cheeks, the little sparks that made her brown eyes glitter when she was aroused. Take her in as she was right now, instead of the icy wraith that had been walking through his castle recently.

But he forced himself to stand there, just a little behind her.

After exactly thirty seconds, she looked up at him. Determination written into every line of that achingly lovely face, she nodded at the plastic tube he was holding. He dropped to his knees by her thigh.

Awareness jolted into him at the aching beauty of her up close. Like an exquisite painting that bestowed some new boon every time he looked upon it.

Chin tilted up defiantly, she presented him with her back. He pushed up the messy tendrils from the nape of her neck, while tugging at the two fragile strings holding the bikini top there with the other. And then the one below.

Her forearms rose to hold the loose top in place, thrusting those perfect breasts into a cleavage that he could unwittingly see perfectly from his vantage point. He didn't know if he should feel like a voyeur or be glad that his libido was back with vengeance. Shuttling those thoughts aside, he poured the sunscreen liberally into his palms and began to rub it down her back.

Smooth golden skin and toned muscles under his palms— he shouldn't have felt such sensual, sensory pleasure in the simple action, and yet Nasir could feel himself getting harder by the second. The contact was innocent and nonsexual, and yet heat seem to arc between his fingers and her flesh, something he could tell she tried her best to hide, but failed.

"As long as I have your attention," she started, and Nasir smiled, because he knew she was trying to distract herself. Was it all simply want on his part and hate on hers? Or was there more?

"If I had known you were looking for my attention, I would've insisted that you stay on for dinner after Zara goes to bed."

She shivered under his hands. "I'm taking the evening off."

"When?"

"Tonight."

On an upward sweep of his hands, he found tight knots at her shoulders. "For what?"

"I need a night off."

"Has Zara worn you out?" When she stiffened, he quickly added, "Quite the prickly thing, aren't you? Anyone would be worn out and begging for adult company when one spends most of their waking hours endlessly running around after a five-year-old."

He pressed his fingertips gently into one stubborn knot and heard her soft moan. The sound went straight to his groin. Thank God she couldn't see him because at this point, he must look obscene.

"I have castle fever," she finally said.

Somehow, he infused humor into his words when all he felt was a tsunami of inappropriate wild urges. "I thought you loved castles."

"As a fanciful teenager, Nasir. Castles are all well and good, especially when you think a charming prince lives in them but—"

"I'm the devil. Is that it?"

"More like a beast." Her answer was immediate.

He grabbed the bottom ends of the bikini top by reaching around to the front and almost grazed the underside of her breasts. Breath shallowing, he tied the strings at the bottom, and then took hold of the ones at the top. His fingers lingered on her neck, as he tried to keep the damp tendrils of her hair from getting into the knot. Her shoulders trembled as he touched the jut of her clavicle, marveling at how much passion was contained in such a fragile body.

Shooting to her feet all of a sudden, Yana jerked back. And he saw it then—the pink flush that shimmered under all of that golden-brown skin. And not just her cheeks or neck, but dusting the tops of her breasts. Her throat moved in a hard swallow that rippled down her chest.

"I apologize for hurting you," he said, transfixed by the sight.

Gears turned in his head, mostly driven by the molten desire in his blood. Truth dawned and held him in thrall—she definitely wanted him.

"I'm not going to break apart because you caused a little pain."

"But I should not cause it in the first place," he said, coming back to himself.

Knowing one of the most beautiful women in the world wanted him was a trip all on its own. But it was also a sop to his masculine ego that had taken enough dents with a partner who'd cheated on him as if she was picking a different weekly flavor of her frou-frou coffees.

But knowing that someone like Yana—vulnerable and innocent and full of heart and fragile—wanted him...was a honey-coated thrust to his insides. "Yana, I should like to talk to you about what you said the other day."

Grabbing a sheer white robe, she tied it at her waist with a fierce tug.

He had the most insane urge to pull those ends with his hands until she fell into him and he could burn the edge out of them both in the best way he knew.

"It's not necessary. As I've proved to you over the last two weeks or so, I'm very much capable of having a polite relationship with you, Nasir. Please, let's not dig back into the past and play the blame game again."

"Even if it's only so I can admit to you that I've been inexcusably wrong?" he slipped in.

For a second, just a second, it looked like she would give him a chance to talk. Something almost like longing flashed in her eyes.

But then she was shaking her head, and her messy bun fell apart, and long, wavy dark gold strands of hair framed her face. In that moment she looked very much like a beautiful, naive prize that had been grabbed up by the beast. He was beginning to hate that damned fairy tale.

"A friend of mine will be here to pick me up around five this evening. I've already prepped Zara so you don't have to worry. She knows I'll be back tomorrow morning by the time her Arabic lessons are done. If you'll just inform security to let him through the electronic gates—"

"No."

"What do you mean, *no*?"

"I mean my security won't let him in."

He turned around and started walking away. That was not the end of it, he knew. But he'd had enough of kidding himself that he didn't want to explore this thing between Yana and him. Enough of his own lies that somehow he'd keep away from her.

Right now he simply wanted her company. Her forgiveness. Her wild laughter. Her eyes on him.

She grabbed him by the shoulder and turned him and thrust her face close to his, all warm, golden skin and exploding temper. "Is old age affecting your brain cells? Because I wasn't asking for permission."

He laughed.

That lovely, lush lower lip fell open as she watched him, drinking him in. Warmth crested his cheeks at the open, artless way her eyes stared up at him, as if he was exactly the tall, cold drink she needed after a swim in the afternoon heat.

"Oh, believe me, every faculty, even those I thought were faulty or dead, are now functioning at peak capacity. Thanks to you, *habibi*."

Her mouth opened, closed and then opened again. Curiosity danced across her face and he willed her to give in, to ask him what he meant. But he lost. "Are you saying no to my friend coming here to pick me up or are you saying no to my going out?" Tiny lines pinched at the corners of her eyes. "What gives you the right to say no to me for anything?"

"No to both. For one, I don't want some random friend of yours finding out where I live. And second—"

"Have Ahmed drop me at the nearest village, then."

"You never asked for a day off when we were talking terms." There was no way he was going to let her go off and see some male *friend*. He didn't care to examine his motivations just then. Maybe never. Maybe there was a freedom in going all in into becoming this ruthless, arrogant, uncaring beast she thought him to be anyway. "If it's not in the contract, Yana, it's not happening."

She pushed at him with her hand on his chest, but he didn't budge. And he saw now how volatile and touchy she got when her temper was riled.

Raising his hands, he gave her a sweet smile that he knew would only push her closer toward the edge. He wanted to see the explosion, the thundering temper, the impulsive, self-destructive step she might take.

And then he wondered what it would be like to be in the path of all that destruction she wreaked, to let himself be devoured by the storm that was this woman.

She stomped her foot, much like Zara did when she didn't get to eat her dessert before dinner. "Oh, how I hate you sometimes!"

"I prefer hatred to what you've been serving me up this past fortnight or so."

She colored. "I'm keeping my end of the bargain. I spend most of my time with Zara. I love spending that time with her. It's only for an hour or so during her nap, and then again after she has her dinner and goes to bed that I leave her. So why are you—"

He stepped closer to her, determined to not let her run out without giving him an answer. "Where is it that you disappear to? And what do you do? Don't tell me the party girl, supermodel extraordinaire, retires to bed at only seven in the evening?"

"That's none of your business." She shut him down so hard that it only made Nasir more curious. "As you've just mentioned, I'm not used to being tied down to one place for too long. I need a night out on the town."

"Where do you want to go?"

Her response was the cutest twitch of her nose in distaste. Something in his chest melted and he wondered how much of him had been frozen over the years to be constantly melting at each taunt and expression that she threw at him. And what would eventually happen to him if he didn't stop her?

"A nightclub. I want to go dancing... I have all this energy I want to get rid of." There was something so sensuous and yet, unpracticed in that little wiggle of hers that all Nasir wanted to do was see her do it again. And do it because she wanted his eyes on him. Do it because she wanted to please him.

"Give me a few days and I'll take you."

She laughed and it was like watching a sunrise captured in one of those time-lag videos. It was beautiful, and breathtaking and made his breath falter in his throat.

"You at a nightclub?"

"You sound more scared than excited at the prospect. What are you so afraid might happen?"

She swallowed and didn't meet his eyes. "If you come, it will become a big thing. I don't want to be photographed with you again."

"I thought you didn't care about being photographed with me. Your sisters know where you are, right?"

"It's not my sisters that I'm hiding from."

"Nobody can get to you here. I promise you that. You don't have to be scared, *habibi*." The endearment fell from his lips as easily as if he'd said it a thousand times.

"It's not what you think," she said. "It's just... I don't want Diana to know where I am."

He wanted to probe the source of the argument between them. Not that he was surprised at her wanting to hide. Diana had never been a good parental figure. For now he let Yana be.

Soon, though, he would have all her secrets. He'd lay her bare, see through to the real Yana she hid under the party-girl persona. Maybe that was the way to break this fascination with every facet of her. Maybe then he could go back to viewing her from afar with a mild interest at best.

"Have dinner with me in a few days. We'll have guests over, since you're scared of being alone with me."

"I... Who?" Suspicion marked that single word.

"A few good friends of mine. You'll have good conversation and dancing choices other than me."

Her eyes widened. "Really? You're going to let your friends see me here at your forbidden castle? Has hell frozen over?"

"You're the one making all the assumptions here, Yana. And you won't give me a chance to dispel any of them. One might wonder why you need to retain them. Almost like armor, one could say."

He left her standing there, with her mouth open, incredibly frustrated with her and even more so with himself. But he'd brought temptation into his life, into his house, into his very bed even, and he had nothing left in him to resist her.

CHAPTER EIGHT

YANA WAS SEARCHING through her wardrobe for something to wear to Nasir's dinner party when she heard a knock on her door.

For a second she wondered if it was one of the staff to tell her that Nasir had rescinded the invitation. Because nearly a week later, she still couldn't process his change of heart.

Tolerating her for Zara's sake was one thing. Actively seeking her company was another. Although, she didn't doubt that he thought he was being all protective and honorable by keeping her out of trouble. Whatever his motive, though, she was far too tempted by this chance at a glimpse into his life to refuse.

She opened the door to find an army of people. Surprise made her gasp as Ahmed and a younger woman rolled in a dress stand, followed by Zara, her hand tucked into her grandmother's bigger one.

Yana followed Ahmed and the colorful display of dresses on the stand. "What's going on?"

"Nasir Sir thought you might need help with getting ready for tonight."

"Did he?" Yana asked, somehow keeping her bitterness to herself. "Does he think I'd embarrass his highbrow friends, Ahmed?" she hissed in a whisper so the others couldn't hear.

He shook his head. "This is my daughter, Huma," Ahmed said, beckoning the younger woman closer. "If it's okay with you, she wishes to dress you for the party."

"I was just going to wear something from my wardrobe," Yana added, wary of Nasir's new behavior. But the crestfallen expression on the younger woman's face made her feel horrible. "Of course, I didn't pack for one of Nasir's fabulous dinner parties. I'd love a chance to try one of your creations." She ran her fingers over a couple of evening gowns made of frothy chiffon and cut in simple, classic lines. Nearly a decade and a half in the industry had given her a discerning eye when it came to fashion. "These are gorgeous. Did you design these yourself, Huma?"

Pride and joy shone in Huma's eyes. "Yes, I'm studying fashion."

Ahmed gave his daughter a nudge. "Nasir Sir has already paid for her education. But she refuses to leave because she thinks her old papa cannot take care of himself."

Yana's heart warmed at the obvious affection between these two. Suddenly, she could see why Nasir might have suggested to them that Yana needed help. It wasn't a big surprise that he was a wonderful human being when it came to other people. It was only her he held in such low esteem.

Even if it's only so I can admit to you that I've been inexcusably wrong...?

His question had been haunting her. Did he truly want to apologize to her? To begin a different sort of relationship? Could she bear that? Or was she letting him mess with her head again?

"I'd love to wear one of your creations, Huma, as long as you let me pay you for it."

Huma shook her head. "Not at all. It's a dream come true to see you wear one of my designs. If you'd just let me take a picture once you're wearing it," she rushed on. "I wouldn't share it with anybody. Not on social media. I just... I want proof that the gorgeous, stunning Yana Reddy wore one of my designs."

Yana squeezed her hand. "Of course you can share it. Between you and me, I'm kind of getting tired of the modeling world, but I still have my foot in the door there. I know a lot of photographers and design houses. I'll get you in touch with people I trust," she added, noting Ahmed's expression.

"I'm not worried about the kind of people you will introduce her to, Ms. Reddy. If they're anything like you, my daughter is in good hands."

Yana had no idea what she'd ever done in her life to deserve such genuine affection from him but she let it drape around her like a childhood blanket. "Now…" She clapped her hands, picked Zara up and settled her on her hip. "Let's see. Zuzu baby, do you want to help me pick a dress for tonight?"

Like an octopus, Zara wound her hands and legs all around Yana, as if she never wanted to let her go. For all the hours they spent together, Yana was still dreading the goodbye that would eventually come at the end of three months. As much as she hadn't wanted to be here, under the same roof as Nasir, she'd found that she liked living at the castle.

Especially since, whatever her son had said to her, Amina had kept her distance from Yana, too.

"To turn you into a pwincess?" Zara asked.

Yana laughed. "Maybe. Although I'd like to be a princess who saves herself."

Zara nodded, as if she understood the intricacies of adulthood and wanting to be someone who saved themselves. "But I'd love Huma's help with a dress and yours with my hair so that I can be a perfect princess. Even the brave princess needs all the love she can get."

"Yay, did you hear, Gwandma? Yana Auntie said I can do her hair."

Dragged into the conversation by her granddaughter, Amina offered a tentative smile. "Are you sure you want

Zara's fingers on that lovely hair of yours? She's going to mess it all up."

"Oh, I don't really care, Amina. It's not like I'm going to walk the ramp tonight and face a thousand cameras." And yet, even the wildest, longest, hardest events of her career hadn't caused this...constant flutter of butterflies.

Was she a fool to look forward to the party this much? Where were all the promises she'd made to herself that she'd treat Nasir as just another employer?

"You will look beautiful whatever Zara does to your hair," Amina added, always wanting to have the last word, just like her son. "You're leaving modeling, then?"

Struggling to keep her shock off her face—the older woman had the hearing of a bat—she said, "Give or take a decade, Amina. It's not like I know how to do anything else."

The words left a bitter taste in her mouth.

She had to stop with the negative talk. And yet, the fact that she'd not been successful yet in placing her children's novel with an agent had left her in knots.

She wanted it so bad—this new, fluttery dream to be an author, to fill some child's life with escape and adventure and love, as Nasir's stories had done for her. But...she was terrified that she'd never make it. Never get it right. Never have what it took.

She could share the manuscript with Nasir and get his feedback and advice. And yet, the thought of him finding her talentless, or worse, laughing in her face, made bile rise up into her throat.

With Zara still on her hip, Yana moved to the huge vanity table that had been moved into the bedroom the second day of her arrival. It was the most beautiful thing she'd ever seen, and she had seen a lot of beautiful things in her life. With three different panels of mirrors, it was truly a princess's possession. She had no doubt Nasir had acquired it in some rare auction, but she wondered every time she sat in front of it why he'd had it installed in here when she was still using his bedroom. "First, I'm going to do my makeup, okay? Something soft and…"

"No, Yana Auntie. Glittery… Pwincesses have glittery makeup."

Everybody laughed and Yana groaned. "Oh, pumpkin, you don't want your papa's guests to make fun of Yana Auntie, do you?" she said, unable to keep the biggest fear that had been haunting her ever since Nasir had issued the invitation, out of her voice. More dictate than invitation, though, she thought wryly.

Whatever she heard in Yana's voice, Amina came to stand behind her. "First rule of being a woman—never let men decide if you're good enough for them."

She gave the older woman a quick nod in the mirror and wondered if she'd imagined the glint of satisfaction in her gaze. "Well, let's get started," Yana said, truly excited now at the prospect of getting ready for the night ahead. "With this many fairy godmothers, I'm sure I'll look beautiful tonight."

Yana entered the dining room and came to an awed stillness.

An otherworldly quality permeated the room with its grand sweeping ceilings and archways leading off to yet more rooms, like it belonged in an old film with its brightly lit sconces, gleaming chandeliers and the black-and-white-checkered marble floor. Through a huge archway, the room segued into an open, airy ballroom, where a couple was already slow dancing. With jazz playing on a record player and a low hum of conversation, it looked like one of those intellectual soirees she'd never felt good enough for.

The hum died as every gaze turned to her.

A huge stone fireplace blazed on one side in contrast to the French doors opening into a wide terrace with a view of the mountains. Cigar smoke drifted in from the terrace through the doors and lingered, adding to the dark, mysterious atmosphere of the room. Along with smoke, cold fluttered in, making one side of her deliciously chilly versus the warmth on the other from the fireplace. It was as magical as she'd imagined.

First impressions bombarding her, she noticed that it was an intimate group of guests. That meant less chance of losing herself. Her nervousness grew, thrashing it out with the excitement she'd been feeling all day.

It felt like an audition she was entering to find herself worthy of Nasir's highbrow group. And even if she didn't fit in, so what?

Bolstered by those thoughts, she straightened her shoulders. Her gaze moved over four couples, finally landing on Nasir, standing next to the huge hearth. His gaze swept over her, gleaming brighter than the amber liquid in the decanters on the bar cart.

The bright pink chiffon cocktail dress she and Huma had agreed on showed off her tan perfectly. It dipped low in the front with a beaded corset hugging her breasts tight, leaving her back bare all the way almost to the upper swells of her buttocks. It wasn't the most daring dress she'd ever worn and yet, maybe it was the most daring for this company.

It was cleverly held together by two straps tied at her neck, and that had reminded her of Nasir's fingers on her nape as he'd reknotted her bikini strings, and the delicious sensations that had engulfed her.

She didn't know how long they stood like that, gazing at each other across the room, quiet murmurs all around them while the jazz crooned to a soft, sinuous beat, and the sounds of the night drifted in from outside. All of it felt like an inspired, perfectly orchestrated soundtrack for this moment.

"So this is why you've been avoiding us, Nasir. You've got this beautiful creature hidden away in your castle." A deep voice quipped from her side, breaking the pulse of tension between her and Nasir. For a fanciful moment, she wondered what kind of vision she'd need to see it arc between them like a rainbow, fizzing with electricity, tugging them closer.

A second voice chimed in. "Our Mr. Hadeed is not as conservative as he'd have us believe."

Yana turned to face the two men, their arms around each other, both stunningly good-looking in completely different ways. She nodded, her mouth curving into a smile at the easy camaraderie they offered.

Nasir was moving closer. Only years of faking a snooty haughtiness helped her swallow the awed gasp that rose to her lips.

Dressed in a casual black jacket, white shirt and black trousers, he looked like one of those larger than life heroes of the silver screen. Hair slicked back, that long beak of his nose standing out, a cigar dangling from his fingers, there was a magnetic quality to him that made her greedy for every detail.

Yana let herself look to her heart's content, let herself feel the sensation of desire drench her, let her senses fill with the sheer sexual appeal of the man. She could live for a hundred years, and she knew she'd never find a man more attractive to her than he was.

Reaching her, he tucked one braid that kept falling out of its clip behind her ear. "Your hairstyle is…enchanting."

Yana laughed, trying to cover up the heat she felt at his casual touch. "Only a dad can come up with such compliments for his five-year-old's handiwork."

His brows rose. "You let Zara do your hair?"

She nodded.

"Ouch. She gives me head massages and I know how painful those can be. Somehow, I managed to talk her down to once a month." He watched her with that intense scrutiny. "I finally told her that her poor little papa will lose all his hair if she continued in that vein."

Instantly, her gaze moved to his thick, wavy hair. The gray at his temples had only added to the appeal of the blasted man. Her fingers itched to sink in and tug and stroke, until he was putty in her hands. "I see no risk of that."

"You look…delicious enough to eat." He took her hand in his. A casual touch but his fingers were rough against her soft ones, and Yana felt the contact deep in her core. "No, not just eat. Devour."

She stumbled, a helpless longing slithering through her, as if he was a sneaky snake charmer determined to wrest out all her secrets. His palm at the small of her bare back was a warm, steady weight.

He hesitated, just for a second, and then took a look at her bare back. Yana smiled. She knew she looked good most days in most outfits. Her beauty had long ago lost any personal meaning to her, if there ever had been any. It had become a tool—even a weapon to wield if Diana had had her way, a means to earn a livelihood, something to oil and feed and care for so that it ran smoothly. For a long time she'd even felt a strange dispassionate apathy toward it because she'd thought it had led her to make bad decisions, starting with this very man.

But hating oneself—one's body, one's mind, one's weaknesses—she'd learned was one of those toxic traits that hollowed one out. She'd always thought her little sister Nush was the most perfect, achingly loveliest, woman and yet Nush, she knew, thought she looked odd and weird, just because she didn't conform to some arbitrary beauty standard.

So Yana had learned to at least respect her body, her looks, her face, even if what she showed the world wasn't exactly what she felt inside. But tonight… Tonight sheer pleasure fluttered and tightened low in her belly when Nasir looked at her. She reveled in the soft grunt of his exhale, in the stunned expression that had come over his face when she'd walked in, in the way his long fingers danced tantalizingly over her bare back.

Already, she felt drunk on pleasure.

"That dress should come with a warning label." There it was again—a husky timbre to his voice that he made no effort to hide.

"It was our unanimous choice for tonight. Huma's and mine."

"No wonder she was so eager to dress you. You look sublime in it."

"All these compliments… You make me wonder what the price is going to be." Instantly, she wished she could take back the words. She wanted to enjoy tonight, didn't want to dilute it with acrimony and accusations about the past. And yet, she was the one who'd gone there.

"There is a price," he said with the smoothness that made her feel like a gauche idiot. Her temper had always gotten the better of her. And she'd never been more aware of the fact than when she was with him, enveloped in his cool control and stoic rationale. "I wish for you to simply enjoy the evening."

Shocked, she darted a look at him. Found him staring back at her. Swallowing, she nodded. Something in her responded to his offer of truce. "I'll try. Believe it or not, the last couple of years haven't left me a lot of time or energy for living in the moment, or any kind of enjoyment, for that matter."

She wanted to smack her forehead with the heel of her hand. Apparently, she couldn't do artificial banter. Either she went too far with her anger or too deep with her confidences.

His fingers tightened over hers. "Come, let me introduce you to this rowdy crowd. Stick to me, and you'll be safe."

When he patted her on the back of her hand, it made her giggle.

His gaze dipped to her mouth, an eager frenzy to it, as if he wanted to taste her smile. "What is so funny?"

"You? Rowdy crowd?" She taunted him, even as she wondered exactly how he would introduce her.

A new swarm of butterflies took flight in her tummy. Who would he say she was? Zara's extra nanny? His ex-wife's BFF? His problematic, once-upon-a-time stepsister he couldn't wait to be rid of? His employee? Or a woman forever in his debt?

Her nerves jangled as he nudged her toward the grand table in the center of the vast room. As if he had beckoned them, his friends moved up from their various lounging positions across the room.

He didn't let go of her hand or loosen his grip around her waist. If she wasn't so nervous at the prospect of meeting his intimate friends, she'd have called his hold of her possessive.

"This is Yana, a close family friend. She's doing me an enormous favor by helping Zara settle down here after the last year."

A close family friend...

She liked the sound of that less than she should. Actually, she loathed it for how...sensible and correct it sounded. How it hovered in the space between them—a label, a barrier, the drawing of a line that shouldn't be crossed. And every inch of her rebelled at that boundary and she wondered if she'd ever be cured of this madness. Of wanting to be more to a man who'd never really seen her as a woman.

CHAPTER NINE

YANA FELT NASIR'S appraising gaze on her, as if it were a finger on her cheek. Somehow, she managed to keep her smile locked tightly in place.

His guests spoke at once, their greetings effusive enough to move the moment along. She shook their hands and couldn't help gushing when one of them was Nasir's longest standing friend and editor.

"Close family friend is so droll, Nasir. Especially the way you've been eyeing her from the moment she walked in," he said.

Before Yana could tuck his comment into a corner never to be opened again, one of the women spoke up. "This is the stepsister you're quite protective about?"

A chorus of reactions ensued, taking the whole secret stepsister idea and running with it. If it wasn't for the fact that she was tied up in knots about which one of her shenanigans Nasir had shared with the woman, she would've enjoyed the flights of fancy.

As if sensing her distress, Nasir's fingers tightened on the bare skin at her back.

The woman, sensing the current of tension pinging back and forth between her and Nasir, said in a whisper, "Nasir just wanted to know about what kind of emergency measures one might need to take with type-one diabetes. As the castle is quite cut off from immediate medical centers."

Yana couldn't help but send a glance at Nasir, perplexed yet again by his motives.

"I have made similar inquiries about Ammi's heart condition, Ahmed's ulcers and one of the staff's recurring back pain," Nasir said calmly.

She relaxed immediately.

Another gorgeous man, dressed to the nines, grabbed her by the waist with the charming insouciance she knew well from working in the fashion industry.

"Yana Reddy!" He kissed the back of her hand with a regal flourish that made her laugh. "Now I know why Nasir demanded that I come to this party. Usually, it's my partner James that he can't do without," he mock-whispered. "He knows the rest of this crowd is too boring and fuddy-duddy for a glorious creature like you."

Yana turned to the man who wouldn't bore her if they lived together for a hundred years. "Is that true?"

Nasir raised his palms in surrender, his gaze holding hers in a silent siege. "Before you misunderstand my intentions yet again, I simply wanted you to have fun tonight."

Before she could respond, a short, squat man approached them. Recognition flared even as James introduced his famous musician partner.

"Where have we seen her before?" asked Dimitri.

"Other than the fact that she's a hot supermodel?" James quipped and then clapped. "Ilyavich's paintings. Her nudes were the best he ever did."

Comprehension dawned on Dimitri's face. But instead of the usual mockery or disdain, excitement lit his eyes. "That's it! You know, I've tried so hard to get my hands on one of those paintings. After that first private buyer got hold of them at the initial auction, they never surfaced again."

"I'm glad they didn't," Yana said. "I don't regret doing

them, but the whole episode was ruined for me thanks to the dirty accusations I had to face afterward."

"It's almost like the buyer was looking out for you," said James, casting a pointed look at Nasir.

Yana's response misted away when she caught Nasir's reaction. Her skin pebbled into goose bumps. He knew who had those paintings? How? The next thought came like a torrent after the first. Strike that—he didn't just know where the paintings were.

He *had* the paintings.

Then she was being dragged away by a smug-looking James. But she couldn't help casting a look behind her.

Sure enough, the answer to her dilemma danced in Nasir's eyes. And Yana suddenly knew that she was in a lot more danger than she'd ever realized.

It was past midnight, and most of his friends had drifted off to various bedrooms when Nasir stubbed out the one cigar he'd allowed himself for tonight and sought the woman who filled him with adolescent anticipation.

His mother's warning about how necessary Yana was for Zara buzzed like background noise in his head, but made no difference as he walked toward her. Slow jazz was still drifting up from the record player and Yana was sandwiched between James and Dimitri, the three of them swaying to the soft beat.

"My turn," he said, taking her hand in his, and spinning her away from his friends. Despite her surprise, she came like a feather, light on her feet. Her delicious scent sank its tendrils into him, filling his chest.

She stiffened for a second before settling her hands on his shoulders. He wrapped his arms loosely around her waist, the bare skin there an irresistible temptation.

All evening it had been impossible to look away from her.

But he also felt a kind of savage satisfaction in seeing the real, tempestuous, funny woman come out of that ice cocoon she'd spent the past few weeks wrapped in. She'd engaged in a rigorous discussion with his editor about books, given James and Dimitri a run for their money when they suddenly decided to start singing old melodies, and had generally been a warm, wonderful, passionate hostess, even if she didn't know she'd played the role so naturally.

Not even a month in, and already Nasir didn't remember what the castle was like without her. Without her and Zara's giggles and running around and playing hide-and-seek and making the staff join in and just generally filling the empty spaces in his life. But he was only an audience, as he'd wished to be for so long, instead of a participant.

Even the space and time between him and Zara was filled with how wonderful Yana Auntie was. It was as if she was a witch who'd cast a spell on all of them—even his mother. Proving every day what Zara and he had been missing, even before Jacqueline had died.

And now she was in his arms, a perfect, soft landing at the end of a lovely day.

They danced for he didn't know how long, simply letting their bodies move to the slow beat of the music. It was a sweet exhilaration even as tension buzzed and fizzed every time her thigh brushed his or his fingers found another patch of warm, bare flesh. His heart thundered as her hands drifted from his shoulders to his neck, then back again to his chest.

When she pressed her cheek against his heart as Ella Fitzgerald crooned, Nasir felt a sweet, poignant pleasure like he hadn't known in forever. The night was perfection, one he'd needed for so long. But what had made it even sweeter was that this woman in his arms was a mysterious, interesting puzzle that he couldn't stop wanting to unravel.

Sudden laughter from behind them made them both look

at Dimitri and James, who were now singing at the tops of their lungs while clutching each other.

A soft sound fell from Yana's mouth and she looked down. To hide her expression from him, he was sure.

"What?" he asked, wanting to know every thought that crossed her mind, every emotion that made her sigh. His fascination was fast turning into an obsession.

"Nothing."

"Remember our truce?"

She seemed to come to some sort of resolution because her mouth narrowed into a straight line. Bracing for either his criticism or his mockery, he realized. "They are so… gloriously in love, aren't they? It's enough to make one…"

"Nauseous?" he asked, threading humor into his tone when he felt anything except laughing.

She slapped his arm playfully. "Why am I not surprised you find two lovers nauseous?" Her gaze dipped to his mouth, and then away. "I think it's magical. I've seen that kind of love between my grandparents. I think Thaata died so soon after her, because he couldn't bear to live in this world without her. They'd been through so much—my dad's alcoholism, bringing up three granddaughters… But their faith in each other sustained them. I see that in James and Dimitri. They're so lucky to have found each other and—"

"You think it's luck that they found each other?" he asked, genuinely curious.

"A stroke of luck, that initial meet-cute, where their eyes met across a raucous crowd, knowing James…" She laughed. "But I'm sure they work at it every day. I used to think it was magical when people just came together and stayed together. Now I know better."

"I don't think I'm interested in the formula, but I do want to know how you have learned that."

"I've seen my sisters. They're wonderful, accomplished,

bright women. Caio and Aristos clearly adore them. But it hasn't been a cakewalk for either of them. There have been tears and drama and grief and pain…"

"You talk about them as if they're more deserving of love than you."

She shrugged and he thought his once petrified heart might crack open at the expression on her face. He pulled her closer, anger and tenderness twin flames in his chest. "You know that's not how it works, right?"

"I thought you weren't interested in love."

"I'm not. But it doesn't mean I don't understand it." Fury against everyone who'd wronged her, who'd led her to believe such utter nonsense, including himself, colored his words. "There's no metric you use to measure someone's worthiness. You should get that into your pretty head."

"You're lucky I find you sexy when you're all growly and bossy."

The husky half-mutter, half-whisper dropped into the space between them, sounding like what it was. A defense mechanism, a distraction. Not that it didn't get him all hot under the collar, egging him on to act.

"Are they okay now?" he said, curious to know how she fit in between them. How she talked of them betrayed how she saw herself, and he wanted to know more. And the more he learned, the more he realized how one-dimensional he'd made her in his head. For his own purposes.

"The difficulties they faced only proved that their relationships were worth working on, I think. Worth fighting for."

"You want this…grand, glorious love, then?" A faint tremor laced his words even as he told himself her answer wouldn't make a difference to their relationship. It wasn't anything he had to offer her.

"Yes," she said, blinking. "Although it took me a while to figure it out."

"You're not out there looking for this love?"

"As you know, dearest stepbrother," she said, her breezy smile not hiding the ache, "I'm trying to fix me first. No one wants a mess in progress."

"There's nothing to fix, Yana," he said, tucking another stray braid behind her ear. A strange sort of helplessness speared him that she should think herself less than any other woman or man. "Messy and imperfect and tempestuous and volatile and stubborn is all its own kind of perfection. I'm the intellectual fool who didn't see that."

The bodice of her dress shimmered as her chest rose and fell, tension shimmering like a dark cloud around her. "*Enough*, Nasir." Her eyes flashed at him, her cheekbones jutting out. "I've let you seduce me with words and compliments all evening. But the farce ends now."

"James?" Nasir called out, knowing that the storm was about to break. He wanted no witness to their sparring or her temper. He wanted no one else to see her like this—unraveled and glorious.

His oldest friends waved goodbye and stumbled out of the room. The thud of the double doors was a loud gong in the bitter silence.

"I'm going to bed, too."

"No, you're not. Not until we have this out."

A flicker of fear flashed through her eyes before she notched her chin up in that characteristic belligerence that only aroused his baser instincts. "I'm not having anything out with you."

"I assumed a lot of things about you, Yana. Most of them in error, to my own detriment. But I'd never thought you a coward."

That stopped her, as he knew it would.

"How dare you? I've never in my life backed away from anything."

"Then why are you so intent on running from me?"

"Because I'm tired of dancing to your demands. Because I don't trust you."

And because I still don't trust myself with you.

Yana swallowed that last bit, though.

The whole evening, Nasir dancing with her, talking with her, laughing with her, arguing with her about important topics, asking her opinion—all of it had possessed a dreamy, surreal quality. His friends welcoming her as if she was a part of them, as if they were privy to the secret but well-known knowledge that there was a *them* that was made up of Nasir and her, had gone straight to her head and heart. As if she'd inhaled a hallucinogen that provided her with a real-life version of her deepest hopes and secret fantasies.

She should've never agreed to the evening. Never dressed up for it. Never enjoyed his gaze on her. Never agreed to the truce and flirted with him all evening. Because now she was standing in a quagmire that only pulled her in deeper and deeper.

She'd never been able to resist Nasir—even when he'd misunderstood her, castigated her, loathed her—for some right and some wrong reasons. Now he had an agenda to win her over, which seemed to require her surrender, and she was definitely not ready for that.

Not again, not when this temporary fascination ended and she'd once again stand alone with her shattered heart in her hands.

"What's there to not trust?" he asked in a low, grumbly voice, and she knew that it was his truly annoyed voice. The angrier he got, the lower his tone, as if he was turning himself into a statue, determined to keep it all inside.

"Why can't you leave this alone? Leave me alone?" she

said, and one of the braids done by Zara lashed against her cheek yet again. Having had enough of the charade, she gathered her hair and tied it into a messy knot on top of her head.

"I wish for things to change between us."

If he'd lobbed a grenade into her face, she'd have been less shocked. Breath didn't come to her lungs, much less words to her lips. Her entire body felt like it was seizing up on her, seizing on sensations and images she shouldn't be feeling or thinking.

She stepped back, away from him.

It didn't matter because he took a step forward, too, and Yana thought he truly looked like a beast then as he stalked her across the vast room, with the glittering sconces casting dark shadows on his saturnine features, iron-hard resolve etching itself around that luscious mouth.

"There's been too many years of misunderstandings and dislike that we've both nurtured with a lot of care. It doesn't wash off easily and I don't even want it to," she protested.

"No, you'd like to paint me as your villain for the rest of our lives."

"I don't have a different role for you. The die was cast long ago." Her words came out as shaky as she felt. "It's enough to be polite acquaintances, considering we have a child we adore in common."

He raised his palms. All evening he'd been reeling her in with his compliments and kind words but it was a false surrender on his part. Or a fake one. "What exactly is your complaint, Yana?"

"Why do you have those nude paintings of me?"

"I told you I felt responsible that I didn't warn you about Ilyavich. But when I saw them—when I saw how gloriously he'd captured all the different facets of you, that urge to protect you from all the other, greedy eyes only became stronger.

Even without knowing then that this persona you carefully cultivate is all a mask, I felt an overwhelming compulsion to protect your true self."

If he'd had the words scripted to cause maximum damage to her heart, he couldn't have done it better. His reasons were why she'd felt such relief that the paintings had never surfaced again. Still, she tried to fight the spell he was weaving over her. "Why go to such lengths just so that I had a good time tonight? Why are you being so nice to me?"

If she thought he'd laugh at her irrational questions, she had him wrong once again. His frown graduated to a scowl. "That's what's sending you into a tailspin? The fact that I'm finally treating you as you've always deserved to be treated?"

"That's not an answer, Nasir."

"Fine. I want you to feel comfortable in my home. With my friends. With me. I want you to think of my home as one of your main bases in Europe."

Her heart thrashed itself in its cage. "Why?"

"Because I want you to be happy." An exasperated breath rattled out of him.

Yana knew he could be infuriatingly stubborn—a dog with a bone, really, when he got stuck on something—it was one of the qualities they shared, but she'd never expected to be at the receiving end of that resolve.

It scared her that she'd caught his passing fancy, or his sense of fairness. And where it would leave her when he'd had enough. "When you visit us, at least," he added as an afterthought.

She was shaking her head, excitement and something headier washing away the dread and fear and insecurities and the little rationality she possessed. "Don't do this. Don't trap me. Don't—"

And then he was reaching for her, and his hands clutched

her arms and there was such sheer urgency, such reckless, naked desire in his eyes, that she was the one rendered a statue now. "You're the most confounding woman I've ever met. How is it trapping you if I want to do the right thing by you?"

"Because it's all pity and for God's sake, Nasir, I don't want your pity," she said, sidestepping the minefield she'd created herself.

How did she explain to him that her stupid heart had never been able to distinguish pity from liking when it came to him? That she'd take the little interest he showed her, turn it into hope and hang herself with it?

"It's not pity if I want the best for you or if I want to share your burden or if I want to tell you that I'll be here for you when you come out of rehab for your gambling addiction. I want to be the friend I should've been to you years ago."

Yana saw the trap then and it was of her own making.

Lies and half-truths and misunderstandings…she'd built them so tall and high that he didn't even see the real her. He saw the illusion she'd created, felt sorry for the mess she'd showed him, because he'd decided with that arrogant self-righteousness that he'd had a hand in it, too.

The illusion not only didn't serve her anymore but also threatened to make her worst nightmare come true. "I lied to you, Nasir. Those were not my debts. I'm not addicted to gambling and I never was."

He blinked and she braced herself for his disbelief and doubts. But he recovered fast with, "Then whose debts were they?"

"Isn't my word enough?"

"Of course it's enough. But now that we're dispensing with the smoke and mirrors, I want the whole truth. How were you in such a financial hole, then?"

"It was Diana." The words were wrenched out of her from some deep cavern, and yet immediately freed her of their dark weight. Until this moment when she'd made it real, she hadn't realized how much the secret had gouged her soul. How the pain it brought had stayed inside her, pulsing and throbbing, hollowing her out.

He sighed. "Diana took advantage of you, again."

"Yes. She…cleared out my bank accounts last year. I took measures then. But she still managed to get hold of my credit cards, and she…maxed them out. All our assets are jointly owned since I started modeling before I was legally an adult. I'd thought I could trust her, but she forged my signature and sold the apartment in New York and the house in California. Even the few rare pieces of jewelry I owned…she completely cleaned me out."

"While you were busy looking after Jacqueline," Nasir said, finally connecting the dots. Seeing a picture emerge in which he'd been so eager to find fault with her when there was none.

"I don't regret it one bit," Yana said, memories softening her mouth. "I know she wasn't perfect, but Jacqueline showed me more love and acceptance and concern than Diana ever did."

"Your loyalty is laudable, *habibi*. Is that why you covered up her affairs?" He wasn't angry but his bitterness was clear. "You had a just reason to hate me anyway."

"That's unfair. I didn't let our past color my actions, Nasir. Even when you treated me as if…" She tugged at the neckline of her dress in a nervous gesture he was beginning to recognize. "Jacqueline was desperate to save your relationship."

"And yet, she kept cheating on me."

"You've no idea what it is to be in love, do you? And to be found wanting?" she said, vibrating with emotion.

"Love was never supposed to be a part of our relationship. She knew that."

"Don't tell me the great observer of humanity's foibles and flaws thinks relationships can work based on a chart and a few conditions?" Even now, sympathy and affection filled her words. "Jacqueline made mistakes. It doesn't mean she ever stopped loving you. She begged me to help her, to..."

"You must have known it was a sinking ship, Yana. She abandoned Zara to you to care for."

"By that time, she was drinking a lot, her modeling dropped off and her business took a dive and...then came her diagnosis. She became bitter, different from the warm woman I'd come to adore."

"You still looked after her."

"Is it friendship if we only show up for the good times?"

Hesitation flickered in her eyes before she took a deep breath. Steely resolve hiding a fragile heart—he was beginning to understand her now. And himself clearly, too, in her words. He had had all these rules and plans and conditions for his marriage and not a single one had served them well. Not with Jacqueline and definitely not with his own daughter. There was no way to shut himself out of the world without making his daughter think he didn't love her, either. Without the risk of losing her.

And here was this woman he'd thought he'd pushed to the margins, gloriously in the center of it all, lashing him with truth after truth. Instead of gentling his pain, all the rules he'd lived his life by had only alienated him from Zara and his father.

"And since we're on the topic," she said, straightening her shoulders, "I had no idea she was considering filing for solo custody of Zara. You spent little enough time with Zara back then. But she talked so much about you whenever she returned from the trips you took her on, and she sounded so happy that I knew whatever your complaints about Jacqueline, you were trying your best to be a good father."

Her words were a vindication to Nasir's ears.

Or maybe even a benediction and approval that he hadn't even known he needed. From the moment he had learned that Jacqueline had been planning to take solo custody of his daughter, using his alleged indifference to his own child, he had wondered if there was any truth to it.

He'd never planned to be a father, something Jacqueline had been fully on board with when they'd met. And he'd done his best to keep their marriage together even as they'd grown apart by the time she'd conceived.

So many sleepless nights, and he'd even wondered if he'd done such a good job of turning himself into stone that he felt less than he should for his own child. He'd wondered if Zara would be better off with her mother.

"I think Jacqueline never told me what she was planning because she must have known that I'd never agree to it," Yana added.

Nasir forced himself to meet her eyes. "I should have known that, too. My entire world felt upside down when I realized how I'd made my own child doubt my love for her. I was so angry and scared that I'd lose Zara that I lashed out at you. Not that it's an excuse."

He ran a hand through his hair, marveling at how wise she was even as she thought herself messy. But that was the magic of Yana, he was realizing.

She lived her life fully, loved so thoroughly that it was like watching a thunderstorm. Both spectacular and dangerous at the same time. And Nasir remembered when he'd lived life like that once, when he'd loved freely, lived dangerously close to the edge. And suddenly, he wanted to be there again.

There were two things he had to do. The first came easily enough.

"I'm sorry, Yana. On so many levels. For all the sins I heaped at your feet, when they were all mine. For being a beast to you."

But the second—to let her go when he knew what she wanted out of life was something he could never offer her—felt impossible to even contemplate. For the first time since Fatima died, he felt an overwhelming need to lose himself to his selfish desires. To drown himself in pleasure. To live dangerously just once more, even if that meant Yana would burn him through.

CHAPTER TEN

YANA DIPPED HER HEAD, unwilling to let him see her confusion and the little flicker of fear. Nor did she feel any vindication or relief from his apology. It was disconcerting to discover that his compliments had more than their fair share of an effect on her, though. Disconcerting to discover that all of her defenses were falling away, like the castle Zara had made out of rainbow-colored sand.

No, he was attacking her defenses, laying siege and shredding the lies and half-truths she'd surrounded herself with. To what end, though? Did he simply want to clear the air between them now that she was going to be a permanent part of Zara's life? Or was there more?

"What other secrets and half-truths are you using as ammunition against me, then?"

"Demands and more demands," she said, deploying her silken protest even as she was quivering inside. "And here I thought you were not the usual predictably powerful man who wants what he wants when he wants it."

"You've no idea what I want, Yana."

His angry tone was like a shot of adrenaline. When he treated her as his equal, when he took her on as she was, there was no bigger high. She tilted her chin, letting him see her fighting spirit. "You have not earned the right to my secrets, Nasir. Nor to my dreams or fantasies."

"And yet, if I cover this last foot between us and touch you, I'd bet I'd find you far too willing and ready to voice at least one fantasy, *habibi*."

She watched him, every word acting like a leaping pulse within her body. Every step of his creating an ache between her thighs. "And why would you want to do that?"

"Because I have this insane urge to corner you and catch you and strip you bare until I know all of you. You're a maddening puzzle I want to unlock."

"This is about your ego, then? Because I managed to trick you—"

"You and I both know this isn't to do with my ego or pity or friendship or Zara or the past. It's about you and me." Another step and she could see the scar that bisected his upper lip and raked its finger upward toward his cheek. And she saw the naked desire in his eyes and the steely resolve of his mouth, and every cell within her reverberated.

"So will you dare let me test my theory?"

He was close now, so close that she could breathe in the heady scent of his aftershave—another weapon in an arsenal full of them. Her breath was a shallow whistle in her ears.

She should've burned, or melted, or ignited with him this close to her after all these years, and yet, the moment seemed to spring out of her deepest, wildest dreams, and suddenly, she didn't know how to be, how to act, in this reality. Did she run or did she stay and see this through? Did she dare steal this moment and live it with all she had, or did she bind herself and back away from a lifetime's temptation?

Something hard dug into the small of her back, and she pressed herself into it even more, hoping the sharp pain would be an anchor tying her to the ground when all she felt like was flying away. And then he was within touching distance, and she stared helplessly like the naive, inexperienced virgin that she was.

All the roles she'd played in her life at being a brazen seductress who lured men to make bad decisions and led them to their doom hadn't taught her any tricks or tools to get through this. She hadn't let any man get this close to her at all, because she hadn't wanted any man like she wanted Nasir.

If he'd grabbed her and kissed her to prove his point—as so many men had done before, thinking her volatile temper and confident words meant that she would welcome their crude attempts at seduction, if he'd touched her and smiled that infuriating, winning smirk of his as if this was nothing but a game they'd been playing for years, if he'd taunted her with one more word—Yana would have been able to resist him. Could have told herself that after all these years, after all the pining and longing that had become an intrinsic part of her, she was better than he was; she was better than this moment.

His palms on the dark wood on either side of her head, he leaned closer and pinned her like a splayed butterfly with his gaze. And said the one thing that was her Achilles' heel, that shattered all of her defenses.

"I see you, Yana, the real you." His breath feathered the side of her cheek in a warm caress, his amber eyes gleaming with a feral glitter. "Finally, I see all of you. And the things I want to do to you…" A self-deprecating sigh fell from his lips. "We've come full circle, no?"

So long, for so many years, with so many people in her life, she'd longed to be seen, to be accepted, even as she'd hidden the greedy, needy parts of her away. All her struggles, all her pain, all her victories, all her defeats—had they led her to this moment with this man? Was life worth living, worth beginning at all, if she backed off now?

She braced herself as if one could brace oneself for drowning in a tsunami. Leaning closer, she pressed her mouth to the corner of his. "Test your theory, then." Then she took that lush lower lip of his between her teeth and bit down and said, "This, however, isn't surrender."

Tingles of shock and tendrils of sensation swooped when he returned her favor with a matching nip of his white teeth over her own lower lip. "Ah, *habibi*, I've finally learned my lesson. I'll never underestimate you again."

He smiled then and it was a roguish, hungry smile and it built into something more possessive and molten as his hands started moving over her willing flesh and she swallowed all of that, too, along with the heat and hunger of his lips, because he was kissing her and kissing her and kissing her. As if he, too, had been waiting for this moment for a lifetime.

She was spinning stories yet again but even her lies tasted sweeter when he kissed her like that. He tasted of cigars and chocolate and like the darkest decadence she could ever imagine. They went at each other like horny teenagers—nipping and licking and sucking and fighting for dominance, and it was exactly like she thought it would be. But also somehow better.

There was magic in the very air between them and she let it seep into every pore. His jacket was discarded, necklines were tugged aside for better access, for more. His mouth seemed to stamp his possession all over—her lips, her temple, her pulse, her neck, the spot below her ear, and still, he wasn't done kissing her.

She groaned as he sucked at her pulse, arrows of sensation skittering straight down to her pelvis.

"Who knew such a prickly thing could taste so sweet?" he groaned.

She grabbed the lapels of his collar and pulled in opposite directions until buttons were flying and she could palm the taut planes of his chest and then slide down to explore the ridges of his muscled abdomen. He was warm and hard, with a silky coating of hair that she loved running her fingers through already. She kept petting and stroking every inch of flesh she discovered as he buried his mouth at the crook of her neck and shoulder.

Within seconds he already seemed to know where to hit her the hardest. When he dragged his teeth against the pulse fluttering already at her neck, she groaned and wrapped her leg around his hip.

They stopped then, tuned in to each other on a level that terrified her. He was so deliciously hard against her, and she instinctively rocked herself into him, the need for completion a much more primal drive than fear or sensibility.

Somehow, he'd shuffled them across the marble floor, the cold tiles on her now bare feet a welcome relief against the heat pouring through her. She wasn't laughing anymore as her back hit the plush padding of the chaise longue that was tucked against the far wall.

Nasir was on his knees on either side of her hips, gazing down at her.

It was a new angle to find herself in, a new angle from which to look at him. Except for the sizzling sparks from the fireplace and the fast, erratic whistling of their own breaths, everything was dark and still and silent.

Reaching her hand up, she clasped his cheek, rubbing the pad of her thumb over that scar. Allowing herself one, *only one*, moment of tenderness. She wasn't sure if she would get another chance like this. And she wasn't sure if she would survive another one anyway.

His nostrils flared when she dragged her thumb to the center of his lower lip and pressed. His teeth dug into the pad before he closed his lips over it and sucked, and she felt the strong pull of his lips somewhere else.

She arched her body, chasing the pleasure, and he granted it. Heavy and warm, the heel of his palm rested against the sweet center of her entire being. She writhed under that warm weight, begging him with her hips to make it more. His fingers snuck under the fabric of her dress, caressing the silky skin of her thighs, and then they were pushing away her thong and tracing the outer lips of her sex.

Sensations and need forked through her, winding her tighter and tighter. Finally, finally, his clever fingers found her most sensitive place, and slowly, softly, rubbed the bundle of nerves up and down.

Her language became gasps and groans and filthy expletives as she chased the tantalizing caress of his all-knowing fingers. "What else do you need, sweetheart? Ask me. Tell me."

His gaze pinned her in place, a dark need glittering there, when her body itself seemed to be spinning away from her. She rubbed a hand over her breasts, the tight corset covering them adding to her torment and pleasure in turns. "Touch me here, please."

Bending low, he plucked at the beaded corset and when it didn't budge, he cut it open with that damned knife he kept on himself all the time. Her entire torso arched up like a bridge rising out of stormy waters as he rubbed one taut nipple between his fingers. "Every inch of you is perfection," he said, almost to himself.

Then his mouth was at her breast and he was doing some swirly thing with his tongue. His teeth were there, too, and his thumb kept drawing those mindless circles around her nub, and suddenly, she was right there at the edge of the world.

And when she fell, splintering into so many different parts, he held her and kissed her and soothed her and he put her back together again. Yana thought she might already be addicted to those strong, knowing hands, those wicked, wanton fingers and those sweet, taunting lips. And she wondered if she might ever do this with another man, even though she already knew the answer.

But right then, tremors of aftershock still quaking through her in soft ripples, with his scent lodged deep in every pore, with his arms enveloping her in a perfect cradle as if she was precious and fragile, she didn't care. She couldn't care about the future or that she didn't have one with him.

"Come, *habibi*. Let me walk you to your bedroom."

Those long lashes fluttered as she looked around herself like a baby fawn. As if she didn't know where she was. And still, in that state of near comatose bliss, her body leaned into him, gifting him with a trust Nasir didn't deserve but was selfish enough to revel in anyway. Just watching her climax with that reckless abandon was more sensuous than any carnal act.

After several long beats, she rubbed the back of her hand over her mouth and looked up at him. For a split second, he saw a strange kind of longing for him that he'd once seen in another woman. A woman he'd failed to protect despite her absolute trust in him.

Drowning in the madness that Yana effortlessly weaved over him, it was quite possible he was imagining things he had no right to imagine, much less should, if he had any sense. He'd never meant for his dare to get this far, either.

His body was strumming with unsatisfied desire, Yana was looking at him as if he was the answer to every dark desire she'd ever had, and he simply gave in to the sheer sensuous luxury of the moment.

"You're good," she said with a smile that stretched her lips.

He was struck by a tenderness he hadn't felt in so long,

that he'd thought parts of himself had petrified out in that war zone years ago.

"I'm glad you think so," he said, tugging the sides of her sliced open dress together, but she slapped his hands away.

"The last thing I want to do right now," she said with a sudden sharp clarity to her words, "is walk through the castle like this, let everyone see you've dismissed me yet again and advertise my walk of shame."

Irritation he should have mastered colored his tone as he brusquely said, "We're two consenting adults. There is no shame here, Yana."

Her feathery brows came together in a bow. "I thought the same thing a long time ago."

"Yana—"

"If there's no shame in this, then why are you so intent on walking me back to my room?"

She was such a mix of calculation and vulnerability, a complex puzzle he'd never stop delighting in. But, he had to remind himself, she wasn't his to delight in. Come tomorrow morning, in the clarity of daylight, she might even regret this moment of madness and freeze him out.

Wasn't that the best idea, though, seeing as they could have nothing more than this one night? There was no future for them; he should make that clear to her, as he had no intention of committing to a third woman and having it go wrong again as it inevitably would. And yet, he had no taste for fracturing the satiated smile on her lips just yet. Or was he thinking with his ego again, imagining she wanted some kind of future with him? What if all Yana wanted was to get this madness out of their systems? Would one night be enough for her? With all their misunderstandings—mostly on his part—cleared up now, and with her place in Zara's life permanent, couldn't they just be two consenting adults with sizzling chemistry? Or was that him thinking with his painfully hard erection again?

"You have to know—"

She leaned up and claimed his mouth with a possessive hunger that decimated the little honor he had left that he was trying to keep. On and on, the kiss went, with her nipping at him, licking him, then running away and having him give chase.

"Why do we have to leave when we aren't finished yet?" Leaning back against the chaise, she giggled. Contrary to that light laughter, her gaze swept over him leisurely, full of desire and need and unabashed lust. She scraped a long nail over his Adam's apple, and down his chest, running down each scar on his chest as if it were a map to some long-lost treasure.

"Unless it's because you're an old man and can only 'do it—'" she used quotes as if anybody could misunderstand her right then "—missionary style on the bed?"

He arrested her fingers when they fluttered near the zip of his trousers. "You're mad," he said, bringing her hand to his mouth and placing a kiss at the center of her palm.

She shrugged it off. That thread of irritation flickered again as it dawned on him why she did that. She didn't want tenderness from him. Only sexual touch was welcomed—an arrangement that should've suited him just fine given where his thoughts had been moments ago. And yet, that thorn was under his skin again. Although he was getting used to that, too, that painful, stringent awareness, like new skin on an old wound. Like he'd never be sure of his own desires and thoughts when it came to her.

"I feel drunk. That's the first time I—"

He stilled.

She peered at him from under her lashes, something calculating flashing across that stunning gaze.

He cupped her cheek, a sudden urgency driving him. "What?"

She leaned into his touch as if his fingers weren't circling her neck with a possessiveness he could not control. "The first time I felt that kind of pleasure with a partner. Usually, I need my—" that cute little frown appeared between her brows again "—tools."

Awkwardness dawned at that strange word, and she shrugged. Something wasn't adding up. Under his continued scrutiny, color stole into her cheeks, dusting them a pretty pink.

"I meant my battery-operated devices." She rolled her eyes, as if he was being thick on purpose.

And then in a move that was clearly supposed to distract him, which it did successfully, she dragged a finger over the outside of his trousers, tracing the shape of his shaft. His erection leaped under her touch. When he went to arrest her fingers, she kissed his chin.

Eyes wide and soulful and full of longing studied him. "Now who's intent on shutting this down? Or are we still only dancing to your demands?" She pouted, to hide the very real emotion in her words. "Have you solved the puzzle that you labeled me? Is your fascination with me over now because I've thrown myself at you the moment you beckoned?"

"Shut up, *habibi*."

He closed his eyes and that was a bigger mistake because with him deprived of that sense, now all of his being was focused on her palming his erection. He grunted his assent, giving himself over to her curious fingers.

She wasn't urgent or greedy or fast now, but devastatingly thorough. The smack of her lips had him watching her again.

Pushing her hair away from her face in a gesture that was sensuality and innocence combined, she gave her full attention to the task of undoing him. The tip of her pink tongue stuck out between her teeth as she unzipped his trousers and then her fingers were sneaking under his boxers to fist his shaft with a soft, hungry growl that pinged along his length.

Breath hissed out of him in a guttural whisper, his hips automatically pumping into her hand like a schoolboy being touched for the first time. Her own mouth fell open on a soft gasp, calling his attention back to her.

Eyes drunk with passion, tongue licking her lips, she watched him with an artless abandon that was as arousing as her slow, tentative strokes.

"You haven't done this much, have you?" he said, trying his damnedest to put brakes on a situation that had long been out of his control. From the moment he had seen her again at the nightclub, in fact. Wasn't that why he'd fought begging her for help?

Something almost like anger flashed in those gorgeous brown eyes. "Stop trying to pin me down, looking for reasons to stop," she whispered in a voice that was so husky that he felt a surge of all his possessive instincts.

Hair a mess around her face, the silky corset falling apart again to reveal small, high breasts with plump tips, and acres of smooth, golden-brown flesh…she looked like his darkest fantasy come true. He wanted no other man to hear her like this, or see her like this—messy and unraveled, and so tempting that his mouth was dry. He wanted no other man to know her like this.

A filthy curse exploded out of him when she rubbed her thumb over his sensitive tip, gathered up a droplet of liquid and brought it to her mouth. She rubbed it over her lower lip, all the while holding his gaze in a challenge that undid him.

The last of his honor evaporated. Or maybe he'd had enough of his own lies and half-truths. She was right. He'd started this, and as always, she'd risen to the challenge of his dare, proving that she was magnificent in a way he'd never previously understood.

Because now he could see the invisible scars life had left on her and how she still walked through it full of heart. A heart that was unwillingly beginning to fascinate him as much as her body did.

Holding his gaze, she licked that lower lip, even as she cupped her own breast with her free hand. In between her fingers, the dark pink nipple peaked, beckoning for his mouth.

Hands on her hips, he lifted her and reversed their positions until he was sitting back against the chaise and she was straddling him, his erection pressed up against her slick, hot sex.

Instantly, her spine moved in a sensuous ripple, mocking all the constraints he'd use to bind her. Head thrown back, the cut-open remnants of her dress baring her to her navel, she was the wildest thing Nasir had ever seen.

Wrapping the fingers of one hand around the back of her neck, he stroked his tongue into her mouth, even as he filled his other hand with her small yet perfectly lush breasts. She moved again until the width of his shaft notched against her core. Sensation skewered his spine and his body threatened to give out. He laved at her swollen lower lip, ran his palms all over her smooth back, the tight dip of her waist, reveling in the soft, raspy growls that seemed to escape her mouth every time he let her move a little. He touched her everywhere and it only inflamed his desire further. The more he had of her, the more he wanted.

"I have no condoms. But I swear to you I'm clean," he whispered against her throat.

"I'm on the pill," she said, whimpering as he bit down on

the madly fluttering pulse. "Please, Nasir. No more teasing. I need you inside me. Now."

The sheer naked need in those words was the last thing to shatter his control. Taking his shaft in his hand, holding her still with one hand on her hip, he thrust into her inviting warmth in one long stroke.

His grunt sounded euphoric to his own ears. The tight clasp of her sex made lights explode behind his eyes in a kaleidoscope of sensations.

Sweat beading over his forehead, heart pounding loudly in his ears, he reveled in the tight sheath of her body. Without even moving, he was already close. He held back, determined to wring another climax out of her. He'd leave her so boneless with pleasure that she never thought of doing this with another man.

He was so far gone, so deep inside his own head, his senses so deeply entrenched in pleasure, that it took him several grasping breaths to realize that Yana had gone awfully still.

He opened his eyes to find her looking a little shocked, one lone tear streaking down her angular cheek. He closed his eyes and cursed himself for eternity. Even then, comprehension escaped him. In his hurry to relieve her pain, he took hold of her hips and jostled her slightly, and then heard her soft gasp.

Finally, the truth dawned on him, and with it came indescribable anger.

Of course, even in this, she would make a villain out of him. He'd hurt her, unknowingly, and he needn't have. "You and your childish games," he bit out, a gravelly bitterness coating his words. "How clever you must think you are, *habibi*. Is this some kind of revenge, then? Are you winning yet, Yana?"

When she reared back to look into his face, there was pain and want and a host of things he couldn't read. She nuzzled her face into his neck, dampness seeping from her skin to his.

And then she licked at the hollow of his throat and clutched him harder with her arms and below with her sex and that, too, was a pleasurable torment.

All of her was a weapon and she wielded it with such innocence.

But buried deep inside her as he was, even his anger was only an irritating hum and a tight knot in his chest that he could easily ignore beneath the unparalleled sensation streaking through him as she adjusted herself. She moved as if she meant him to burrow deep inside her and never come out.

When he clutched her hips again, this time to gently pull her off him, she seemed to come back to herself. A half-growl, half-groan fell from her lips, and she was truly the wildest thing he had ever seen then.

"No, you're not going to leave me like this. Not again. Not anymore." One hand sinking into his hair, she tugged imperiously, as if she meant to own him. "Finish this." Without waiting for his response, she took his hands and brought them to her breasts.

Questions tore through his brain, even as fresh pleasure zigzagged through him. She was warm and soft, and with her hands on his shoulders, she undulated her spine in such an instinctive ripple that he was suddenly nearly all the way out of her slick clasp. Again and again, she wriggled her hips in a sinuous dance; figuring out her own rhythm and letting her use his body to seek out her pleasure was both a delight and a torment to him, and the slip-slide of their bodies created a symphony wholly their own.

She was trembling now, and Nasir stroked her, petted her, whispering nonsensical words into her skin, even as she gained momentum and confidence. Her rhythm was crude, a little erratic rather than smooth, and yet it was still the most erotic thing he'd ever known.

"At what point is this going to be less painful and more

about pleasure?" she asked with a smile, and that husky voice pinged on his nerve endings. He laughed then, and he kissed her as if she was the most fragile, precious thing that had ever come to his hand. It wasn't that hard because she was the most fragile, the most achingly lovely, thing he had ever held.

Slowly, softly, he thrummed his fingers all over her body, noting when she leaned in to the touch, and when another soft gasp escaped her mouth, feeling when she ground down. A more natural rhythm built as he started thrusting up when she brought herself down. The slap of her thighs against his, the tight tug of her fingers in his hair, the erotic slide of her breasts against his chest made his spine burn with his approaching climax.

Holding her back from him, he lifted her breast to his mouth and sucked until he could tell her own need for climax chased her. Fingers, lips, words, caresses, tongue, teeth... He used everything in his arsenal with a ruthlessness he'd long ago given up to drive her to the edge again, even as he held back his own climax by the skin of his teeth.

And then she was shattering yet again, calling out his name, as if he was the benediction, and not her, and her sex was milking him.

Nasir pushed her down onto the chaise still shuddering, and instantly, she wrapped her legs around his hips, creating the perfect cradle for him to sink into. They could have done this a hundred times before and it couldn't have been as perfect. So right. So good.

He began with slow, deep thrusts, willing himself to enjoy this moment, even as selfish desire urged him to go faster, harder, to show her how needy he could get, to somehow mark her as she was doing him with such little effort. Hair billowing around her head, pupils blown up, her lush mouth trembling with explosive breaths, and his name on her lips... she took him straight over the cliff with her.

He came inside her, and it was the most explosive release he'd ever had. All he wanted was to do this over and over again. He wanted to make her fall apart again and again. He wanted to lose himself in her. He wanted to *keep* her. And the arrogant thought released a host of other thoughts.

What a grave blunder he had committed just because his ego refused to be perceived as the man who'd done her wrong. What else could this be except a predatory urge to conquer her anger and her distrust and her wildness and *her*, in essence? Where else would this lead but to her pain and more scars at his hand when their relationship inevitably ended? What could he do to avoid that? What choices were left to him?

He'd closed himself off to feeling the very thing she wanted out of life, because he had nothing to offer her. Especially now he knew that beneath the numerous masks she wore, she was as vulnerable as a baby bird.

Contrary to the confusion wrecking his mind, though, he gathered her soft, trembling body to him, buried his nose in her neck and whispered sweet nothings into her skin long after she fell asleep like the fragile, trusting, wonderful woman she'd always been.

CHAPTER ELEVEN

IN THE END, Nasir ended up carrying her to her bedroom, and Yana was sure a battalion of people had noticed her disheveled and thoroughly seduced state. Hiding her face in his neck, she thought she might have even heard Amina's loud, disgruntled huff at seeing her son parade about the castle with his virgin lover in his arms, like a dark sacrifice he was bringing back to his lair.

And that made her giggle uncontrollably. So much so that it skated the edge of hysteria. Nasir tapped her lightly on the cheek as he placed her on his bed.

"Care to share what's so funny?" he asked, locking her between his forearms, his torso leaning over her like a tantalizing shadow.

Yana writhed on the bed, loving the cool comfort of the sheets against her bare, overheated skin. The slick wetness between her legs coating her inner thighs and lower made itself known.

"I was trying to imagine how we must have looked to your mother."

His mouth twitched. "That's the last thing I need in my head right now." When she continued to smile, he ran his thumb over her lower lip. "Tell me."

"Like you were a beast bringing your virgin sacrifice to your lair."

He bopped the tip of her nose even though his jaw tightened. Still sore about that secret of hers, then.

"You have quite the imagination, *habibi*."

"You don't know the half of it," she said, desperate to tease him out of the dark mood.

He straightened and watched her. A sliver of moonlight illuminated his own features for her. *Just for her.* All sharp slashes and hard contours and even with that scar ruining his lovely mouth…he'd always struck her as the epitome of sex appeal.

But she tended to forget that he'd achieved it by living a whole other life before she'd even grown to adulthood. He was always going to be out of her reach, if she thought like that. If she sought to put him on that pedestal.

But he wasn't, by his own claim. He wasn't a statue, either, however much he claimed that. And with the open sides of his shirt flapping about, his hair ruffled and made unkempt by her fingers, his chest bearing the slight scratches from her nails, he was *so utterly hers* then that her breath stuck in her throat. Possibilities fluttered through her heart, bolstered by the soreness of her muscles and the tender ache between her legs.

"No, I don't know the half of it. Or you."

And with that pointed remark, he was walking away. When every inch of her wanted to run after him like a half-naked, lovesick wraith, ready to prostrate herself to keep her with him for the rest of the night, Yana rolled away to face the other side of the bed instead, a strange kind of lethargy stealing over her.

His anger was a familiar companion she'd lived with before. Could live with again. But she did an emotional check on herself like Mira had taught her and Nush to do.

All through that long walk across his vast castle—no, even

before that, when he'd roared his climax in her ears and she'd hidden away that sound in some deep part of her psyche, to be taken out in private and examined again and again—she'd been trying to muster up some kind of regret.

Or anger, or shame or guilt or any number of darker emotions that she was used to drinking up like a toxic cocktail when she made bad decisions. Because he was her darkest weakness and deepest want, and when he'd beckoned a finger, she'd gone running, hadn't she? She was a pushover if ever she knew one.

But the bitterness of regrets, the acidic taste of failure, refused to come this time. Not with the sweet, pulsing ache between her thighs or the swollen sensitivity of her lips or the soreness of her muscles to distract her... Instead, she felt alive and thoroughly debauched and gloriously loved. Maybe she should listen to her body more often and refuse to poison it with negativity, she thought.

Burying her face in the pillow, she gave in to the languid smile that fought its way through. If she put the *shoulds and shouldn'ts* aside, it felt like fate or the universe or some inevitable course she'd set herself on through the years that it should be Nasir who ultimately destroyed her fear and distrust in herself. As if all the previous wrongs had led to this one right.

But that way also lay the trap of romanticizing not just the sex they'd had but also the entire episode, the entire evening. Attaching meaning and expectations to it when there were none. The whole evening had built to this moment—no, years of attraction and dislike and even shared grief had all led to tonight. A once-in-a-lifetime thing, a self-indulgent, luxurious experience, a reward for all the bad things about her old life she was shedding, enabling her to move on into her new life. Having sex with Nasir was not a mistake, but it wasn't a new road to explore, either. There, that explanation suited her. She hoped her silly heart got on the same train.

"Turn around, Yana."

She rolled onto her back to find Nasir kneeling on the bed. Had she been so deep inside her head that she hadn't even noticed that he hadn't actually left, he'd just gone into the bathroom?

Hands on her knees, he gently opened her. A cool, wet washcloth on her sex made her hiss out a deep sigh. It felt damned good and that, perversely, made her resentful. "Have you done this a lot, then?"

"What?"

"Ministered to virgins after debauching them?"

His laugh was a booming sound—gravelly, with no hint of actual humor. "Yes. The sacrifice will come next."

Her mouth twitched. She let out a long, shuddering exhale, so that he knew that she was merely tolerating him. The wet splash of the cloth as he chucked it back into the bathroom made her eyes pop open.

"Nasir, I can look after myself."

"Of course you can, *habibi*. I'm under no illusion about what you are capable of anymore. But indulge me, just this once."

With that terse dictate, he began to pull at the sad remains of the dress from around her tired limbs. With an efficiency that reminded her that he'd once been a journalist covering the most dangerous places in the world, he briskly gathered her hair, pulled her up and dressed her in a T-shirt of his.

"Underwear?"

"Nope," Yana answered without missing a beat.

"Better and better," he whispered at her temple and then retreated again.

Only then did she realize she hadn't felt an ounce of hesitation at giving him a straight answer. As if they were an old married couple, used to the small intimacies that made up the best parts of a relationship. She had this strange sense that this should've been awkward and sticky and messy, and yet, it had that ring of inevitability about it again.

"I think you should leave now," she said, trying to cut the strings of the parachute of her dreams before it flew away into some magical fairyland where the messy, volatile princess conquered her beast with the all-consuming power of her love.

"I think differently." He returned, dressed in loose pajama bottoms and nothing else. All of his tautly muscled chest and back with its myriad scars beckoned her.

Pure, irresistible temptation.

"Scoot over."

"I don't think we need a postmortem, Nasir. It happened. It was fantastic. Now we move on."

When she didn't give in to his ruthless demand, he gave her a playful shove to the middle of the bed, and by the time she'd recovered from her quick roll, he was sitting up next to her, with his fingers pushing her hair away from her face.

Under the guise of straightening herself under the rumpled sheet, Yana gave herself a moment to fight the inexorable urge to stay like that, with his fingers raking through her hair with a tenderness she'd craved for so long. She also wanted to push off the duvet, shrug off the T-shirt he'd put on her and arch up into his touch. To dig her fingers into his hair and bring that sinful mouth down to her breasts again. At the mere thought, her nipples tightened, sending tingles straight down somewhere else. It was a weird state of arousal and languidness, and it took all the willpower she had to not just give in to the moment. To not just give in to him.

Shrugging his hand away, she sat up.

"Who said anything about a postmortem?" His voice was silky-smooth but with a hard undertone to it. "Maybe I'm looking for a repeat. Maybe I'm the beast who's finally got his filthy hands on the virgin princess and would be cursed for the rest of his life if I let her go."

She sent him a shocked look—his narrative was perceptively close to the one in her own head.

What was real and what was made-up fantasy between them? What was attraction and interest on his part and what was just a bunch of baggage he wanted to be rid of, in order to right his mistakes? And worst of all, why was this intimacy so easy between them? Why did the dark quiet feel like it was weaving a spell around them?

"Why all the lies, Yana? Why make yourself out to be someone you're not?"

"So I'm suddenly more valuable now because I still had my V card?" She combed her fingers through her hair, quickly braiding it to the side. "I thought you a better man than that."

"I have committed enough sins without adding that one to the list, *habibi*. It doesn't matter to me how many men you'd slept with. It does matter to me that you've created a certain image for yourself and today you've decided to reveal the real you."

"Ahh, gotcha. You're worried that I might think you're special because you're my first lover?"

He clasped her chin between his fingers, an angry frown turning his face dark. "My point is that you decided to keep lying to me, even to the last second. Maybe you thought this would all be a big laugh, proving me wrong about you. Maybe it's just a grand game to you. But I won't make the mistake of assuming that tonight meant nothing to you."

And you? Did tonight mean more than nothing to you?

"No, you'll just assume that I want more from you than this. Isn't that why you are here now—to set the record straight? To make sure I don't see some big, bright future together?"

"Yana—"

"And people say women are the illogical ones. I won't cling to you, Nasir. How can I make that clear to you?"

"Why is even having a conversation with you a fight?" He sighed, the back of his head hitting the headboard. "This talk was coming, even if we hadn't had sex tonight. I'm not a man who bears the weight of his guilt easily, even when it's justly deserved." His tone hinted at volumes of grief and loss that shut her up instantly. "I'm here to appease my own conscience, to cater to my own ego, to make sure I don't fall off the pedestal I tell myself and the world I stand on. Pick whichever of those you feel best applies."

She laughed then and he glanced at her—her eyes, her mouth, her neck—and desire danced there, more than just a burning ember.

A whole conflagration waited there. Just that one look and everything she'd buried deep inside her heart awakened. In that moment she adored him more than she ever had, more than she'd ever thought possible again.

Here was the man who'd always been able to laugh at his own weaknesses and faults and yet had still tried to do better.

"Amina is going to hate me all over again," she said, searching for a safer topic.

"That tactic won't work."

"We have decided that it's your fragile masculine ego that begs to be tended to. What else is there to talk about?"

"What else about you has been a lie?"

Yana looked at her tightly clasped fingers and loosened the grip.

He had no idea what he was offering her. How burdened and cut off and lost she'd felt in the past few months. How she hadn't realized that her stubbornness to do it right finally, to take charge of her life in a meaningful way, would nearly be her undoing.

She'd be even more beholden to him, but outside of the sex, she was beginning to believe that he cared a little about her. Even if only to right past wrongs.

"You know more about me than Diana knows, more than my grandfather did. More than even my sisters." It didn't even surprise her anymore that he was the one who'd ended up being the witness to all of her failures and flaws but also the one who'd see her strengths, who'd give her the validation that she shouldn't still need but longed for anyway.

"Yana—"

"If you're going to spend the rest of the night here, I propose we do something fun, at least."

When he grinned like the careless, charming rogue she'd known once, she shook her head. "Not that, you rogue."

"Ahh… What do you have in mind?"

"Since I've given you my virginity and my deepest secrets—" although there was something else she'd fight with her last breath from giving him this time "—I think a favor's fair."

Something about the naughty twinkle in her eyes, the sheer enthusiasm in her words, made Nasir want to kiss her all over again. Instead, he leaned back and gave a beleaguered sigh. "You've already robbed me blind, *habibi*. What else would you have of me? More importantly, I don't believe you've given me all your secrets." He grabbed a thick lock of hair and tugged until she arched up toward him like a bow and his mouth hovered over hers in a tempting tease. "I think you like keeping me hanging."

With a flourish that made him laugh, she pushed him away, then sat up cross-legged, shoulders straight, readying for battle. His T-shirt fell off one shoulder, baring silky-smooth skin and drowning her in it. Hair in the messy bun again, face scrubbed of makeup, she looked utterly different from the sophisticated, elegant Yana she'd been earlier at dinner.

Even more beautiful in his eyes, because this was the real version no one knew.

Maybe no man should ever see her again like that, his possessiveness crowed, joining in with the irrational crowd of voices rioting in his head.

No maybe about it, said the part of his brain glutted on endorphins.

She should be mine. Only mine, the deepest corner of his heart announced, aided by his arrogance.

And how he could bring it about danced vaguely at the back of his mind. A solution would tie a bow around two of his dilemmas.

"You can ask me whatever you want," she said, her nose held high as if she was granting him a favor, unaware of the scheming his libido and his brain were doing together, "and I'll do my best to give you a truthful answer."

"Wow, and you think you're not a hard-nosed business-woman? I don't want the most truthful answer, Yana. I just want the truth."

She frowned. "I have a pretty big thing to ask of you, so fine."

"Where do you disappear to in the evenings after Zara goes to bed? The whole damned staff knows but won't tell me. Loyalty to Ms. Reddy and all that. I should fire Ahmed because I think he's the one heading up that rebellious campaign."

The easy humor of two minutes ago evaporated and a heart-twisting vulnerability shone in her eyes. "Don't fire anyone on my behalf."

"Then tell me what you're doing."

Yana knew he was only joking—his staff was his family, so she should keep this particular truth close to her heart. But that reckless, defiant part of her wanted to tell him and test him and...

"You're scaring me, *habibi*. And that has happened only twice in my entire life. What secret is so dark and deep that you look like I'm asking you for a piece of your soul?"

With one perceptive sentence, he'd disarmed her all over again. "It costs a piece of my soul to tell you."

"Let's make you feel better, then. What do you want from me in return?" he asked, knowing that in that moment, he'd give her anything she asked for. It was only the high of good sex, he told himself, but the claim felt hollow.

Her face glowed from within as she softly whispered, "I want to read the advanced copy of your next two novels."

His chest warmed at the childlike fascination that made her eyes glitter like priceless gems. "That's it?" he teased and then said, "Done." Pulling her to him, he kissed the tip of her nose. "Now, give it up, *habibi*."

Her chin lifted and a new kind of light shone from her. He was a writer but he had no words to describe the exquisite expression in her eyes. It was hope but brighter, shinier, more radiant.

"I'm writing a book. It's actually the second in a series and I think it's good. Like, really good. I also wrote a fantasy horror that's based on Indian mythology in the last few years. Thaata used to tell me all the scariest stories, you know? He used to say I was the only one among the three of us sisters who didn't scare easily." Pride he'd rarely seen danced in each word. She drew in a fast, shallow breath as if she couldn't stop talking now that she'd started. "I don't know if you've noticed but I had quite a rigorous discussion with your editor Samuel earlier tonight. I kinda ran the premise by him and he said he'd take a look at the book. How fantastic is that? Which reminds me that I should thank you for inviting me to today's gathering and—"

He laughed then and tackled her onto the bed until they were all tangled up in each other and the sheets, and there was nowhere she could escape to. He didn't remember the last time he had laughed so much, when listening to another person had brought him such joy, when he had felt such an overpowering rush of tenderness that he couldn't think straight.

"What's happening?" she said on a husky moan, when he covered her with his own body.

Ya, Allah, she fit so well against him—all soft curves and prickly edges and silky skin and sleek flesh and trembling thighs and tremulous moans. And those big, dazzling eyes reflecting everything she felt straight at him.

"You're so adorably sexy when you talk about your deepest dreams that I've been overcome by uncontrollable lust once again, *habibi*," he whispered at her ear and then followed it up with the filthiest words he could speak to her.

She blushed even though she didn't fully understand him and then those sleek legs converged around his back and she was lifting her hips up and Nasir ground his erection into her with no self-control.

A trail of damp kisses followed from her mouth, licking and nipping at his flesh. With one hand, she tugged up her T-shirt and through his silk pajama bottoms, he could feel the heat radiating off her sex. Pressing herself up against him, she writhed with a wanton pleasure that had his rock-hard length twitching.

"Please, Nasir. Now."

He took her mouth in a gentle kiss. "You will be sore, *habibi*. It might hurt a little."

"But after it passes, you'll make me scream with ecstasy, won't you? Twice at least."

And then without waiting for his response, she pushed down his pajamas and freed his shaft and then he was there at the center of her sex.

Reaching for a control he wasn't sure he possessed anymore, Nasir played with her soft core. Stroked her own wetness all over her until she was moaning his name like a symphony. Taking it slow with his fingers, letting her get used to him all over again. With all the skill he had, he teased her over and over and only when she began to fall apart, calling out his name, did he slide himself into her.

Slumbering heat built and built in his spine as he went slow and deep and shifted her pelvis up until he could hit a different spot and she was moaning that she couldn't go again. But he saw the need and greed in her beautiful face and he hit that spot over and over again, dragging his abdominal muscles over her sensitive nub and it was all an erotic tango that made his muscles clench and sweat bead all over his skin. When she screamed in pleasure and went over the edge again and buried her teeth in his pectorals, he followed her and fell apart along with her in a way he hadn't allowed himself in a long, long time.

After they'd showered, despite her complaints that she wanted to sleep, and he'd fed her pieces of crisp apples and cheese and nuts, she'd wrapped herself around him like a vine. When he'd tried to give her a little space, she crawled back to him and over him, limbs akimbo, aggressive and prickly even in sleep.

When he held her against his chest, she kept throwing her legs and arms around. And when he finally got her to settle down with a long, drugging kiss, she mumbled sleepily that she'd thought it would be like this, that she'd known that it would be him. That he was worth the wait.

Nasir thought his petrified heart might have cracked open at that vulnerable admission. And he wondered if stones could be turned back into men and even if they could, if they could relearn the most human thing to do again—to love.

Or if it was all too late for him. But he knew one thing about men; that they were selfish. He was one, too, and he knew he wouldn't give her up when she fit into his life so perfectly. Not ever.

CHAPTER TWELVE

THE NEXT SIX weeks were as close to paradise as even Yana's wildest dreams could have conjured them to be. It had felt unbelievable when she'd looked at her calendar that morning and realized there were only three weeks of her stay left, as per the contract she'd signed with Nasir. Of course, the contract had no meaning left between them except as a joke Nasir used when she'd ask something of him and he'd say she'd robbed him blind already.

Time seemed to rush at an indescribable speed the more she tried to double down on it. Or was it her grasp of time as a construct that was slipping because she'd never been happier, or for the first time in her life, that she was truly thriving and flourishing on all fronts?

She'd had to finish up the last of her modeling contracts already in place, so she'd done those. She and Nush had squealed with joy at learning recently that Mira was pregnant with twins—*twins*—and the sisters had managed a weekend for a much-needed girls get-together arranged by Mira's clearly besotted husband Aristos. *And* to top it all off, she was making good progress on the second book she was working on in her series.

It was still hard for her to trust Nasir with reading her work. Or maybe it was her insecurities? But she managed to reveal theoretical scenarios to him because his mind was a maze and he was the best at brainstorming. While it rankled him a little that she refused to share more, he always indulged her outlandish inquiries and they ended up discussing craft and the industry and research so often that Yana began to fall for him all over again.

Between quick one-day or overnight jaunts to different locations for a magazine ad shoot, a perfume ad and the opening of a new night club in Amsterdam, she'd spent the past few weeks soaking in the sun, swimming in the pool and wandering the woods with Zara in tow.

Nasir, to her shock, had shown up at the same hotels as she had for almost all of her work trips. To her unending delight, he was one of those people who'd been to every damn city in the world and always knew the best places to eat, knew the real history that books seemed to forget and then there were those glorious nights of passion and tenderness and more to explore between them. The best part was that she felt as if the trips were slowly bringing out the true explorer of life Nasir was at heart.

After that first night, they didn't try to label what was between them again or set an expiration date on it, and that was perfectly fine with Yana.

Clearly, he still wanted her with the same fervor and madness she felt. In this, finally, they were equals. They were lovers and confidants and shared all the ups and downs of loving and caring for a little girl.

She was living the life she'd once dreamed of and during those glorious moments where they were playing with Zara, or reading quietly together in the evening, or talking about her book, it felt like it was more than enough. At least that was what she told herself, trying her best to not give too much thought to the future.

Not confiding in her sisters when she wanted to share the

real relationship she was finally having with Nasir, hurt her heart. But they would only ask about where it was all leading, out of pure concern for her, and then Caio and Aristos would be dragged into it, and she didn't want to force the issue when it was, in the end, all a precarious house of cards.

For now their *affair*—for want of a better word—still possessed that dreamy, magical, out-of-this-world quality to it and she was loath to disrupt it with talk of reality and future and stupid, silly organs getting far too involved when they should know better.

It was the same when they were at the castle, too—as if the whole scenario and the actors had truly emerged out of a dark fairy tale into a happy romance. She didn't know if the instructions not to mention it had come from Nasir.

She was only thankful that the staff and Ahmed and even Amina acted as if they didn't notice anything. Nasir's mother had been excessively, exactingly kind to her, and Yana had cautiously returned the courtesy because Amina seemed to finally realize how much Yana had loved her husband. How real her mourning of Izaz was.

But sometimes, Yana saw a calculating quality in the older woman's eyes and it unnerved her. She kept pointing out with a tone to her voice that Yana couldn't pin down, that Zara was flourishing, thriving, blooming, under the attention of the two adults she loved the most.

Especially since she must know that her son ended up back in his bedroom—which Yana still also occupied, every night without fail. Though Nasir left before dawn at the latest—immediately after sex sometimes—to return to the bedroom he'd used since she'd arrived.

Yana had initially found both injury and insult in his leaving right after sex until he'd explained to her, with that charmingly wicked smile of his, that inspiration for his next novel had been coming to him in waves around midnight, right after he'd made love to her. That if he didn't want to be ditched by his frustrated editor or his agent, he had to capitalize on it. And that he'd been making the trip back to her bedroom after his writing session, only to leave at dawn again because they didn't want to be caught together by his curious five-year-old.

Acting the seductress—a bad habit that Nasir demanded she'd better *not* give up because it made her say and do outrageous things just to provoke him, she'd prettily suggested to him that he'd better dedicate the book to her for her part in getting it done.

His reply had been, "I wouldn't want to shock my loyal readers with all that went into finishing the book, *habibi*. Those particular details are only for me to savor. Especially the time you decided you wanted to be on your knees."

She'd blushed so hard that her cheeks had burned. But she'd also been secretly glad—not because she believed sex with her had some magical writer's unblocking properties, but because, for the first time in years since she'd known him, Nasir genuinely looked relaxed. Content. Happy, even.

And she wanted to think at least some of that—a tiny, little part—was to do with her.

The summer sun had already started to set, immediately bringing a cool chill that particular evening as Yana hurriedly packed up their picnic supplies. Especially since they'd ventured farther than the boundary of the woods they usually stuck to. It was her own fault for giving in to Zara's continued request for more playtime. Between keeping up with her and her own flagging energy, Yana hadn't checked the time.

Yana pushed to her knees and lugged the heavy tote bag— Zara had to bring all the rocks she'd collected today, onto her shoulder just as the little girl, in her hurry, slipped over something and fell facedown into the knee-high grass.

Dropping the bag where she stood, she rushed to Zara. The five-year-old's cry—a sudden, spiraling wail—told Yana it was more shock and fear than real pain. Fighting the worry in her head, she squatted on the floor and gently pulled Zara into her lap.

The little girl attached her arms to Yana's neck with a hic-cupping cry, without letting her check her face. Sighing, and loosening her arms so that she didn't communicate her own fear to her, Yana rocked from side to side even as she whispered that Zara was okay. When Zara finally let her look at the small cut on her cheek, Yana set about dealing with it.

She wasn't sure how long it took, when suddenly Yana noted that complete darkness had fallen. With the forested area at her back, and the castle at least a mile in the opposite way, it would be easy to get lost without light.

Pushing onto her feet, she talked Zara into wrapping her arms around her neck and her legs around her back like a little baby monkey they'd seen on a nature show not a few days ago, clinging to its mother.

Wiping her tears on Yana's T-shirt, Zara instantly cheered up.

Turning around with her lightweight baggage, Yana walked back to where she'd dropped the tote. She found her cell phone and turned on the flashlight, although there was no signal to call Nasir this far out. The sky was a dark canopy of stars she'd rarely seen and she stopped several times to show Zara this star and that constellation.

Her arms and legs hurt from all the day's exercise but soon, Yana could see the shadowed outline of the castle. She blew out a long breath, imagining herself in a hot bath with Nasir in it, too, hopefully, once they'd settled Zara into bed. It was a ritual she hadn't planned on getting involved in and yet, had been roped into when Zara had begged that they both read her a story and tuck her in for the night. As if even the little girl could sense the current of happiness between the adults who adored her.

Now, with her departure rushing at her with every day that passed, the ritual and so many more like that had gained weight and gravitas. Yana didn't want to leave. There, she'd admitted it to herself. For the first time in her life, she was happy and content and...she felt like she belonged here. Like the castle walls themselves were imbued with her very joy.

"Where the hell have you been?" Nasir's question tugged her into the present with a firm jerk.

Taken aback by his tone, Yana stared at him.

"Do you know how worried I've been? It's dark and you weren't at your usual spot."

"I didn't notice the time and then Zara—"

"You should know better than to venture out so far and for so long after sunset," he said, plucking Zara from her arms into his. "That was careless of you, Yana."

Yana froze, struck by the criticism in his voice. But whatever defense she wanted to provide was drowned out when the entire staff came toward the high entrance from all directions surrounding the courtyard, clear relief on their faces. And then she was being tugged inside, by Amina of all people, who checked her arms and legs and worried over her dirty T-shirt and shorts, and all through it Yana kept looking at him, but Nasir wouldn't meet her eyes.

Suddenly, Yana felt as if she'd been permanently pushed into a cold, dark place, shunned from all light. All her doubts about how she'd leave when the time came turned into something else.

Finally, they were all in the full foyer illuminated by one

of those blasted chandeliers with a million little lights and her gaze fell on the small cut on Zara's cheek just as everyone else's did.

"You're hurt, Zara," Nasir's voice cut through the commotion around them, like a knife slicing through. And Yana heard it then—his fear. Saw the tension carved into his face. The sweat that had gathered over his brow.

"I didn't listen to Yana Auntie, Papa," Zara said, scrunching her face up. "She told me not to go too fast but I thought I saw a dragonfly and then I fell over." Her thick curls dancing around her face, she drew in a long breath. "It doesn't hurt, Papa," Zara piped up, looking for Yana among the crowd that surrounded her. "Yana Auntie alweady cleaned it and put a gel on it. She said I get a medal because I only cwied for thwee and a half minutes. She said I was so bwave when she cleaned it that I could eat chocolate cake in the morning. Can I have chocolate cake for bweakfast, Papa?"

The tension dissipated from Nasir's face and he pressed a kiss to Zara's temple. "Yes, pumpkin. You can have anything you want for breakfast."

"Will you and Yana Auntie wead me two stories each tonight, Papa? Since I fell and hurt myself?"

Nasir laughed and hugged his daughter tight. "Manipulative little thing, aren't you?" When Zara frowned and pushed out that lower lip she deployed like a weapon, he hurriedly added, "Yes, two stories each, Zuzu baby. After that you have to sleep, yeah? And then..." He looked up over Zara's head and met Yana's eyes. "I have a very important thing to do."

"What, Papa?"

"Eating crow, baby," he said with a sudden, heart-wrenching smile aimed straight at her heart. Zara pounded him with more questions and he went on to elaborate that her papa was a blockhead who forgot his manners when he was upset. And he had been upset, he told Zara and an arrested Yana, at the thought that his two bestest, most favorite girls in the world might have been lost and hurt in the forest in the dark.

Yana's heart swelled in her chest, overflowing with emotion. And she knew, just knew, that she was going to leave pieces of herself behind when she left.

They ended up spending more than two hours not only reading to Zara but also watching some anime with her. Even though, for the first time in his life, Nasir wanted his little energy bunny to fall asleep fast.

In the end, he left Zara and Yana cuddling in Zara's bed, both of them suddenly fast asleep together.

He went back to his own bedroom, made some quick arrangements in the bathroom, changed into pajamas and waited. He couldn't blame her if she didn't join him tonight, could he? He'd been so eager to criticize and blame her for a small hurt Zara had received.

He pushed a hand through his hair and tugged at it roughly. Of course, five-year-olds got hurt all the time. Why hadn't he controlled himself better? And now here he was, once again, wondering if he'd hurt her.

He'd worn down the carpet when the connecting door finally opened and Yana came in, locking it behind her.

They stared at each other—her expression wary as she watched him, and he…he didn't know what he looked like. Only that he wanted to make more than simple amends. Reaching for her, he took her hand in his and tugged her into the bathroom.

Her eyes widened as she saw the full bath he'd filled with her favorite lavender oil and scattered with rose petals, and the lit candles and the bottle of wine with a glass, waiting on the rim. "Nasir—"

Forestalling her argument or a justly deserved complaint, he said quietly but firmly, "Raise your arms."

He was more than surprised when she complied. Tugging her T-shirt off, he gathered her hair and gently tied it into a knot at the top of her head, like he'd seen her do. Then he stripped her of her bra and shorts and panties.

Eyes wide in her face like a gazelle, she stood there, utterly naked.

"Into the tub," he said gruffly, before his desire overtook his common sense.

She complied silently. Again.

He watched with sheer fascination that apparently refused to even simmer down into something manageable, as her limbs disappeared beneath the water and she threw her head back with a soft moan.

He swallowed when he caught sight of her tight nipples playing peekaboo under a rose petal. Needing to give himself something to do, he uncorked the wine and poured it into the glass.

She took it from him wordlessly and then took a sip. She murmured appreciatively and she wriggled her shoulders as if to dislodge a knot there. His guilt intensified. "Once you get out of the bath, I'll work those kinks out of your shoulders," he said, wriggling his fingers at her.

"No, thank you," she said, not opening her eyes. "Especially if your massage skills are no better than your daughter's."

"Try me and then pass judgment, *habibi*."

Another exhale left her. "Thank you for this. It was exactly what I needed at the end of a long day."

Seating himself at the edge, he watched the overhead lights play with the angles of her face. "I shouldn't have snapped at you when you got back. I was worried, terrified, that you both were hurt. I... I was suddenly reminded of everything I once lost..."

"It's okay, Nasir," she said, lightly tapping her fingers over the back of his hand and then retreating. "I got that from your face. But just so you know, Zara's five and she's going to get hurt sometimes. Under my supervision or someone else's."

"I know that, in here," he said, pointing toward his head. "And the amazing thing is she knows that, too, doesn't she? She's completely fearless with you. But I do worry about her, Yana. All the time. Especially since I've already messed up with her once, so badly."

Opening her eyes, Yana watched him with that silent gaze. Asking questions without asking them. Waiting for him to reveal his darkest fears.

"I never planned to be a father, Yana. And yet, ever since I held her that first day, I've loved her. I know I can't keep her wrapped up in cotton wool, surrounded by staff who watch her twenty-four hours a day."

"You can't. And as much as you'll hate me for saying this, she'll be six in three months. She needs kids of her own age to play with, Nasir, to learn social skills, to learn boundaries. Even if you decide to homeschool her. You can't keep yourself shut out from the rest of the world and also be a good father to her. Kids need to learn about the world, and Zara's a pretty social kid."

"I don't hate you for saying it. In fact, I..." He swallowed the words, loath to unburden himself to her when he hadn't broached the topic in his head yet with her. He was aware of days dwindling at a rapid rate, of her looming departure. And yet, he held out. Told himself he and Zara would manage. Told himself that Yana would return to her normal life and yet they would still be able to resume their affair and fall into some kind of a sticking pattern, long distance.

He'd never been an indecisive man before in his entire life and he hated that he was waiting for time or something else to decide for him when he'd never done that. The certainty of time passing and the uncertainty of his own plans were eating through him.

He looked up and met her gaze. "I hope you won't ever stop saying that, Yana."

"Saying what?"

"What you think is right for Zara. Even if you're afraid that I'll get all grumpy and grouchy with you."

"I'm not afraid of you, you beast," she said teasingly, splashing water on him.

He went to his knees and then cradled her neck. Pressing his mouth to her temple, he whispered, "Even after you've left here?"

She grabbed his forearm. "I won't," she whispered earnestly and he heard the promise in it.

"Am I forgiven, then?" he said, trailing his mouth to the shell of her ear.

Her questing hands went straight to his erection. She palmed him and Nasir forgot all about the world outside. "Only if you get into the bath with me."

That was an invitation he could never resist.

CHAPTER THIRTEEN

YANA'S THREE MONTHS were up as if someone had taken the hourglass and shaken it up to make time go faster. She had an assignment in New York, then she was going to visit her mother in California and then return to be with Mira for almost a month before the twins were born. Of course, she'd promised Zara that she'd visit her, too, whenever possible in the midst of her hectic schedule. And she'd meant it. For once, everything in her life had the patina of normality and it left her feeling out of sorts.

She was at peace with herself, with where she was going in her life. She'd continue to pick up small contracts here and there until something definite came up in her literary career. Just thinking about that sent a ripple of excitement through her.

In the meantime, she had two sisters she adored and two billionaire brothers-in-law who were forever inviting her to visit and meant it. And Yana decided she would. She'd worked in one way or another since she'd been sixteen and she would take it easier now that she was already at a crossroads.

She'd kept waiting for the bubble that Nasir and she seemed to live in to break, for reality or some other ugly life thing to fracture their almost fantastical happiness. When it happened, it did so because, once again, she couldn't help herself bringing up the past.

Because the seeds of the future had already been sown somewhere in the past and, in the end, because she'd realized the truth that had never changed.

That final day, Amina and Ahmed had taken Zara to meet Amina's sister in London, leaving Yana and Nasir behind. At his dictate, she'd learned later. To make it easier on Zara when Yana left the castle, but she wondered if he thought she'd also cause a scene.

Dread and something else curled around Yana's chest. She'd miss Zara with all of her being. She'd miss the staff, Ahmed's gentle care, Huma picking at her for ideas and even Amina, who'd thawed so greatly that she'd once said Yana was the daughter she'd never had. As skeptical as she'd wanted to feel, she'd thought the older woman had actually meant it.

As if her dark fairy-tale romance had to continue the theme, a great storm darkened the skies that last evening, chasing her and Nasir indoors. As if someone had set a background score, a hum of anxiety had thrummed through her all day.

As usual, Nasir and she ate together, then worked for a little while on their respective laptops in the great big library in quiet, comfortable silence. He put the gramophone player on, and she stood up to stretch and suddenly, he was behind her, clasping his arms around her and leading her in a slow, sensuous tango around the room.

She had no idea how long they danced like that. How long they stayed silent even as their bodies communicated freely and easily and effortlessly. In her three-inch heels, she was at perfect height for the V of her thighs to feel his thick erection. She'd gone braless and her nipples felt deliciously tormented pressed up into points against his hard chest.

He tilted her chin up with insistent fingers and Yana read

his raw desire as easily as she could hear the thundering pulse of her heartbeat in her ears.

She went with a willing wantonness as he pressed her upper body over a centuries-old side table full of crystal decanters and expensive candlesticks. She moaned like a brazen seductress when he pulled up the hem of the icy-blue cocktail dress she'd worn for him because he'd whispered once when he'd been deep inside her that he loved seeing her in it. She turned her head and let him see her greedy abandon with an eager push of her hips when he tested her damp readiness. She slammed her palm onto the dark wood when he thrust into her with one long, deep stroke. The decanters and the candlesticks rattled, the table hit the wall with a rhythmic thud and the entire castle felt like it was standing witness to them, and she wondered just who was seducing and who was surrendering.

And then she realized it didn't matter anymore.

Her breath came in sharp pants and shallow gulps when his thrusts began to gather speed, but suddenly *lost* that finesse. Then his fingers were at her core, and his mouth was at her neck and he was demanding she come for him and he was telling her she was the sexiest thing he'd ever beheld and he was all over her and around her. The clever, wicked man that he was, he hit the exact spot where she could see glorious stars and soon, she was climaxing so hard that she thought she might never come back together in the same way ever again.

Yana felt undone, unraveled, as if he'd wrested away parts of her. Her legs wobbled when he helped her straighten and she thought he was on shaky legs, too. She turned and smiled and then he was kissing her and telling her what a good, quiet, biddable lover she was and she was thumping him in his chest with her fist because he was deliberately provoking her all over again before he kissed her.

She had no words to describe the tender reverence with which his lips touched her. How they said so much that he couldn't or wouldn't say. She buried her face in his neck and let herself drown in the delicious scent of the man.

They stood like that, while the storm raged outside the castle, and Yana wondered at how perfectly it mirrored everything that was happening inside her.

"Come back to me, *habibi*."

"I'm here," she said and yet she felt like parts of her were going to stay behind forever with him. "I'm leaving tomorrow morning."

"I know."

"Thank you for giving me tonight. With you. With just you."

"You think it was a favor to you? It was a selfish man's selfish desire. To have you all to himself for one final night."

"Then for the first time in our lives, I think we're in agreement," she said, forcing a humor she didn't feel. "I'll return whenever I can."

"I know."

"I'll call Zara every day."

"I know."

"I'll let you know when you can drop her off with me. Mira would love to see her, too. And Aristos. And Nush and Caio. I want Zara to meet them all. I want her to think of them as her family, too."

"You're very generous, *habibi*, and Zara is lucky to have you."

"Are you mocking me?" she asked.

"Do I dare?"

She looked up and ran her fingers over the scar almost obsessively and then pulled back. "I'm sorry."

"You're welcome to touch me anywhere, Yana. Even the scar. I don't mind."

"I know," she said this time, and he smiled, and she smiled back, and it was a moment of perfect communion.

Age had only made him more handsome, more distinguished. Laugh lines crinkled out at his eyes even as grief and loss had permanently etched themselves onto those stern features.

It came to her then how much he'd changed after the incident that had given him those scars, how a shroud of grief had hung around him. With her usual foolish naiveté and a reckless urgency because it had pained her to see him like that, she'd not only trodden on his raw, wounded emotions but also declared shamelessly that she was in love with him and that he belonged to her.

God, had she ever read a situation so badly?

Whatever had happened on that trip had changed him—inside and out. Now she wished she'd asked him about it instead of throwing herself at him, that she'd kept a safe space for him like he'd done for her. Like he was doing for her again now.

But as much as she tried, she couldn't be mad at herself for her grand avowal of love back then. She'd sensed something was wrong with him and with her usual all-guns-blazing attitude had desperately wanted to fix it for him. She'd thought herself enough to fix him.

But it didn't really have anything to do with whether she'd been enough or not. Something else had happened to him on that trip. Now she realized it, and like that saying, the truth did set her free.

It was life affirming to have someone who loved you by your side when you went through hard times. But in the end, one had to save oneself. One had to decide to live and love despite the pain and pitfalls life threw at you.

"Who did you lose on that trip when you came back with all these scars?" she asked, twisting her fingers so that they cast shadows on his white shirt when what she wanted to do was look into his eyes and see the answer for herself.

The atmosphere dropped to frost instantly even though he was warm around her.

She closed her eyes, cursing her impulsivity. Just because he'd found her good enough for an affair didn't mean they were going to exchange every painful secret. But to her surprise, he answered.

"A photographer I'd been training for a while. Fatima was—" a small smile painted his mouth "—young, and brash and defiant and wanted to change the world for the better. I brought her with me on an assignment I shouldn't have. She died in my arms."

"You loved her," Yana said, stating the fact rather than asking him, the final puzzle pieces that made up Nasir suddenly falling into place.

"I did. And I should've done a better job of protecting her. I was more experienced than her. I should've done a better risk analysis—"

"Weren't you yourself hurt by the blast?"

"Yes, but—"

She laughed then and it was an empty, mocking sound that rivaled the storm's fierceness. "How heavy your ego must be, Nasir. Don't your head and your shoulders and your back hurt from the weight of it?"

"You don't understand—"

"No, I understand it perfectly. I see it, finally. I see all of you, too," she said, throwing his words back at him. "I see now why you shut me down with such brutal cruelty."

Suddenly, his marriage to Jacqueline—which had had disaster written all over it from the beginning—his withdrawal from the world, from his first career, from his father, and even from her, made complete sense now. It was what Izaz had meant when he'd said his son was lost.

After that trip he'd seemed colder, harder, flatter even, with none of those soft edges that added such charm to his incisive brilliance, none of the quirks and awareness that had made him...larger than life. Her own naive stupidity had been but a cinder in the sacrificial pyre he'd already built for himself.

"You don't understand how terrible it is to have someone you love die in your arms. How utterly powerless you feel. The memory itself would haunt you forever."

His words were a death sentence to her poor heart's tentative whispers. But she was damned if she let him believe he was right. That somehow, he had to live through this punishment, forever alone. "No, I haven't lived through that exact scenario. But I know about loss and grief and...screaming at the universe for just one last chance. One do-over. I'd give anything to have one last minute with Thaata, to tell him that I was sorry, that I finally see what he'd been trying to do all along. That I loved him so much."

Nasir took her stiff hand in his and clasped their fingers tight. But still, Yana wasn't done. She was furious, actually, on behalf of herself and Jacqueline and the woman he'd lost. Not to mention Zara.

"I'm sure Fatima would have loved to know," she said, crossing all lines, venturing once again into that forbidden zone, her reckless tongue bashing out truths he'd hate to hear, "that her death has been conveniently reduced to the reason you have turned away from living a full life. And you dare call me a coward?"

"It's not cowardice if I want to leave emotions out of my decisions. Not that I succeeded with you, I admit."

"Ha! Then why hate me for so long?"

"Because you were right. I lost the battle against myself over you long ago. Don't you see how that must have driven Jacqueline crazy? My dislike for you was far more potent than anything I ever felt for her. It didn't matter that I told myself to stay well clear of you. You were always there at the periphery of my life, teasing and taunting me. I wish I'd just admitted defeat sooner. You and I both know we were heading here, one way or the other, for years now, Yana."

"Because you were so sure that I'd throw myself at you again?"

A pithy curse was his aggrieved response. "Because as much as I fought it, a few days ago, a few months ago, a few years ago, when you were Jacqueline's maid of honor, even when you were my nineteen-year-old stepsister with the body of a goddess and the innocence of a locked-up princess, I was attracted to you. I wanted you all along. You have no idea how close I came to taking what you offered all those years ago. How I wanted to use you to bury my grief, to relieve the guilt I felt about Fatima."

"And why would that have been so wrong? Why do you talk of it as if it fills you with horror to even think it? I was only nineteen, yes. But how do you measure adulthood? How dare you take away my agency? I'd been through loss and neglect and rebellion and wrong influences and bad parent-ing…so much already. You were a good thing in my life. Loving you was a light in a place of shadows and mistakes and I'll never ever regret it."

"Don't, *habibi*."

"I don't want to play games or fantasies, Nasir. In this, I've never been able to dupe even myself."

His forehead pressed against hers, his exhale exploding over her lips, washing away her fears all over again. His hands cupped her shoulders and held her to him, hard and tight. The contact was nonsexual, seeking and giving comfort, and yet she felt it pass down through limb after limb, vein after vein, reaching the deepest corners of her and staying there. Rooting her to the moment, to the man, to herself.

Bringing her back full circle to her own truth. That she still loved him. That she'd loved him for all the yesterdays of her life and that she'd love him for all the tomorrows yet to come.

And this time her love didn't feel wrong or bad or forbidden or immature or selfish or demanding. It simply sat in her heart, fitting in, settling into place. It felt like coming home.

"You're punishing yourself for a mistake you didn't even commit. With me and with Fatima."

"I'd have discarded you afterward. I had nothing to give you back for your declaration of love, Yana. I'd have simply used you."

"And now?" she asked, even though she'd promised herself she wouldn't go there.

"And now, I still have nothing to give you." He held her gaze, and she saw it coming before he said, "Except marriage."

She jerked back. "What?"

"Marry me, Yana. I'll give you every happiness that I can, make every dream of yours come true. Marry me because Zara needs you and I need you. Marry me so that you never have to say goodbye to us again. Admit it. It's killing you to leave. Admit that you're happy here with us."

Tears and smiles came at her together as she gazed at him. She couldn't lie to him now, even if she wanted to. Because it was her most sacred truth. "I've been happy here. Happier than I've ever been in my life. And yes, it's killing me to leave you. The thought of coming back as just a friend into your life, of not calling this castle home, kills me. The thought of not seeing you and Zara for months on end…kills me."

"Then stay and marry me. Make a life with me." He took her mouth in a hard kiss, and she felt herself melting. Falling. Weakening. But she had to remain strong against temptation. "Stay, *habibi*, and I'll be yours in all the ways that matter."

"No, you'll be mine under conditions and caveats." Regretful tears drew paths down her cheeks. "You're still trying to pin me down. To take everything from me without giving me anything in return."

He flinched, and her chest felt like it would cave in. Because she knew he was standing there, with one foot on the precipice, ready to fall with her, but he just wouldn't take that last step.

"Only you could make me consider marriage again after the nightmare with Jacqueline. Why can't you see that?"

"I don't want the little crumbs you can manage. I don't want anything from you," she said, trying to cover up the thundering of her thudding heart and rolling belly with a small smile. Who'd have guessed that her teen fantasy coming true would be such a horror in real life? Who knew she'd walk away when her deepest dream was finally within her reach? "Because whether you admit it or not, you're already mine. You've always been mine, by your own admission. I've owned you for a long time and I just didn't know it."

She felt free then. Free of fears and shackles and incessant demands and made-up rules. Because her love for him was a simple truth. Like the sun rose in the east. Like the storm that was raging outside but would leave the world renewed come tomorrow. Like the pain that was crashing through her right now but would settle into another scar in the months and years to come.

What she refused to do was to twist herself inside out ever again, with the foolish hope that she'd finally be loved the way she deserved to be. Not even for Zara or for him.

She clasped his cheek then and licked into his mouth. The taste of mint exploded in her mouth, fusing with her very cells. She let her hands roam the broad chest, the tapered waist, the hard planes of his back; she snuck under his shirt and traced all of his scars and…then she kissed him all over again, hoping it would last her at least until the dark dawn and the long day ahead.

"Goodbye, Nasir."

CHAPTER FOURTEEN

NASIR FOUND HER at a fashion show in Athens, Greece. He'd followed her there after learning, from his mother of all people, that she was with her sister Mira, who'd just given birth to twins.

It had been four months since she'd left.

He hadn't called her or texted her or even snuck a glance at her as she talked to Zara on a video call, stubborn and hardheaded to the end. But thoughts of her consumed his every waking and sleeping moment.

His bed felt cold and empty. His life felt colorless. His words had dried up again as had his imagination. He'd thought of a million questions he'd never asked her and wondered at her answers. That a lifetime wasn't enough for her to surprise him and delight him and annoy him and bring him to his knees again and again. And he was beginning to think it wasn't a bad idea to be on his knees for the woman he clearly adored.

And she, apparently finally wising up to what an extraordinary, incredible woman she was, didn't even steal a glance at him. Even his mother got screen time. As did Ahmed and Huma and his staff. Never a question or a comment about him or for him since she'd left them.

Not Zara. Never Zara.

Just him. She'd left him because he'd been a coward. And in one of those petty moments, Nasir found himself envious of his own six-year-old for the generous, lavish, unconditional love she got from her Yana Auntie.

All he'd wanted to do for weeks was storm through her brother-in-law Aristos Carides's lavish mansion like a bull on steroids, making claims and commitments that made him come out in a full sweat, and announce to anyone and the world and her, especially, that she was his.

He wondered yet again how long their red-hot affair would have lasted if he hadn't brought up marriage. Clever and perceptive as she was, she'd seen it for what it was—another contract he'd use to bind her to him, without opening his heart. Without actually committing to anything. Without giving her, the glorious creature she was, her due.

Now he was ashamed of how he'd attempted to manipulate her, even if he hadn't done it on purpose. Dangling the mirage of a dream as if it was some prize she would leap at.

Even though she'd made it clear that she wanted all the fireworks and passion and roller coaster of true love. Finally, it was the thought of another man giving her what he'd refused to that had spurred him into action. The thought of spending the rest of his life wondering where she was, who she was bestowing that warmth of hers on, felt scarier than the risk of opening his scarred heart to her, hoping she wouldn't deal it a death blow.

So here he was in Athens at a fashion show, the buzz that it was Yana Reddy's last show—another fact he hadn't been privy to because she wasn't talking to him, letting himself be photographed by media and paparazzi, giving rise to all kinds of speculation just so he could have one glimpse of her.

He wanted to see her shine and dazzle and sizzle. He wanted to be a part of her dreams coming gloriously true.

Whatever Nasir had imagined about how she'd look when she strutted onto the catwalk had nothing on the reality. The music, the crowd's energy and the sensual beauty of each model highlighted by carefully orchestrated lights and makeup and music…it was meant to bamboozle the audience.

Having been to a few shows in his twenties, and the couple of shows he'd been to during Yana's stay at the castle, he knew how this worked. And yet, when Yana walked onto the stage—the last of the models to do so—in the French designer's magnum opus: a glittery, rainbow-colored pantsuit, he was captivated anew.

Without a bra, the lapels of the jacket were stuck to her skin, baring most of her breasts, and she looked like a queen.

No, she was his prickly, fierce princess. And he'd been stupid to turn away from the best thing that had ever happened to him. To turn away from the incandescence of Yana's love. A coward, as she'd called him.

But there was no turning back now, because she'd brought him back to life.

He was bemoaning his habit of not drinking alcohol when the doors to the penthouse suite of the hotel opened and she stepped inside.

Smoky eyes and a pale glossy lipstick and shimmery glitter over her chest…she looked like a dark, alien goddess full of fire and passion. Her hair had been plastered to her scalp in some weird hairstyle that served to highlight the stark sharpness of her features. All angles and edges that were soothed by the promise held in that lush, wide mouth.

"I wondered if it was you I saw out there," she commented coolly, still standing there.

That explained her lack of surprise at seeing him in here now.

He nodded and swallowed and ran a hand through his hair. She watched him, and he watched her.

"Not a fan of the after-parties?"

"Not really," she replied.

He stole a glance at his watch. He hadn't expected her for hours, not until dawn. Suddenly, he felt woefully unprepared for all the words he wanted—no, needed—to say, after a lifetime of employing them. "I thought you'd be there."

"You were the one who had me upgraded to this penthouse suite?"

He shrugged, waiting for her to slam the doors in his face and run off.

Instead, she walked into the suite, grabbed a bottle of water from the mini fridge and emptied it out. Then she opened another one, stood over the sink and poured it out over her hair and face. Her breath came in sharp, bracing spurts as the ice-cold water made goose bumps rise on her skin. "That's better. It feels as if all those lights and sounds are stuck to my skin."

He grabbed a hand towel from the bathroom and handed it to her.

She pressed her face into it and when she emerged from it, there was a resolve to her mouth that spelled his doom. "Will you tell me why you're here? Or can I go to sleep? I've been on my feet for eleven hours straight."

"Catch some rest. I'm not leaving until we've talked," he finally said, following her to the sunken living room.

"I won't catch a wink knowing you're out here." She plopped onto one of the sofas and before she could stretch her legs onto the marble coffee table, he sat down. His hands were shaking when he took her foot in his hands, pulled the lethal-looking heels off and pressed his fingers into the arch.

"God, I've forgotten how good you are at that," she said, throwing her head back.

He repeated his actions with her other foot and an electric silence built around them.

"I've brought you good news," he admitted finally.

She sat up, pulled her feet from his lap. "What?"

"Samuel loves your book. He wants exclusive rights to it. This is big, Yana. You're going to be incredibly successful."

She threw herself at him so suddenly that his heart rushed into his ears. "Oh, my God! That's…awesome. I didn't… I can't tell you what it feels like to hear that. I…" Then she grinned, and there were tears in her eyes, but she rubbed them away quickly with the back of her hand. "Wait, of course you know how it feels. Thanks for telling me, Nasir. It means a lot. And it means even more that you came all this way to tell me."

"When Samuel told me, although I know he shouldn't have, I begged him to let me be the bearer of good news."

"Why?" she asked, her mask falling, a sudden belligerence to that one word.

"I wanted to see your happiness. Your laughter. Your victory. Your passion. I wanted to see you, Yana." And before she could probe him further, he said, "Do you have an agent yet?"

"No. I do have a pile of increasingly promising rejections from two years ago. They'd gotten more personal, came with more feedback. But after the last round a year ago, I stalled. I worked a bit more on the book and rejigged some major plot stuff. With Diana's games and Thaata sick, my head wasn't in the right space to start querying all over again."

"Do you want me to recommend you to mine?"

"Why?"

"Why what?"

"Why would you recommend me? As a bonus for sleeping with you?" she said, half-laughing, half-mocking.

"You're never going to stop taunting me, are you?" he said, knowing he deserved it. "My agent is amazing and will do a fabulous job negotiating you the best contract with Samuel. Fair warning about Samuel as an editor, though. He's brilliant, but he might make you rip the book apart until you hate him, the book and yourself. Just stay…strong and keep your vision for the book at the forefront, okay?"

Yana nodded, feeling a rush of joy and something almost like pride well up inside her. "You believe in me, then? That I could do this author thing?"

"Of course I believe in you," he said. "I'd love to read it and get a real sense of your work but I understand that you're nervous about letting people read it."

"Only you."

"Only me what?"

"It's only you that I'm twisted up about showing it to. I've given copies to both my sisters and brothers-in-law."

His jaw tightened. "May I ask why?"

She shrugged. "Before, I was afraid that you'd mock it. Mock me."

"You really painted me as a monster in your head, huh? And at every step, I added color to your rendering by confirming your worst impressions."

"I think it helped to paint you like that."

"Helped who, Yana? Because it's been eating me up."

"Me. It helped me. Every time I wanted to give in, admit defeat, throw in the towel, give up on myself, I'd get this image of you. I'd see you looking down at me full of anger and contempt and I'd tell myself, *no way*. No way am I going to give Nasir a chance to think less of me again. No way am I giving up. You were kinda like a fire under my butt."

"I'm horrified yet again by my cruelty toward you and how it has—"

She came to him then and clasped his cheeks with that bravery that colored her every action. "It was a good thing, Nasir."

"From which damned perspective, *habibi*?" he retorted, with an angry flush.

His fingers moved over her cheeks, soft and slow and reverent, as if he worried that he might mar her.

Yana leaned into his touch. "Even when I loathed you, you were a positive force in my life. I loved you. I wanted to be worthy of you. I—"

"You're worth a million versions of me, Yana. You're fiery and beautiful and worthier than a thousand sunrises and a thousand sunsets. Your heart is beauty and joy and life itself, *habibi*."

"You're making me cry."

"Par for the course, then," he said with a twinkle, and then he was kissing her, and every nip and lick was lust and reverence—two such opposing shades of the same sentiment. "I wanted to be the bearer of good news. Even that was selfish. Shall I tell you why I'm here, truly?"

"Yes. Now, Nasir. You've stripped me of all my roles and defenses. I can't be strong for too long. Tell me now. Please."

"The second piece of good news first. I had three pieces."

"There's more?" she said, wiping the back of her hand over her cheek with a vulnerability that squeezed his heart.

"I'd fill your days and nights with all the good news I can muster, *habibi*. But these are small in the scheme of things."

"Tell me, please."

"I have finally convinced Diana to enter rehab."

"What? How?" Yana pressed her hands to her mouth, disbelief a giant balloon in her chest. In all the months since she'd agreed terms with Nasir, she hadn't been able to make any progress with her mother, who had broken down and admitted that she had a problem but wanted no part of the solution. Yana had seen shades of a woman she'd once adored, and her resolve to help her had only intensified. But her efforts hadn't borne fruit yet.

He shrugged, as if it was indeed a small thing. "I tried to

persuade her. Offered her incentives. Then I…" He rubbed a hand over his mouth, as if unsure of her reaction. "I sort of threatened her with being completely cut off from the rest of her family. I think it was a culmination of all three that finally brought success."

Yana laughed and then cried, feeling as if gravity had been stolen from under her. She knew how much he disliked her mother, how many bad memories were associated with her. How much he'd have hated even talking to her. And yet, he'd done it. For her peace of mind. For her happiness. She took his hands in hers. "I can't thank you enough."

"Now for the third piece," he announced, as if her gratitude made him uncomfortable.

"I'm ready," Yana said, her words a mere whisper compared to the loud thundering of her heart.

He placed a sheaf of papers on the coffee table in front of him. "These are custody papers. If you sign them, we'll share custody of Zara. You can have her for more than just a month. You can course correct me when I get it wrong. You and she can have each other without me in between."

Whatever high she'd been riding deflated and she crashed with a hard thud back into reality. "Why are you doing that?"

"Because I know how much you love her and I want you to have everything you want, Yana. I never want you to doubt your place in her life."

"Everything I want, Nasir?" she said, throwing his words back at him.

"Yes, everything. Including my heart, if you still want it."

Yana stared wordlessly.

"I'm in love with you, *habibi*." His gaze searched hers, studied her, seemed to devour her. Even now, confusion danced in his eyes and she wondered if he felt as untethered without her as she felt without him. "You're a sorceress, like in the dark magic tales of the old. Only instead of cursing me to a wretched existence, you brought me back to life. And if you'd let me, Yana—" now he was on his knees in front of her, his large hands on her thighs, his amber eyes glittering with such pride and devotion and love "—I'll show you how much I love you for the rest of our lives. Life without you is like words without emotions. You are my heart and soul, Yana. And I'm sorry it took me forever to realize that you were already and always mine. I was the one who had to grow worthy of you. Do you see?"

Tears filled and overflowed down her cheeks and he still couldn't stop talking. "And I'm so glad that you came to me, *habibi*. That you found me all over again. That you gave me another chance because now, finally, I see you and I'm so ready for the exquisite, fragile, prickly and precious thing that you are, love. I'm ready for all of you, sweetheart."

And then she was crying in earnest then, falling into his open, waiting arms, her shoulders shaking with these great, heaving sobs that seemed to rush out of her in a torrent, and Nasir just held her, feeling his own heart break and tear and come back together again, in some kind of loop, as if it could be made and unmade by her tears and her laughter and her joy and her promises.

It was a long while before she raised her head and looked at him. Her eyes and nose were all pink and splotchy and she was so achingly beautiful that a flicker of fear flashed through him. "Do you want to marry me?" she asked.

"Yes. Now. Tomorrow. I… I've wasted enough time as it is."

Then she hid her face in his chest and held him so tight that he was reminded of his daughter's hugs. "Zara's already your child as much as she's mine. Just give me a chance, too, Yana," he said with growing alarm that she hadn't really given him an answer. "Give me a chance to do this right."

"And if I have lots of demands and conditions and nego-tiations?"

"Only if you agree to all of mine."

She was kissing him now and laughing at the arrogance creeping back into his words and she thought she loved him most like this. "And what are they?"

"You'll hire a wedding planner so you don't get stressed out. You'll sleep in my bed even before then. And if you want babies, *habibi*, then we'll have babies, even if it means I turn old and decrepit by the time they go to college. But the wed-ding will be in two weeks, Yana. No more. I won't wait, not even for your sisters. And it will happen on the castle grounds."

Yana couldn't help smiling at how he'd tried to make it sound like a request and utterly failed.

"The castle? The whole world will know where you live, then. Because I don't want a hush-hush affair, Nasir. I want a big bang of a wedding. I want the whole world to see you're mine. At least a thousand people."

His eyes widened and he flinched and then recovered fast. "Fine. It will be gloriously extravagant and beautiful and loud, just like you are. And afterward, we'll move to a dif-ferent castle then and we'll have two different ceremonies and you can invite the whole damned world if you want."

He picked her up and carried her to the bedroom and Yana buried her face in his neck, her heart full of joy. "I'm all sweaty," she said, offering a token protest, but Nasir was al-ready unbuttoning his shirt and she pushed his hands away because that was her job.

And then he was inside her and they were laughing and she was still crying a little and she wondered if one could explode out of sheer happiness.

Hours later, in the dark of the night, Yana sat up and looked at the man next to her, deep in sleep. She'd tired him out with her incessant demands, she thought with a smile. Switching on the night lamp, she pulled her clutch open and took out the letter she'd been keeping for just such a moment.

Her heart was full of love and happiness and courage and she wanted to greet her Thaata like this. Settled in her own skin. Finally, accepting all of herself. It was all he'd ever wanted of her.

To my wonderful Yana,

You're funny and brave and loyal and contrary and argumentative and reckless and messy and I know you keep stealing my cigars. But my darling girl, did I ever tell you that you're perfect just as you are?

You're loved so much, Yana, I promise you. Try to love yourself a little, too.

Thaata

Tears filled her eyes and fell down her cheeks, the world blurring and reforming and blurring all over again. Yana pressed the note to her chest, laughing and crying and wishing she could hug her grandfather just one more time.

"Yana?" Alarm crossing his face, Nasir gathered her to him until she was drowning in the familiar scent of him. His mouth was at her temple, tension vibrating through him. "What's wrong, *habibi*? What happened?"

Yana showed him the letter and buried her face in his bare chest. "He loved me all along, Nasir. I gave him such a hard time, and still, he loved me."

"Of course, he did, my love. As I keep telling you, you're perfection indeed and your grandfather was a wise man to see it. As am I," he added with that exaggerated pride in his voice that he knew got her back up. "But if you still don't believe it, I'll tell you every hour. And show you every hour."

His hands on her shoulders, he flipped them until she was straddling him and she could see those sparkling amber eyes fill with such tender reverence that she fell onto his chest.

"I love you, Nasir. And you're right. Let's get married. But I need at least a month, okay? Mira and Nush and Amina will kill me if I don't give us all enough time to look spectacular. Huma could design the dresses. Would you be mad if I wore black?"

And then while he grumbled about being thrown over for her sisters, she sat up, pressed her back to his chest and decided to call her sisters and share her good news.

When they arrived at Mira and Aristos's home a few weeks later with Zara in tow, Nasir made good on his promise to put up with her shenanigans whatever they comprised. He greeted Mira and Nush with that solemn look in his eyes, withstood Aristos's and Caio's inappropriately territorial questions about his feelings for Yana and then picked up her niece and nephew Eira and Eros in the cradle of both arms with a reverent care that only confirmed her own wishes to make their family bigger.

When he looked up and their eyes met and he showed that he understood her most urgent and fervent wish with a raised brow and a hungry look, Yana knew that her life couldn't possibly get any better.

* * * * *

PLAYING THE SICILIAN'S GAME OF REVENGE

LORRAINE HALL

MILLS & BOON

CHAPTER ONE

SAVERINA PARISI HAD spent the past year proving her brother wrong. She loved her oldest brother, but that didn't mean she didn't celebrate this victory.

When she was fresh out of university, *he* had thought she should take a gap year. Spend time thinking about what she really wanted to do with her life. The only thing Saverina had wanted to do was belong in her billionaire brother's company.

She had made him a deal. She would be his assistant, where he could keep an eye on her, for six months. If she did a good job and still wanted to work at Parisi, she could stay. If she hated it, or was terrible at it, she would have to go take that gap year.

Maybe she should have taken the gap year as so many people weren't afforded that luxury, she knew, but all she could think was at this age her brother had been building empires—all to save the family. She wanted to be part of the material thing that *had* saved them from the awful poverty they'd grown up in. She wanted to help Lorenzo in some way that might be a *little* repayment for all he'd given her.

So for six months she had been an *excellent* assistant. Never afraid to take an angry phone call, to soothe ruffled feathers, to tell someone to wait. She had no problem working her way up in her brother's company, any more than she had a problem with people whispering about how she got the job.

The Parisis had come from nothing, so she had no qualms about using all her brother's considerable wealth and influence to do what needed doing. She owed it to Lorenzo and all he'd sacrificed for the family. She owed it to the sister they'd lost who'd never had a chance to succeed.

But mostly, she owed it to herself.

When her six months were up, even exacting Lorenzo couldn't find fault with her effort. She was allowed to stay on. She would remain as Lorenzo's assistant until the end of the year, then decide what direction she wanted to go in within Parisi Enterprises.

She'd planned to dive into the different sides of the business and decide where she wanted to put her talents to use. IT would have been the best fit for the skills she'd learned and honed at university, but it also had a lot of room for error.

Saverina Parisi didn't do error.

Instead, she'd been distracted. And now Teo LaRosa was much more than a distraction. The handsome executive currently zooming up the ranks with no connections whatsoever had gone from an ill-advised date to a full-fledged relationship in the course of a few whirlwind months, even if they were still keeping it a secret.

Which was why she was purposefully ignoring the fluttering butterflies in her stomach and the way her pulse seemed to *pound* in her neck while she waited for Teo to give his assistant the go-ahead for her to be let into his office.

She needed to speak to him briefly for work. Her

brother was on an extended holiday with his growing family, so Saverina's duties took her to Teo's office often. Each and every time, they behaved perfectly professionally...

But all the man needed to do was smile at her to have her knees going a little weak.

It was strange to be this woman. When she had flicked *boys* off at the slightest irritation all through university. She had *never* felt out of control of her own heart, let alone impulses.

Only Teo twisted her into a million knots she didn't understand.

Saverina considered herself incredibly world-wise. She'd lost her mother and sister under tragic circumstances and had been nothing but relieved when her father had drunk himself to death. All before she'd hit her teens. Since then, she'd been raised by a workaholic brother. She thought she knew just about everything—or certainly enough—until Teo had kissed her.

Now the world was different, and she wasn't quite so sure of her place in it. But she knew without a shadow of a doubt that she wanted to be next to Teo.

"Ms. Parisi, Mr. LaRosa will see you now," Teo's stiff, stern assistant offered. Mrs. Caruso had been working for Parisi since its inception. Saverina had watched her be nothing but warm and kind to Teo, to Lorenzo, and a cold wall of ice to literally everyone else.

So she didn't take the woman's cool gaze—all the way through the door—as an offense. Mrs. Caruso was doing her job and wasn't easily swayed by the Parisi last name.

Saverina much preferred that to the type of people who sidled up to her or sucked up to her simply because of her connection to Lorenzo. Besides, she'd learned how to live under scrutiny in a million different ways as the sister to a self-made billionaire, especially when his supposed bad deeds had been splashed across gossip sites years before.

Inside Teo's large office, new in the past month thanks to all his hard work, the man in question sat at his desk, head slightly bowed as he finished typing something on his phone.

His dark hair was swept back, ruthlessly styled always—well, except after hours when she got her hands on it. His shoulders were broad, something that was evident even with him sitting down behind his desk. He glanced up, his dark eyes still half-distracted by whatever had been on his phone.

His face could have been sculpted out of marble. High, sharp cheekbones, an aristocratic nose. All edges and angles except for the sensual promise of his lips. She loved the way that mouth felt against her skin.

She kept waiting for that breathless, foolish feeling to go away in his presence, but it never did. And every time it didn't, it caused her daydreams to get more out of hand. Trusting him enough to let him into her bed—well, *his* bed, since she still lived at Lorenzo's estate—had been one thing, but now she was thinking toward things like *love* and *forever.*

She despaired of herself. But when he smiled at her and got to his feet, all despair was replaced with a warmth and longing so tangled and deep it threatened to make her forget *everything*, when she was a woman who always had her wits about her.

Or had been. Before him.

She cleared her throat and moved forward, taking the seat opposite him at his desk. She looked up at him, fixed her most businesslike expression on her face, and tapped the notebook she'd brought. "Lorenzo has extended his vacation, so we'll have to discuss moving some of next week's meetings further out."

Teo stood there, staring down at her for a moment, before he said anything. A moment when she felt his eyes take a tour of her body—as she'd hoped.

She had dressed knowing she would have a meeting with him today, opting for a skirt over pants and a blouse the color of strawberries that skimmed her figure rather than hid it.

It was all very professional, but it definitely wasn't sexless.

"You have access to my calendar, do you not?" he finally said, that dark, delicious voice of his threatening to turn her insides to absolute *mush*. "You couldn't have just changed the meetings?"

"No," she replied, feigning—perhaps a little exaggeratedly—shock and disdain. "Not everyone is prudent about filling out their schedules, and you know how Lorenzo is about changing things. We need to make certain no more reschedules happen." Which was, of course, ridiculous, because Lorenzo was the one rescheduling in the first place.

But she liked having an excuse to see Teo at work, and it *was* often easier to meet face-to-face to make schedule changes rather than trade endless back-and-forth emails. Or so she told herself.

"We must behave ourselves at work, Saverina," he said, and she supposed he meant it to sound scolding, but the curve of his mouth and the heat in his eyes undermined his words.

"I don't recall suggesting otherwise," she responded brightly. This man had turned her world upside down, sure, but she was still *herself.* Inwardly she might quake a little, but even when Teo got under her skin, under her defenses, she didn't let *him* know that.

She hoped.

Teo LaRosa was not a good man. He knew this every time he put his hands on Saverina Parisi and did not tell her the truth. Every time he watched with too much interest as she crossed her legs in his office.

As he did now. She was a beautiful woman. Smart, and so quick-witted it nearly knocked him off his axis on a daily basis. Even if he had not targeted her, he might have found himself interested in her.

But he had targeted her. From the start. After this job, she was the key to his plan for revenge. Retribution would always be more important than goodness or truth.

No matter the surprise of Saverina Parisi.

"I believe your *eyes* were suggesting otherwise, *bedda,*" he said, enjoying these interludes when they were just alone enough to flirt, arouse, seduce…but at work and unable to go through with any of it. Until tonight.

After.

It had been no hardship wooing her. She was beautiful. Clever. He hadn't even really *planned* to take her to bed. It had just sort of…happened. The chemistry was undeniable.

It was hard, sometimes, to remember that she was a means to an end over someone to be enjoyed. But at the end of the day, he always remembered.

Just as he always remembered what Dante Marino had said to him the first and last time Teo had approached him.

I will crush you if you try.

Teo would never be crushed. He would use everything in his power—this job with Dante's worst enemy, a soon-to-be engagement to said worst enemy's sister—to not just flourish, but to crush Dante first. In every way that would hurt the man's substantial pride and reputation.

Saverina was a tool, but this would not hurt her in any real way. Her beloved brother also hated Dante Marino. So Teo did not consider this *using* her, exactly. They enjoyed each other. And when she married him, he would be a suitable husband. He would provide for her in the lifestyle to which she was accustomed. He would be kind—or his version of kind. He would never drag her name through the mud or embarrass her, and he would certainly never treat her in a way that would make her fear for her life.

That was a Dante Marino specialty, and Teo had promised himself the moment he'd discovered the truth that he would never be anything like his biological father.

Perhaps he could not love Saverina as such a young, beautiful woman deserved to be loved. He had no use for love, for children, for families...all those delicate things that could be lost. But he would give her a good life.

She would never need know that she was a tool or a pawn.

They rearranged the necessary schedules, and Teo fixed them into his computerized calendar himself while simultaneously noting them down in his paper planner as that always helped him remember things without having to look at them again.

He had not risen in the ranks at Parisi Enterprises by being careless or relying on anyone else, even an assistant, though he had one at his disposal now. He had worked hard, kept all his cards close to the vest, and given

Saverina space and time to arrive in his orbit rather than go after her so obviously.

Teo knew how to be patient. He knew how to lay a trap. But most of all, Teo LaRosa knew how to survive.

Now he was on the precipice of *thriving*. As he'd promised his mother he would after she'd made those world-altering deathbed confessions.

He had the unwanted image of his mother, small and frail and wasting away in a hospital bed, lodged in his mind, and needed to erase it. The way he'd been doing for the past two years.

Focus on his revenge.

"That should be all," Saverina said, rising from her seat. He rose too, enjoying the way she didn't quite meet his gaze. He knew if she did, her cheeks would go pink, and she didn't want to leave his office flushed and flustered.

It filled him with an emotion he could not quite identify that he could do both to her.

"I have a meeting tonight," he told her, walking her to his office door. "But I'd like to take you out to dinner tomorrow." Usually he gave her more details, but tomorrow would be special. Tomorrow, all his plans would start to stitch together.

She would say yes to his proposal. He had no doubt. But he also saw the little flash of suspicion in her eyes at this moment. Since she had privy to his schedule and knew the meeting wasn't business, she was suspicious. She likely thought it something as mundane as seeing another woman behind her back.

Teo was not mundane.

He smiled at her in the way that usually had her softening. And it was intoxicating to make this woman soften.

She was young enough he'd thought she'd be naive. Bid-dable.

Saverina was none of those things, but luckily she'd taken to him anyway. And tomorrow, she would agree to be his bride.

But tonight, he had some things to set in motion.

"The meeting is with the lawyer of my mother's es-tate," he explained, even though the explanation was a lie. "It shouldn't take all evening. If you'd like, you can let yourself into my place, and I'll text you when I'm on my way."

His mother had no estate. There were no lawyers. There were only the men he'd hired to get the DNA from Dante required to then test it against his.

Proof was the first step.

Destruction was the second.

Saverina was a tool, a means to an end, but one he was prepared to lie to for the rest of his life, if necessary.

When she smiled up at him, a silent agreement to be waiting for him, he knew that he would succeed.

Thrive, he told himself. Because what was better suc-cess and satisfaction than revenge against the man who'd made his mother's life hell?

Teo would pay any price to win that game.

CHAPTER TWO

SAVERINA WALKED INTO Teo's luxury apartment after being let into the building by the doorman, who knew her by sight now. Since she lived with Lorenzo and his family—because she loved spending time with her niece and nephew, and because Lorenzo's estate was big enough that she could *feel* like she lived on her own if she wanted to—Teo had never met her there.

Maybe she should broach going public with him. She'd been just as keen to keep their relationship a secret at first—both because of their positions at Parisi and because…well, she'd wanted to make sure this was something…real first. Deep down, she knew it was a little silly, but she couldn't stand the thought of *failing* in her brother's and sister-in-law's eyes.

And maybe, in the dark of Teo's lavish apartment, she could admit to herself it wasn't just failing in front of Lorenzo. It was failing…*period*. She didn't think anyone—even her brothers and sisters—knew just how hard she worked to make her entire life look like effortless success.

She felt as if she owed them that. After all they'd sacrificed, so much more terrible things they'd seen during their traumatic childhood, and the loss of her eldest sister—Saverina wanted them all to believe her life was *easy* and everything she wanted. She hoped they thought her spoiled and frivolous and successful. Without a care in the world.

She blew out a breath, frustrated at the serious tone of her thoughts today. Ever since that meeting with Teo this afternoon, she'd been out of sorts. He'd never mentioned this "meeting" of his until today, and she didn't know why it had felt...off.

It wasn't right to be suspicious. He'd given her no reason to be, and he had every right to be a little...strange regarding a meeting with his late mother's estate lawyer. She knew he had no father in the picture, and his mother's death had been a long, drawn-out affair—though he'd never been specific about what illness had taken her life.

Saverina hadn't pressed because she knew not just the pain of losing a mother long before you were ready, but the way the circumstances behind it could twist inside of you. The way it felt better to hold it in some dark place inside rather than discuss it ad nauseam.

Besides, if he was really off doing something that would damage their relationship, would he have invited her to be here tonight? She liked to think *no*. But a little voice inside of her that had never trusted a man outside her family before whispered *maybe*.

Frustrated with herself, she didn't bother with the lights. She walked through the apartment and out to her favorite part of it. The curving balcony that looked out over the city. In the daylight, you could see the Madonie Mountains stretch out beyond the ancient spires and sleek lines of Palermo's architecture. At night, the city sparkled until it all went dark past the beach and in the midst of the Gulf of Palermo.

Saverina stepped into the cool evening and breathed

in deep. She'd long planned to spend her life alone. Happily single. Like Lorenzo. But then he'd gone and gotten himself married and built a family. And if *Lorenzo* could believe in something like love, then surely it existed. Surely it could exist for her too.

No one had warned her it would be *terrifying.* No one had explained to her that she might have a riot of feelings inside her she didn't know how to put to words. And worse, that she might not have any idea how the person on the receiving end felt about all this emotion.

Sex was easy, she'd found, and suddenly in retrospect understood a lot of her classmates better. Love, on the other hand, was complicated.

Did she love Teo? She was almost certain she did. Did he love her? She thought he *acted* as though he did, but he never gave her the words.

Should she tell him first? Part of her knew she should. Silly and old-fashioned—something she refused to be— to wait for him to say it first.

But she supposed that fear of looking like a failure, like something might be *effort*, like she was putting something on the line…well, it wasn't just about her siblings. The idea of telling Teo she loved him to be met with anything other than fall-to-his-knees gratitude left her feeling sick to her stomach.

Luckily she didn't have to dwell on those conflicting thoughts any longer, because she heard the apartment door open. Forcefully. He stepped inside, the anger vibrating off of him.

Until he saw her. He stilled. It was only the flash of a second, that fury in his eyes, but the daughter of an alcoholic father and drug-addicted mother knew how to look for flashes. How to brace for the storms that might come in the aftermath.

She entered the room carefully, aware of every inch of her body. It wasn't that she was afraid of him like she'd been afraid of her father. Teo had never been anything remotely close to violent. But temper and words could hurt, and though he'd never unleashed those on her, she knew the potential existed.

"Is everything okay?" she asked, keeping her voice carefully neutral.

He stared at her for a moment in complete silence, and she watched him put it all away. With a breath and some internal control, all those storms calmed into peace.

She found she didn't believe that peace, even when she wanted to. All she could do was want to help him find the real thing.

The meeting had not gone well, and it delayed his many plans and put Teo in a foul mood. So foul he'd forgotten he'd told Saverina to be here in the first place. He'd forgotten about her entirely, so he was not at all prepared to deal with her as he usually was.

This was what came of being too confident. He'd gotten cocky and made a few missteps this evening. Now he had to deal with the consequences. He knew better, and that twisted his self-directed anger more than the rest.

He hid his fisted hand in a pocket. The role he played for Saverina was not an angry man, not a man with a temper. But it boiled inside of him tonight, and he did not know how to tame it.

Because they had not gotten the necessary DNA. The men he'd hired said it could be another week before they had a chance. A *week*. Now he didn't know if he should postpone the engagement or go forward with it. He didn't know whether to hire new men or stick with the ones who'd promised him careful, clandestine results.

He didn't *know*, and it left him wanting to *rage*. He had to get rid of her without raising any suspicions or concerns, because he did not wish his anger to concern Saverina. And he needed quiet solitude to reconfigure his upended plans.

"Teo?" Saverina said, a little hesitantly. She didn't act *afraid*, but he saw her concern and endeavored to beat back everything roiling inside of him.

"Everything is fine," he said, but his voice was not convincing. Even he knew it sounded hard-edged and mean. "I thought this would be my last meeting with the lawyer, but he informed me we are not quite done yet. I was eager for it to be...over." He didn't see the problem with a little truth mixed in with the lies. That's how he'd won her over, after all. "It's put me in a foul temper."

She let out a little sound, like a sigh, then fully crossed the room to him. "It must be very hard," she murmured, reaching out to him. Ready to soothe.

She did not. If anything, she did the opposite. She was merely a pawn, but she was here in his space, offering kindness, and he did not deserve it. He could not *take* it.

He grabbed her hands before she could wrap her arms around him, stopping her in her tracks. "I will have to apologize and excuse myself. I'm in a terrible mood, and I cannot see putting it to rights tonight. Perhaps you should just go home." He'd tacked on the *perhaps* because if there was anything he fully understood about Saverina, even in this mood, it was that she did not respond well to *demands*.

"Perhaps," she agreed easily, but she just stood there,

his hand enclosing her slim wrists. She did not attempt to pull away or push forward. She simply stood there, a bit like a prisoner.

It clawed at him, along with the sympathy he saw in her eyes. Not pity. Just warmth and kindness and everything she should not give him. Did she have no sense of self-preservation?

"But perhaps," she continued softly, "I should stay, as I am not only here to enjoy your good moods and happiness."

For a moment, he had no words. He could not move at all. He had careful lines, and they all led to *revenge*. Not complications. He had already blurred too many personal lines with her—having her in his bed, discussing his mother's death no matter how superficially, and if he did not get rid of her *now*, he would no doubt cross yet more lines.

Disastrous.

But insisting she leave, drawing that hard line, would also be a problem. She would not care for it, and if he was to go through with his proposal plans, he could not afford to make her angry or upset. If he lost her now…

No. He would not fail this. Perhaps he had to alter his other plans, but he would not alter the ones that made him a Parisi by marriage. *That* would hurt Dante as much as anything else. So *that* was what Teo lived for.

He forced himself to release her, to breathe. He could not will the storms away, but he could steer the ship through them. "I'll just get myself a drink. Would you like something?"

He started to move for his kitchen, but she stopped him, her palm sliding up his chest as she hooked her other arm around his neck.

"How about this instead." She lifted to her toes and pressed her mouth to his. It was sweet, but he only felt fire. A dangerous mix of frustration and want. The offer of something he wanted, after the denial of what he needed.

It made the kiss dangerous. Untethered. So often the chemistry between them surprised him into going further than he'd planned with her, wanting more than he should from her. But this was different, because the lack of control was both about her and what had happened earlier tonight.

He wasn't at his best. He wasn't thinking straight. He could not control that careful line he walked. So the kiss became wild. He held her too tightly, dove into the taste of her too deeply, lost in everything she offered. He had never allowed himself such an utter lack of walls built against his needs.

This would threaten everything.

Still, he couldn't gentle the kiss, his grip on her. Everything in him resisted the knowledge he needed to pull away. Set her back. Wait until he could control himself. Take this step by step. Slake his lust, and hers, knowing he was in control.

Control. Always control.

Finally he managed to wrench his mouth from hers, their breaths mingling in harsh gasps for air. Her mouth swollen, her eyes heavy-lidded and needy. It took every last ounce of willpower to resist.

He had to resist. Didn't he?

"If I take you to bed tonight, Saverina, I do not have it within myself to be gentle," he growled. The best warning he could muster as needs and wants and thwarted desires jangled in his gut like a dangerous concoction set to explode.

Her dark eyes studied him for a long moment before she spoke—not pulling away in the slightest. "Who said you had to be?" She nipped at his lip, teeth scraping just enough to cause a quick, sharp stab of pain underneath a potent arrow of pleasure. "I'm not made of glass," she continued. "I'm certainly not fragile. Is that what you think of me?"

He had no answer for that shocking response, no reason over the roar of his blood, the tightness in his body that she'd put there. He tried to hold on to all his control, all his plans, everything he was.

"Be honest with me, Teo. If that's rough, so be it." Then she pulled his mouth down to hers once more and… if this was what she wanted, if this was all her doing, he wasn't losing his control. Ruining his plans.

He was only enjoying what she offered. He could not give her honesty in all things, but he could give her the honesty of how he wanted her in this moment—because she wanted it too.

So he didn't bother with the buttons of her blouse, simply tore as he ravaged her mouth with his. He tried to pull the shirt off of her, but it got caught there, trapping her arms behind her back, stuck in the sleeves of her shirt.

He pressed her against the wall, needing something he could not articulate, could not find. He pulled back from her mouth, but there was no anxiety in her gaze, no tightness in her shoulders. She didn't shake her head or warn him off. She met his gaze, direct, intense.

"Well, don't stop," she murmured.

So perfect, boldness and fire at odds with the delicate form of her. He kissed her once more, her mouth, her cheek, her neck. Then went ahead and used his teeth, scraped down the slim, elegant curve of her neck. Her sigh was a shudder as he jerked her skirt up.

Need was a molten river. There was no finesse. Just a race to be one. To chase all of these tangles inside of them to some precipice that felt, in the moment, as if it might solve it all.

He didn't bother to remove her undergarments, or any more of his clothes. He simply freed himself, moved her underwear out of the way and slid home. When he lifted her, she wrapped her legs around him, and in one thrust she came apart there in his arms, shaking and shuddering, his name on her lips.

It was wrong, and yet it felt as right as anything ever had. The soft give of her—fire for fire. Turning all this rage into something not so sharp, not so all-encompassing. Her hands in his hair, her body bowing to meet every desperate thrust.

"More," she demanded of him.

So he gave her more. He took her to that edge, flung her over it until she was weak with it, limp with it. A shuddering mass of everything he could do to her.

Him.

He roared out his release, and in the aftermath of it all, he knew he'd solved nothing. And yet he felt as though he'd solved it all.

CHAPTER THREE

SAVERINA HAD NEVER spent the night at Teo's place before. Though they often spent time here, in his bed, she usually she made her excuses somewhere near midnight, half hoping he'd ask her to stay, but he never did.

Last night, though, they'd worn each other out—over and deliciously over—and she'd dozed off before she could make her customary offer. So this morning she woke up tucked next to him, warm and sated and…happy.

It was a step, surely. Instead of shuttling her away, he'd let himself feel his feelings *with* her. That had to mean something. Something positive. She certainly felt *positive* this morning. Blissfully, pleasurably used and spent and worshipped.

She sighed into the memory, snuggled closer to his warm form. But he was a bit like a very hard, immovable furnace. Maybe he was still asleep, but she got the feeling he was awake. Lying there next to her. Making no effort to pull her close, to drop a kiss to her forehead, to do anything.

Almost as if…he didn't want her here. Almost as if last night was different for him than it was for her, no matter how many times they'd happily destroyed each other.

Saverina kept her breathing carefully even as anxiety began to creep in. He could have *told* her to go. He could have done a lot of things. So she wasn't going to cata-strophize. She was going to open her eyes and be *happy*.

When she did, she noted he was in fact lying there wide awake. Staring at her. He had an expression on his face that reminded her of last night. Not angry, but all those things he put over the anger to hide them.

Happiness drained away quite quickly, anxiety seeping in easily, but she was a woman with pride. She did not let anything show in her expression, she hoped. She even smiled. "I'm sorry. I must have fallen asleep."

She made a move to roll away when he said nothing, but he held her there. So she could not make a casual slide out of bed and far away. She steeled herself to look over her shoulder and raise an eyebrow at him. Cool, regal, *sophisticated*. God, she hoped.

His gaze was as impenetrable as ever, but he made no move to let her go. Or to explain himself. Saverina, usually quick with a quip or *something* scathing, found herself...unable to find her voice. Everything felt too tenuous, like if she spoke or breathed or moved, it would all break and crash apart.

Maybe she should let it, but she didn't *want* to. She wanted him to love her. Plain and simple. And she had never thought herself much like her mother, never understood her mother's destructive need to earn approval from a husband who was never going to give it.

Now, terrifyingly, Saverina thought she understood. But before she could do anything about it, Teo took in a deep breath, released her and got out of bed. "Do not go anywhere." Then he pulled on pants and strode out of the room, storms in his eyes.

He didn't seem angry as he had last night, but there was none of his usual smile or charms or easy way. Something was bothering him, eating at him, and it wasn't just the lawyer issue of last night. She was sure something darker simmered underneath *that* frustration. Which wasn't about her or wanting him to love her.

While he was gone, Saverina sat up in the bed, pulling the sheet around her as she was pretty sure all her clothes were out in the living room.

She didn't know what she was staying put for, what he was doing, but she didn't think she wanted to be completely uncovered to deal with it.

When he returned to the room, he was exactly the same. His pants were not fastened, he'd pulled on no shirt. His hair was wild.

From her hands.

There was *some* satisfaction in that as he approached the bed. She worked very hard to keep her cool expression in place, to give absolutely no hint of the way her heart was pounding in her chest or nerves had flooded every inch of her.

What *was* this? Was he…? Surely he wasn't going to break up with her while she sat here *naked* in his bed? The very thought had twin types of feelings rushing through her. Fear and pain and sadness so deep it threatened to make her cry.

And a roiling, dark, violent anger, the vicious temper handed down by her father that she worked very hard to keep on a leash.

Nevertheless, if he broke her heart right now, she'd *eviscerate* him, and she refused to feel an ounce of guilt over it. Sometimes fury *was* the answer. She just had to be careful about when that was and who it was aimed at.

But before she could say anything, tell him *all* that he'd be missing if he walked away from her, he knelt right next to the bed. This was strange enough, but then he held out his hand. He held a small box.

A jewelry box.

That pounding heart in her chest dropped straight down to her stomach, and she felt lightheaded, like all of her muscles had suddenly gone to jelly.

"Marry me," he said. Stern and earnest.

Saverina could only stare. He had a ring. Two simple words. *Marry me*. She thought she should want to jump at the chance, scream yes and throw herself at him. And part of her did, just as part of her was in the tears threatening to fall over.

Marry meant commitment. A life together. And she loved him, so much, she could admit to herself *now*. She could see wonderful and happy years stretched out together, making a family, just like so many of her siblings were doing.

But she didn't speak because something was…missing. It took her a moment to understand why it all felt a little…hollow, even with a symphony of other emotions running through her.

He offered no declarations of love. No promises of a future. Nothing soft at all. She didn't need over-the-top gestures, but was it wrong to want more than a demand to stay put, then a statement and a ring?

She didn't like being commanded, and she didn't like the nearly emotionless way this was all going down. A marriage proposal should be…about all that future they would make together. All the feelings that had led him here.

Shouldn't it?

She *wanted* to say yes. She *wanted* to marry him. To throw herself into all they were, but could she do that when he'd never once said he loved her? When no one around them even knew they were together? Was this leaping too far ahead, too quickly?

Her brain whirled in circles and still he just knelt there, ring outstretched, waiting for her answer like they had all the time in the world.

She looked into his dark eyes, but they gave nothing away. Like there was nothing inside. Like this was a business transaction. He wasn't nervous or excited or felled by love or even lust.

But last night hadn't been devoid of *feelings*. It had been full of them. Waking up to him meant something, it *had* to. And *she* loved him. He clearly cared for her or he wouldn't be proposing marriage. This was not her mother's experience. Saverina was too strong for all that.

So maybe she didn't *need* the words. Maybe, if she loved him and wanted to marry him and he was asking, the only thing to do was say yes. To take what she wanted.

Unless you're setting yourself up for unmitigated failure.

Saverina did not respond. She sat there, naked in his bed with the sheet wrapped around her. Tempting and beautiful and resolutely *silent*.

When he was altering his plans. All because he'd woken up to her gently asleep next to him like… He shook away the strange sensation he'd had with her tucked up against him, breathing quietly.

He'd thought to himself that she *would* be his bride, one way or another, so why wait any longer? Why not propose right now? Insist upon it after last night? Surely she'd fling herself headfirst into it the same way she'd flung into his anger—turning it into something else entirely. Renewal.

But she sat there now and said *nothing*. Gave away nothing. Frustration and anger started to mix with some other emotion he refused to acknowledge. Was this just another thing that would go wrong? Another wrench in his climb for revenge?

He wouldn't allow it.

"It is a yes-or-no question, *bedda*," he said, and was quite happy with how smooth his voice came out sounding. Instead of as rough and frustrated as he felt.

She looked up from the ring, eyes cool but oddly bright like there might be tears in them. And something too close to fear for comfort. "It wasn't a question at all, Teo," she said in that crisp way of hers—a tone she usually only used at work. "It was a statement."

He smiled in spite of himself. Perhaps all his plans weren't ash after all. Perhaps Saverina with her cool command and insistence on being *asked* could be the shining star that saved it all. Before he had met her, he'd been so sure she would be weak-willed and naive, and only now, with so many of his plans within reach, did he realize that wouldn't do at all.

He needed her strength. Her poise. Even that little flash of temper he saw sometimes. She would be able to handle all that came with aplomb. Because she was perfect.

And so was his plan.

"Ah, my little *principessa* does not like a statement. *Scusa*."

She got all prim-looking then, chin in the air, looking down her nose at him.

"So regal," he murmured, getting up off his knees because he'd be damned if he was going to grovel. He moved onto the bed next to her, ring still outstretched. He let the hand closest to her slide down her shoulder, over her elbow and to her hand, which he took in his while he worked to make sure he sounded…whatever way a man was supposed to sound when he did something as foolish as propose.

Gentle and besotted or some such. He lifted her hand to his mouth, pressed a kiss to her palm. "*Will* you marry me, Saverina?" he asked, infusing as much warmth into the *question* as he could manage.

She sucked in a breath, and for a moment, her expression went open, vulnerable. If he looked too deep, he saw a longing that had a twist of guilt vising his lungs. Which wouldn't do.

Thankfully, she blinked it away quickly, and then her lips slowly began to curve. She cleared her throat before she spoke. "Now, that's a question I think I can answer." She looked down at the box. The ring was flashy, expensive, and he'd thought it suited her personality the moment he'd seen it. She was not a shy woman, not afraid of demanding the attention of an entire room.

All those flashes of vulnerability and fear were figments of his imagination. Or his guilt. *This* was her. She would say yes, and he, in return, would ensure she had the best. He would treat her well. It did not need to be love or real to work. To be fair enough.

She smiled at him, all bright and far too…hopeful to land in him well. "Yes," she said, her voice little more than a whisper. "I'll marry you, Teo."

That vise on his lungs was back, but he ignored it. He was an expert at ignoring those unwanted, unwieldy feelings. Maybe it was dangerous to have them around Saverina, but he knew what he was about. He knew his goal.

So he pulled her forward, pressed his mouth to hers. And refused to sink into the soft promise of her. Because he had work to do. He pulled away. "We really shouldn't be late to work. Particularly both of us."

She glanced over at the clock, then waved it away. "I've got about ten minutes left to bask." She held the ring up and let it sparkle in the light of the room. She settled in against him, like casual intimacy would be a part of their future, when he had no plans for that to be the case.

He should stop this.

He did not get up.

"We haven't even told my family or *anyone* we're dating," she said with half a laugh. "How am I going to explain this?"

"We don't have to tell them about the engagement straightaway." He had a timetable for when they needed to announce it by, but last night had given him more time on that score.

See? Not a mistake, not a failure, not even a misstep. His revenge would not be thwarted, because he had promised to enact it. Nothing would stop him. Not even a few setbacks. They would end up, always, working in his favor. One way or another.

Saverina laughed again, leaning her head against his shoulder, still admiring her ring. "I kind of love the idea of springing it on them with no warning, but Lorenzo and Brianna are away, and I'll want to get as many of them home as I can to tell them in person. So we'll keep it under wraps for now." She moved the ring from one finger to another so that it no longer denoted engagement. She stared at it for a moment, then looked up at him.

Teo had to swallow against the ocean of hope he saw there in her dark eyes.

"Are you sure about this? That this is what you want? Forever?" she whispered, tears sparkling. So unguarded he felt as though she'd cut him off at the knees. "I'm going to have to insist on forever if we're getting married."

He was not a good man, he reminded himself. Guilt and being cleaved in half did not matter if he got the necessary end result. The revenge he'd promised. The revenge Dante Marino deserved.

"Of course, I am sure."

He would have everything he wanted. Guilt be damned.

CHAPTER FOUR

BEING ENGAGED WAS strange when it was being hidden, because it was supposed to be something momentous, or so Saverina had always assumed. But nothing in her life had *really* changed. Even if she scanned wedding dress websites on her lunch break, or found herself thinking about cakes, flowers, color schemes, it was all internal.

Everything external remained the same. She'd even spent the past three nights at home rather than at Teo's after having dinner with him and enjoying his bed.

Which didn't bother her—she was refusing to let it bother her. She'd been the one to want to keep the relationship a secret, and now that meant the engagement had to be. She couldn't bear the thought of Lorenzo hearing about it from someone else. Maybe he was her older brother, but he'd also been the closest to a real father figure she'd ever had. And she wasn't fully sure how he'd take this.

He liked Teo—as an employee. He *never* liked secrets. So she would have to address this all…very carefully. Once he was back from his well-deserved holiday.

Teo respecting that, keeping this a secret with absolutely no pressure to do otherwise, was just another sign of the way he cared for her. Maybe she'd spent too much time the past few days fretting about why he'd never once uttered the words *I love you*, but she was too much of a coward to say them either, so maybe that was her fault.

Some people were bad with words, she told herself, night after night on her way home. She'd never considered Teo one of them, but…maybe it was deeper. Something to do with his mother, his childhood, some hidden trauma he'd never let her in on.

It didn't matter. Him saying the words didn't matter if he wanted to *marry* her. That was the same as love.

Wasn't it?

She thought about asking her sister-in-law when Lorenzo and Brianna called from their babymoon to check in, because Brianna obviously had experience with difficult men allergic to feelings. But she was too afraid of what Brianna might say. Like, *No, Saverina, he does not love you if he cannot say it.*

Or what Brianna might tell Lorenzo, Teo's *boss*.

She wasn't about to worry her other brothers or sisters over the conundrum as she much preferred everyone to think of her always in the driver's seat. She was on her own—the way she always was, because *she* chose it.

Besides, Brianna had once told her love was work, not a fairy tale. So Saverina supposed that's all this was. The work Brianna had been talking about.

She decided to walk down to the sandwich shop for lunch, hoping the exercise would clear her head. Maybe it wouldn't be clear until she could tell her family. Maybe secrecy—which she'd rather enjoyed up to this point—was now more weight than fun.

Before she ordered her sandwich, she began to paw through her purse and realized she didn't have her wallet. She tried to think of the last time she'd had it. She'd bought dessert on the way to Teo's last night, wanting to surprise him with his favorite cannoli.

She must have left the wallet at Teo's when she set the dessert down. She wasn't usually so careless, but she recalled—with heat flaming into her cheeks—he'd arrived a few minutes after her, and she'd soon forgotten about both the wallet *and* her dessert surprise.

They'd made a dessert all their own.

She glanced at her watch. If she took a taxi, she could make it to Teo's, grab her wallet, and be back in her office before her lunch break was up. And hopefully cool the heat in her cheeks at the memory of last night's activities.

She smiled to herself as she hailed a taxi and gave the driver Teo's building's address.

See. Things were *good*. No need to feel confused. She should focus on the happiness, the excitement. Because she felt those too.

Of course, she felt a little…uncomfortable going to Teo's apartment without his permission. But she had a key. She often was there without him if he was running late. It was not *unheard* of.

And she refused to ask her *fiancé* for permission to enter his place and look for *her* wallet. If he needed that, well, they were going to have a discussion about what it meant to join their lives together.

Shouldn't you have done that already?

She shoved that annoying little thought out of her head and pulled out her phone. She knew he was in a meeting, so she fired off a quick text.

On a search for my wallet. Headed to your apt. Need anything while I'm there?

There. Casual. Informative. Certainly not asking permission. And since he was occupied, he likely wouldn't answer until she was done.

She paid the driver, then walked into Teo's building, waving at the doorman and greeting the elevator attendant politely. They were all paid to be discreet in an apartment building such as this, so they knew her. Knew exactly where she was going. The attendant pushed the button to Teo's floor, and quickly enough, she was letting herself into Teo's apartment.

Feeling a bit like a burglar. Which was *ridiculous*. She marched straight for the kitchen, quickly finding her wallet. She slid it into her purse, and considered grabbing something from his fridge since she now didn't have time for lunch.

But then she heard an odd *ding*. Confused, she moved out of the kitchen and looked around. Surely he hadn't left his phone or laptop behind, but if he had, she could always bring it to him. Maybe they were *both* out of sorts.

Because engagement was a *big* step, a life-changing one. Not because it was the wrong one, but simply because it was *momentous*.

There on the coffee table *was* a laptop. The screen had lit up with the ding. But it wasn't a Parisi computer. It was a personal one she'd never seen before.

None of her business, she told herself…even as she stepped toward the couch. He could, of course, have a laptop she'd never *once* seen him use. Why wouldn't he? She needed to head back before her lunch break ended.

She lowered herself onto the couch. The password window had come up with the *ding*, but in the corner was a banner with the subject and sender of the email that had come through.

Veritas Lab. DNA Sample Received.

She didn't breathe. For a moment, she just read the subject over and over and over. Then she forced herself to suck in air.

He was probably doing one of those silly ancestry tests. He never spoke of family besides his late mother. Maybe he was searching farther afield.

It would make sense.

What didn't make sense was worrying that it was worse. That maybe he had a child out there. Maybe some woman was suing him for paternity. Maybe…

So many *maybes*.

And most of them were perfectly innocent *maybes*, so she should let this go. If it was something bad, he would tell her.

Unless he doesn't.

"You're being foolish," she whispered to herself. Out loud here in Teo's living room.

But that of course did not change the anxiety spiking inside of her.

She knew what would, though.

No one knew about her computer skills, certainly not Teo. Lorenzo knew she had *some* experience because even in university he'd kept up with what classes she was taking, what her grades had been. But he didn't know about her side hacking projects, all the below board things she'd learned off at university because computers were interesting and hacking could be fun.

She had kept quiet about that because she didn't think her family would approve, but also because if they knew her skill level, both Lorenzo and her other brother, Stefano, would pressure her to join the IT department at Parisi.

She didn't want that kind of pressure. The internet security of their entire livelihood? No. Too much room for error. For failing them.

But there was no pressure in seeing if she could get through Teo's private computer security. There was no pressure in seeing what he was keeping from her. There was only the moral issue.

It was wrong to poke through his personal computer. It was wrong to sift through whatever he might be keeping a secret, because he would tell her if it was important. She trusted him.

But if she reversed the situation, and she had *nothing* to hide, she would not care if he sorted through her things. Because secrets were dangerous. Secrets were poison. There had been so many secrets during her childhood—how her mother and sister had supported the family through prostitution, her father's drinking problem, her sister's death and the way Lorenzo had handled *everything*—carefully kept from her because she was the baby.

Too weak. Too delicate. Too whatever.

If Teo had a secret...she had to know. Fair or not, right or not, she *had* to know. So she hit the keystrokes necessary to hack into his system—beyond the password, the security, the files he'd saved encrypted. She set herself a deadline—allowing some time to be late from her lunch, but not so late as to raise eyebrows.

She scanned emails, documents for mentions of DNA. At first, it seemed he was just trying to find out the identity of his father—and though she knew he wasn't in Teo's life, she'd had no idea he didn't even know the man's *identity*.

She began to feel slimy and gross and wrong as she dug. She'd have to confess everything to him and hope he could forgive her for poking into his private—

And then she saw a name that had her entire body turning to ice.

Dante Marino.

Her brother's number one enemy. A man who had spent years trying to ruin Lorenzo—his company, his reputation, his family. Lorenzo mostly brushed it off these days—it was hard to make rumors stick when Lorenzo was so dedicated to his family and was careful with his hiring practices at Parisi.

But there was no way Dante had given up. None of the Parisis thought so, even if Lorenzo was particularly philosophical about the whole thing.

"Let him try to drag me through the mud," Lorenzo had once said. He'd been sitting with Brianna on one side of him. She'd been nursing their new daughter, Gio—his oldest, snug on his lap. *"I have everything I need."*

Saverina tried to keep that sweet, unbothered memory in her mind, but her blood was boiling.

The only conclusion she could draw to finding Dante's name in Teo's personal files was that Dante Marino had sent Teo LaRosa to hurt her family.

Her phone dinged, causing her to jump. Teo had replied to her text.

The only thing needed is you naked in my bed.

She stared at that text. So incongruous to the moment. Twenty minutes ago, it would have sent a bolt of heat through her—and she wasn't immune to the physical reaction of knowing what he could do with such a premise.

But now she had a sneaking suspicion as to *why*. He was connected to Dante somehow. He wanted to hurt her brother somehow, no doubt. *Through* her.

Teo had made her a pawn.

He'd made her a fool.

She signed out of the computer, put it back exactly the way it had been. He'd never know she touched it. He'd never know what she knew.

Because she would not confront him with this. No.

She would make him pay.

Teo was on cloud nine. Dante's DNA had finally been collected and dropped off with the testing site. He would have his proof within the week. Which meant he needed to get Saverina moving along on the relationship front.

He rather liked having her to himself, having everything be a secret so every night together felt like theirs and theirs alone.

But this was not the plan. The plan was revealing to everyone he was Dante's son. An illegitimate son—painting Dante the adulterer, child abandoner, which was bad enough.

But then, to twist the knife, show the Parisi family as his saviors. Lorenzo, the man who'd given him a chance to raise to the lucrative position he was at now. So kind and generous and *such* a family man he'd even allowed Teo to fall in love with his prized sister.

Media channels would eat it up, exaggerate it beyond the telling. Dante would forever be ruined—his traditional, family-friendly, upstanding reputation in tatters. While the Parisis soared.

Teo nearly laughed alone in the elevator. He needn't

have worried last week. Everything was working out just as it should.

Not that he was getting cocky. He wouldn't do that again. Just that he'd enjoy each little step toward success.

For you, Mamma.

The thought of his mother was always sobering, but more than that these past few days, it seemed to twist into his mother *and* Saverina. They weren't much alike, but still he could see, if she'd lived, them enjoying each other's company. Saverina's sharp wit, his mother's kind soul. Saverina would have made her laugh. Mamma would have eased those strange hints of fear he sometimes saw in Saverina's eyes.

But it was of no matter. His mother was dead. Saverina's fears were her own.

And his plan was all that mattered. The elevator stopped at Saverina's floor—because he'd pushed that number. He strode out of the elevator when the doors opened, then stopped short, looked around, as if he hadn't meant to get out on this floor.

This was a farce they'd played a few times. He knew she rather liked it—the secrecy, the sneaking around. Now he hoped someone saw him. Saw a pattern. Began to wonder.

Because they would need to announce this engagement by the end of the month.

He looked down the hall to Saverina's desk, politely smiling at anyone who passed or made eye contact with him. Then he turned back to the elevator—once the doors had closed—and pushed the down button once more.

Like clockwork, Saverina exited her office. He didn't look her way, but in his peripheral vision, he watched her approach.

"Good afternoon, Ms. Parisi," he offered quietly when she came to stand next to him, as if also waiting for the elevator and *only* the elevator.

"Good afternoon," she replied.

When the doors opened, they stepped inside in tandem. He hit the lobby button, then waited for the doors to close before turning his grin on her.

But she did not look at him or sidle closer as she usually did.

Odd.

"Are you going to the charity gala the art society is hosting?" he asked, hoping she would enjoy his new plan. "We should go together. Not as an engaged couple, of course, but start moving the wheels toward the idea that we are indeed a couple."

She didn't say anything. Didn't meet his gaze. There was a frown on her face. The elevator doors would open soon, but still he could not resist, reaching over and brushing a hand over her hair.

"Are you feeling all right, *bedda*?"

She smiled up at him, and it was her normal smile, but something… Something in her eyes was not right. Like a dimming. "Just a migraine. I think I'll go home and lie in a dark room for the night." She looked down at her purse. "I know we had plans, but you don't mind, do you?"

The doors opened, and she stepped out first. He followed, dogged by a strange confusion. "Of course not." It would give him time to work on his timeline, his media contacts. Ensuring his whisper network never pointed back to him as the source, because that was just another way to twist the knife for Dante. Make it look like Teo himself had been willing to keep such a thing secret.

Saverina hadn't answered his question about the gala.

And she strode toward the lobby doors with clear, quick purpose. So quick, he was practically tagging along after her even though his natural stride was much longer than hers.

They did not share goodbye kisses here at the office, but still something about the way she headed for her car without a goodbye or a smile left him feeling…concerned. Was she angry with him for some slight? Women, he supposed, were forever doing that sort of thing.

But before she fully reached her car, she turned and shaded her eyes against the setting sun to look at him.

"Lorenzo asked if I'd join them on the last leg of their trip. The children are wearing Brianna out."

"Do they not have nannies for that kind of thing?"

"I enjoy the children, and it would give me the opportunity to tell them about us. Explain everything so they don't think the engagement is too quick. I'd hate to have Lorenzo disapprove." Again she gave him that smile that was dimmed.

By the migraine, obviously. She was in pain. It made sense. And she was talking of breaking the news of the engagement to the person keeping that news from being spread far and wide, so this was good. Once Lorenzo knew, the plan could move forward. "I hope you have a wonderful time, then. When do you leave?"

"Early tomorrow morning."

This shocked him, and he didn't think he did a very good job of hiding it. Because her smile changed. Sharpened, ever so slightly.

"I'm sorry for the short notice," she said. She lifted a hand, and for a moment he thought she would reach out. Offer something physical with her goodbye.

But she only made an odd waving motion. "I'll text,"

she offered, then turned to her car. She slid into the driver's seat and closed the door behind her. No extra smiles. Nothing.

He found himself watching the car drive away. Unsettled. Frustrated. With the strangest sensation battering his chest and the errant and incomprehensible thought that he'd miss her while she was gone.

CHAPTER FIVE

SAVERINA DID NOT go to meet Lorenzo and Brianna on their vacation. That had never been the plan. Subterfuge was the plan.

Crushing Teo LaRosa was the plan.

She called off work for the week and spent the next few days hacking into Teo's personal and professional emails and systems to gather more information, but she was still mostly left with the fact Teo was DNA testing to see if Dante Marino was his father. And he had befriended quite an array of media professionals over the past year—mostly from anonymous accounts.

She wasn't quite sure how or if these things connected, but they were the only two facts she could be certain of from his digital communication.

She found no evidence Teo and Dante had ever spoken, but she could think of no other reason for a connection to her family's enemy than that Teo was working *against* Parisi. She found no evidence Teo had done anything to hurt Parisi on a professional level, so corporate espionage seemed a bit of a stretch.

After a few days, she accepted she'd scoured every computer avenue—now she had to do some real-life digging. She needed more information before she knew how to proceed. How to crush Teo into tiny, jagged, destroyed bits and wished he'd never even *looked* at her, let alone fooled her.

She'd considered hiring someone to follow him, but she hadn't been able to get over the desire to hear it herself. From his own mouth, whatever he was trying to do to her family. So tonight, she would set out to follow him herself.

Maybe he would recognize her, maybe it would destroy her revenge, but she needed to do this herself.

Her fury wouldn't allow anything else. Besides, she had some experience trying to move through the world without being seen. When she'd been at university and Lorenzo's false misdeeds had been plastered about, she'd wanted to keep a low profile, and she had. All it took, often enough, were baggy clothes, an unflattering hairstyle, and making certain to engage eye contact with no one.

If she failed in this, there would be other ways to get answers, to thwart him, to ruin him. She was an intelligent woman with computer skills and a hefty trust fund and well-paying job. She would use every privilege in her arsenal to eviscerate the man who'd broken her heart.

She waited at the little restaurant patio across from Teo's apartment that evening, picking at a salad and waiting for him to arrive home. He did not have anything on his digital work calendar, but he'd had a little note on his personal one. No time. No date. Just an untitled entry.

She was going to find out what it was.

She had expected to be bored to death, waiting around, but she was so twisted up with anger and a hot, dangerous sense of purpose that watching for his car's arrival felt like watching a movie.

When he finally appeared, sliding out of the slick luxury car and waving off the valet, she felt a surge of too many conflicting emotions to wade through. If he didn't have the valet park his car in the garage, he was planning to come back out and use the car again.

He was so tall, so sure and handsome. It twisted inside of her hard and sharp, like grief, when the only thing she would allow herself was fury.

Besides, why should she grieve a love that was a *lie*?

He disappeared for half an hour, and in those ticking minutes, she pictured walking across the street and slapping him when he came down. Going up to his apartment with sultry smiles and dirty invitations—just to see if she could sway him from his purpose. She pictured herself doing all sorts of things, and every little daydream ended in his embarrassment and begging her forgiveness.

Perhaps if she had not watched her brothers conduct business with cool clarity, she might have indulged in any of those flights of fancy. But that was not how you won.

Clearheaded thought, follow-through, and surety were how you won.

When Teo reappeared, she paid her bill by leaving cash on the table and moved swiftly to her own car—well, Brianna's car, which she was borrowing. When Teo pulled out of his parking spot, she did so as well. She wondered if he'd be paranoid enough to notice Brianna's run-of-the-mill "mom car" tailing him.

She wasn't sure she cared. Part of her almost *hoped* he noticed. Confronted her. Part of her was dying to cause a scene.

But they drove through the glitzy, nicer parts of Palermo to the rougher back alleys. To a hole-in-the-wall bar she'd never been to. It was hard to picture Teo spending much time in this rough establishment either, but then again, she didn't know him.

He was a *liar*. A fake. A rat.

She waited in her car for a good ten minutes after Teo went inside before she got out of her car, and then took time to lock her car, check her reflection in the window, waste time until she saw a group of large men approach the door. She hurried her steps so that she could enter the bar, hidden behind their bulky forms.

Inside, she immediately spotted Teo even though the room was dark. He was sitting at a table in the corner, eyes on the door. But if he could see her through the crowd of men, his eyes passed right over her—likely thanks to the baggy clothes and her hair back in a braid that hid her usual soft waves—which was why she never wore it like this.

She kept her body as much behind larger men as possible as she worked her way through the crowd. She had a target. A booth right behind Teo's table. She would have to walk by him—so close he could reach out and touch her—but his gaze was so hard on the door that she decided she could take the risk.

She edged around the table, keeping her face tilted away, and calmly slid into the booth close enough to be in earshot.

He didn't even glance her way. His gaze never left the door. He was clearly waiting for someone very specific.

She let out a slow breath and stared hard at the wall. Her back was to him now, so she could not see him. Could not do anything but sit here and wait and hope that when his meeting partner came, she would be able to hear their conversation over the buzz of voices and the steady thrumming bass of the music playing over the speakers.

"You sure you want to wait for your friend?" a woman's voice asked. Saverina didn't twist in her seat, but she carefully angled her head so she could see Teo's table out of the corner of her eye.

A waitress was leaning over, trying to entice Teo to order something. Flirtatiously. Saverina watched, stomach twisting in knots, expecting him to smile, flirt, or charm her right back.

He did not. He ordered two drinks—clearly to get the waitress to leave him be—his gaze never leaving that door.

It didn't matter whether he was flirting back or not, so she would *not* be relieved. They would never, ever be together now. He could entertain himself with as many women as he pleased.

And damn her breaking heart for throbbing there in her chest like a weak virginal *youth* at the thought.

She sucked in a breath, focused harder on the wall, and reminded herself what all this was for. For her brother. For the Parisi name. For *herself.*

"You're late." Teo's voice, low and cutting.

Saverina dared a look over at the table. A large man sat across from Teo now.

"Here are the results." The man slid a large envelope across the table. "They are what you hoped. How do you want me to proceed?"

She watched his profile as Teo took the envelope. He sucked in a breath, but no real emotion showed on his face. Knowing him made it clear to her that whatever was in the envelope was of the utmost importance to him.

"I'll deliver copies of this report to you when we're ready to go public. You'll distribute it to your contacts to go far and wide. It cannot get back to me."

"It won't."

"Then let's raise our glasses in a toast," Teo murmured.

"To the destruction of Dante Marino." Teo's smile was cutting and harsh. His eyes glittered with that revenge he'd spoken of.

Not against Lorenzo and her family, but against her own enemy.

Saverina looked back at the wall, trying to understand...any of this. He wanted to destroy Dante. Who was...his father, apparently, because getting revenge on a man whose DNA did *not* match didn't make sense. So, this was about his parentage? He was Dante's illegitimate son, and wanted some kind of revenge over that?

Perhaps she should be relieved, but she couldn't quite get there. Why was he tricking her when they wanted the same thing? Surely he knew she'd be more than happy to see Dante crushed. Nothing about this fit any of the scenarios she'd come up with in her mind, and she had *no* idea how to proceed.

Leave, and regroup. That was what she had to do. But before she could even think about getting up, someone slid into the booth across from her.

Teo.

She could only stare at him. No words, no excuses, no *thoughts* formed.

"I hope you heard all of that, *bedda*," he murmured silkily. "I'd hate to have to go over it again."

Teo would give her credit. Saverina didn't wilt when he slid into the booth across from her. She didn't look the least bit abashed. She looked coolly furious once she got over her shock.

And beautiful.

He couldn't think about that just yet. Too many things were problematic now. He wished he'd noticed her just a few minutes earlier, but he'd already made his toast when he'd caught sight of her profile in the booth.

How she'd gotten there, what she was doing, he did not yet now. But he knew he had to play his cards very carefully.

His revenge would not be thwarted by her now.

She met his gaze, chin up and regal. All icy princess. Something painful twisted in his chest. He wanted to reach out. Touch the soft velvet skin of her cheek. Press his mouth to hers. He hadn't tasted her in days, and no matter how Dante and revenge had absorbed his every waking hour, he hadn't been able to put her out of his mind.

Unacceptable.

"I heard enough, I think, but not enough to understand quite what this is."

"I guess that's something we have in common this evening, because I cannot fathom why you are here, Saverina. When you told me you were away." When she should know nothing about his connection to Dante.

For a moment, she only held his gaze with a blank one of her own. "I suppose I never told you how much I abhor secrets, Teo. How I would go to any lengths to find the truth when I suspect I or my family might be in danger."

"I pose no threat to your family, Saverina."

"Anyone who connects to Dante Marino is a threat to my family, and apparently you have quite the connection."

He could not fathom how she had found this out, but he gave none of his surprise away. He thought he should be furious, but there was a different sensation plaguing him, and he did not understand it.

A kind of relief laced with pride. She knew, so he did not have to keep twisting the lies and secrets around someone who was now in so much of his life. She knew, because she was keen and smart and strong enough to suss out any threat.

But he was no threat.

"My revenge on Dante has nothing to do with our relationship—"

"Don't." And she sounded just hurt enough under the icy fury that he could not continue the lie he'd always meant to tell her if she began to have suspicions about his motives. "Perhaps I don't understand what you're after, or why you'd use me to get it, but I know you were using me. It is not *coincidence*. Your job at Parisi. Your engagement to me."

"You don't know that."

"I do. Because you don't love me, Teo. That is very obvious."

"Then why did you agree to marry me?"

For a moment, he saw those vulnerable hurts of hers he was forever pretending weren't there because they so quickly disappeared. Tonight, she simply looked down. "I thought… I came here tonight because I thought your connection to Dante was about hurting my family."

"I have no wish to hurt your family, Saverina." Not that he had any plans to *protect* them, either. It just happened they had the same enemy, so they could all give each other things they wanted.

She nodded. "Well, that is a relief. But you're going to have to explain to me what your plans *are*, or I am going to have to make some of my own."

"Like what?"

She met his gaze, and he did not wish to recognize any of the feelings swirling in there. So he did not.

Then her gaze dropped to her hand. She pulled the ring he'd given her off and pushed it across the table toward him.

He stopped her forward movement with his hand over hers. "Let us not be hasty," he murmured. "Why don't we return home and—"

"Do you think I would marry you now?" she asked. "You must be delusional. Your best option at this juncture is to convince me not to tell Lorenzo everything I know, and so far you are failing in that."

Temper poked, Teo smiled and leaned back in his booth. He left her hand and his ring right there at the center of the table as he looked down at her with as much disdain as he could muster. "Ah, yes, run home to Daddy, is it?"

Everything in her expression sharpened—anger, disgust, hate. He welcomed them all. Better than hurts and vulnerabilities that poked at things he dared not look directly at.

"You are an adult, Saverina," he said, keeping all the scathing in his tone. "Behave as one. Think this through. Dante has hurt your family. Now, I can get my revenge on him alone, for just myself. I have no issues doing such. But won't it be better, more satisfying, if we work together to destroy him? Once and for all."

He thought she might look shamed or hurt, but she leaned back in the booth as he did. His ring—which likely cost more than everything in this bar—sat on the sticky table between them.

She raised a regal eyebrow, crossed her arms over her chest. He should have known she would not be so easy to mold. "You have me confused with someone else, Teo." Then she slid out of the booth as if she owned this entire low-end bar and sauntered out of the establishment, with more than a few eyes watching the sway of her hips as she left.

CHAPTER SIX

SAVERINA BLINKED BACK tears as best she could. The evening outside the bar was cool and dark, and she wanted nothing more than to make it to the car and sob all the way home.

Everything was a lie. She'd known this for days now, but something about having to deal with Teo, something about it being not quite the betrayal she had thought it was, made all her defenses crumble.

But she heard footsteps behind her, and she would be damned if she would cry in front of this scheming, lying, horrible *bastard*. She sucked in a breath and blew it out hard, then turned to face him. She shook her hair back, looked up into his dark flashing eyes.

His expression was one she'd never seen before—except that night he'd come home angry. The night they'd...

She could not think about all the ways she'd let this man into her heart.

"I am not through with you, Saverina," he growled.

"What a shame for you." She jerked her car door open, unsurprised when he grabbed it and blocked her entrance. She didn't rage—though she wanted to. She met his fire with ice. "I'm not sure it would be a good look if I called the police, Teo. A harassment charge would certainly complicate your plans, I would think. Or is this a bit like father like son?"

It landed like a blow, as she'd hoped, and half feared would not. He was so smooth, so totally in charge, even when she'd clearly uncovered a secret he hadn't wanted uncovered. But *that* comment hit where it hurt. It flashed in his eyes, in the way his mouth went slack for just a moment.

She curled her hands into fists and assured herself it was *satisfaction* she felt at the arrested look on his face.

Quickly smoothed away.

"I could turn this on you, *bedda*. I could make things equally as uncomfortable for Parisi as I do for Marino."

A threat? She wanted to *laugh*. "And I could *destroy* you, and your sad little plan for revenge," she returned, unable to hold on to her ice. She *seethed*.

For a moment, they only stared at each other in the dim, unflattering parking lot light.

"I see we are at an impasse," he finally said. Cool and in control, which made her want to rage. But she held on to the tiny thread of composure she had left.

"Why don't we talk this through somewhere less public and more comfortable?" he said, as if this were a reasonable suggestion. As if they were in a boardroom. As if he was her *boss*.

"Follow me back to—"

"I will never step foot in your apartment again." Maybe it was showing her hand too much, but she knew he had the upper hand if they went back to his place. She wanted to believe herself immune, but if she went back to where they'd created far too many memories together, she was afraid she'd soften—to him, to his plan, to the chemistry between them.

She refused. But she couldn't ignore the fact his plan of destroying Dante Marino was...intriguing. Especially if it helped Parisi. Especially if Lorenzo never knew. She should likely send Teo off right now, but if there was a chance she could cut Dante Marino off at the knees... "If you simply must continue this fool's errand, then you can meet me at my house."

"Your brother's house."

She didn't even falter. "Yes, indeed."

"If I am seen at Lorenzo's home with you, people will talk. And they will talk in a direction that helps *my* plans."

"How shortsighted of you to think so," she returned. "You can either meet me there or not." She shrugged, jerked the car door out of his grip and slid into the driver's seat. She half expected him to try to keep her from closing the door, but he didn't.

Perhaps her threat to call the police was enough to keep him in line, but she doubted it. As she drove back the Parisi estate, she noted Teo followed in his own car very closely.

When she pulled through the gates, she clicked the button to keep them open for Teo's car, then drove around the twisting lane toward the garden—rather than the main house or her private entrance in the back.

No one would see his car here, and even if they did, they would not tell anyone except maybe Lorenzo. She wanted to keep as much of this from Lorenzo as possible, but if she had to tell her brother a version of events, she would.

She parked and slid out of the car. The moon and stars shone above. The smell of earth and flowers in the cool night air should have made this all a very romantic setting. She almost regretted never sneaking Teo in here back when...

When what? When he'd been lying to her? Talking her into his bed even though he had no feelings for her whatsoever? She had to breathe through her fury to keep herself from slamming her car door. Instead, she closed it quietly and moved over to the little bench among the plants and statuary.

Teo followed suit, though he did not sit with her on the bench—smart man. He stood before her, hands in his pockets, studying her like he'd never seen her before.

"I'll admit, the idea of destroying Dante Marino has me intrigued," she said, copying what she'd always called Lorenzo's *boardroom* voice. Not complimentarily, of course. Usually she was poking fun at him.

But the cold, detached way her brother spoke in business meetings would certainly help her conduct *this* one. Because that was all it was now. Business. The business of revenge.

"I cannot understand how tricking me into an engagement is part of such a plot, though. So why don't you enlighten me?" She looked up at him, hoping all the aching hurts swirling inside of her were hidden behind the wall of fury.

She half expected him to argue with her use of the word *tricking*. When he did not, she had to admit to herself that she'd *hoped* he'd argue with the word. It hurt that he didn't. That he launched into an explanation instead.

"I have spent the years since my mother's death perfecting my plan. And it *is* perfect. This is what we will do." He spoke as if there was no question that she would hop into this *we*. But he kept on, so clearly impassioned she couldn't even interrupt to correct him.

"We will announce our engagement. We will enjoy *that* attention for a short period of time before the rest begins to leak. People digging into my past. Into who I am. And slowly but surely, an image of a Dante Marino will emerge. A new image. A man who refused to acknowledge the son he created after coercing an employee. Who threatened her with his considerable power and privilege to never reveal a thing. He did everything he claims to stand against. Not just in the past, but now, when he refused to even see me."

"So… I'm just a plant to get people interested in you, Teo?" Had she really expected this to not make her feel worse and worse? Had she really expected this to *ease* things? She was a fool, but she'd never let him know she thought so. "How sad for you that you are that boring without me."

He didn't even spare her a quelling glance. "Expand your imagination, Saverina. While people are digging into my past—regardless of *you* and having everything to do with our impending union—it will be made quite clear through my many media contacts that while Dante ignored me, threatened my mother, made our lives hell— Parisi welcomed me with open arms. A job. A family. So much so that when I fell in love with the youngest Parisi, nothing but approval, welcoming, and acceptance was given to me. And everyone, finally, will see that Parisi is everything Marino isn't."

Too many emotions battered her then. She couldn't believe a heart could feel this bruised over someone she'd been involved with for a short time. How stupid she'd been to let him in there in the first place. How stupid she was to let her next words slip out. "That is the first time you've used that word. *Love.*"

He had no quick response to that. She didn't dare look at him, too afraid she would feel his pity. Too afraid this failure would swallow her whole. Because it was a failure on her part. To believe a liar. To fall in love with one.

Her chest got tight, not just in pain but in that telltale sign she was heading for a panic attack. If anyone ever found out she'd been so fooled, if her siblings found out she'd been so *stupid*. That she'd failed so spectacularly. That...

She took in a breath through her nose, counted to three. She used all the tools her university therapist had taught her for dealing with her panic. She would not lose her composure in front of *this* man.

"Why do you care about Parisi?" she managed to ask him, though she felt her tight throat and heard the strangled way she spoke a bit like she was floating up above herself.

"Because Dante cares. And wishes to see your family destroyed. Destroying him isn't enough for what he did to my mother. I will see his enemies lauded, his business ruined and handed over to his rival, while his reputation is ruined beyond the telling. I want everyone he hates dancing on the grave of the Marino name."

She breathed deep a few more times, stemming the tide. For now. It made a strange kind of sense, she supposed. How did you hurt someone irreparably? Not just take away everything he held dear—for Dante, his reputation—but also give his enemies everything he wanted. That positive media attention. That lauding. Any clients Marino lost would go to Parisi, no doubt.

The engagement to Teo wouldn't be real anymore—not that it ever had been, but now it would be an act for her as well as him. Could she go through with it? Was

she that good an actress? Could she set her curdled feelings about Teo aside if it meant Dante Marino would get
what he deserved? Perhaps he had not hurt Lorenzo the
way he'd hurt Teo's mother, but he had tried to ruin Lorenzo's reputation, Lorenzo's business. All because Lorenzo had stood up to him.

Saverina breathed in through her nose, out through her
mouth. Counted. Calmed. She didn't know if she could
do this, but she knew she wanted to try. But first, she
had to know… "Tell me one thing. What was the plan if
I never found out?"

Teo had lies. Contingency plans for everything that was
happening. Yet looking at her now, he struggled to voice
them. He realized he wasn't quite as sure as he once had
been that she would believe them.

He knew she was quick and sharp, but he supposed
he'd still underestimated just *how* much. He wanted to
find it annoying. A speed bump. But mostly he was im-
pressed.

And other things he didn't want to acknowledge. Other
things that reminded him too much of the days around
his mother's death. Helplessness and failure and grief.

No, those feelings didn't belong here. "There was no
plan. I would have been a husband to you. A good one at
that. We would have had a perfectly nice life together. I
have no need for a real marriage, no belief in things like
love. So why not have it be a business arrangement?"

"While *I* thought it was love?"

He would not touch that question with a ten-foot pole.
"There is chemistry between us, Saverina."

"Ah. A woman in your bed at your disposal was one

of the things that wasn't a *lie* in this whole debacle. How comforting."

"I could have many a woman at my disposal should I so choose, *bedda*."

"But you chose me. For my last name. This is not quite the compliment you seem to think it is."

He scowled because she was taking this off the rails. While *he* was being reasonable and rational. "Regardless of how you feel on the matter, this was the plan. This *is* the plan. And you are here listening to it because you want to see Dante suffer almost as much as I do."

She frowned a little, but she did not argue. Because she wanted this too. Maybe he'd have preferred her to be in the dark. Maybe that would have been easier. It certainly would have given him more control over the situation, but nothing needed to change just because she knew. He still had his plan. He still had her.

Now he just needed his revenge.

He held out the ring she'd left on the table. "Things do not need to change, Saverina. We want the same things. It only involves a few well-placed pretends, and while we pretend, I can offer you anything you want."

She let out one of those odd long breaths, like a swimmer gasping for air. Yet she was perfectly calm and in control when she spoke. "No, you can't."

"Name it."

"Love, Teo. I want to marry someone I *love*. Like Lorenzo and Brianna love each other. They make each other happy. They make each other *better*."

He turned away from her then. His only experience with love was that it hurt. That it meant loss—of control, of hope. He had loved his mother—and to what end? There had been nothing he could do to stop Dante from ruining her life. Nothing he could do to stop cancer from ending her life. Love did not matter. It was the most inconsequential thing on the planet.

"Love is what I want, and that is what you cannot give," she said.

Before he could think of anything to say to that ridiculousness, she stood and moved around so they were facing each other once again. She reached out, and he nearly backed away. He did not want to feel the soft brush of her comforting touch in this disorienting moment with the word *love* echoing about.

But she only uncurled his clenched fingers and took the ring from his hand. "But I also want to see Dante suffer for what he's done to Lorenzo. And since Lorenzo won't wage this war himself, I will. We will fake this engagement, Teo. I will play along with your plans. But I will not marry you. Once we have destroyed Dante, we will dissolve the engagement in a way that does not reflect poorly on either of us. That is the offer I'll extend to you. It's the only one I will, and you must decide now."

He surveyed this woman he could not seem to get a handle on. He didn't think he'd underestimated her, exactly. He'd known she was clever and might, at some point, begin to wonder about his motives, but he'd never expected her to understand his plan so quickly.

He'd never expected all the flashes of something *else* in her expression to exist, or to bother him. To have him hesitating. It would be easy enough to lie again. To agree to her little counterplan knowing he had every inclination of talking her out of dissolving anything—for a few years at least.

But he was beginning to see that even if he could *per-*

suade her, that route came with…uncomfortable and unusual pitfalls.

"I cannot agree to this plan, as I think a marriage will be necessary to prove my point, to twist the knife. However, I will concede that the matter shall be left up in the air. If you can convince me a dissolution of our engagement can work once enough time has passed, I'll agree."

"And if not? I'll just be *required* to marry you?"

Teo lifted a shoulder. "I see no other way."

"You are ridiculous, Teo. I am in charge of saying 'I do.' Well, in this case, *not* saying it."

The sparring put him back on even ground. Re-cemented his control. He even managed a smile. "If you are so certain, there is no harm in agreeing, Saverina."

"There will be ground rules," she said fiercely. "*Reams* of them."

"You may come up with whatever rules you wish," he returned, and his smile got more genuine by the second.

She only scowled. "You must follow them."

"We'll see." Which he figured was a perfect time to make an exit. Let her consider it overnight. She would come to his way of thinking.

And if she didn't, he would simply convince her.

Because they were as close to Dante's ruination as he'd ever been. So there was no turning back.

CHAPTER SEVEN

SAVERINA HAD KNOWN she would not sleep well. After she had finally accepted that she would not sleep at all, she'd gotten up and begun her list of ground rules.

The first thing she wrote down was the most important.

No physical contact unless expressly required to prove a point in a public setting.

She knew it gave away the fact that his touch affected her even after finding out his secret, but no doubt he already knew that. Protecting herself was more important than her pride in this *one* instance.

She was taking a risk, and she tended to avoid those, but if she failed in front of Teo... Did she care? He didn't matter to her—not anymore. Not the way her family did. So the most important thing to remember about all this was that as long as her family remained in the dark about her failures, everything would be okay.

She told herself this, over and over again. Through her lists of rules, through her morning routine of getting ready. She went down to breakfast and missed her brother and his little family because the noise would have distracted her from all the things twisting inside of her.

It was probably best they were enjoying their vacation, far away from what she was doing. She went to work, focused on the necessary tasks for her morning. Then, when it was time for her lunch break, she took the elevator up to Teo's floor.

She could have forwarded him the memos via email, but she'd printed them out because she wanted to deliver her carefully written rules to him—in as public a place as she could manage—without raising any eyebrows. So he understood she was serious, that *he* had to toe *her* line.

Mrs. Caruso eyed her as she approached. "Mr. LaRosa is very busy today."

Saverina smiled. "I'm sure. I only need to speak with him for a moment, and was hoping to catch him on his way out to lunch." Saverina made a rather over-the-top production of looking at her watch. "He *is* about to be on his way to lunch, isn't he?"

Mrs. Caruso only scowled, but she didn't stop Saverina from approaching Teo's office door or stepping inside. Since it wasn't a meeting, she didn't close the door behind her.

Or because you're a coward.

He sat behind his desk, gazing at his computer. He didn't even look up at her as she walked in. Which was good because her footsteps faltered for a moment. How could she still look at him and think he was breathtakingly handsome? How could she sit here and think about how his hair would feel if she raked her fingers through it after what he'd done?

She *hated* him. When was her body going to accept that?

"I have a few memos Lorenzo asked me to forward to you," she said, probably too loudly, moving toward his desk. Once she was close enough to speak quietly so her voice wouldn't carry to his likely listening assistant, she whispered, "And my list of ground rules."

This caught his attention. He flicked her a glance, then got to his feet. "Perhaps you could read them to me on our way to lunch." He moved around his desk and began to stride for the door.

Saverina stayed exactly where she was. "I cannot go to lunch with you in public," she said in another whisper that just barely avoided being a hiss.

"Why not? It is time, Saverina." He stalked back toward her until she had to lift her chin and remind herself she was *strong*, lest she back away or scramble behind his desk just to put space between them. Just to be able to breathe the same air as him.

Because of *rage*, she assured herself. That was the heart-pounding, pulse-quickening sensation moving through her. Whatever vestiges of attraction she felt for him, they were just mixed up with all this distaste for him. And they would fade.

Wanting to touch him had to fade.

"We must begin to set the stage," he said quietly. "Lunch today. The gala this weekend. You may tell your family we've been seeing each other whenever and however you wish. My gift to you."

Gift. While he was standing there telling her what to do like *he* was in charge. "Have you always been this arrogant?"

"Of course. You just thought it was charming when you wanted it all to be real."

The dig hurt, but she looked at his easy expression and knew he didn't even *mean* it to be a dig. In his world, it was just a truth. Because he felt no shame for what he'd done. For how he'd tricked her. He didn't even fully understand *why* lying the way he had would hurt her.

She honestly did not know what to do with that. Had

no one ever taught him right from wrong? Was he so blinded by revenge that he just couldn't consider it might be *wrong* to use her? Was he so unaccustomed to love he couldn't fathom it could hurt when it wasn't reciprocated?

She did not know. Wasn't sure she wanted to.

Then he took her by the arm. She narrowly resisted jerking out of his grasp. Instead, she carefully and coolly stepped to the side so his hand had to either tighten or drop.

It dropped. "It seems there are a few rules we must go over *before* lunch, Teo. First, you will not touch me." She set the memos she'd brought on his desk and held out the piece of paper with her carefully written and considered list of rules.

He sighed. Heavily. Then took the offered piece of paper. His eyes skimmed over the writing.

"So, you will not come to my apartment under any circumstances," he summarized. "We will not be alone together—anywhere. I must run all plans by you before I do anything." He fixed her with a pitying gaze. "Come, Saverina, you do not really expect me to follow these foolish attempts at control. *I* am in the driver's seat. This is *my* plan."

"One you need me for."

"Very well. I will agree to let you in on all the plans you're a part of before I enact them. I will keep my hands to myself, and under no circumstances invite you back to my apartment." He handed her the list and smiled, slow and devastating. "Even when you beg me to do just that."

She was so shocked—because clearly her entire body heating through and through was *shock*—that her mouth hung open, and no pithy retort came out.

"Come. We can argue over lunch. We will walk down

to the restaurant on the corner. Sit on the patio." He walked toward the door, glanced over his shoulder and raised an eyebrow when she did not follow. "You do want to hear the rest of my plan, do you not? Put your stamp of approval on it."

A stamp of approval he clearly did not want or need. He was going to keep steamrolling right along.

Well. She was going to find a way to put a stop to that. Or at least keep one step ahead of him. This lunch wasn't it, but she didn't know how to say no. If this plan was to work, they *did* need to start going public.

And she would need to explain to her brother that she was dating one of his top executives in Palermo. So that when she announced her engagement, Lorenzo wouldn't *totally* flip.

She followed Teo out to the hall.

"I will be on my lunch for the next hour, Mrs. Caruso," he told his assistant. He glanced at Saverina. "If you would hold my calls, I'll get back to anyone upon my return." He smiled at Saverina, that devastatingly charming smile she'd once fallen for.

Now he did it in clear view of Mrs. Caruso, who frowned. But voiced no argument.

Saverina didn't want to think about how that might have thrilled her just a week ago. How she would have taken it as a sign of his *love*. It made her entire stomach turn.

"If we are to be believed, Saverina," he murmured as they stepped into the elevator, "you're going to have to stop looking like you've swallowed a lemon."

She glared at him as the doors closed. "Pretending not to hate you is going to take a level of acting that would win me an award."

"Ah, but you do not hate me. You're not a hateful person, Saverina. Perhaps you'd like to be, but you're too... soft."

"Soft?" It was so ludicrous, she scoffed. Which helped wipe the scowl from her face as they left the elevator for the lobby. "I suppose believing you listened to me was just another fiction."

"I listen."

The serious way he said those words made her shiver, but she fought through the feeling as they stepped into the sunshine. He was lying. Everything about him was a lie.

And now that she knew, she'd never forget.

Teo arranged for a table out on the patio, in a corner and a little bit away from the other tables so they could speak freely. He wanted to be seen, and he liked the way the afternoon light dappled Saverina's dark hair. The patio was quite full as it was a pretty, sunny day. The sidewalks just outside were bustling with people. But they had their own corner.

Once they were seated and had ordered their lunches, Saverina looked around. "If anyone we know sees us, they will only assume it's a working lunch."

"Will they?" He leaned forward, did his best impression of a besotted fool—a look he'd seen her brother give his wife more times than he liked to count. "Perhaps your no-touching rule will make it more difficult to get my point across, but you'd be surprised what people will read into the right kind of *look*."

She angled her chin away from him. He didn't bother scolding her for not *acting* like they were on a date. He might need her to exude something less edgy and angry to convince people they were *happily* together, but telling her what to do wasn't working quite the way he'd imagined it would.

He'd need a new strategy. "Tell me how your weekend was, Sav."

She scowled at him, presumably for shortening her name—so that was not the strategy. Clearly.

"We aren't friends, Teo. I see no reason to *pretend* we are."

"Ah, but the enemy of my enemy *is* my friend. Particularly in this case."

She shook her head and took a sip of water. She wore a yellow top today, buttoned up practically to her chin. Like she'd known she'd see him and wanted to keep as much of her body covered as she could.

It gave him a strange kind of thrill. He supposed because it meant she thought about how he could make her body feel. Her no touching and no alone time "rule" also pointed to the fact that while she might be frustrated with him, angry that he'd lied to her and kept things from her, she still wanted him.

He studied her now. She would be in his bed again— willingly and happily. He had no doubt. Once she got over her somewhat childish hurt, she would realize that their situation was much better than any sort of *love*.

"Well, I spent much of my week hacking into all your systems, discovering you to be a scheming liar, and then confronting you about it, so it was quite full."

"Ah, but you did not confront me, Saverina. I caught you." But it brought up an interesting point. How she'd gotten the information she had. Hacking. He studied her. Was his Parisi princess *that* skilled? "You're claiming to have gotten into my personal computer?"

"And phone. And tablet. Basically anything you've ever connected to your network—or Parisi's."

She said it so conversationally, he frowned. "My security is quite solid."

"I'm sure you think so. I'm sure the Parisi's IT department thinks so as well. But it only takes one person with a decent enough set of skills and a target to get through all that *solid* security."

Wasn't she a delightful surprise? If all this was true... He leaned forward, lowered his voice. "Could you hack into Marino's systems?"

She didn't say anything at first, didn't look at him, but he saw the flare of interest in her eyes. The subtle relaxing of her shoulders. When she finally met his gaze, hers was cool. But he saw the eagerness. "It wouldn't be the first time. Why didn't *you* hire someone to do it before?"

"I'd considered it, but in the end I didn't find anyone with the necessary skills who was also as trustworthy as I preferred. Surely I can trust you, Saverina."

She smirked. "We'll see, I suppose."

She really was a delight. Their meals were set in front of them, and he watched as she picked at hers. Not wearing that frown that did something uncomfortable to his insides. More like wheels were turning in her head. "I never found anything damning on the Marino systems before. What kind of information would you be looking for?"

"Anything that might reflect poorly on him. Questionable finances. Correspondence that points to secrets. Anything and everything."

"You were quite careful to keep most things out of your emails. I couldn't put your plan together simply from your digital footprint. Dante has been just as careful."

"Perhaps. But it doesn't hurt to look again, does it? Especially if you can go back into the past, when his security might have been more lacking, or he understood less about computers and the like."

Saverina considered this. "I couldn't do it on company time. Or at my home. It can't connect to Parisi."

"I know it is one of your little rules, but my apartment is the best option. We are portraying an engaged couple. Why shouldn't you spend time there?"

She frowned and said nothing—clearly understanding it was the best option and clearly not wanting to give in. "It would not be wise. You were right last night. There's chemistry between us, but I won't be engaging in it any longer. Best we keep our space."

He sighed, finally realizing he'd never understand this stand of hers. "I simply don't understand, Saverina. Why must things change? We can enjoy each other's company—in and outside of the bedroom. Accomplish all our goals and revenges. We get along, and we are attracted to each other. Perhaps the relationship isn't 'real' in any romantic way, but is working toward a common goal and enjoying each other not better than most romantic relationships that end in heartbreak and anger and theatrics?"

He was sure these words would change her mind. She had always behaved as a rational, sensible woman.

Instead, she took a long sip of water, then leaned forward and fixed him with a hard glare. "Have you ever been in a romantic relationship, Teo?"

He did not have a quick response for that. He'd never had any desire to complicate the enjoyable pursuit of sex with the trap of feelings. So, *no*, but he also hesitated to give her ammunition for whatever onslaught she was currently planning. "Probably not by *your* definition."

She rolled her eyes. "All right then. Did you love your mother?"

He cooled considerably at the mention of his mother. He'd told Saverina a bit about her, but mostly just that she'd suffered a long disease and then passed. "I cannot fathom what my mother has to do with any of this."

"Clearly she factors into your revenge. You're doing this because Dante refused to acknowledge you, but that has to connect to your mother. The question is, did you love her?"

He leaned back in his chair, resisting the urge to get up and leave. But retreating just because she poked at a wound wouldn't get him what he wanted. Which was things back to the way they were on his road to revenge. "Are there people who don't love their mothers?"

She let out an odd sigh. One that made him want to reach out, skim a hand over her hair. The part of him that wanted to break her rules earlier was quite glad they were in place now.

"Toward the end of my mother's life, I'm not sure what I felt for her," Saverina said softly. Then she let out a bitter kind of laugh. "I've never told anyone that. Not even my therapist. I guess enemy-friends are good for something after all."

"We are not enemies, *bedda*."

She ignored that. "You asked me about romantic relationships. Before I can answer, I need to understand something. The point of my question is, have you ever loved anyone?"

"That is not *my* point."

"Humor me, then, Teo. Tell me about how you grew up. The normal things engaged people might know about each other."

"You mean the things you did not know when you agreed to marry me?"

She looked at him for a long second that made him want to do the unthinkable. Shift in his seat. "Perhaps I should just go."

He wanted to be unaffected enough to invite her to do just that. But his *plan*. He needed people seeing them together. That was the only reason he considered her request. The only reason he began to speak of a time he did not care to remember.

"Our lives were very isolated. Mamma was afraid of retribution from Dante. So she steered clear of her family, lest they get involved. She stayed here in Palermo. She cleaned offices in a large building, and I worked alongside her."

"What about school?"

"She educated me as a young child. When it became clear I wanted to go to university, she put me in public school. I was old enough to be focused on my studies by then. The only thing I was concerned with was doing what I could to create the potential to save my mother from her concerns. I did not make friends. I did not *date*, if that is what you're asking. I had only one goal. To keep her safe."

"And then she died anyway."

It hit like the slice of a knife. Sharp and so cold he could scarcely manage an easy breath. "How kind of you to point that out," he returned, his words utterly devoid of any inflection.

"Both of my parents were dead by the time I was eleven," she said. "I didn't have a great relationship with either of them, and still, it's world-altering when a parent dies."

"Perhaps. But I was not a girl of eleven. I was a man of thirty."

She lifted her elegant shoulders. "I don't think it matters, Teo."

It mattered. Because her death had given him a new purpose. A name for his nameless father. All the revenge he needed.

"While you were lying to me—"

"I was not—"

"You were lying to me," she cut him off sharply. "You led me to believe you loved me and wanted to spend your life with me."

"I don't recall ever using those words."

She inhaled sharply—and made him wish he hadn't said that.

"No, you didn't." She shook her head. "The point of all this, the reason it can't just *go back*, is because a real relationship is based on trust and respect and love. It ends poorly—with those theatrics you mentioned—when one of those things are broken. You want me to forgo the pursuit of love, trust, and respect in order to protect myself from those things being broken. I think I even understand why you'd feel you must avoid those things. For me? I can't simply...decide I don't want those things. Protect and insulate myself from those things because they might *hurt* in the end."

He did not care for the word *avoid*. It painted him as a coward when what he prided himself on being was *rational*.

"I will never trust you, Teo. Not now. So there is no hope that this turns into what *I* want. I can't go back. We can only move forward with our mutual goal and my carefully considered ground rules." She pulled a paper from her purse—the ridiculous *ground* rules she'd written out in her pretty, precise handwriting. She pushed it across the table to him. "If you cannot agree to all of these, I cannot agree to be part of your revenge."

Teo ran his tongue over his teeth in an effort to remind himself to be as rational as he prided himself on being. Irritation with her—with the *loss* of her—was pointless. Because revenge was all that mattered.

"Very well," he said when he trusted himself to speak calmly. "Then you will have to follow a few of *mine*." He pulled a pen from his pocket, flipped her paper over, and began to write.

CHAPTER EIGHT

SAVERINA FROWNED AS Teo wrote. *His* ground rules.

As if he had *any* right.

She considered leaving again. She did not *have* to do this. Lorenzo had told her for years he didn't need Dante to pay, so maybe she shouldn't want that either. Maybe she should leave this for Teo. Perhaps Dante had spent years dragging Lorenzo's name through the mud, but that was not nearly as awful as refusing to acknowledge your son. Creating an environment where the mother of your child lived in fear in isolation.

But she couldn't let the idea of revenge go. Not just for Lorenzo anymore. For a little boy who'd been raised the way Teo had outlined. Saverina was well-versed in sad and bad childhoods. They came in all shapes and sizes, and she could never be immune to feeling compassion for those who found ways to succeed in spite of their upbringing.

And more… Oh, she hated herself for it, but Teo's story of his childhood had softened her. Not enough to change her rules, of course. Just enough that it was hard to hate him. That she thought…he wasn't so much hard and cold and mean.

He was misguided. He didn't understand love. He'd only known it from his mother, and no doubt her death had made it feel like more weapon than joy. Saverina might have felt that too...if she had not had her siblings. If Lorenzo had not found Brianna. If she had not watched love and family change him.

She blew out a breath, knowing this was a dangerous line of thought. She could feel sympathy for him, she could work with him, but she could not under any circumstances believe she could *change* him. That she could teach him how to love.

Right?

Teo handed her his list of rules, and she tried to shake her traitorous thoughts away. She took the paper and skimmed over the harsh ink strokes, trying to use this ridiculous farce as enough of an insult to harden her foolish heart to him.

Any information gathered on Dante Marino will be immediately shared with me.

Well, she didn't really care so much about that. As far as she saw it, they needed each other to create the worst-case scenario for Dante.

We will attend any and all events I see fit.

She tried not to scowl. He did not get to dictate when she went *anywhere*.

I will have wardrobe approval at such events.

She nearly laughed out loud, though she kept it in. Clearly he was trying to make her mad.

We will eat lunch together every workday from now on.

Smart, but she didn't like it. Spending all this time together? No, she didn't think that was wise at all.

I will drive you home from work every day—except on evenings we attend an event together.

Over her dead body.

It was an utterly absurd list, but when she looked at his

self-satisfied expression, she knew it was on purpose. He thought her rules were silly, so he would make a few silly rules of his own. He probably thought she would explode over the wardrobe approval at the very least.

Well, she wasn't going down without a fight, but it would be the fight *she* chose. Not the one he expected. She slid the rules back to him. "Teo, this is ridiculous."

"Why?" he asked, too much innocence in his expression for anyone with a brain to believe.

"We don't need to be in each other's pockets for people to believe we're engaged. The only person we have to fool is Dante Marino."

"All of this will aid in our efforts to do exactly that—because for Dante to believe it, the media must believe it and report upon it. They must be interested enough to take our picture, to dig around. Now, if you will not come to my apartment, if you will not allow *touch*, then I'm afraid time is what you must give me to accomplish my goal." He paused. "*Our* goal," he amended.

But she didn't believe he really saw it as *our*. He saw her as a tool. Maybe it hurt a little, but she didn't have to be the tool he wanted. She could be the tool she chose. Right now, she chose to be calm and rational. "Driving me home breaks *my* rule of us being alone together. You'll have to cross that one out."

"Then I refuse your no touching rule."

She didn't react immediately. She made sure her expression was stoic. Throwing a fit or getting angry only seemed to play into his hand. She had to be as calm and collected as he was. As much of a strategic game player as he was.

When she spoke, her voice was cool and breezy. She hoped. "Why should you want to touch me, Teo? Surely you can slake your manly lust elsewhere." The thought made her want to *die*, but she'd never, ever let him know that.

"Not as long as we are engaged, *bedda*." He reached out, took her hand. The one with the fake engagement ring on her pointer finger. So much faking. So much pretending.

She wished the heat that seeped into her at his touch was either of those things. That her heart wouldn't soar at the idea he might be faithful to her when all he was being faithful to was his revenge.

"You have my word," he said, pulling her hand to his mouth. Pressing a kiss to the top of her hand.

For *show.*

She hated it. *Hated* the way it made her want his mouth on hers. *Hated* how it made her feel young and vulnerable and insipid—such a little fool who'd be fooled by him once then still allow attraction to cloud her thinking. Who—despite knowing better in a million different ways, many that had played out before her in the hovel she'd grown up in—thought she might be able to *change* him.

Wasn't that her mother's fatal flaw? Believing that her father would change? Would suddenly love her?

Saverina refused to let someone have that kind of control over *her*. Never. Ever. If she ever fell in love again—if she ever married—it would be for *real* love. The kind that was reciprocated. The kind you didn't have to fight for.

Control. In this moment she had to find some. "Very well. I will amend my no touching rule. You may engage in public displays if necessary." She withdrew her hand from his with a little jerk against his grip. "On the condition you will cross off driving me home every night. If we arrive at events together, we will use a driver."

"Whatever you say, *principessa*."

She wouldn't bristle at the way he said that. Wouldn't think about the way he'd used that term when proposing. *Fake* proposing.

"Any other quibbles?" he asked, again with the feigned innocence.

"Not at present." She even managed to smile.

If he was taken off guard, it was only a flash of a second before he settled into a distantly amused expression she refused to let affect her. "I have to admit, I expected you to have something to say about the wardrobe approval."

She smiled over at him with all the fake sweetness she could muster. "But I've lived all my life for a man to tell me how to dress for an event." She batted her eyelashes at him. Because she knew the first event—the gala— she'd wear something that would make him regret such an attempt at control.

Teo did not appreciate being ordered about. He could not fathom why he was following Saverina's instructions to the letter.

It is all for the end result. Revenge.

Right. He straightened his jacket and walked to Saverina's front door. He'd texted her, per her instructions. *Imagine.* It was the modern version of honking at a woman's door and hoping she emerged.

The driver of his car stood at the passenger door, ready to open it for them. Another one of Saverina's demands. Couldn't be alone, even for a second.

Ridiculous. The whole thing was ridiculous, and

maybe he was playing along because he needed her for the severest form of revenge, but that did not mean he had to be a *lapdog*. She wanted to believe she had something over him, that she had some power here.

She did not. This was *his* revenge. *His* plan. He would do it his way, and if he made any accommodations along the way, it was because he wasn't a monster. He could be *quite* charitable. Always better to bend a little than break something.

Breaking things was the purview of Dante Marino, and Teo would not be like his biological father. He had been raised by Giuseppa LaRosa. He would always do her kindness and sense of fair play justice.

Fair play did not mean bowing and scraping to Saverina like she was in charge. It meant *compromise*. So he did not storm into her home. He did not bang down the door. But he also did not wait by the car as instructed.

He moved to wait by the door. Technically not alone, because the driver stood in view. But he would not be able to hear anything said should Teo and Saverina have a conversation before walking down to the drive.

He meandered up the walk, enjoying the gardens in the moonlight. The scent of flowers was earthy and exotic. The cool night settling in over the heat of the day a nice contrast. It was a pretty place. The kind of home he envisioned for himself once he and Saverina were married.

Because she would marry him, and she would play the dutiful wife. A Parisi-LaRosa union that would be a constant reminder to Dante and anyone who supported him that *Dante* lost at everything. Even revenge.

He heard the telltale creak of a door opening and turned to watch Saverina emerge. She stepped onto the little porch full of potted plants and flowers. The outdoor lights landed on her like a spotlight, and that's exactly where she should be. Looking like *that*.

She turned to lock her door, not yet seeing him there just a few yards away down the walk. When she was done and faced him once more, she came up a little short as their eyes clashed.

He could hardly think beyond the sudden fire in his body.

The outfit she wore was a bright, violent red. The top did not connect to the bottom. It was just a band around her generous breasts, baring her entire midriff. The skirt was long and flowing, but the slit in the fabric went dangerously high on her thigh.

He could not think past the onslaught of memory. The way she tasted. The way she felt when she came apart around him. He enjoyed sex—who wouldn't? But it had never become an insatiable hunger until *her*.

A thought that didn't do to dwell on.

She kept her distance, but she smiled at him now. "Does this dress meet with your approval?" She pretended to look at her watch. "We have time for me to go in and change should it not."

"Dress?" He laughed, irritated at how raw that laugh sounded. "That is hardly a dress."

She rolled her eyes. "It is high-fashion, Teo. Would you rather I dress like a nun?"

"I'm sure you'll be the talk of the gala," he managed to say, despite the raging of his own body. Moonlight dappled her dark hair. Her eyes seemed to shine, an otherworldly glow out here among the flowers and stars.

He wanted his hands on her so badly he had to curl his fingers into a fist. Fight back the cloudy haze of lust and want like he was doing real physical battle.

"That's what we intend, is it not? People to talk, wonder, and poke into things?" She fished around in her little purse.

"It is exactly what we intend."

She looked up at him, her eyebrows furrowed. "And yet, you seem…tense. Is everything all right?"

It was *not* a genuine question. She was playing a very dangerous game, and he had two choices. Call her out on it.

Or play along.

He moved closer to her now and watched the wariness creep into her eyes. But she did not back away. Did not hold him off. Even as he stepped up onto the porch with her.

She angled that beautiful face up, all regal condescension. "Then we should be on our way."

He looked down at her, let his gaze take in the elegant curve of her neck, the enticing line of her shoulder. The way that little strip of fabric held her breasts in place and on display. Particularly when she inhaled a little more sharply than she had been. Because heat arced between them, raw and potent. An electricity he did not understand why she was so intent on denying. All over something as pointless and unpredictable as *love*.

Her perfume wafted around him. Something spicy and sultry and intoxicating. When his eyes finished their tour of her body, he met her dark gaze. Warm and needy. Pink stained her cheeks—not from the elaborate makeup she wore, but from *desire*.

"You want me, Saverina," he murmured. Still not touching her, no matter how much his body demand he did just that. "Why deny it?"

She let out a careful breath. It didn't shake, but he could tell that was hard won.

"It's not *wanting* you on a sexual level, since heaven knows that's all you mean, that I deny, Teo," she said, clearly if a little breathlessly. "It's allowing a liar to have access to my body that I deny. You can trust that is not much of a punishment on *my* end."

She was an excellent liar, but he knew she lied. Because she could hate him for his subterfuge. She could spend the rest of her life not trusting him. But she knew and felt as well as he did what they could create together. And denying it was a physical pain, even if a necessary one.

"Trust, *bedda*, I know just how much pleasure I offered you. You can pretend you don't miss it, if that makes you feel better." Then he stepped off the porch and held out his arm for her. "Now, we have places to be. Let us not be late."

CHAPTER NINE

SAVERINA REFUSED TO consider the dress a mistake. She'd been waiting for an appropriate place to wear it, and this gala was just such an event. Yes, she'd hoped that the way she looked in it might *punish* Teo, and she liked to think it had. She'd seen the flare of desire in his eyes. She knew he *wanted* her, in a physical way, if nothing else.

She just hadn't thought about the fact that it would punish *her* as well. Because the way he looked at her—not just outside her home, but here at the gala—made her wish it was his hands not his gaze on every last inch of her.

She did not understand how she could be so hurt by someone and still *want* them. She was beginning to realize she'd still had a child's black-and-white outlook on life. Now she had to adjust to something more...complicated. Gray areas and moral complications.

She hated it.

Still, she smiled. She chatted. She didn't stick to Teo's side or vice versa, but they had arrived together, and at strategic points throughout the night they shared a chat, got a drink from the bar together, cozied up with each other in a corner.

Saverina could feel the interest from some people—mostly the people she worked with. The way eyes followed them when they were together, when they drifted apart.

She would have to call Lorenzo tonight as most of those people were his employees and would no doubt find a way to pass along what they'd seen the minute Lorenzo returned if not sooner. She supposed she could tell her brother the truth about pretending with Teo to get revenge—without the little bit about how Teo had fooled her for so long—but he'd no doubt tell her to stand down. Not important or too dangerous or *whatever*.

No, she would have to lie to her brother. Pretend she was desperately in love with Teo. She glanced across the large ballroom, her eyes landing on his tall, impressive frame. He spoke with two other Parisi executives, but she didn't even notice who. Because her heart twisted in her chest.

It wasn't a lie that she loved him, no matter how she wished it was. The lie would be that he loved her back. She blew out a breath and took a sip of her champagne. She should drift closer, give Teo a reason to break off from his business associates, but she liked her little corner where no one really noticed her. Where she could *breathe* and fortify herself against the next Teo attack.

You want me.

The dark way he'd said that there in the pretty evening in one of her favorite places. Looking so handsome it hurt. If she would have left her answer at *yes*, opened her door, they'd be back in her room rather than here.

And that would have been a mistake, she reminded herself harshly.

Maybe she'd enjoy the moment of being with him again—okay, no maybes. She *would* enjoy it. Until it was over. Then she would have all the same hurts, and even more regrets.

She didn't want that.

Suddenly Teo was at her elbow. He leaned close. "Dante is here," he murmured.

She scanned the crowd. Dante was over by the bar talking to a few men.

"Did you know he would be here?" Saverina asked.

"No. He was not on the guest list." There was a grimness to Teo's expression that Saverina didn't think would do well for the overall plan. She slid her hand up to his shoulder and tried to harden herself against any reaction.

"Come, let's dance," she suggested. When he raised an eyebrow at her, she shrugged. "You can't spend the rest of the gala glaring at him or people will talk in a way you do not want. Yet. Come." This time she took his arm and tugged him forward to the dance floor, where a nice slow song was playing.

He did not precisely wipe the glare off his face, but when he pulled her into his arms for a dance, some of that grimness faded. And then they danced. Easily and in time, like they were perfectly matched to do just this.

Part of her wanted to lean her head against his chest and just…give in. Allow his pretend. She could love him and he could not love her and would it really be so bad?

She thought of her mother toward the end of her life. Ragged, used, lost. All because she'd loved a man who wouldn't love her back. Saverina didn't think she was *that* weak. She could go into this knowing Teo's limitations.

Then again, the hope of his someday understanding love might eventually kill her.

"Perhaps we should make an early exit," she said, because it turned out pretending to be who she wanted to be on the outside, while knowing she couldn't be on the inside, was *exhausting*. And Teo kept looking at Dante when he should ignore the man all together.

"To be chased away by *him*?"

"So people might talk about *why* we left early and together after slow dancing, Teo." She looked up at him, trying to get through that vibrating anger. "Your plan, remember?"

The plan. Never before had Teo wanted to damn the plan. Stride across the room and strike the man. *This* was why he steered clear of spaces Dante was in. His fury overrode all attempts at control. Being in proximity to the man who'd harmed his mother, who'd threatened to crush him if he revealed his parentage always threatened to undermine the plan in a blatant explosion.

If Teo thought that would be satisfying in the long run, he'd give in to it. But Dante would twist it. Teo would likely end up in jail for assault, and Teo would never have his revenge.

So, yes, the plan was essential. "Very well," he muttered. "We will make a hasty exit. Keep your hand in mine."

He half expected her to argue, but she'd been surprisingly obedient—a word she'd no doubt hate to be used on her—this evening. She smiled, she touched, she danced. It was an act. He could see that by the shadows that lingered in her eyes. But it was a *good* act. Only someone who knew her would notice those shadows.

He did not interrogate why *he* did.

They left the dance floor hand in hand, and Teo headed for the door, but he made a *slight* detour. He steered Saverina right toward Dante. Not for a confrontation, no. In fact, he turned his head away from Dante and pretended to nod at a colleague on the opposite side of the room as he moved Saverina farther toward the door.

"Is he looking?" Teo asked under his breath.

"Oh, yes."

"Good." It was *good*. Dante had to know who Saverina was by sight, and if he did not, surely someone would inform him. From there, Dante would begin to wonder. He would begin to worry. The son he wanted to crush. The sister of the business rival he hated. If Dante did not start seeing him as a threat now, he would be a stupid man.

Teo thought many unflattering things about Dante Marino, but he did not think the man stupid.

Teo escorted Saverina to their waiting limo. Once inside, she watched the city pass by as the vehicle headed for her house. Teo was too lost in his own plans and machinations to worry about conversation, but about halfway through the drive, she turned to him.

"When did you find out about Dante possibly being your father?"

Since it brought back unwanted memories of his mother's deathbed, he hedged. "Why do you ask me this?"

"Humor me."

He did not *need* to humor her, but he found himself giving in anyway. "Almost two years ago. Mamma informed me of my biological father's name with her last breath." He could have left that detail out. He did not want her pity, but he also wanted her to understand that his revenge would always come first.

For his mother.

She was quiet for a long moment. He could see her only in the way lights flashed through the window as they passed other cars and streetlights. He knew she looked at him, and he was more than happy to find himself mostly shrouded in the dark.

"How did you find out the rest, then?" she asked quietly. "About him threatening her, and what you told me the other night?"

"Careful research and study. Putting together stories from speaking to her family, from what I dug up on Dante, and so forth. I tracked down an old employee of the Marino household who had known my mother, and she filled in the remaining gaps. She had no love lost for Dante."

Another silence stretched out between them, and he assumed that would be that. Assumed it so much he refused to say anything else. He would not tell her what the past two years had been like.

But he *wanted* to. All those words on the tip of his tongue. It was a twisted desire in him. So Saverina would see. So she would understand.

He did not need any of these things from her, no matter what his traitorous heart whispered. All he needed from her was what they'd agreed upon.

When she spoke again, her tone was still quiet, careful. He did not like how close it sounded to *pity*.

"You say *her* family, but if they were hers, they are yours too."

Teo shook his head before he realized she couldn't see him. "They did not know I existed. They live in northern Italy. To them, my mother was long dead before she died—and I inconsequential."

"Are you sure about that?"

Since he was not—he had not left any possibility for some silly reunion. Why should they care for him or about him? Too many years passed, too much... *Dante* in him. He'd felt they'd be happier not knowing he existed. "When I spoke to them, I did not mention who I was or what exactly I was after. They do not know my mother had a son. They did not need to."

"But—"

"No buts, Saverina. This is not a fairy tale." He refused to believe in such things. "For thirty years they did not know of my existence. They thought my mother simply turned away from them. Best for everyone if that does not change. That is the end of this discussion."

"You don't think they'd want to know their family *didn't* turn away from them? That they have more family? A piece of her?"

A piece of her. That twisted inside of him like shrapnel. But she was no longer here. There were no pieces left. "That is the end of this discussion, Saverina," he growled.

There was a considering silence, and he thought she'd let it go. Thought she'd *listen*. He should have known better.

"It's painful for you," she said softly. She even reached out and touched his arm. Initiating touch even though it was against her rules. This was not public because the driver was separated from them by the screen. This touch was not an act.

He blamed his surprise over that for not stopping her before she said the rest.

"But pain is not such a bad thing, Teo. Dealing with your pain and grief often leads to beautiful things on the other side."

There was no other side of the loss of his mother. There was only revenge. He pulled his arm away from her touch. "I do not know what this is, Saverina, but I will never give you what you want."

She inhaled sharply, jerked her hand back, and scooted into her little corner where he couldn't see her expression even in the passing lights. "I feel sorry for you, Teo," she murmured, her voice icy now.

"You should not. I soon will have everything I've ever wanted."

"No, you won't. You will get your revenge, *we* will get our revenge, but then your whole life will stretch out in front of you, and then what?"

"I will enjoy it."

She laughed. Bitterly. "You wouldn't know how. You isolate yourself from anything and everything that might be *enjoyable*. You refuse to look at all the hurts you've been dealt. You think pushing them away will make them go away, but trust me, they won't. The hurts linger until you deal with them."

It was his turn for a bitter laugh. "You'll have to excuse me, *principessa*, if I do not take a pampered heiress's word on *hurts* and *grief*."

He thought that harshness would shut her up. Perhaps he was even desperate for it to.

"That might hurt my feelings if it were true, Teo. But you know my story. You know it has not all been pampering and easy. Which leads me to believe you're nothing more than a lion with a thorn in its paw. Roaring and lashing out because of your *own* pain."

"I haven't begun to roar and lash out, *bedda*."

She only made a considering sound, and they spent the rest of the drive in silence. But he could not fully erase her words, her experience from his mind. And *that* was unforgiveable.

CHAPTER TEN

SAVERINA COULD HAVE kept arguing with him, but he would only build walls there. Where it hurt and he didn't even *realize* it. So blinded by his revenge—by this thing that he thought took the grief away.

But the grief never went away. Whether you loved a parent or not. There was always grief—whether they were gone or whether they'd never been what they should have been. She wished this understanding would help harden her heart to him, but all it did was soften it.

He was a grown man with the world at his fingertips, and she'd been a young, confused girl working through her grief. But the real difference between them was even in the absence of her parents—both when they'd been alive and after they'd died, after Rocca had died—she'd had her family. Not just Lorenzo, but all her many brothers and sisters who'd looked after one another, made sure they were all okay.

Teo had *no one*.

But pushing at him would make it impossible to ever get that through to him. Maybe it was a pipe dream to think if she was careful, she might be able to help him. The way she and her siblings had once helped Lorenzo realize that loving Brianna was a gift—not a punishment.

But sometimes a woman had to believe in a pipe dream to get through the day. As long as she didn't pin *everything* on him reciprocating, she would not end up like her mother. She tried to assure herself of this.

The car pulled to a stop in front of her private entrance to the sprawling Parisi estate. She should immediately say her goodbyes and get out, but... There had been something she'd wanted to broach with him before they'd gotten on the subject of his lost family.

She glanced at the partition between them and driver. No doubt soundproof, but she couldn't be too careful with this.

"Come inside. I'll have someone bring us a nightcap."

"A nightcap." She couldn't see him in the dark, but she could feel the sarcasm of a raised eyebrow all the same.

"It's not *that* kind of invitation, Teo," she said on a sigh. "We have something to discuss."

She got out of the car when the driver opened her door. She offered him a smile, then strode for her entrance without looking back to see if Teo had followed.

Of course he followed.

She swept inside, smiled at Antonina. "Could you fix up a tray for us? Bring it into my parlor?"

Antonina nodded and disappeared to do as she was asked. Saverina kept walking through the hall, refusing to look back at Teo. She wasn't breaking her own rule. She was bending it. For business. Besides, any number of staff people were about... They weren't *alone* alone as long as they stayed in her parlor.

She led him into said room, a wide-open affair full of plants and windows and no privacy whatsoever. It was as close to a greenhouse as she could get inside the house. The plants were something that steadied her when she was feeling precarious. She loved this room, and while she didn't really want memories of Teo in here, it was the right room for her purposes.

She trusted Lorenzo's staff with everything, even secrets. They might *mention* Teo's attendance here, but they would not listen in on the conversation. They would not act as *spies*.

She settled herself on the little settee. She finally steeled herself enough to look at Teo and smile. "You may sit there," she said regally, pointing to the same settee she was on—but the opposite side.

His expression was one of bemusement, and he said nothing as he sat himself where she pointed. Of course he was so tall, the spread of his legs meant there was very little space between them.

This could not matter. She kept the pleasant smile on her face as Antonina entered with a tray of the little sweets Saverina preferred, along with a small collection of expensive alcohol bottles and glasses.

"Would you like me to pour?" Antonina asked.

Saverina waved her away. "Thank you. I'll handle it."

The woman nodded and then left them alone. Saverina fixed Teo a drink to the exact specifications she wished she didn't know, but there were more important things to discuss than her feelings. Or his.

So she got right down to it. She handed him a drink, didn't bother with one for herself.

"Did you ever hear about the attack on Dante's oldest son about five years ago?"

"Yes, I read about it. They never found who did it, but Dante tried to blame your brother."

Saverina nodded, angry all over again even though the accusation had never truly stuck to Lorenzo, no matter how Dante had tried. It *had* hurt Lorenzo's reputation at the time, though. He'd been painted as a violent monster. And he'd *let* people paint him that way.

She'd never understood how Lorenzo could just…accept that. Step into that. He'd been right in the end. Eventually the rumors had ceased. Nothing had come from it.

But even the memory of what the papers and gossip sites and such had said about her brother made her angry.

"Yes. Not the first time he tried to pin something on Lorenzo, but possibly the most successful at the time for swaying public opinion. Lorenzo lost a few clients, but he didn't fight back. He knew it wasn't true, so he didn't see the point in fighting Dante at his own game."

"Pity."

Saverina laughed. She couldn't help it. It *was* a pity.

"Dante's pattern for blaming your brother for the bad things that happened to him or his business is why I targeted getting a position at Parisi. Clearly he has a vendetta against your brother. Do you know why?"

Saverina sighed. "No. Lorenzo has always maintained he has never understood a reason other than the fact that Parisi was a business rival that wouldn't be crushed like the rest. Dante is a textbook narcissist who can't stand the fact he once lost a client to my brother. Of course, these days Lorenzo says it's simply because he has everything Dante wants."

"What's that?"

Teo would not care for the answer, but Saverina considered it more deeply than she ever had. "Happiness," she said gently. She'd thought that was Lorenzo being blinded by love talking, but now…

She just wondered if it were true. Could happiness

and not worrying about revenge and competition really be the answer?

Teo's scowl told her, *Not with this man.*

Happiness. Teo grunted irritably. *Happiness.* A man like Dante wouldn't know what to do with happiness if it landed in his lap, so how could he be jealous of it in Lorenzo?

Teo glanced at Saverina. Dangerously close on the fussy little sofa. The smell of her perfume seemed to wrap around him, as it had done on the dance floor. The memory of her in his arms as they danced tonight was too potent.

Happiness.

Would *he* know what to do with it?

Well, he'd find out when he got his revenge. Because it was the only thing that could bring true happiness. That couldn't shatter and break. That couldn't leave a hole so big and wide it hardly mattered the good that had come from it.

People died. Revenge didn't.

"I had just started university at the time," Saverina continued, clearly focused on something he couldn't quite follow yet. "Furious someone would print such blatant lies about my brother, obviously. Lorenzo was also angry, I could tell, but he wanted to keep me out of it."

"I'm sure you took that equitably," Teo muttered. He knew her too well. She would not have taken that easily.

She laughed, and Teo found himself leaning toward that sound. He missed her laugh. Her genuine smiles. He missed...

Well, nothing he wouldn't have again. She'd get over this foolish, naive need for love. They'd have what they had before, and everything would be quite simple and easy. He was sure of it.

He always got what he wanted these days.

"I know he was worried *I* would become a target if I waded in. Lorenzo knew Dante could be ruthless even if the public didn't. I understood his reticence to let me in. He's always taken my protection quite seriously."

For a strange moment, Teo felt…arrested. Deep within. The idea that Saverina being in Dante's orbit might make her a target… He closed his hands into fists. He would kill first. But this was ridiculous, as he wasn't putting her in any danger at all.

"But no, I did not take his warning me off well. I was determined to get to the bottom of the perpetrator of the attack. I'd already been developing my computer skills at that point, so I used them. To determine the police's suspects, to track where Dante was getting his information."

"They never even found a suspect for the attack."

"No, but with what I did gather, I developed a…theory. I've never been able to prove it. It's totally a theory of my own making based on circumstance, but perhaps it's a theory we should consider once again."

He knew he should focus on her story—it might lead him to an even stronger thread of revenge. Leverage. Everything he wanted. But all he could focus on was the part of her background that didn't make sense.

"Whyever don't you work in the Parisi IT department, Saverina?"

This question clearly surprised her. She made an odd little noise, then lifted her hand to flutter it in a strange gesture he'd never seen her use before. Almost as if she was flustered. Over a rather straightforward and easy question, all in all.

"It doesn't matter," she insisted. "What matters is, though I couldn't prove my theory at the time and I let it go since I couldn't, his wife stopped attending events with him after the attack on their son. Dante only ever comes to these sorts of things alone now, but before the attack on their son, she was always at his side, or she and his boys. They were always the picture-perfect family. The perfect contrast to Lorenzo's singlehood and complicated background before Brianna."

"The reports are that she suffers from some kind of condition." Though Teo had never spent much time digging into Dante's wife. She'd seemed rather inconsequential, especially since she did not attend events with the man anymore. The former staff member who'd once filled him in on what had happened to his mother had only sung Mrs. Marino's praises.

"This very well could be, but I've always wondered. Could Dante have ordered the attack on his son himself? Could he have *done* it himself? Could his wife have found out about it? Is *that* why she stopped attending events right after the attack and has continued all these years? Is *that* why no perpetrator was ever found?"

Teo could only stare at her, sitting elegantly on her elaborate sofa, that excuse for a dress making her skin seem to glow gold. It would have threatened to be a distraction if the bomb she dropped was not quite so big.

Could Dante have attacked his own son? And for what? Just to blame Lorenzo? It was cruel and insane, but Teo was not above believing those things of Dante. And if it was true...

He reached out, all her rules be damned, and took her hand. Squeezed. "We must prove it, Saverina. *You* must prove it."

She swallowed and looked away. "I will see what I can do, of course, but if I couldn't find proof when it happened, how could I find proof now? Maybe you should hire someone else. Someone with real experience in investigation."

She sounded oddly...insecure, when she'd always been so sure of herself. She was a confident woman, and she'd stood up to him time and again. Hell, she'd hacked into all his systems, followed him to that bar. Why should she seem...fragile now?

"It was years ago when you tried. You were a *teenager*. You're older, wiser. No doubt you have access to better equipment. You can do this. You will do this."

She shook her head and withdrew her hand from his, lurching to her feet. "N-no. That's...not the deal." Her breathing was coming in little pants, the words sounding a bit strangled. He stood too, reaching out for her without fully understanding why. Just the instinctive need to calm her.

But she stumbled backward, only keeping herself upright by pressing against the wall. Her eyes were wide. She was gasping like a drowning person. Panic radiated off of her in waves.

"Saverina," he said, careful to keep his voice even although her panic sliced through him. But demanding to know what was happening certainly wouldn't calm her. "*Bedda*, breathe."

"Can't," she gasped. Her gaze was wild.

"Yes," he returned as he stepped closer. "You can. You are fine and well and safe. Come, Saverina. Hold on to me." He held out his hand, heart hammering in his chest. He knew he could not simply grab her. It could cause whatever panic was hurting her to expand.

She had to make the choice. For long, terrible moments she just stood there, struggling to breathe and staring at him with wide eyes. Then slowly, very slowly, she reached a trembling hand toward his outstretched one.

He grasped it quickly, then didn't bother with the rest. He swept her up in his arms. She shouldn't be on her feet anymore. "Come, *bedda*. We will sit, and all will be well," he murmured with more certainty than he felt.

He carried her to the little couch, kept her safe in his lap as she shook and gasped for air. He could not give her air, and that about cut him in two. But she held on to him, trembling and struggling.

The only other time he'd ever felt so helpless was watching his mother fade away. The memory should have filled him with anger anew, but he couldn't get there past all his worry for Saverina.

When she finally began to settle, he skimmed a hand over her hair, setting it back to rights. "Explain this?"

"N-nothing." Her shoulders slumped, and she leaned into him. He held her close. It wasn't nothing. That much was clear. But he didn't prod her, just held her until she was breathing normally again.

CHAPTER ELEVEN

WHEN THE WORST of the attack was over, Saverina was too exhausted and wrung out to even feel embarrassment. Yet. It would come, but not tonight.

All in all, it wasn't the worst one she'd ever had, though it had come on more quickly than they usually did. Usually she had time to remove herself, time to access her coping skills. This one had hit hard and fast and with no warning.

The way he'd grasped her hand, so certain, so impassioned. *"You will do this."* It had just set off an immediate panic inside her, because she had *tried* to prove this once before and failed. No one had known, so while it had been frustrating, it hadn't been a failure.

Now it would be. The panic threated to curl around her once more, so she simply breathed in the spicy scent of Teo's cologne and enjoyed—when she absolutely should not—the feeling of utter safety in his arms.

It was embarrassing but not terrible. She'd rather have an attack in front of Teo than have one in public or in front of her family. She did not have to worry about Teo blaming himself for her own issues like she did with all her siblings.

"Come. Explain," he said. He spoke gently, calmly, but it was a demand. She found this was one of the rare instances when a demand kind of worked rather than made her angry. It gave her a clear next step, helped her brain focus on the answer, not the panic still fluttering around inside of her.

"I…have panic attacks sometimes. An old vestige of a traumatic childhood. It is nothing to concern yourself over. I spent some years in therapy dealing with the worst of it." She wanted to get up off the settee, his *lap* for heaven's sake, but her legs were shaky. Every part of her was shaking.

"How have I never seen such a thing?" he asked, not in accusation, but with a kind of confusion. Still, he just held her against him like sitting curled up with each other was the most natural thing in the world.

It would *never* be, she reminded herself harshly, no matter how much she liked the feeling of being held and looked after. "It is rare that I have them these days. I have gotten help, and I know how to avoid my triggers, for the most part."

"Triggers. Such as?"

This question was enough to have her pushing against him. She couldn't stand just yet, but she managed to maneuver off his lap, out of his arms and to her own side of the settee. Discussing her triggers was *not* avoiding them.

"It is of no consequence." Did he really need to know all her weaknesses? He'd no doubt exploit them to his own ends.

"How can I avoid them for you if I do not know them?"

This seemed like a reasonable question, but they were not friends. He was not her real boyfriend or fiancé. He did not love her or care for her anyway. At best, he was attracted to her and didn't *hate* her. At the end of the day, he was just a man using her to aid in his revenge.

He'd made that very clear.

"Why would you care to avoid them, Teo?" She rubbed at her temples, where the usual after-attack headache was beginning to make itself known. She did not have the energy to guard herself against him. She had to find some way to finish their conversation and send him on his way.

He did not answer her for a long time. So long it felt like she *had* to look at him. Confusion was etched across his beautiful face. She doubted that was a very common feeling for him. "You are not my enemy, Saverina," he said, very seriously.

"You say that like it's a positive." And she could not go believing neutral statements were signs of love. She knew too well the path that led down.

"What triggered you this evening?" he pressed. Maybe confusion was rare, but giving up was rarer.

She was too tired to fight, so she simply gave in. "I don't like to fail."

"Who does?"

She shook her head. "I cannot explain it. The idea of certain failures…certain expectations…the pressure of it. I cannot handle it." She tried not to think of it as a weakness. Therapy had taught her that it was a natural result of a traumatic childhood. Not her fault, something to work through with no shame.

But sometimes it was impossible to leave shame behind no matter how aware she was that she *should*.

"This is why you do not work in the IT department? The pressure."

She could deny it, the logical leap he'd just made, but why bother? Maybe if he knew all her embarrassing little secrets, she'd stop being in love with him.

"Yes. I tend to put the most pressure on myself when

it comes to my family. They…" She could not quite believe she was saying this, but why not lay it all out? It
would never matter to him. It was freeing, almost. To
say the things she'd only discussed with her university
therapist out loud, to someone who was in her life. No
matter how temporarily. "They sacrificed so much for
me, particularly Lorenzo. I would never want them to
know I struggle. With pressure, with anything. Lorenzo
would blame himself."

"It seems who he would blame is his problem. Not
yours."

"You don't have a family, Teo," she said. It was mean,
she knew, but she thought it would get him to stop poking into her softest parts. "You cannot understand."

"Perhaps not. But the way other people blame themselves—or don't—is hardly your responsibility. And Lorenzo dotes on you. He would not be hard on you in a
position in the IT department."

She shook her head. "You don't understand," she repeated. Because no one ever did. "It's not about whether
he would be hard on me. It's that I don't want him to be
disappointed. I know I can be an excellent assistant—or
whatever else I end up deciding to do at Parisi. A mistake as his assistant, in marketing or sales or whatever,
would be embarrassing, but…inconsequential. A mistake in the IT department? It's the security of the entire
company. He could lose everything. The consequences
could be catastrophic. I couldn't…" The panic was closing in again. She breathed through it, focused on one of
the hanging plants over by the window. The way the ivy
twisted down toward the ground. Her little sanctuary
where she was *safe*.

But there was a man here. A man she loved, who did

not or would not love her back. And too many old hurts in the air around them.

"Very well," Teo murmured, as if he sensed she was on the edge of losing it again. "But you looking into Dante potentially being the one to attack his son is not pressure, *bedda*. We have a plan. Consider this…icing on the cake. If it does not come to fruition, it hardly matters."

But it did matter. She could see it in his eyes. He wanted this *so* badly, and she *shouldn't* feel obligated or pressured to give it to him. Not after what he'd done to her. But in a way that felt far too much like her childhood—her feelings and her rational thinking weren't meshing.

"You don't have to be kind, Teo. I know what it would mean to prove this."

He straightened out his jacket, brushed at lint that was most certainly not there, and *scoffed*. "No one has ever accused me of being kind."

But he was. Perhaps that was the heart of him. Behind all those walls and that need for revenge, he had a kind, bruised heart he'd rather harden than ever deal with. Hadn't she gone through that season in her life too?

She wished she were back in his lap. Wished she could just stay there in the circle of his arms where she'd felt protected and safe even as she struggled to breathe.

But she'd been protected her whole life. She'd spent university and the past year trying to prove to Lorenzo *and* herself that she could protect herself. That she could handle her life, her triggers, herself.

If only she could handle her heart. "I'll see what I can do."

Teo spent the next few days not allowing himself to consider Dante's possibly even larger downfall than he'd planned himself. He would not put that kind of pressure on Saverina. Every time he even considered the old story about Dante's son, he could only picture Saverina struggling to breathe.

So he tried not to think about it.

He did not consider the lack of pressure a kindness. He did not consider it anything but smart business. You did not ask something of someone that was more than they could handle. That would only ever end in disaster.

It was not *kindness*. It was sense.

He told himself this day after day, lunch after lunch, when he did not push her on the matter. Did not ask if she'd attempted to find anything regarding Dante's wife or son. He focused on his original plan. On how they would announce their engagement.

What he did *not* focus on was how much more he preferred these past few days *with* Saverina—no matter if she went home alone every night—than the one week he'd spent thinking she was off holidaying with her brother.

What he did *not* focus on was how every day at work, he looked more forward to his lunches with her, so much so that his work suffered in the mornings.

These things were frustrations, but they did not signify in the greater scheme of things. It was only good that he enjoyed the company of what was, essentially, a business partner. Revenge was a sort of business, after all. How nice they could share it.

But he would not grow to depend on this feeling. He would not tolerate it. His joy, his *happiness*—that thing foolish people put so much stock in—would only come from things he could control.

Never the fickle nature of *life*.

Or so he told himself. Even as he found himself wandering down toward Saverina's office a full fifteen minutes before her lunch break would begin. He convinced himself it was for the optics of it all. People would see him and gossip.

This was the goal.

Her office door was open when he approached. She stood with her back to the door, a phone cradled at her ear. She wore a silky shirt the color of sunrise and a skirt that skimmed the flare of her hips.

Something potent and raw slammed into his chest. Uncontrollable, but not as simple as lust. Lust was easy. But he knew now—having had her and knowing he wouldn't at the moment—that this lust lingered. Twisted. Sank into his bones until it felt like nights without her were torture.

Too close to grief to bear. *"The hurts linger until you deal with them."* She had said that to him, and those words, too, lingered in his head like a curse. Like she'd foisted *hurts* and *dealing* upon him when he knew *exactly* what he was about.

What he would do. What he wanted. But he wasn't above altering his plans when just cause presented itself. When this was over, maybe he would let her break off the engagement. She did deserve what *she* wanted, after all, and he had no interest in *love* and *families*.

Yes. That would be the new plan. The plan that would be *best*. Not because he was kind. Not because there were hurts not dealt with. But because... *Because*. He didn't need her. He did not need to force anyone to stay by his side.

He was Teo LaRosa, and he would *never* lower himself to such things. So he would let her go because her staying would not give him what he wanted.

Peace and fulfillment in the wake of his revenge.

He wouldn't tell her that just yet, or maybe at all. He'd give her the illusion of it being her own decision later on. He would magnanimously agree. Let her go.

Be without her.

He scarcely realized his hands curled into fists.

When she turned, setting the phone down on the desk and lifting her gaze to see him there, her expression softened. He could not decide what it meant, but in a flash, her soft smile turned into that cool professionalism she wielded so well.

It felt like a punch to the gut. Like pain and hurt when it was just…business. The business of revenge and her finding out the truth. Which seemed like a better and better turn of events as days went on.

"I still have a few things to tie up before I can take my lunch break," she said, looking down at her desk rather than at him. "Perhaps I could meet you at the restaurant?"

Except that question felt as if it was posed to someone else. As if he was floating above this exchange, existing in a strange cloud of pain and a realization trying to break free.

He refused the realization, refused the feelings. He was Teo LaRosa, and he was in control of everything, and *everything* would lead him to destroying Dante Marino.

Saverina Parisi was *inconsequential*. Always.

She took a few steps toward him before she stopped herself. She clutched her hands together. Her expression was cool, but he saw concern in her dark gaze. "Teo, are you all right?"

"Of course." Of course. He was always all right. He had a goal and he would meet it. What would ever *not* be all right about that? Maybe his throat felt tight and his words were raspy, but he was *excellent*.

Everything hinged on this goal, and for the first time, an uncomfortable little flare of uncertainty tried to find purchase in his gut. Like this was not smart, to twist your entire life to accomplish one thing.

But he'd made a promise. To himself even more than his mother.

Dante would pay. If nothing else mattered besides that simple fact, he would not worry about *after*.

CHAPTER TWELVE

SAVERINA WAS GETTING too used to lunches with Teo. *Time* with Teo. That had been all fine and dandy when she'd thought this was real, but no amount of knowing he saw this as little more than a business deal could stop her heart from aching for more.

Case in point, the leap her heart had taken when she'd looked up and seen Teo there early. It was just impossible to get over someone when you shared so much time together, no matter how much you understood it could go nowhere.

Harder still when, the further they got into their plans of revenge, the less she could blame Teo for how he'd gone about things. It was so easy to see he had used his plans for revenge as a replacement for grief. That he had not considered *her* feelings, because he was so deeply in denial about his own.

She worried for him now—when he got his revenge, what would be on the other side of it? Would he simply find something else to focus on while his denial grew stronger, or would he finally have to experience all those feelings he was trying to stave off? Both options seemed a terrible thing to deal with alone, and he was so very alone without her.

He is not your responsibility.

She walked next to him on the sidewalk to their regular restaurant and wondered what it said about her that she could not get that through to her soft, vulnerable heart.

They were seated as they almost always were in a little corner of the patio, with the exception of when the weather was bad. Today was bright and sunshiny, and it was nice to get out of the office and enjoy the breeze and people-watching.

They didn't only speak of Dante at their lunches. Sometimes they were seated too close to others to get deep into their plans. Sometimes there was just nothing else to say.

And sometimes, she tried to engage him in conversation about his mother, because she couldn't just let it go no matter how she knew she should. If he actually *dealt* with that grief…she wouldn't let herself *count* on things being different, but she didn't see the harm in acknowledging it was *possible*.

Maybe Teo didn't love her. Maybe he never would. But he certainly *liked* her well enough.

Today he seemed…distracted. Grumpy. She almost laughed to herself at how little he'd enjoy that description. It didn't matter, though. She had a very specific topic of conversation to go over with him today regardless of his mood. "I spoke to Lorenzo and Brianna last night."

He'd been looking off into the distance. Brooding. Now his eyes were sharp and on her. "And?"

"I told them we'd started seeing each other. That we had been for a while, but it was getting serious, so we had decided to tell people. They'd already heard some rumblings after the gala, so they weren't exactly surprised."

"Were they approving?"

She hesitated. Even now, she wasn't sure *what* their

reaction had been. She'd expected a little bit of…something. She wouldn't have been surprised if Lorenzo had even thrown a tantrum about her being too young, or that Teo working at the same company was out of the question, or *something*.

But they'd been very…distant about the whole thing, which was not like *either* of them. "They were not *disapproving*."

Teo raised an eyebrow. "Is this something we should be concerned about?"

"No, I don't think so. I've never told them about anyone I've dated before. I suppose they weren't quite sure what to do with it." Which was true enough. She'd understand better once they were back home and she could gauge their expressions. The phone conversation had just felt…careful, when Lorenzo and Brianna were never careful with her.

"What would your mother think of all this?" she asked. It was not the most subtle of topic changes, but it was the only way she knew how to deal with the *yearning* inside of her. Maybe if she pushed him too far, he'd break, and she could go back to her solitude. She could have the space to get over him.

And maybe…

She could not let herself finish that thought. She could not dream of happy endings. She would not allow herself delusions. Only practicality and self-awareness would get her through this, happy or at least accepting of whatever outcome occurred.

His frown deepened, and he looked off into the distance again. "I cannot fathom."

But based on his expression, she thought maybe he was fathoming right now.

"Would she approve of the revenge plot?" Saverina continued, posing it like a general question as she focused on taking a bite of her pasta.

"No," he said quickly. "She…she was too softhearted to want such a thing. I think she had told me his name in hopes I'd let it go. Or perhaps to ease her conscience. It was not for revenge. That was not in her."

"But you won't let it go, even though she might have wanted it?"

He fixed her with a sharp gaze. "I will not. I am my own man. I do this in her honor, because it is what is right. Not because it is what she'd want. She isn't here."

Saverina pretended to contemplate this. "Do you believe that? Death is the end?"

"What else would it be?"

Saverina shrugged. "I took a philosophy and religions class at university. There are all sorts of theories on what happens after."

"Theories. Because there are no facts except bodies in the ground. Now, we need to talk about the museum opening Saturday. If you've told Lorenzo we are dating, there's no point to pretending these things anymore. We will arrive together, stay by each other's sides, and leave together. Everyone will know we are together, no questions."

He was very good at that. Giving her just enough leeway in a conversation to think she was getting somewhere, and then shutting her down. She studied his face in the dappled sunlight. She'd always *let* him shut it down. With everyone else in her life, she was quite happy to poke and poke and poke until she got what she wanted.

But she'd always been just a shade afraid to do it with Teo. He sent out warnings, and she heeded them. Because, in that heady beginning, she'd been afraid he wouldn't love her. She hadn't realized it at the time, but realizing it now was embarrassing. She'd always prided herself on being so strong, so blunt and fearless with people.

She hadn't been those things with him in the beginning. She'd been more like her mother, who she'd vowed to never be like. She couldn't keep going down that road, because this was no longer the beginning. Saverina was no longer under the illusion it was real.

So she needed to be herself. To keep poking at him. Especially since a little flutter of panic wriggled in her stomach at the thought he might end this—when she should relish the thought. No more backing off. No more being afraid. It was time for her to...listen to her own mind, and her own heart. No matter the consequences.

She carefully twisted pasta onto her fork, lifted it. Steeled her spine and mustered some courage that had sorely been lacking on her end in this relationship. "Why are you so afraid to discuss it?" she asked him before popping the pasta in her mouth.

His affront was truly a thing of beauty. The way he straightened. The way his expression grew very cold and he seemed to somehow grow taller. No wonder he'd been so successful at Parisi. He knew how to wield his expression like sharp, deadly weapon.

But since she'd been attempting to get a reaction from him, the weapon caused no damage.

She smiled instead of wilting.

"I cannot fathom why you would consider my rational disinterest in *philosophy*, of all pointless, irrelevant topics, *fear*, but I assure you, it is not fear that causes me to have no patience for such banal conversations."

"Then what is it?" Saverina asked, imbuing her voice with as much innocence as she could muster.

"Pointlessness. Waste of time. I abhor both."

She pretended to think this over. "That's funny. All these lunches and evening events feel like a waste of time to me. People are whispering about us. My family knows. Dante no doubt knows after the gala that you are cavorting with his sworn enemy's sister. Yet here we are, still dancing about. If I didn't know you so well, I might think you actually liked spending time with me."

She wasn't fishing. A few days ago, that's what a question like that would have been, but now… Something had changed the other night. She'd been so vulnerable in front of him. Her panic attack. Explaining why she didn't want to work in the IT department. He was the only man she'd ever shared her body with. He knew more about her than just about anyone. She had opened herself to him.

She would let him go when this was all over. She was *determined* to let him go if that's what he demanded. She would not beg. She would not twist herself into her mother.

But what she would do in this time between now and then was demand more of him. Without fear. As they worked toward that end, she would work toward…answers. Simplifying the complicated things that lay between them.

The truth was, everything between them was complicated. By his lies, his issues, and her own insecurities. She knew he'd put up with her for his revenge even if he didn't like her at all, but she wasn't sure he was quite as good an actor as he thought he was. Because if she looked back on their relationship now, she could tell how different things were in the beginning.

She'd chalked it up to her own nerves, the awkwardness of the beginning of a relationship, but he'd been playing her. Using fake charm and smooth lines. He'd been gauging her every response, then adjusting for it. He'd swept her up and away, yes, but she couldn't help but think he'd been a little swept away too.

Something had happened that first time they'd kissed, then again when he'd taken her to bed for the first time. Everything had gotten messier. Less calculated. Sometimes he'd said the wrong thing, or they'd bickered. Sometimes his temper had flared—and he'd tried to hide it, but couldn't fully.

She couldn't say he'd gotten *careless*, but he'd gotten less *aware* that every moment they spent together was his own fiction.

She knew in his head he simply saw these things as attraction. Probably luck of the draw he'd chosen someone for his revenge who suited him well enough. He did not see it as real or love or anything she couldn't seem to let go, but that did not mean some reality and some love weren't *there*.

Saverina would not let herself *hope* for him realizing that. She would not sacrifice herself at the altar of *maybe he will love me someday.* But what she *would* do was acknowledge the chance that Teo cared for her more than he was willing to admit to himself.

"I *did* like spending time with you. Once," Teo said pointedly.

She realized how that might have hit her like a blow just a few days ago. Certainly a few weeks ago, when she'd believed in his unspoken love, that comment would have hurt.

Today she stayed relaxed, even smiled at him as she clucked her tongue. "Come, Teo. Doesn't it get a bit exhausting lying to yourself? Pretending you do all this to honor your mother's memory when it's only your own ego you're trying to salvage?"

It was a low blow. She knew it, but she was beginning to think that was the only way she ever got through his impeccable control. The only way to find out what truly lay in his heart. Low blows had gotten her through life, through to her brother when he'd been particularly stupid about Brianna.

Teo shoved back from the table, his chair scraping against the ground loud enough to have a few people looking their way. Which she supposed was the only reason he didn't stand.

She leaned across the table and spoke very quietly. "I'm not sure getting up and storming out in a childish temper tantrum are the optics you're hoping to achieve," she said, keeping her voice low, her expression calm. Fiery temper leaped in his eyes, but he did not get to his feet.

Triumph washed through her.

"I am not certain what you are trying to do with this new little attitude, Saverina, but it changes nothing."

Saverina nodded. "Yes, I agree. I suppose that's why I'm doing it. If nothing changes, I might as well be myself. I might as well *enjoy* myself, and watching you dance around your inevitable existential crisis is entertaining enough to try to push you over the edge."

Anger was like hot, fiery lava in his veins. Anger. Fury. Rage. Certainly not hurt. Teo would not account for *hurt* when the opinion of a billionaire's pampered little sister mattered to him not at all.

She was fooling herself into believing he might have feelings for her. Using obnoxious tactics fit for a *child* to get a rise out of him.

He would not allow it. But as he tried to even out his breathing, unclench his hand from the arm of the chair, he found the usually simple task of calming himself down difficult.

Existential crisis? Ridiculous! This was the purview of pampered, feckless fools. His revenge being about *ego*, after what that man had done to his mother? An insult of the highest order.

He did not need to react to every insult, though. He choked down the rest of his meal, and then they left the restaurant. He maintained his silence, but she chattered on as they walked out. He hoped it gave the illusion of a happy couple, but he wasn't sure his expression would fool anyone.

He was determined to get his temper under control on the walk back to the office building, have a foolish, *love drunk* smile on his face by the time they entered the building, but his temper only seemed to be stoked higher by the sunny day, by her cheerful, inconsequential chatter, the way everywhere he looked there seemed to be a couple holding hands, taking ridiculous selfies, *kissing*.

He wanted to destroy the image of every last one of them. Instead, he had to walk into their office building, and not snap at anyone who greeted them or spoke to them. He had to get into an elevator with her, the sweet smell of her perfume scenting the air like a drug that threatened to make him forget everything.

When the elevator stopped on her floor, she made a move to say goodbye, but he stopped her.

He got off the elevator with her. "We have something to discuss," he said under his breath. He thought of leading her to her office with a hand on her back, but something about the silky fabric of her shirt made him think of her skin under his hands, and if he touched her now…

She had her rules, but she had broken *his* rules by poking at him. She deserved a little turnabout. He would prove to her that she was not in control. She was *never* in control.

She swept into her office, and he closed her door, him still inside. She turned to face him, all challenge and some inner amused *knowing* that angered him to no end.

He did not move. For ticking minutes he stayed where he was, looked down at her, and finally watched her swallow in response. She still held on to her bravado from their lunch, but he saw wariness creep into her expression as he took a step toward her and then another.

But with that wariness was the spark of something else. She did not back away. She did not ward him off. She lifted her chin as he approached, as he crowded her. As he took her in his arms.

He said nothing. Words would not get his point across. *Words* would prove nothing. Kissing her and walking away unmoved would prove it all.

So he crashed his mouth to hers, damn all her ridiculous rules, and devoured. She did not push him away. Her hands slid up his chest, and then her arms banded around his neck. It was proving everything he wanted. She was weak for him.

But proving things and winning points seemed to dissolve as he tasted her again, as she pressed her soft body to his. It had been so long. He felt like a man in the desert, and she was the water he'd been seeking.

Her warmth, the soft give of her mouth, the way she threw herself into a kiss like nothing else could ever matter, and he got just as lost. All that coiled anger and tense frustration leaking out of him. So that the kiss was no longer weapons drawn, a gauntlet thrown, *war*.

It was peace. It was soft, swirling relief. She melted into him, and he held her as gently as he had after her panic attack. Her hands slid down his back and up again like she was offering comfort. And he found it, there in her mouth, by combing his fingers through her soft hair. She *eased* all those barbs inside of him so that he only wanted to stay here, exactly here.

Dimly, he heard the sound of his cell ringing and felt the vibrating in his pocket. He might have been content to ignore it if enjoyment had been the point of this endeavor, but he'd lost the point.

He'd *lost*.

He wrenched his mouth away from her, disgusted by the weakness he'd just discovered in himself. He had been *punishing* her, but he had *failed*.

Her eyes were dewy, her lips swollen from him, her hair mussed. She was the most beautiful thing he'd ever seen, so perfect in his arms he *ached* there in his chest. Like a heart could be fooled into believing in love after knowing how it ended.

No. He would never be fooled. He would never love. Life was nothing but a blip, and in that blip *he* was in control. Never something as useless as a heart.

"You may think you have the upper hand, *bedda*. But you want me, and it makes you *weak*. You will always be fooled by me because you want me to love you, but I do not love. I will not love. I do not know what weakness fools humans into thinking love means a damn, but it is as ephemeral as life."

Her eyes were bright, but her expression did not look devastated the way he *wanted* it to. And he still held her.

"Yet we live our lives anyway, Teo," she said softly, her arms still around his neck. "Ephemeral or not."

He removed her arms, stepped away from her. Shut it down. Iced it out. He did not look at her when he spoke, determined it was because she was *beneath* him, not because it hurt too much.

"If you mention my mother ever again, I will end this. Here and now. I will end it in the most embarrassing manner I can fathom. And I will get my revenge on Dante without you."

"But you'll have gotten your revenge on him, which means I'll still win too."

"Trust that if you do not do what I say, I will make sure you *never* win." He jerked her door open, but before he could take his leave, she spoke very softly.

"I thought you didn't care, Teo. These are very big emotions for a man so derisive of them."

He turned, faced her down this time. The anger so ripe inside of him he knew it was only that. He leaned down, got his face very close to hers so that she would understand the fury she'd unleashed. So no one out there in the hall would hear him speak to her this way. "This is strike one, Saverina. You do not want to get to strike three." And with that, he turned and left. He told himself it was a power move, but deep down…

He wondered.

CHAPTER THIRTEEN

SAVERINA DID NOT see Teo for two full days. He had his assistant cancel their lunch date both days. Saverina knew she should not read into that, but she wondered if this might actually be a good thing.

If he was avoiding her, that meant he had to feel *something* for her…didn't it? Certainly her words had caused some kind of reaction that made him not want to see her despite all his many *very* important plans.

They were supposed to attend an event tonight at a museum, and she had yet to hear from Mrs. Caruso about Teo canceling it, so she decided to head down to his office and face him before she went home at the end of the day.

She whistled to herself the whole way there. She hadn't been this happy and light since the beginning of their relationship. Back then she'd been drunk on the possibility of love, and now she was drunk on the truth. On being herself.

On poking at him until he breaks.

She laughed to herself in the elevator. It was so fun watching him get all cold and remote, because she could see it hid the fact he was *flustered*. Teo LaRosa might hide it well, he might rage and deny and cut down all his enemies, but when she was honest with him, when she refused to back away from his soft spots, *she* flustered *him*.

Heady stuff.

It wasn't that she wanted to hurt him. That wasn't the source of her joy at all. Her heart *ached* for him half the time. But she knew, from personal experience, things often had to hurt before they could heal.

He would never be *over* the death of his mother. You didn't simply heal grief. But Saverina wanted him to have a healthier relationship with that grief. And though it hurt, a painful, aching wound deep inside, she could stand the idea of never having him if it meant she got him to deal with that denial.

It was strange how everything inside of her had twisted into this new kind of appreciation for their situation. Strange how doing the most embarrassing things she could imagine—being fooled by him, having a panic attack in front of him—had showed her there was nothing to fear.

She could be herself in front of him. She could even *love* him. She could not control *him*—his responses, his feelings, his denial—but she didn't need to when she acknowledged her own.

When she allowed herself to release those fears, and the fear of repeating her mother's mistakes, everything seemed easier. She loved Teo, yes. It was quite possible he'd never return that feeling, and it would hurt. It would be devastating, even. But just like always, she would survive. She wouldn't be alone. She had her entire family to support her.

The idea of telling them the relationship had failed— or worse, that Teo had fooled her at first—had a little kernel of panic sprouting in her chest, so she set it aside. Because today was about dealing with Teo. Not about potentially looking like a failure to her family.

She smiled brightly at Mrs. Caruso, ignored the woman's usual admonitions with a pleasant wave, and waltzed right into Teo's office since the door was open.

He looked up, and she studied his expression. A flash of something—a bit like anger, but not quite that simple. Then he cooled it all off into ice.

"Saverina," he said, her name devoid of any inflection.

"Good evening, Teo," she said with all the cheerfulness she had inside her. "How are you?"

He eyed her warily, looking her up and down before turning that gaze even colder. "Can I help you with something?"

It was such a strange realization to find that exact tone of voice might have made her wilt before she'd found out about his lies. He would have pulled that out and she would have thought she did something wrong. She would have left—chin high, because she'd always had her pride—but she would have gone home and cried a little.

It seemed the truth really *did* set you free. Maybe it helped that she didn't believe his icy stares and harsh words had anything to do with *her* now. She understood the way he reacted to her was all about his own issues.

It was freeing.

"I'm on my way home, but since you're so fond of canceling our plans lately, I wanted to make sure we're still going to the museum event this evening. Together. I did not get a cancelation from Mrs. Caruso, but you've been absent the past few days. Have you been ill?"

He stared at her with cool eyes. "I have been busy."

She nodded as if she understood perfectly. "Of course." She even smiled at him and *didn't* point out that he'd never been busy for two straight days when it came to her before. "Too busy to go to the museum event? I could always go alone, but I'm afraid there *would* be talk now that our relationship is public and we haven't been engaging in our usual lunches."

"I doubt anyone pays that much attention," he said through clenched teeth.

But she kept her sunny smile in place. "I think you know they do, or you wouldn't have set this whole plan into motion in the first place. I know you're very busy, and not at all a coward, but we did say we'd be there tonight."

His expression went very nearly volcanic when she said the word *coward*. She had to bite her tongue to keep from laughing. Who knew keeping a cheerful attitude in the face of someone's fury could be so entertaining?

"If you're still planning on attending, and still wanted to approve my outfit, you should come by the house a little early. I'll have Antonina let you in."

His gaze grew skeptical. "Is that in adherence to your little rules?"

He meant it to be insulting. Too bad he failed at that. "I've been thinking about my rules. I set them up to protect myself."

"You would be smart to do so. Always."

She nodded along. "It made sense when I was heartbroken and embarrassed," she said. Then gave an insouciant shrug. "But I'm not anymore."

His eyes narrowed, temper flashing in their dark depths. It really was hard not to laugh in his face when he was so easy to rile up. When she knew he would only care about that statement if he *wanted* her to be heartbroken. Which would likely mean his heart was a little more involved than he wanted.

"Seven thirty work for you?" she asked sweetly.

A silence stretched out, his dark and vibrating with portent. Her smile never faltered. His dark-as-night act didn't faze her now, and what a gift that was.

"Very well," he agreed eventually.

She skirted his desk, watched the little war in his expression. She had the feeling he wanted to lean *away* from her—which was a victory indeed when it came to a man like him. Even if he ended up holding his ground.

She leaned down, brushed a kiss across his cheek. "See you soon." Then she walked out of his office, feeling lighter than she had in weeks.

Teo was too smart not to see this was a trap. He just couldn't quite fathom what trap Saverina was laying for him. *Yet.*

Not heartbroken anymore. What rot. If she'd gotten over it that quickly, her heart had never been involved in the first place.

Not that it mattered, because his heart did not exist and was certainly not involved and never would be. He rubbed at the odd pain in his chest as he walked up to Saverina's door.

Too much stress. Not enough sleep. Perhaps he should see a doctor. Revenge was inching closer, and it was a delicate business. That's what kept his mind going in circles at night, certainly not memories of Saverina in his apartment and the frustration of her not being there anymore. Not missing their lunches even though it had only been two days.

No. He was not so weak and childish. Wouldn't allow himself to be.

When the door opened, it was indeed the woman who'd served them drinks the other night. Teo forced himself to smile. He was in control of his face, his feelings, all of it. And if he'd had to remind himself of that more the past few days than he had in years, well, again.

Stress.

"Saverina said to send you on up to her bedroom." The woman led him down a hall and pointed at some stairs. "She's the first door on the right."

He did not trust this letting go of her rules. The soliciting his opinion on her outfit. The inviting him to her *bedroom*. Alone. He took the stairs and braced himself for some kind of…attack. But a man only fell for a trap if he didn't see it coming, and Teo saw this coming a mile away.

Whatever it was.

The first door on the right was open, and as Teo stepped over the threshold, he came up short.

The room was an explosion of color…and mess. He looked at it all in shock. She'd always been very neat at his apartment, never leaving a thing out of place. Her office at Parisi was always elegant and tidy. She herself was always well put together.

What was *this*? Clothes everywhere. Plants in every corner, hanging from the ceiling in some places. Piles and piles of notebooks, jewelry, makeup.

A door deeper in the room opened, and out she came, her hair piled on top of her head in curling spirals. She was dressed, but barefoot. When she saw him standing there, her smile bloomed.

"Oh, good, you're here. Zip me up, will you?"

She turned her back to him, the zipper of the dress gaping open. The band of her bra was a bright, vibrant pink against the demure black of the dress. His gut tightened.

He studied her back, the elegant curve of her neck left

naked by the updo of her hair. Was this some game of…
seduction?

She looked over her shoulder at him. "We don't have
time to waste, Teo. I still have to decide what shoes to
wear. *If* you like this dress."

It wasn't anything like the red one she'd worn at the
gala. This one was not meant to hit a man over the head
with her raw sex appeal. No, this little black number was
meant to be a demure display of all the exquisite beauty
she possessed. A tease, all in all.

Particularly now that he knew she wore a bright pink
bra underneath. But he was no fool. He would not fall
prey to her little game. He crossed the room to her and
found the zipper there at the small of her back.

He did not resist touching her. She could put on this
little act, she could claim lack of heartbreak, but chemistry did not lie, and she felt it just as much—if not *more*—
than he did. He skimmed his finger along her soft skin
as he pulled the zipper up.

He felt the intake of breath, heard the little shudder of
it as she exhaled. But when she turned to face him, she
was all sunny smiles. "Thanks!" Then she did a little turn
in her dress. "Approve?"

It plunged in the front, but not outrageously so. The
straps were mere suggestions of fabric rather than anything substantial, and the dress's shape swept around her,
outlining the perfect hourglass of her figure.

He could not seem to come up with *words*. Why should
such a simple garment affect him so? Because she had
set it up thusly, laid down rules, and was now breaking
them on purpose. It was *all* a game.

One he had no designs on winning, because he had
no desire to play.

"It's fine," he returned.

She didn't even pout. Just turned to an array of shoes spread out all along the floor. "Which shoes do you think I should wear?"

He did not know why this question enraged him, but he knew he could not let that frustration show. "Approval is not playing fashionista, *bedda*."

She shrugged as if to say, *your loss*. Then spent far too long in silence contemplating the pairs of shoes. She chose an open-toed pair that showed off the pink nails that matched her bra.

Like a *dare*.

There'd never been a question that she was a beautiful woman. He'd never had to feign attraction for her. So she could not use those wiles against him, because they weren't *weapons*. They were just her.

And he was immune. He would be *immune*.

He took his time before speaking to ensure he was as cool and detached as he was determined to be.

"I do not know what game you're playing at, Saverina, but I can assure you it is not one you will win."

She sighed. Heavily. Then crossed to him and patted his chest. Like he was a misguided *child*. "Teo, it is no *game*. What you are now dealing with is simply *me*."

"And what, pray tell, was I dealing with before?"

She seemed to consider this, moving over to a vanity. She poked around in little bowls and boxes filled with jewelry. "Insecurity, I suppose. When I thought this was all real, I was very careful around you. I didn't change my whole personality, lie about the things I like, change who I am at my core, or anything like that, so I thought it was fine. But I was careful with the truth. Careful with how readily I showed how much I enjoyed your company.

Maybe I was just taking cues from you at first, but in the end, I was so afraid you would not love me if I pushed too hard, that I simply didn't push at all." She attached one dangly earring that sparkled in the light, and then the other, as she studied herself in the mirror.

When she finally turned, her expression was one of complete control. He didn't want to believe this little speech of hers, but it was hard not to when he realized he'd never seen this expression on her face before. He'd seen what she spoke of. Always just a hint of being careful.

"I have to thank you, I think," she said. "For lying to me. It taught me a valuable lesson. Because if I'd been honest, if I hadn't been so afraid of...failing at relationships or whatever, I would have been *fully* myself, and maybe this would have gone differently. If I'd been open and honest about my feelings. Then again, maybe it wouldn't have. Maybe you have it in you to lie and manipulate someone who's in love with you, but I don't think you do."

"You'd be surprised, *bedda*." He would do *anything* for his revenge. That had always been the plan. Whatever it took. Maybe he'd lost sight of that, but she had reminded him. *This* had reminded him. He was not nice. He did not care for her feelings, her panic attacks, *her*. The foolish fiction of *love*.

All he cared about was his revenge.

"Maybe," she agreed, so damn readily he wanted to rage. "But it is of no matter. Because my lesson is learned, and now I will not fear being myself, feeling all my feelings around you. If you do not like that version of me..." She lifted an elegant shoulder. "It is your problem. Not mine."

CHAPTER FOURTEEN

SAVERINA HAD NOT fully realized how many eggshells she'd been walking on all this time with Teo. A shadow of herself. It should be embarrassing, maybe, but it was hard not to chalk it up to a learning experience. She was young. All in all, it had not been the most traumatizing first love a person could endure.

Now that she had let most of her anger go, now that she saw this whole experience as just that—an *experience*—to learn and grow from, she could sit back, relax and enjoy.

Oh, she was still in love with him. That wouldn't be easy to get over. But it was *possible*. And maybe, just maybe, she'd be able to get through to him. Show him that his grief was not the enemy, and his revenge could never assuage it.

She wouldn't shrink herself to make that happen, and *that* was the difference between real love and what her parents had done to one another.

She watched the city go by, content with Teo's brooding silence tonight. The fact he *was* brooding, *was* irritated with her, was only a good sign. Much like the realization she'd come to earlier about him lowering his guard with her after the first few weeks of wooing her with fake charm and smiles. When Teo couldn't control his anger, frustration, or whatever this was, that meant there was something deeper at play.

Poor hurting man. So determined to fight away all those feelings. Maybe they needed to get their revenge over with so he could get to that other side and *realize* he needed to deal with his grief.

She'd done some digging on Dante's wife, Julia. She'd gone back over everything she'd found when the attack had first happened and tried to coordinate a plan on what she could hack into that would give them answers. She had a lead to tug. She hadn't told Teo the work she'd done, not just because he'd been playing scarce, but because she'd wanted to get *something* for sure before she admitted to him she was trying to.

She might be growing, maturing, *evolving*, but it was a process, not an immediate cure. She'd likely always have panic attacks, so mitigating her triggers wasn't *cowardice*.

Or so her therapist had told her.

The limo joined a line of cars in front of the museum. The wealthy and elite glittered as they got out of their cars and made their way up the lighted walk to the museum.

Before the limo came to a full stop at the dropping-off point, Teo took her hand.

Every time he touched her, her heart still leaped. She still *hoped*. But that didn't make her a fool. She wouldn't let it. She would not fall into the trap of believing love was inconsequential any more than she would allow herself to treat it like a drug.

As she'd once told Teo, it required trust and respect. She would not settle for love without it. But that didn't mean she had to abandon *all* hope she could help him, open his eyes, find the heart of him.

He took the ring he'd once given her and moved it from the pointer finger to her left ring finger. "Tonight there will be no doubt."

Her breath caught, too many things fighting for purchase in her gut. It wasn't *real*. But, oh, this ring and his serious expression made that easy to forget. "But I've *just* told my family we're dating. I can hardly—"

"The timetable has moved up." He got out of the car before she could mount an argument.

She inhaled deeply, let it out. She wouldn't scramble after him. She wouldn't be predictable. How would an emotionally mature person handle this? She got out of the car when he opened her door, took his offered hand.

When she got to her feet, she met his gaze with a bland, calm one of her own. "I don't *have* to do this, Teo."

"Then don't."

Calling each other's bluffs. But the time for bluffs was over. The time for careful and tiptoeing and *plans* was over.

He tucked her arm into his, smiled at someone who greeted him, and pulled her forward. She went, not wanting to make a scene, but once again, she chose to see this as a good thing. Proof he was rattled.

"Why did we move up our timetable?" she asked, plastering a social smile on her face as they moved forward into the museum.

"You accused me of wasting time. Well, perhaps you were right. Perhaps I was being too careful. Now we'll move. Full steam ahead, because that is my plan, and my plan is the only one that matters."

"You seem very adamant about that. So angrily sure that it's all you could possibly want or care about."

"Almost as if I have been crystal clear about that for a

while now, *bedda*." He moved them toward a man with a tray, handed her a flute of champagne. "Why not find some of your little friends who love to gossip about Parisi?" he said dismissively. "Make sure to flash that ring about."

Saverina thought about being difficult, but doing it here wouldn't suit their revenge narrative. As much as she thought Teo needed to understand there was more to life, more to *him* than this revenge, she also wanted to see Dante pay.

Especially if her theory that he'd attacked his own son turned out to be true. So for the next few hours, she would play her role. After the event, she would try to poke at Teo again.

She found a few of the biggest office gossips, started up a conversation, until they inevitably noticed her ring. Some just got wide-eyed and didn't mention it, though they'd no doubt take it back to their friends who might care about such things.

However, Nevi, one of Saverina's least favorite people at Parisi, immediately grasped her hand. "Oh, my! Look at *that*!" She looked up at Saverina, eyes all wide…but calculating. "Who?" Nevi demanded.

Saverina found that a little odd. She knew it was all over the office she and Teo were dating now. Their lunches had done that. For Nevi to act like she didn't know who Saverina might be engaged to was a bit suspicious.

"Teo, naturally," she said, tugging her hand free of Nevi's.

"Teo *LaRosa*! But…he's so handsome."

As if that meant he wouldn't be interested in Saverina? She tried not to scowl, but this was exactly why she didn't like Nevi. She was the queen of trying to make everyone else feel small. "That he is."

Nevi chewed on her bottom lip, leaned forward as if they were confidants. "Aren't you worried?"

"About what?"

"Well, we all know who your brother is. This was a bit whirlwind. Aren't you worried he's just using you to get to your brother?"

Saverina looked at the woman a full, silent minute until a faint blush began to creep into Nevi's cheeks.

"Sorry. I guess that was insensitive."

But she didn't look *sorry*. She looked embarrassed. Like Saverina was supposed to have just answered the inappropriate question, not made it awkward.

It didn't matter that Nevi was correct, in a way. Teo *was* using her to get things. And if—*when*—they broke off the engagement, this is what people would assume. She would have to live with that very public embarrassment. And likely all her siblings' pity.

She could let herself panic over that, or she could focus on the evening. What mattered was Nevi not getting a win in this little game of immature posturing.

"I guess you never really know a person's true motives," Saverina said, attempting to sound very *worldly*. And like Nevi couldn't possibly understand. "You can't read their mind or anything. But I think I know him. I understand him as well as anyone can. This isn't about Lorenzo." It wasn't even about Dante anymore. But Teo *would* hold on to the belief it was.

Until she found a way to *prove* to him that he was in a deep denial. Until she could hold up a mirror to all his hurts and *insist* he face them.

So while he played the game of revenge, while Nevi and whoever else played their middle school lunchroom games, Saverina would find a way to save the man she loved.

* * *

There was a reason Teo had wanted to come to *this* event. A reason he hadn't let Saverina in on. Which was why he'd sent her off to make certain the gossipmongers saw her ring, on *that* finger, and went to work spreading the news.

News that would be the talk of Parisi tomorrow. Far more than the gossip should anyone notice that he was talking to Dante Marino's wife at the event.

Because Julia Marino was set to attend. He'd never met the woman, but once he'd learned of her RSVP to the event—and Dante's regrets—he'd studied up on her, made sure to look at a few pictures so he would know her when she appeared.

She was speaking with a small, slight man in a shadowy corner when he sent Saverina off to stoke gossip. Teo didn't make a beeline. He took the roundabout approach to putting himself in her orbit. He watched her the entire time, even as he greeted people he knew, or pretended to study a display. Eventually, he positioned himself in just such a way so she would *accidentally* bump into him. All it took was watching her out of the corner of his eye, then stepping back just as she started forward.

She ran right into him. "Oh, goodness. So sorry." She reached out to steady herself, and he took her by the elbow. "I didn't spill your drink, did I?"

He smiled kindly, released her arm, and held up the mostly empty glass in response. "All is well. Pardon me. I must have been distracted. Lovely display, no?" he said, pointing to the bronze sculpture from some centuries ago he'd been pretending to admire.

She just kept staring at him for a full minute before she seemed to remember herself. "Sorry. You've taken me a little off guard. You look…familiar."

"I'm sorry to say, you do not." He offered a sheepish shrug. "Perhaps I just look *like* someone you know."

She nodded. Slowly. "You have a rather striking resemblance to my sons, actually."

He made a considering noise. No wonder. They would share DNA, would they not? Did she say that knowing it was true? A stab of fury tried to take purchase, but he iced it away. "Teo LaRosa," he said, offering his hand. "Perhaps we are long-lost relatives," he said with a laugh.

She didn't even feign a smile in response. "LaRosa. I knew a woman by the name of Giuseppa LaRosa once."

Teo's eyes widened. He slapped a free hand to his chest. "My mother."

She looked him up and down, then managed what appeared to be a very forced smile. "It's been years. How is she?"

"Passed, I'm afraid."

"Ah. I am sorry. She was…" Julia trailed off, looking around the room as if to escape.

"And you are?" Teo asked.

There was another hesitation. "Julia Marino. I believe your mother once worked in my household."

Teo pretended to be confused by that. "Hmm. It's possible, I suppose. In my lifetime, she always worked cleaning large office buildings. Oh, but your husband is Dante Marino, is he not? Perhaps she cleaned his building?"

Julia's expression got more and more…closed off, Teo supposed. "You work for Parisi now," she said. Flatly. Ignoring his questions altogether.

"Yes. Oh, dear. We're a bit of your husband's rivals, aren't we?" Then he gave a little chuckle. "Ah, I suppose I should not be seen cavorting with the enemy. Or vice versa."

Her blue gaze cooled. Considerably. "I suppose not. I'm...sorry about your mother, Mr. LaRosa. Enjoy your evening." Then she turned on a heel and strode away.

Teo could not let the self-satisfied grin that wanted to spread do so. He had to keep his expression bland, maybe faintly puzzled. He turned and scanned the room, looking for Saverina. Or at least hoping that's what anyone paying attention would think he was doing.

He had planted the seeds he'd intended to with Julia. What might grow from them? So many options, but any of them would give him exactly what he sought.

When his gaze landed on Saverina, she was laughing with a man Teo knew worked in Parisi's IT department. For a blinding second, he forgot about Julia. Dante. Revenge.

All he saw was her smiling at another man. Too close together. For a strange, out-of-body moment, he imagined himself *bodily* removing said man from Saverina's orbit, but the man was already walking away from her by the time Teo could see past the immobilizing rage that pummeled him.

He breathed out, his face hot, his heartbeat a rapid, rabid thing in his chest. If he stepped back from this situation, looked at the whole thing as an outsider, he might worry that this was *jealousy*.

But of course, this was all revenge, so he had nothing to be jealous of. It was about the *image* of it all.

What he found most disconcerting about the moment was that his usual denials *felt* wrong. He couldn't fully accept that he was mad about image when the very idea of another man touching her made him want to tear down the foundations of the earth.

But he would get it under control. He would...he would

find a way to undo this. To reverse these strange, unnec-essary, *impossible* feelings.

Saverina made her way over to him, and he was glad he'd stayed where he was. Proud that he had stood his ground. Maybe a few wayward feelings had escaped, but he hadn't acted on them. That was all that mattered.

"I think news will be all over the office on Monday," Saverina said, sliding her arm into his, easy as you please. "I'll have to call Lorenzo when we get home and let him know the happy news." She was close now, her per-fume in its normal dance with ruining him entirely as she leaned in closer. "Were you talking to Julia Marino?"

"Yes," he bit out, his gaze following the man who'd been talking to Saverina.

"Why?"

"We will discuss it later."

She frowned at that, but she didn't argue. They made the rounds. Enjoyed different displays. She made him laugh with her insightful commentary about some mod-ern art that didn't make any earthly sense to him. Then she made him uncomfortable when she got teary over an old artifact of a child's toy displayed with bits of blanket and earthenware.

"It's kind of amazing. The things that never change, no matter how many centuries have passed, don't you think?"

"I don't think about the past."

She pursed her lips and looked up at him. "Perhaps you should, Teo."

"I do not see why. I live in the present." Case in point, the man who'd been standing far too close to Saverina was *presently* talking to someone but looking at *her* while he did so. Teo angled his body to block the man's gaze from Saverina. He pointed at the ancient artifacts. "What does any of that have to do with now?"

"You live in a present informed by their past and your own, and if you don't know what any of that has to do with now, perhaps you should consider it."

"I don't see why I'd waste my time."

She sighed heavily, clearly frustrated with him, but it was a foolish conversation. Besides, they'd done what they came to do. They could leave now. Far away from anyone's too hot gaze. Once he dropped her off, he could leave these twisted, unwelcome feelings behind. He could focus on his plan. On his revenge.

On the only thing that mattered.

When they got into the limousine, Saverina immediately turned to him. "What were you talking to Dante's wife about?"

"Nothing really. Just gauging her reaction to my name, my face. She mentioned I look like her sons."

"Oh." Saverina slumped back into the seat, pushed a palm to her heart. "Oh, how awful for her."

"I doubt it was a surprise, Saverina." He didn't want to consider Julia Marino's feelings or Saverina's response to those feelings. It was just the business of revenge. "And if Dante really attacked their son, and she knows he did, I hardly doubt my existence will change her perception of her husband."

"Maybe. Maybe she knew. Maybe she hates him. But it can't be an easy thing to know your lawful husband had a child with someone else."

He did not know why this made him think of the man she'd been talking to. But as he was not jealous, and he did not care, he pushed it away. "She is still married to him," Teo pointed out. "It cannot be that hard on her."

Saverina shook her head. "You can't begin to know what she might feel or think about it. You don't know…" She let out a long sigh. "You are a brick wall sometimes."

"Sometimes?"

She chuckled a little. "I suppose it's my own fault for constantly flinging myself at it."

"There has been a decided lack of *flinging* lately, *bedda*. Toward *me* anyway."

Her eyebrows drew together, like she didn't understand. "Have I been flinging myself elsewhere that I don't know about?" she asked, as if she genuinely had no idea.

Which infuriated him. It made him feel as though he was overreacting when, of course, he was not. He'd seen her too close to that man with his own eyes, in front of all those people who were supposed to believe she was engaged to *him*.

Something had to change. She had introduced these changes, this *being herself*, and he had not pivoted yet. He needed to sort out his response, shore up his defenses. He could not let her get to him like this.

"I would simply like you to consider the optics of cozying up with another man when we're trying to convince people *we* are engaged. I did not think it needed saying before tonight, but apparently you need some educating on how to behave like an engaged woman."

She stared at him for a full silent minute. He wanted to look away. He—inconceivably—wanted to move his body in what could only be called a *fidget*. Unacceptable.

"I don't recall cozying up to anyone. Except the odious Nevi, and I don't think she is who you mean." She kept *staring* at him, like she could see through every last brick wall she claimed he had. "The only man even remotely my age that I spoke to at that event was Carlo.

Who happens to be my sister-in-law's cousin. And married. We were talking about his impending fatherhood."

"It is my experience none of these things prevent a man from wanting what he should not have." Those words felt damning…but not toward her. Toward himself.

Again, her silence dragged out, even as the limo came to a stop outside her home. His skin felt too tight, and everything inside of him too tense, like he might simply explode. He did not understand anything that was happening inside of him.

"Were you jealous, Teo?" she asked softly. All silky promise.

He barked out a laugh, too loud in the condensed air of the limo's back seat. "I am worried about how it *seems* to those we need to convince in order to achieve my only goal." He wanted to add that he did not care who she laughed with, who she touched, but the very image had his throat closing so tight he could not force out the words.

"Ah." But she did not sound convinced, and this pounded through him like an uncontrollable fire.

She turned to him then. Her knees brushing his, those eyes flashing with something he recognized all too well. A softness he did not want from her. Ever.

"You were my first. You have been my only." She reached forward, brushed a hand over his tie, the words, the gesture sending all that fire straight to his sex. "Does that make you feel better, Teo?"

"I am quite sure I do not care one way or the other," he ground out, but something primal roared through him in direct contrast to his words. He wanted to reach out. Take. Hold. Keep.

"Would you like to come in for a drink?" she asked,

still playing with his tie. "We could discuss jealousy. Flinging. Brick walls."

He raised an eyebrow at her, not at all trusting what she was up to. Or maybe it was the roaring need inside of himself he did not trust. "You really *have* thrown the rules out the window."

"Like I said, those were about protecting myself. I think…is it really living if you're always protecting yourself? Never risking? Never feeling? I suppose you get injured constantly flinging yourself at the brick wall, but sometimes you break through. And it's worth the bumps and bruises along the way."

He did not like this analogy. For a great many reasons. "You have attached a lot of *philosophy* onto sex, Saverina."

She didn't even falter. "Sex is what you make of it, Teo. I don't mind it being a little philosophical. Not with you. So, do you want to come in?"

She wanted him to say yes, clearly. She wanted some admission of jealousy. He would not give her those things…but that did not mean he had to all-out resist. As long as it was her idea. Her choice.

Because if *she* chose it, it did not have to be about any of those things he did not want it to be about. It could just be sex. Something they were very good at together. "Are you inviting me in?"

She sighed heavily and shook her head. "Teo, I'm asking you. Is that what *you* want to do? Regardless of revenge. Would *you* like to come inside and share a drink and some time with *me*?"

Words seemed to jumble. *Regardless of revenge* when he was only made of revenge. When nothing else could *matter*—not her, not wants, not something as foolish as jealousy. *Nothing.*

"I'd be happy to invite you in, to take you upstairs, to enjoy all this heat between us, Teo. I'd be happy to forget *all* my rules, but you'll have to come out and say it, Teo. Do you want me? Is a night together what *you* want?"

She was trying to…break down his supposed brick walls. But there was *nothing* behind his walls. Just a void. "It is of no matter to me, *bedda*."

She nodded, then reached for the car door and opened it herself. "Then I'll see you Monday at work."

She was outside in the dark evening before he could muster a response.

He would let her go. He *should* let her go. None of the *feelings* fighting it out inside of him, painful and angry, were things he could ever let win. Could ever let control him. He couldn't control loss…so he could only ensure he won. He couldn't *want* that which would lead him astray. That which threatened all the control, all the walls he'd erected these past two years.

"You have been my only." As if that could ever matter in this world. In his *plans*. The only thing that mattered was his revenge.

But his hand was on the car door handle, and all he could think about was her. *"Do you want me?"* She'd posed it like a simple question, and maybe it should be, but it felt more like he was being cleaved in two. What he wanted. What he didn't. Somehow both the exact same thing.

Want. Want. Want.

Her.

CHAPTER FIFTEEN

SAVERINA HEARD THE car door slam. She jumped at the surprise of it in the quiet night. She really hadn't expected him to...change his mind.

She didn't let herself turn around to look at him. She didn't let herself run for him like she wanted to. He had to choose. He had to put his wants above his plans. She had to *let* him do that.

But it was hard to keep walking. To reach out to put her key in the lock. To pretend she did not hear or feel him approach. She unlocked the door, even turned the knob, but before she could push the door open, his hand clasped over her arm.

He turned her around, and she wanted to close her eyes. The punch of him in moonlight would be too much. She had invited him in because she wanted him, but she needed him to want her too. If it had taken a little unnecessary jealousy to get there, so be it. But she needed some *give*, or she was just throwing herself at the same brick wall, hoping for different results.

That would only leave her shattered. She couldn't allow herself delusions now. She was mature. She was strong. She could fight, but she couldn't sacrifice herself at the altar of his jealousy for *nothing*.

She needed more.

She looked into his eyes, and she was lost. His mouth crashed to hers and she welcomed it, throwing her arms around his neck, kissing him back with wild abandon just as she had in her office the other day.

He'd told her she was weak that day, and maybe she was. But if it felt like this, she would be weak. Just for a few seconds. The dark, dangerous taste of him. His hands in her hair. The way his heart pounded against hers.

Because his heart *was* involved. His *wants* existed beyond his revenge—*this* had nothing to do with Dante. How could it? But she needed to hear him say it. Admit it. Out loud. To them both.

She pulled her mouth free, pushed her hand to his chest. Her breathing was ragged, and her heart felt a bit like an open wound, but she had found herself in all this mess. She wouldn't go back now. She would not turn into someone she wasn't any longer.

She met his gaze, cloudy with desire and tinged with anger and fear.

But she would not be afraid. "Say it," she demanded. She'd set a boundary. He'd respect it or perish. Because this *wasn't* weak. This was a step toward whatever lay beyond revenge.

He'd made his decision already, she knew. That was why he was standing here. Touching her. Still she watched the war play out over his face. When he spoke, it was little more than a growl. "I want *you*."

She threw herself at him then. The desire working through her like a potent, heavy liquor, or maybe like that drug she promised herself love wouldn't be. It was wild and dangerous.

His hands slid over her skirt. Then his fingers curled under the hem of the fabric and began to lift up. Cool air swirled around her now bare legs, but the heat of him, of their kiss, kept her from fully feeling it.

She expected him to touch her, to take her here, so much like the last night they'd been together. Back at his apartment. His anger and frustration biting at his control. She wouldn't refuse—couldn't. This was him at his truest, and that was what she wanted.

But instead he lifted her, smoothed his hands up her legs, and she needed no further urging to wrap them around his waist. To let him carry her inside, arching against him with a needy whimper.

He stepped inside, some mix of a groan and growl vibrating low in his throat. She raked her hands through his hair, reveling in the strength of him, the perfect, tense muscle required of every step. She didn't care who saw, who reported what to Lorenzo. She only cared that she felt his skin on hers.

He walked straight to the staircase, one kiss bleeding into another. Teeth and tongue and his lips never leaving hers. He carried her all the way up the stairs, and there was no sense that his breath was ragged from the effort of doing so. No, that was all from what they made each other *feel*.

He kicked her bedroom door closed but didn't put her down. Though he did stop kissing her long enough to speak. "Your room is a disaster."

She laughed, incapable of controlling the breathless feeling running rampant through her. "Mostly I like things neat, but the room I sleep in I like to feel *lived* in." *Live.* Oh, how she wanted him to live. With her.

This would solve nothing. This was temporary, physical. An explosion of all that chemistry. Or maybe it was an expression of her love. He wouldn't accept *that*, not yet.

But maybe it could be a chip in that brick wall. One he looked back to and realized it had been more, meant more.

Maybe he could believe she loved him, and that it would matter that she did, before it was too late. Maybe he couldn't ever get there. But she'd know she gave it her all. She'd given her love before she'd called it quits.

She gentled the kiss, her arms. She unhooked her legs and slid down his body until she was on her own two feet again. She didn't let him go, didn't break the kiss. Instead, she called on all the tenderness she'd ever possessed and put it in her kiss, her touch, even the press of her body against his.

There was a moment, so brief, when she thought she felt him simply...relax. Give in. *Lean* in. Like someone starved of touch...but in this case what he was starved of was *love*. And she had so much to give him. So much.

He withdrew. First the kiss, then his body. He went so far as to take her by the arms and set her back...just a step. But he didn't release her arms. They simply stood there, now a little space between them, winded and staring at each other.

He said nothing. Didn't move. Didn't let her go. Whatever warred within was something he was determined to be his and his alone.

She, on the other hand, was determined he share it. So, even with his hands still gripping her elbows, she reached forward. He didn't stop her. She smoothed her hands up the lapels of his jacket, and his hands dropped from her arms.

She pushed the jacket off, gave it a tug so it fell to the ground. She held his heated gaze as she slowly unbuttoned his shirt. Spread it and pushed it off just like the jacket. He was all muscle, tense and beautiful. That brick wall, but she could feel his heartbeat under her hand. Real and living.

She wanted to show him just *how* real. She got to her knees, reveled in his sharp intake of breath as she unzipped his pants. Freed him. Then held his sharp, needy gaze as she took him in her mouth.

She watched him the entire time, the intent gaze, the harsh cast of his mouth. Here because he couldn't resist. Not her, not the heat between them. Against all his plans, against all his strength of control, he'd gotten out of that car, told her what he wanted, because he wanted *her*.

He pulled her back, hand fisted in her hair. Then he simply held her there, looking down at her, both of them shaking just a little. He said nothing, made no move to allow her to finish or to do more.

"What do you want, Teo?" she asked, her voice a hoarse whisper in the quiet room, barely audible over the harsh echo of his own breath. His scowl hardened at the word *want*, so she smiled.

"I want to take that dress off of you, Saverina. I want to lay you out on that bed and taste every inch of you." The he gathered her up and did just that. With wild kisses and gentle hands.

His mouth roved over her body, stoking fires, teasing, then plundering, then teasing again. She was in some other world made only of nerve endings and a love so big it threatened to drown her where she lay. Until it did, in waving crashes of pleasure that nearly had her crying.

But she wouldn't do that. Not just yet. She rolled over him, positioned herself on top. She looked down at him. "I want *you*, Teo. All of you," she said, then took him. Slow. Deep.

Everything.

Straddled on top of him, looking down at the self-satis-fied half smile on his face. That faded when she reached out, traced a lock of his hair with her finger tenderly. But before he could mount any of his many defenses, she moved against him. And she decided *this* was for her.

She didn't worry about him. What he saw. What he felt. She found her own pleasure. Until she was shaking out a release so potent her muscles felt weak and lax, and she all but collapsed on top of him.

"I missed this," she said, the emotion swamping her. He'd lied to her, she knew, but she thought in this he'd always been honest. They'd always been them, lost in what they could bring out in each other.

He merely grunted and flipped her onto her back, rang-ing over her like some sort of avenging soldier. But she knew it wasn't *her* or even her words that he fought. It was his internal response to them.

So she kept going as he slid inside. As he made the pleasure build again, spiral higher, and deeper. "I missed you. Even when I hated you, I missed you."

His grip on her hips tightened, but he did not stop. He pushed her over that last edge, eyes black as obsidian, the war all over his beautiful face. The orgasm crashed over her, a wave of light and sensation and release. "I love you, Teo," she murmured, pressing a kiss to his neck as he followed her over the edge.

He should have left. Teo knew this in his bones, but he had not. In the aftermath, he'd convinced himself her *"I love you"* was of no consequence. If she felt such things, if she refused to accept he did not—and never would—that was on *her*.

Then he'd fallen asleep, so quickly, so easily. He didn't

wake up *once* through the night—not due to a stress dream, or the strange panic that had sometimes gripped him the past few months. He'd slept free and easy, like he hadn't in years.

It might have been worth it, he supposed. A good night's sleep would help his stress. Help him keep a clear mind as they barreled forward toward revenge. A good night's sleep would keep him sharp and in control when it came to Saverina's *I love you*.

"You have been my only."

But in the pearly light of morning, her hair spread out over her colorful floral sheets. Her even breathing, the soft silk of her skin glowing in the shaft of light that poked through the curtains. His ring on her finger sparkling in that same light. The need to touch her, to drown himself in her scent and never leave, to always be her only, was so big, so deep, so all encompassing, one thing was very clear.

He had made a mistake. She was a danger. Herself. Her love. All of it. It threatened what he wanted.

And still he didn't leave. He could only lie here and stare at her, wondering how she'd done it. How she'd somehow bewitched him into risking everything.

Maybe he hoped she'd press the issue when she woke. Maybe he hoped she'd be angry he didn't return the sentiment. Maybe he hoped...for too much.

When she blinked her eyes open, sleepy and warm, she merely smiled at him. Soft and vulnerable, when she should know better by now. She stretched and yawned and curled into him, even as he kept himself perfectly still.

"I want you to let me take you somewhere this morning," she murmured against his chest, her finger tracing some unknown pattern there above his heart.

Teo felt as though he needed to clear his throat but refused such a weakness. He waited until he knew he'd be able to speak firmly. "I only have the clothes I wore last night."

"I'll get you something more casual to wear." She slid out of bed, and for a moment he forgot all his self-admonitions, the very important need to get out of here, and only watched her beautiful, naked form cross the room, slide on a short silk robe and then move for the door.

She turned in the doorway and looked at him…almost as if she was memorizing the moment of him in her bed. Then she beamed a smile his way before disappearing into the hall.

His heart seemed to be gripped in some sort of vise. He could not find the sense, the wherewithal to get out of bed, to get dressed, and to tell her they had *work* to do. Not places to go simply because she wanted it.

"I want you, Teo. All of you." It had been about sex, he told himself. Over and over again, but he'd seen the look in her eyes and knew for her it was more. *"I love you, Teo."*

Well, he did *not* want that. Avoiding her, however, had not worked. She'd only come back stronger, if last night was any indication of what his withdrawal would do. So he would attempt a different approach.

He would follow along with this little day she had planned, and there would be no *I love you*'s. He would act like it had never been said, as if nothing had changed.

Because nothing *would* ever change. If she pressed the issue, he would make it clear it was *her* issue, not his. If she let things go as they were…well, hadn't that been his plan all along?

He would enjoy it until his revenge was set. And then, if she didn't, he would end things. But first, revenge.

Always and only revenge.

She returned with a little stack of clothes and came over to hand them to him. He took them, against all the declarations in his mind to do otherwise. He frowned at the men's clothes.

"Are these your brother's clothes?"

Saverina shrugged. "He's the only man I live with. Aside from Gio. But I'm not sure a five-year-old's clothes would fit you. Come on, now. I'd like to do this before breakfast."

"What is *this*?" he asked, but he got out of bed and dressed while she disappeared into her en suite bathroom.

"A surprise," she said firmly. She reappeared in black jeans and a pale pink sweater, her hair swept up in a band. She slid her bare feet into shoes and was out the door in under five minutes.

"I have never seen you get ready remotely that quickly."

"I doubt very much we'll be seen," she replied, leading him out of the house and toward a large garage. She opened one of the doors with a button on her key and then led him to a very, *very* small if flashy sedan.

He looked at the car dubiously. "I'm not sure such things were built for men of my size, *bedda*."

"You can push the seat all the way back. It's a short drive anyhow."

She got into the driver's side, and Teo could not fathom the last time some person who wasn't a hired driver or himself had driven him around. It felt completely abnormal getting into the passenger side. Pretzeling himself into the seat that was indeed too small even with the seat pushed back.

Almost as if she was putting him off-kilter on purpose. Well, she was going to find that he did not fall apart quite so easily. Today would be proof. To her. To himself. No amount of weak moments, no amount of pressure in his chest, no amount of her beautiful smiles would change his end game.

He was in charge. Not these feelings she was trying to pull out of him. He'd never let them win.

They drove, as she'd promised, only a short while. Not even venturing into the city limits. She turned into the gates of a cemetery. Everything inside of him turned to ice. His mother was buried here.

"Saverina." But she took a turn—away from where his mother's grave was. Drove to the opposite side of the cemetery and parked. She got out without a word. He knew better than to follow her.

He did it anyway, as though she'd created some magnetic force he couldn't escape.

She walked unerringly down a narrow path and straight up to a well-kept gravestone, shining white in the sun. A delicate angel statue stood atop it.

He read the name engraved on the stone: *Rocca Parisi.* He thought at first it was *her* mother, but the dates were surely wrong as they made this woman only thirteen or fourteen years older than Saverina.

"My sister," she explained, as if sensing his confusion. "Lorenzo did not want her buried with our parents, when they failed her so completely." She knelt next to the stone, wiped at some dirt that had accumulated, pulled at some grass that grew too tall at its base.

Teo could not find words as he stood awkwardly on the path. She had mentioned sisters before, but he did not recall the name Rocca. Of course, she had what seemed like a hundred siblings, so aside from Lorenzo and the other brother he'd met who worked at Parisi in Rome, Teo could not keep them straight. But he knew she had never once mentioned a sister who'd passed away, even when she'd mentioned her parents' deaths often.

"She and Lorenzo were the oldest. Twins. I idolized them both, but Rocca was first. I guess because she was a girl too. My other two sisters are so…sweet. So soft and gentle. Rocca was…fearless. Bold. I wanted to be like her when I was very young, but then…"

Saverina sighed, brushing her fingers across the engraved name. A tear slid down her cheek. "My father never could keep a job, so eventually that fell to my mother. She got into prostitution. When she was pregnant with me, my father forced Rocca to take my mother's role."

Teo had considered himself quite aware of the depravity of humanity, but this shocked him to his core. He knew she'd grown up poor, but the wealth of her brother in the present hid just how much they'd really struggled with.

"Years later, she died by suicide," Saverina continued. "I was twelve when it happened. Lorenzo had begun to build Parisi. He had all these plans to help her, to save her, but he couldn't save her from the pain that made it impossible for her to go on."

"Why do you tell me all this?" Teo asked, his voice rough. His heart, the heart he was trying not to admit existed, ached. An ache so deep, so painful, it reminded him of losing his mother all over again. It was…too horrible. And if he allowed himself to look back on some of the things he'd said to her about her pampered lifestyle, he might actually feel *guilt* over it.

Saverina took a deep breath. She left her hand on her sister's name and looked up at him. Tears in her eyes, on her cheeks.

"I cannot wish her life away, the love I had for her. She meant too much to me even in that short period of time. I struggled with the grief of it, the guilt of it, the *waste* of it for a very long time. The pain doesn't go away, but the struggle gets...lighter when you face it. But I cannot ignore it, wish it away, avoid the *good* that kind of love does in a life. I understand denial, Teo. I have been there. I speak easily of my parents' deaths because I didn't... they weren't good people. I don't speak of Rocca very often, because it hurts so very much."

So this was all about...him. He should feel anger. Fury, really. But he did not recognize the emotion battering him. It wasn't as hot and sharp as anger. It was something far more complicated.

He wanted nothing to do with it. But sympathy warred with a desire to be harsh. When he spoke, he did so carefully.

"I do not know what you wish to do here, and I do not wish to argue in a cemetery, but I am not in need of a secondhand psychologist."

She nodded and got to her feet. "All right then."

And that was it. She did not push the matter. When they returned to her house, he said he had to leave. She gave him a hug and a kiss, said a dreaded *I love you*, and then let him go.

But Teo understood what she'd done, because he could not get the image of the gravestone out of his head. The pain of such a sad story, of Saverina going through all that loss, out of his heart. Of her somehow still believing love could be anything but a weapon made to hurt.

She had cursed him. Again.

And it had to be the last time.

CHAPTER SIXTEEN

SAVERINA DID NOT know what Teo's next move would be, but the silence as Saturday moved into Sunday was clear enough. He wasn't going to *deal* with her *I love you*, or the point she'd been trying to make at the cemetery telling him about Rocca.

But maybe this would be a series of steps. She had pushed him...he'd isolated, and then they'd had their night together and the moment at the cemetery.

He hadn't been unmoved. Maybe he hadn't known what to do with it all, but he'd felt *something*. That was all she was allowing herself to hope for. That was all she was *trying* to allow herself to hope for.

She video chatted with Lorenzo and family in the morning. It was awkward, she could admit. She figured they'd heard through the grapevine about the engagement, but she could not bring herself to tell them a lie. So she avoided the topic, and neither Lorenzo nor Brianna pushed.

At lunch, she received a text from Teo, which was strange. He was not much of a texter. He preferred a call or to speak through his assistant.

But the text was simple.

Dinner. My apartment. Six.

It was not a request, she noted, and a text message didn't feel particularly promising in terms of getting through to him. It whispered too much of cowardice, but the man was a bit of a coward when it came to her. She decided to take that as a compliment.

She was a danger to *him*. Which meant he had *some* feelings. It had to.

She spent the afternoon deciding what to wear. It was a bit like playing chess, she supposed. Taking him to the cemetery had been honest, genuine, but it had also been a move. An attempt to get him to capitulate to his feelings by showing him hers.

Now he would offer a countermove. Maybe he'd attempt to put some distance between them. That seemed to be his MO. So she opted for casual. Much like this morning, she would sweep in and please *herself.* Tell him the feelings she wanted to tell him, and not worry about *him*.

She pulled on some jeans and her favorite sweater because it was soft and she thought the bright, vivid blue looked good on her. Especially when she let her hair down and only did minimal makeup.

Then she drove over to his apartment at the appointed time. She gave a fleeting thought to all those rules she'd laid down to protect herself not all that long ago. It had been a natural reaction to betrayal, but now that she'd stepped back, processed those lies, she could protect herself in the *right* way.

Because there was protecting yourself so carefully, risking so very little, that there was no way of gaining anything, really. That's what she'd *been* doing, most of her life. A bit like Teo hiding away from his grief, she'd been hiding from the potential for failure.

She had to be willing for this to backfire, for it not to

work out, to ever hope that it might work. She had to be willing to feel pain and embarrassment or she'd never enjoy *anything*. Life would be a bland, boring existence and she'd get walked all over.

This entire experience had opened her eyes to that.

She needed to protect herself from letting that fear win, not from the ways the world and people might disappoint her, or vice versa.

She greeted everyone in Teo's building as she made her way up to his floor. He let her in almost right away, but quickly sidestepped so she could not offer a gesture of affection.

Saverina might have laughed, but she was having trouble holding on to that, light, tickled response to all his evasions after yesterday morning. She wanted to find this humorous again, but…she was just getting tired.

"Thank you for coming," he greeted her smoothly. All business Teo.

"Of course," she replied, surveying the apartment. The dining room table was set, and something in the kitchen smelled delicious. She might have deemed it romantic, except there was a laptop open at each spot on the table. A business dinner. She tried to keep her smile in place. She could not control him, only her reaction to him.

"This is an interesting setup."

"I've followed some lines on Julia Marino. There's something I'd like you to try to get to the bottom of for me." He gestured at one of the seats. Opposite the other. The whole length of the table between them.

She studied him as he took the other seat. His expression was carefully neutral. She couldn't help but wonder if he saw this as some kind of punishment. She'd panicked about trying to look deeper into Dante and Julia's son's attack, and he hadn't pushed her...until she'd pushed him.

But in the end, she just didn't think he was that vindictive. Funny when they were dealing in revenge, but his actions regarding her always seemed to boil down to fear...not actually wanting to hurt her.

Hopefully she wasn't fooling herself.

"I can try," she said, keeping her easy smile in place as she slid into the seat across from him.

"I had someone do some preliminary research, and they found an abandoned and wiped legal document of some kind, generated by Julia Marino through a lawyer who is not on Dante's payroll. I was hoping you could potentially tug on this lead and see what you might be able to come up with."

She should not be hurt he had someone *else* do preliminary work. Like she was *incapable*. She'd been on the same stupid lead, but she hadn't told him because of all that pesky *fear*. "Was Francesca Oliveri the lawyer in question?"

His expression gave nothing away, but he paused and studied her for a moment. "You've been digging."

"I told you I would try," she said, keeping her eyes on the computer. She poked around at what kind of software it had, what capabilities. "And so I have been trying."

"You didn't say."

"No, I didn't want to until I had something concrete." She looked up at him. "I'll need a pen and a pad of paper to keep some notes. And some food. You said dinner, and I didn't eat."

"So I did." He walked into the open kitchen, lifted the lid off a pot. Saverina was distracted from the computer for a moment. "You cooked?"

"A chore I do not mind taking on now and again." He plated some pasta and vegetables, and her stomach rumbled. She looked at him in wonder for a moment as he set a plate and a glass of wine next to her elbow.

It was amazing to her, how much they had in common. They'd grown up hard—he'd no doubt learned to cook to help his mother. She had never had to because the existence of her siblings had allowed her horrible beginnings to be shaped in a new, different, safer way, while he had simply been abandoned at his mother's death. He'd only ever had the woman who'd raised him, and then no one. Except a man who refused to acknowledge him.

She wanted to reach out and hug him, but she understood that expression on his face. He'd drawn a line he would not allow her to cross tonight. He would be cold and cruel if he had to be.

She might have considered crossing it anyway, but she felt bruised. She ached for what *could* be if he only let it. She blew out a breath and returned her attention to the computer.

With a pressure-filled task at hand, she just needed to focus on that. Get the revenge over with, then deal with all *this*.

She began to work, eating the delicious pasta as she went without much thought. Digging into the lawyer was just difficult enough to keep her attention on it, rather than on Teo or the pressure to accomplish this. She had already done a lot of the legwork. The next step was a little trickier. She had gone through the lawyer's personal digital footprint, but getting past the law firm's security systems had been a challenge she'd have to work herself up for.

She was irritated enough with the way Teo had set

this up, she felt just up for the challenge now. Of course he'd be *this* prepared.

She hacked into the law office's systems. Worked on dealing with encrypted files most people would never be able to get into. It took time, both getting through the systems and then wading through to find what information she needed. Teo never pushed. Never showed any impatience. He refilled her wine and served dessert.

She barely touched either.

Eventually she found a few documents related to the abandoned case. There was a document the lawyer no doubt thought she'd deleted, but Saverina managed to salvage, that included a scanned written statement from Julia.

It was a complex legal document, but Saverina tried to pull out the pertinent facts. "The day after their son's attack was reported to police, Julia started divorce proceedings. They accuse Dante of being violent with her son, Dantino."

Teo was immediately at her side, scanning the document on her screen himself. "Why did she abandon the case? Why not destroy him then and there? Why go to a lawyer and not the police?"

"I'm guessing because Dante had already gone to the police and blamed Lorenzo the night of the attack. She knew they wouldn't believe her over him."

Saverina dug deeper, trying to find more. Reason for the proceedings to be terminated. Somewhere in writing. Then she found it. An encrypted file, hidden in old deleted ones. It was the lawyer's notes.

Client abandoned case. Assailant bought her out. Ensured safety for silence.

Saverina's heart ached for a whole new reason. That poor Julia Marino had tried to leave her husband, protect her son, but had instead made what essentially was a deal with the devil. To ensure protection for her son. What a terrible situation to be put in.

Saverina looked up at Teo. "We can't use her or this."

"Why not? It proves everything. The worst of the worst. It will ruin Dante forever."

Saverina stared at him openmouthed for a moment or two. "Did you *see* why she dropped the divorce proceedings, Teo? She's protecting herself and her child. We can't just…ignore that for a little revenge."

"I don't see why not. It is the truth. The information coming to light will have nothing to do with her, or her now adult son, so what does it matter?" He walked away from her and toward his own computer, like he was going to start making plans immediately.

He clearly wasn't *listening*, so blinded by his own plans. "You know as well as I do, Dante won't care about *who* leaked this information. He will only care that it has been leaked and hurt anyone involved. He'll blame her because he thinks she's the only one who'll know. If he's capable of hurting his own son, he'll hurt her. She's *afraid*, Teo. For herself. For her son. That's the only reason she dropped the divorce."

"I think he'll be too busy being hurt to hurt them back," Teo said, not even looking at her.

She shook her head, panic and worry moving through her. And something else. Anger. "You are such a man sometimes. With the money and power Dante has, you cannot guarantee that. Even if he gets in *some* trouble, it won't be enough to ensure they're protected. Teo, you cannot use this. We have to stick to *our* plan and leave this be."

"I disagree."

She got up, strode over, and took his laptop off the

table, closing it and setting it aside. "I don't care if you disagree. I will not let you use this."

"You do not have a say. Revenge has always been the plan. He will pay for what he did. To my mother. To me. This is better payment than I could have dreamed. Why should I abandon it just because you don't like it? *You* don't matter."

He said it so...off-handedly, and it cut through her like a stab wound. *You don't matter.* No, she'd been fooling herself to think she could. Perhaps underneath all his issues he might care for her in some way, but it would never matter if he didn't face his issues.

She might have given up and walked out the door if something bigger wasn't at stake. She felt like she owed it to Julia Marino to keep fighting in this moment.

"Your mother is gone, Teo. It isn't fair. It's awful. But hurting Dante won't bring her back."

He stood, his expression nothing but ice. "I have no fantasies about bringing her back, Saverina. I watched her waste away. This is not about *her.*"

But it was. Even if he didn't admit it. To her or himself. She pressed her hands to his chest so he couldn't reach for the computer. "Teo, doesn't this denial hurt? How can you bury it so deep? You lost her, baby. It's okay to grieve that, to feel that."

He removed her hands from his chest, then held them by the wrists, glaring down at her. "Enough. I have what I need. You will go now."

She stepped back. Her heart just *ached.* She couldn't get through to him. Now that he had this slice of an even bigger revenge, he'd just shut her out. Just destroy all these lives because that was the plan.

She couldn't get through to him. "I cannot be a part of this," she said, very carefully, her mind racing for ways she could save that mother and son from this…idiocy. This tunnel vision born of denial.

He shrugged. Unbothered. "I don't need you for this."

Teo convinced himself he was completely dispassionate as he watched her expression fall. He convinced himself the worry and fear and *love* in her gaze was a fiction.

He had his revenge—better even than his plan. Proof the man hadn't just refused to acknowledge his illegitimate son but had *attacked* his legitimate one. It was a boon.

He would not let her guilt him into thinking it was anything else. He would not let her ruin this. "In fact, I no longer have any use for you at all."

He expected anger, that flash of her temper, but her expression just…fell. Like he'd stabbed her clean through. He refused to acknowledge that her expression felt like his own wound.

"I know you want to compartmentalize," she said, very carefully, like every word hurt. She even pressed her hand to her stomach like she was putting pressure on a bleeding wound. "I know you're in denial about your grief. But I know, Teo. This will not change any of that hurt or grief for you. It will not make those feelings you fight away so hard disappear. Putting innocent people in the middle of all this will only cause you more guilt. More pain. At some point there will be too much to ignore."

"I have no need for your continued pseudo psychoanalyzing, Saverina. And I no longer need this engagement. What Dante did to his son and his wife is enough if you cannot fall in line. You're overreacting to think they'll be hurt. This isn't about them."

"You don't get to compartmentalize it all like that."

"Of course I do." He pointed at her hand, because he

could not do what needed to be done with her looking at him with wet, worried eyes. Talking about guilt and grief when revenge was all he'd ever wanted and it was now in his grasp. "I will need the ring back."

The look on her face... He kept his hand outstretched, but he looked at the door behind her. Not cowardice...not hurt... No, something else. Regardless, feelings didn't matter.

"I can see begging you not to do this won't work, so I'll only offer you this piece of advice," she said, her voice raspy. "When you ruin not just Dante's world, but two innocent people's, the guilt will eat you alive. You want to play hard-hearted, detached *stone*, but you are a man. And no matter how you ignore your grief, your guilt, your *heart*, it is there. This won't just hurt me and those two innocent people. It will *destroy* you."

Good, was all he could think. Let it. He forced himself to look at her, at the tears tracking down her cheeks, because love was loss and pain, and that's all it ever would be.

She wrenched the ring off her finger, slapped it in his palm. "If you realize what a mistake you've made, I hope you'll stop yourself. If you regret breaking things off with me in the next few weeks, I hope you'll come apologize. But if you come to me after you've done this horrible thing, once I've gotten over you, I will not take you back, Teo. I will not." She frantically wiped at her cheeks, but more tears poured out of her eyes. Eventually she lifted her chin, met his gaze. "So I would think long and hard about what you want your life—that long, precious thing you have to live no matter what—to be like." Then she turned and left.

And he was glad of it. That's why he went to the table and broke every last dish and glass on it.

Glad.

CHAPTER SEVENTEEN

TEO DID NOTHING with the information that evening. He did not sleep. He did not plan. He sat at the dining room table and looked at Saverina's half-eaten dessert. He could admit, as morning dawned over the city outside his window, that he'd brooded.

He tried to convince himself that this was for the best. Saverina was free to go after the life she wanted. Love and family and hell on earth if she asked him, but she had not.

He could admit, here, he'd rather enjoyed the idea of spending the next few years together. Not because of love. No *children*, for God's sake. Just…friendship. Partnership. A comfortable and enjoyable business arrangement.

Maybe he'd liked an image of all that, but he wouldn't regret it being over. Alone was best. Especially if she'd continued poking at him about grief and feelings. He didn't need that. He was better off alone.

He would begin the leak. Meet with his press point person. Have him withdraw all the rumors about the Parisis and focus on Dante's violent nature. There was no need for Saverina anymore. No need for proving the Parisis were good. If Dante could attack his own son, that would destroy everything.

Poetic justice.

But instead of calling his point person, he got in his car and drove to the address he had for Julia Marino. Because Saverina was wrong. Julia and her son would be *happy* if he leaked this. He would prove it to Saverina.

If he ever saw her again. Maybe he'd quit Parisi tomorrow. He had saved much and invested well. He could go anywhere. Do anything. He had no use for Parisi, for Sicily, for women who haunted and cursed in equal measure.

He would go to the Caribbean. To New Zealand. As far away from Sicily as possible.

When he arrived at the Marino estate, the gates were closed, but there was a little buzzer and intercom system, so he used it.

"Can we help you?"

"My name is Teo LaRosa. I need to speak with Mrs. Marino."

There was a long, long silence. Then the squeak of gates opening. Teo got into his car and drove up to the expansive mansion.

He stopped his car at the extravagant entrance and got out. Something beat in him like panic, but he refused to label it as such. It was simply the realization anew that his mother had struggled all her adult life when she should not have. With this wealth and extravagance, Dante could have at *least* paid her off.

But he'd threatened her, scared her, and left her with nothing.

The door opened before Teo even got up the stairs. Julia stepped out and closed her front door behind her.

"You shouldn't be here," she said as she approached. She began to walk past him, back toward where he'd come from. He found himself following as she stalked away, clutching the cardigan around her tightly.

When they got past the fountain, she finally stopped and turned to face him. Her expression was cold. "The cameras cannot see us or hear us here, but I will need to return immediately. Drive down the street to the park on the corner. I will meet you there. You haven't gone to the press yet, have you?"

He blinked once in confusion, before it dawned on him that Saverina had *warned* her. Fury leaped through him like pain and grief, but he had no chance to ask Julia any questions.

She went back the way she'd come before he could answer. Teo could only stand frozen for a moment or two. Then he began to follow her instructions.

Because he was right.

Because she was afraid of her husband.

And him exposing her secret would save her. Saverina would see she was completely and utterly wrong, and then they could—

Nothing, he reminded himself harshly. His and Saverina's partnership was over. Done. He got in his car and drove to the park. He waited far longer than he should have for Julia to finally arrive. She didn't approach him, just went and sat on a little bench overlooking a small pond.

Teo walked over and took a seat next to her.

"Have you gone to the press already?" she asked again.

Teo could not find his voice right away. Unacceptable. "No."

Julia let out a long sigh as her shoulders slumped. Relief, clearly, and it had that ugly guilt Saverina had warned him about eating away at his insides.

"What do you want, Mr. LaRosa?" Julia asked, her voice frayed by stress and something he could not begin to guess at.

"To expose your husband for what he is. A violent criminal on top of everything else."

She shook her head, then met his gaze. There were tears in her eyes, but they did not fall. "I cannot let you do this."

Teo frowned. "Why not?"

"I don't know how you found this out, but I know who you are. It's impossible to ignore the resemblance between you and my sons, the way your mother left our employ all those years ago. I... I lived in much denial back then, but I don't anymore."

"Because your husband attacked your son."

She inhaled sharply, but she nodded, her hard gaze never leaving the pond. "He was drunk. He and my son engaged in a physical fight that Dante won. It was the first and only time there'd been a physical altercation. And we handled it in a way that is best for my family." Finally she turned to face him, and her expression was pleading. "So I would appreciate your discretion, Mr. LaRosa. Please don't do this to us."

The *please* landed too hard, in a memory of his mother. Begging him for something. He didn't want that memory of her in that hospital bed. A wisp of nothing. Already gone.

"Please be happy, Teo. Please."

"There will be no discretion," Teo said harshly. "I will end him. Not only will his reputation be ruined, but he could very likely face actual charges. He will be put in jail. Whatever you fear, you will be safe from."

She laughed. Bitterly. "No, I won't. And he won't face charges because we won't press them. I understand how you feel. Why you want this. Even if I don't know the details of what Dante did to your mother, I can guess. I sympathize with your feelings, I do. But I will fight you on bringing what Dante has done to light."

He did not understand this. She should be on her knees begging for his help, thanking him profusely. "How can you not want to see him ended?"

"Because with our agreement in place, my son is happy. Free to follow the life he chooses without Dante's say, but with the help of Dante's money. This was my son's wish, and I agreed because this way there's no revenge, no chance of Dante hurting us. I can hurt him worse and better. He stays away, and we get to live free of his threats. I would do anything, sacrifice anything to keep my children happy. Even allow Dante to walk free."

Teo could only gape at her. It made no sense. How could there possibly be a way not to want to see him ended?

"You don't understand," Julia said morosely. "I don't know how to make you understand. I love my children more than I need that man to suffer. Life isn't fair. It has never been fair. We could think we're evening the playing field, make it *feel* fair to us because he loses something. But it isn't fair. *Nothing* is fair. I can let that terrible truth ruin my life, or I can do this."

"And what is this?"

"Love. My children. Myself. Focus on what we have, not what we don't. A mother only wants to see her children safe, and healthy, and *happy*. Would I enjoy seeing Dante in jail? Of course. But it wouldn't last, and he is vindictive and cruel. Trust me when I say that he lives in his own kind of jail. A life devoid of love, empathy, family. He is an empty chasm of wanting more, more, more and never getting it. It will eat him alive far better than any justice system."

It wasn't enough. It couldn't be enough. "I will ruin your husband because he ruined my mother. It is right. It is fair. This...whatever you're doing...is not."

"I only vaguely remember your mother. I don't know you at all. But your devotion to her makes me think you loved each other very much."

He thought back to the day he'd said something to Saverina about everyone loving their mother. Her response about not being sure she did. He had an evil father, so he supposed evil mothers existed, but it struck him as sadder, somehow. But this was not about Saverina. "She was the best person I'll ever know."

"I am glad of it. Let me tell you, as a mother. If she loved you, protected you, got to see you grow into a man who would love her back, who succeeded, her life was not ruined. No matter what hardships she faced. And if you are happy in your life, you have honored her memory in the only way that would ever matter to her. That is all a good mother wants. Her child to be happy and fulfilled."

Happy.

Teo did not know what to say to this. Did not know how to reconcile the fact that... Saverina had been right. Julia did not want his revenge. Did not feel safe in it. And worse, so much worse, she somehow agreed with Lorenzo's philosophy on the whole thing. That love and happiness could be more important than justice.

"Will you ruin my son's life to make yourself feel better?" Julia asked, her eyes full of tears. Like Saverina's had been last night. When she'd begged him not to move forward. When she'd warned him that just this would happen.

When she was somehow right, and he couldn't find

purchase in this moment. He wanted to ruin *Dante*, not these people, but…

"Mr. LaRosa? Teo…"

But he got to his feet. And left without answering her question. Because he did not have an answer. He had nothing now. Only more and more confusion.

So much so that when he drove past the cemetery he'd visited with Saverina only yesterday, he turned in, just as she had. But he drove to his mother's gravesite.

His breath was coming too shallow, his heart beating with painful thuds against his chest. It reminded him of Saverina's panic attack. And worse, made him wish she was here, when that was over.

Over. He had no need for love. It only ended here. Here.

He did not want to do this, and yet some force compelled him. He parked and walked to her grave even as clouds slid over the sun, as thunder rolled in the distance.

Because he didn't know what to do, and when she'd been alive, he'd always known. Always been so sure.

She'd made it clear she wanted simple for her memorial because she'd known she was dying for some time before it had actually happened. Here, he'd given her exactly what she'd wanted.

Simple or elaborate, it didn't seem to matter. She was gone, and her name was etched in stone that would eventually sink into the ground and disappear.

He knelt next to the stone as if someone had pushed him into the position. He could hardly breathe. Everything inside of him was twisted into painful knots. He didn't know what to do except follow Saverina's example from yesterday. He brushed dirt off the stone, picked a few weeds out of the grass.

Rain began to fall, the day turning quickly gray. No sun. No rainbows. Just cold and wet and discomfort and his mother's name etched in stone. Gone. Gone forever. Nothing to be done about it.

So why was he here? "I do not know. I cannot fathom. I know you did not wish me to get my revenge, but I need it. I…need…"

She had loved him. She had wanted the best for him. Had begged him to be happy as she'd slipped away. Julia claimed this meant her life had not been ruined, but how could that *be*?

"Can't you show me what to do? Can't you…lead me in some way? I don't believe in this. Dead is dead, but I need… I need…"

He needed revenge, but the only thing he seemed to be able to really feel was how much he needed Saverina. She would know what to do, to say, to feel. She would know and…

She had once asked him what his mother would think of his revenge. She would not want it. Not for herself and not for him. She'd wanted him to live a life free of that. Live the life that would make him happy.

She'd said that on her last day too. Not just Dante's identity as his father, but messages of love. Of hope.

"Teo, my love, you must promise me to live a good life. A happy life." And he had promised. But he hadn't known what good was. What happy could be. He'd thought it was revenge, but the closest he'd ever come was Saverina. Because plans of revenge had never made him feel *good* or happy. They had only given him a goal. A goal that would one day be over.

And then what?

Without Saverina, that question felt like a prison sentence. Which was not what his mother had wanted for him.

"You would approve of her. I am not so sure you would approve of me."

A boom of thunder shook the ground, followed by the sizzling crackle and flash of lightning. The storm was angry, but his mother had never been. It was no sign from the universe, from the great beyond. It was only weather.

"I do not know how to be happy without you. I didn't want to be." Or he hadn't. Until Saverina had upended everything. She had snuck under his defenses, made him happy against his will. Surprised him with how…nice life could be with someone like her by his side.

And when he was not happy, when he had been hurt with grief and fear, Saverina had put a gentle hand on him. She had *loved* him.

Loved him.

Rain soaked into his clothes, made the ground muddy beneath his knees. Cold permeated his skin until he was shaking.

He did not want to hurt Julia or her son. He did not want to hurt Saverina. He did not want to hurt anyone. Not even Dante, at the heart of it. Because all he'd been searching for was a way to feel better. A way to feel whole. He'd convinced himself it was on the other side of revenge, but Saverina said it wouldn't be.

She'd been right about so many things now. How could he deny she might be right about this?

He tilted his head back, let the rain pour over him. And he made a new promise to his mother.

I will try.

CHAPTER EIGHTEEN

SAVERINA LET HERSELF wallow most of the day Sunday. Her first romantic heartbreak called for a little wallowing, she thought. She looked at her now bare finger and felt the loss all over again.

She let herself cry. She let herself eat far too many cakes. She took a long bath, where she cried all over again. She kept waiting for it to feel *cathartic*, but mostly she just felt wrung out and awful.

She was headed for the kitchen for more cake when she heard…commotion deeper in the other wing. Like… Her heart skipped a beat. She rushed through her wing of the house to the main part, and there they were. Her favorite people.

Helena was having a little toddler tantrum. Gio was covering his ears while Lorenzo held Helena and tried to calm her down. Brianna rubbed her ever rounding belly looking sun-kissed and exhausted. They all looked a little damp.

"You're back."

"Aunt Sav!" Gio ran full throttle at her, so she had no choice but to catch him. Bury her nose in his hair. Hold on for dear life. "You're getting far too big for me to toss in the air." She gave him a tight squeeze, tears threatening. Oh, she'd missed them. Missed this. And…she could be okay. She *would* be okay. Even without Teo, because she had them.

While Teo has no one.

Gio wriggled in her grasp until she had to put him down. Helena, distracted from her tantrum, toddled over to Saverina and demanded the same treatment as her brother. "Up! Sav!"

So Saverina did the same thing. Lifted her niece, snuggled and squeezed until the girl squealed and demanded to be put down.

Usually they made her feel so happy and light. That Lorenzo could have this, when he absolutely deserved it and was an amazing father. But today, she couldn't help feeling bruised. Wistful.

Like children were never going to be hers, when that was silly because she was so young yet. Had so much life to live. She'd meet other men. She'd fall in love again.

It felt impossible in the moment, but she had to shake away these dire thoughts and smile at her brother and sister-in-law.

Lorenzo looked her up and down, frowning as if he could see everything in her expression.

"We decided to come home a little early. Saverina—"

Before he could finish, Saverina crossed the room, flung her arms around her brother, and burst into tears. She had never done such a thing in all her life, always trying to be strong for him. But today...she only wanted to be held and told it would be okay. It would get easier to feel this horrible ache in her chest.

He hugged her close. "Do I need to kill him?" he asked in her ear.

"Yes," she said emphatically into his chest.

"Can it wait until tomorrow? I'm a bit tired from the trip."

It made her laugh, which she figured was the point. "I suppose."

"Come on, Gio," Brianna said, taking her son's hand as she carried her daughter. "Let's let Papa and Auntie Sav catch up."

"But why is Aunt Sav crying?"

"Well, I imagine the answer to that question is *men*," Brianna said with some humor as she tried to drag Gio out of the room.

"But I'm a men," Gio insisted.

"Hopefully a better one," Brianna muttered, and then they were gone.

Saverina looked up at her big brother and sighed. "I suppose you'd like the whole story."

"I do not think I will *like* it, no, but let's hear it."

She explained it all to him. Even the part about Teo tricking her. She laid it all out. The embarrassing parts and the way she'd learned, matured, grown. It made her proud of herself, actually, the way she'd crawled out of that terrible realization into a person she liked better.

"He is so focused on this revenge. But you were right, I hate to admit. When you have love and family and real joy, the revenge no longer feels quite so important."

Lorenzo nodded. "It is a strange lesson to learn, but yes. It is true. However, this is not a lesson you can teach him. He has to accept it on his own terms, in his own time."

"I know. I *do* know that. I can even accept it if he never does. It's just… I know he loves me, but he's…he lost his mother, and he's so mired in that grief he won't deal with. If he would, if he *could*, we could both be happy. Now."

"Well. I suppose men do that kind of thing."

She gave him a sharp look, because he'd done something very similar when it had come to Brianna. His issues had been compounded by being in charge of all of his siblings for so long, for the guilt he felt over Rocca's death, but it was similar.

"I told him that if he didn't go through with this, if he apologized in the next few weeks, I'd forgive him because I love him, but if I got over him before that happened, it was over for good, and he would be sorry."

"And so he shall. Do you want me to fire him?"

Saverina blinked at her brother. It wasn't a joke like killing him. He was dead serious. "Is he good at his job?"

"Naturally. He wouldn't be in the position he is if he wasn't."

"Then it would be highly unethical of you to fire him."

"I'll be as unethical as I please for my baby sister. Hence the offer for murder as well."

"Thank you, but no. I want…" Well, what she really wanted was for Teo to show up right now and confess his love for her and tell her he'd forget all about Dante and revenge. But she needed to accept that wasn't going to happen. "It's a normal thing to have your heart broken, and I want to go through normal things. So I'll be sad and pout for a while, but I *will* get over him."

"Of course you will. The offer for murder and firing stands forever, *soru*."

She moved to hug him again. To feel the solid truth of family that would stand by your side no matter what. She'd been so lucky to have him, her other brothers and sisters. She'd never had to do any of this alone. "I'm just glad you're home."

She tried very hard to lean into the glad, and not fret

about Teo not having *anyone*. She had left the door open for him. She could not make him walk through that door. So she could not be the company he needed, the love he needed, until he was willing to accept it.

"Come, I am hungry. Let us go have some cake," Lorenzo said, giving her shoulders a squeeze. Because he knew cake was her favorite accessory to go with sadness.

But before they could get to the kitchen, Brianna was hurrying up the hall.

"There's a very…wet, angry man at the door demanding to see Saverina," Brianna said with some concern. "Should Lorenzo send him away?"

"Yes," Lorenzo said in a low growl.

"No," Saverina said, slapping a hand to her brother's chest so he didn't march toward the door.

Teo was here. He was… It had to mean something good. It *had* to. "I will handle this myself. If I need help disposing of a body, I shall ask for it."

Lorenzo grunted. "Very well."

Trying to keep her gait casual, slow, Saverina walked down the hall toward the entryway. When she arrived, Teo stood there. Dripping.

He was soaked through, hair plastered to his face, muddy splotches on the knees of his expensive pants. She had never seen him in such a state. And even though his expression was dark and serious, her heart soared.

"I went to your entrance, but Antonina said you were over here with your family. Good evening, Mr. Parisi. Mrs. Parisi."

Saverina frowned and glanced over her shoulder. Lorenzo stood behind her, scowling. Brianna looked more curious than angry. But when Saverina gave her a pleading look, Brianna tugged on Lorenzo's arm. "Come. We have much unpacking to do, and I am not feeling well enough to do it."

Lorenzo's scowl did not leave his face, but he looked from Teo to Saverina.

"Please," she mouthed.

He grunted again, then turned on a heel and disappeared with Brianna. Saverina turned back to Teo.

"Is he going to kill me?" Teo asked calmly.

Saverina pretended to consider the question, then shrugged. "Probably."

"Pity. I was just figuring out how to live."

She looked up at his face, her heart fluttering against all better judgment. "Were you?" she whispered.

He crossed to her and reached out, touched her cheek with a gentleness he'd rarely shown. Certainly not while looking into her eyes like this.

"I went to see Julia. Dante's wife. To warn her what was about to happen." He shook his head. "No, that isn't true. I wanted to prove you wrong. To get her blessing and rub it in your face."

"How mature," she murmured. "But I'd already warned her."

He sighed. "Yes. So she just kept going on and on about how much she loved her son, how that mattered more to her than Dante's feelings on anything. She said...a mother only wants a happy son, and I... I know it is what my mother wanted." He bowed his head. "I did not want to think of it, deal with it. I would have set it aside forever, but between the two of you, I felt...cursed. Haunted."

Saverina couldn't stop herself from frowning, because it sounded rather accusatory, all in all.

But he continued. "I went to the cemetery. I did what you did with your sister's grave. Tidied up a bit. But I did not feel her there. Even when it began to storm. I tried to speak to her, but it was…fruitless."

She swallowed at the lump in her throat. This was why he was wet and muddy. He'd been to the cemetery. "I do not often feel Rocca there either."

"You do not?"

He seemed to need the reassurance, and maybe she was a fool to give it. But she could not deny him this. "Not in the cemetery usually. I think… I think cemeteries are more for the living than the dead. I feel her in other ways. I'll see something that reminds me of her, and it is as if she's there with me. Looking at it too."

He studied her for a long time, his gaze raking over her face. Then his other wet hand came up to cover her other cheek.

"Do you remember the first time I kissed you?"

"I'm not sure where you're going with this, but yes." His clothes and hair were dripping on her, but she did not dare move away from his gentle grasp. "We were leaving the theater, about to go our separate ways. I wasn't sure what to make of you. You hadn't even tried to hold my hand. Then you kissed me."

"You'd told some joke that reminded me of my mother. It would have made her laugh, and my mind drifted to what it would be like for the two of you to meet. I suppose… I felt her there. I did not like it. It made me angry."

"So you kissed me?"

"I thought that would take the anger away." He shrugged. "It did. After a fashion."

"I do not think this is the grovel you think it is."

"But it is. I do not get angry. I do not let it win. Everything is cold and calculated so I can *win*. But you have frustrated me, and I thought I could solve it in all manner of ways, but I never did. I never could solve you."

"I am not a *problem*, Teo."

And then he did something…unfathomable. He laughed. A true laugh that crinkled his eyes and made his entire being seem…lighter. "You are. But problems are not always bad. Sometimes they are something you learn from. Something that changes the course of your life. You have changed mine, Saverina. I cannot let my anger go, but for Julia's love of her sons, for my love of you, I can let this revenge go."

Her heart tripped over itself. "All of it?"

He nodded. "I think I understand what Lorenzo meant. I could hurt Dante, but it would not teach him any lessons. He is an evil man who would hurt his own legitimate son. Why should me hurting him change anything for him? It will only make him a worse person, likely. But one thing that will never make sense to him is me just…living a good life."

"What life do you want?"

He released her face, reached into his pocket and pulled out the ring he'd given her. His proposal had been fake then.

It wasn't now.

"A life with you, Saverina. I love you. It is not easy for me. I cannot promise that it ever will be. Love feels dangerous, so tenuous. Grief is the other side of love, and it threatened to swallow me whole."

She nodded and had to work hard to speak past that lump in her throat. "I'd rather live a life with grief than without all the love that is the other side of it. Grief is bearable when you share it. When you accept it. When you grow from it."

Teo inhaled deeply. "You have taught me this. By being you. By speaking of your own grief. By never being afraid to ask me about my mother, my grief. You have forced me to face that which I did not want to, but needed to. And while you did all that, you loved me. You asked me what I wanted. I was so afraid of what I wanted, Saverina, but I am not a coward. Not anymore."

He took her hand in his. "I want you. A life with you. A family with you. Will you love me? Marry me? Share your life and grief with me?"

Saverina let out a shaky breath but did not answer right away. She loved him, yes, but she had to make a decision that was best for both of them. She looked into his eyes, though, and saw truth. Because love was bright and wonderful and happy, but it came with harder things.

He'd made his peace with that. Finally. She could see it in his eyes. "Yes, I will."

He slid the ring onto her finger, and then she flung herself at him. He was cold and wet, and a mess. But he was hers.

Always.

EPILOGUE

THEY NAMED THEIR daughter after the two people they'd loved and lost too young. Every day, Giuseppa Rocca LaRosa brought her parents a joy that eased the grief that never fully went away.

When their son was born, they named him after the man who'd first showed them that revenge did not really matter when you had a life worth living. Renzo LaRosa was a terror, from the moment he was born kicking and wailing.

"He will either save the world or end it," his uncle Lorenzo had said on his fifth birthday. A bit darkly, but with the kind of love a family bonded by grief and joy understands is the most important thing.

Teo had needed some time to fully sink into that, believe in it, allow himself to express that same kind of love, but with every passing year it got easier. As his daughter grew into a charming young woman, so like her mother. As his son turned into a man who would indeed save whatever worlds he chose.

As his wife never left his side, no matter what they gained, or lost, or fought over.

As he built a relationship with his two half brothers and their mother, so that even they became something like family. As he reached out to the family his mother had hidden from for their own good, and gave them the gift of answers.

Every Parisi gathering grew larger, louder and more boisterous as the years went on. Until it was the loudness and the love overflowing in every room that became Teo's normal, rather than the small, quiet love of his childhood.

Teo appreciated them both. Grieved what he'd lost, and loved what he had in every moment with everything he was.

He rarely thought of his biological father, even when he was with his brothers, and felt only an odd, distant kind of satisfaction when Dante got himself into enough trouble with embezzling business funds to lose his business and spend some time in jail.

But mostly, he did not care what the man did. He only cared that, year in and year out, he had finally kept the promise to his mother he'd made as she'd died.

He lived a good life. A happy life. With more love than any one man surely deserved.

* * * * *

COMING SOON!

We really hope you enjoyed reading this book.
If you're looking for more romance
be sure to head to the shops when
new books are available on

Thursday 15th February

To see which titles are coming soon, please visit

millsandboon.co.uk/nextmonth

MILLS & BOON

MILLS & BOON®

Coming next month

CINDERELLA'S ONE-NIGHT BABY
Michelle Smart

Skimming her fingers up his arm, Gabrielle placed her palm on his chest.

He sucked in a breath. His grip on her hip tightened. The thuds of his heartbeat perfectly matched the thuds of her own.

Andrés was a strictly short-term relationship man. He wouldn't want more than she could give, and all she could give him was one night. It was all she could give to herself.

This was meant to be, she realised, staring even deeper into his eyes. It had been from the start. If she'd known he was single, she would have refused point blank to attend the party with him, would have spent the night alone in her tiny apartment unaware that he held the key to unlocking all the desires she'd kept buried so deep she'd hardly been aware they existed.

For this one night she could put those desires first, and do so with the sexiest man to roam the earth, the man who had the power to turn her to liquid without even touching her.

A man who wouldn't want anything more from her.

She moved her face closer. Their lips brushed like feathers. The heat of his breath filled her senses.

Continue reading
CINDERELLA'S ONE-NIGHT BABY
Michelle Smart

Available next month
millsandboon.co.uk

Introducing our newest series, Afterglow.

From showing up to glowing up, Afterglow characters are on the path to leading their best lives and finding romance along the way – with plenty of sizzling spice!

OUT NOW

Two stories published every month, find them at:

millsandboon.co.uk

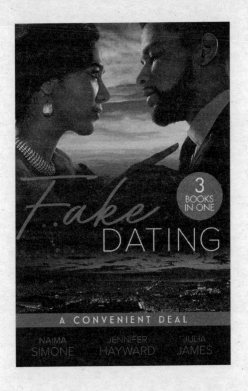

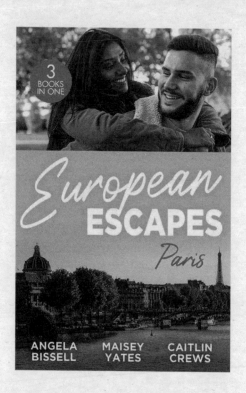

LET'S TALK

Romance

For exclusive extracts, competitions
and special offers, find us online:

f MillsandBoon

X @MillsandBoon

⊙ @MillsandBoonUK

♪ @MillsandBoonUK

Get in touch on 01413 063 232

For all the latest titles coming soon, visit
millsandboon.co.uk/nextmonth